Ascent

The Lit Series
Book 2

Mark Anthony

Dedication

To Charlotte and Andrew.
*"Imitation is the sincerest form of flattery
that mediocrity can pay to greatness."*
Oscar Wilde

Chapter 1

They began to run, the three of them racing down the path toward the buildings, Ellie and Josh to the silo, Sam to the building with the hall. Ellie watched as Sam deviated to his path. He turned briefly to face her, and for a moment, something moved between them. An understanding, a commonality that neither had ever shared before. There were now three of them here and this provided a hint of kinship that neither had ever felt throughout their entire lives. It was for that moment that Sam had gone back for them.

"DON'T LET HIM IN ELLIE! YOU HEAR ME!" he yelled "FUCK HIM UP FOR ANOTHER YEAR! DON'T LET HIM IN!"

As flippant as this was, as brash a statement and as unfamiliar as Ellie was to this way of thinking, she couldn't help but hear those words repeating loudly in her head. She suddenly felt a surge of urgency, energy, and renewed determination.

Across the city a young woman ran quickly down the dark wet street. Her long, auburn hair sodden and plastered across her face. Her dress stuck to her skin from the rain that gushed down upon her. With every flash of lightning the lone figure, confused and erratic, felt the darkness behind closing in. There was no time. Her lungs burned with each icy breath. Her legs were numb.

The blue flame had gone but she knew that this was temporary. She had not managed to get away. Where was it? She couldn't hear it, but that didn't matter. She couldn't hear its macabre voice, though she knew it wasn't far.

It never was. It was always watching. She didn't know what it was. She only knew what it could do. Her husband and his mother had become, just moments ago, its latest victims. Numbers 1 through 14 kept echoing in her mind. She was so used to keeping a tally. It was automatic. Thirteen and fourteen had intruded into the night trying to convince her to go with them. "You need help" they had said, "just calm down."

She argued with them, pleaded with them to listen. She thought she had been covert. She thought they hadn't noticed her increasing anxiety over the last two weeks. They had. Just before she had begun to set the final preparations in place they staged an intervention. They had entered her deceased grandmother's home and found her. They looked at the circle of blood upon the floor. They saw her mounds of camphor upon the old, matted carpet. They had seen the bandage on her arm, covering a fresh, deep laceration and assumed she had lost her mind.

She pleaded with them to leave her alone. The time was approaching. They had to leave. They wouldn't listen, and in her panic, in her desperation to be understood, an argument began. Perhaps it was the fear of this day that had been building up for the past 12 months. Maybe it was their reluctance to listen or the impossible task of explaining it to them in a way that, with the clock grimly ticking, would make sense. She had Lit them. The timing couldn't have been worse. Instead of being in the prepared Circle, which was just metres away, she had to watch as they were taken and dissected by the Doctor. Only then returning to her world with the Circle destroyed, now dead and ineffective. She was open, completely unprotected and *it* had begun.

As hopeless as she knew her situation was, she fled. Driving into the twilight. Fleeing with no plan and the knowledge that it was now all too late. She was overcome with fear, panic, and grief. Wracked with disbelief. How the hell did this go so wrong? It was then that its black mottled face and lifeless white eyes suddenly appeared in the rear-view mirror.

It might hurt a bit.

Its long, drape-like clothes were splattered with blood, coated in fragments of her recently taken husband. In an instant the blue flame engulfed her. Now, it burnt. She threw herself from the vehicle hitting the ground hard. She began to run. Her mind grappled for a plan that she knew didn't exist. Never had she been so awake, so acutely aware of every sensation that bombarded her. The rain hit her skin like pebbles. The searing pain of the burnt skin on her hands and forearms gained momentary relief by the icy water. Lightning gave quick confusing glimpses of unfamiliar streets.

There was silence. Her heart pounded in her ears as she looked about. It was almost peaceful. It hadn't let her rest for days. But now, standing in the rain, in this stark reality, there was the smallest pang of peace. It was short lived as her wet and blurred vision caught a glimpse of the spectacular blue flame sliding towards her.

"Shit… shit… shit" she cursed, struggling to her feet while watching the long wave of flames ebbing towards her. With a defiant grunt she stumbled back. This fire was no longer an illusion. She knew the way it worked. Now, it would sear her skin and char her fingers. The first time she had felt that pain she was barely 7 years old. The first year… her inaugural year. Then helped by a Conduit many years her senior. One who had long since been lost to *them*.

Beyond the flame that swept towards her was something else. It was here. It was tall and thickset, It's head peculiarly small for it's overly large shoulders, with sickly moist black hair parted neatly to the side White eyes were surrounded by what, at first glance, should have been black rim glasses. She knew they weren't. She had seen them up close. The black metal frames were ghoulishly embedded into its mottled, gangrenous skin. From within them shone the luminous white eyes above a weird, almost mocking smile: long, thin, and vicious. It stared straight at her. She took a step back preparing to run. In front of it was held a rusted medical instrument she had seen used on many of its patients. It carefully turned it over, gently caressing it. As its head rolled around, the white eyes scanned the sky when it froze, motionless. An unusual sculpture within the heavy rain. It was listening to the air, feeling the vibrations rising to a crescendo, all racing toward that moment. That's what it was waiting for. The moment when it could take her.

"You fucker… you miserable fucker" she spat, stumbling backwards. "Why?! WHY?!"

The reverbing voices started. Echoes that wafted through the sound of the rain. Its hands became animated as it began striding confidently towards her.

We are going to have to run some tests.

I am going to keep you overnight.

The ground on which she stood burst into the most startling blue. Flames rolled around her. It was hot and it was real. The barriers were down, and she was wide open. It was the beginning. She screamed, turning to run. Her scorched legs stung. A thought, her one single hopeless thought: *Where am I going?*

"Kaylee!" a voice screamed through the dark "KAYLEE HELP ME!" She instantly skidded to a stop and spun about. Once again still, the Doctor stood next to a rusted medical stretcher. Upon it was a man. It was her husband, taken not even an hour before. The Doctor looked down at its bloodied, restrained captive and gave a small, calm nod.

"Michael!" she called tearfully, her hands reaching out to him. "Michael I'm so sorry! I'm so sorry!" She instantly recognised the look on the creature's twisted face. She had seen this sadistic delight before.

It's over now. You cannot help. You cannot help.

This hopeless mantra had worked and had been cruelly accepted in the past. But not this time, not with her husband. Calmly and methodically, the Doctor looked down at its victim. He screamed and bucked as the Doctor twisted a rusted implement into his writhing body.

Ah yes!... I think we have a diagnosis.

"Leave him alone! Get off him you son-of-a-bitch! Get off him" she screamed enraged. There was no use in holding in the anger anymore. She knew the way this worked: on this night, from the time that the winter sun dipped below the horizon, she was its target. The onslaught would be relentless. It was not a fight. It would be a cruel and vicious assault. She was doomed. She knew she was doomed but she would resist. There was nothing to lose. It had already taken everything from her. She wasn't going to make it easy.

"Hey! Hey!... freak I'm over here!" she screamed defiantly. "Here! You've waited years for this so come on!"

With a quick turn of the head, its dead white eyes met hers as its hands remained buried within its gurgling, powerless victim.

"That's right," she panted. "Here I am, come on you miserable piece of shit... come on"

It stayed motionless beside David. Its pale white eyes mere slits staring at her from the dark road. A stand-off the woman knew she couldn't win. She couldn't fight it. She couldn't escape. The moment seemed like forever. She had no plan and somewhere in the back of her mind she realised that all those years had all been leading to this. Soon it would have them both. There was nothing she could do. To hell with the consequences… The outcome was already written.

Her breathing began to calm. Her eyes glanced first to one side of the road and then the other. Then back to the Doctor before her who slowly, expectantly stood upright and waited.

Explosively she dashed forward, screaming in rage. The stretcher, the rain, the beast wearing white, they all raced towards her in the sprint that she was powerless to stop. With hateful rage she threw herself upon the creature, grabbing its head, screaming into its face. She saw it up close, its rotten flesh, its yellowed jagged teeth, its abnormally wide mouth. She stared at its eyes, inches from her own. White, dead marbles. Empty. She pounded its head with everything she had, with every fibre of her strength but it felt nothing. She knew it felt nothing, but the gratification was instantly euphoric. Hit it, tear it. As impotent as it was, the feeling was sublime.

With one smooth sweep of its arm, Kaylee was thrown to the wet road. Numb, and shaking with adrenaline, she lifted her bleeding face as blue fire wafted about her. She could see them now, shapes, humanoid forms staggering towards her from the darkness behind the flames. A brilliant flash of lightning exposed them, confirming her fears. The twisted and gnarled victims from her past were staggering towards her. Some shuffled, some crawled. Various implements of torture were embedded in them, contorting their naked bodies, their faces, and limbs, into unnatural and absurd positions. Demented screams of suffering left their torn and tortured faces. It was too late.

There was no Circle around her. There was nowhere to hide. The sun had now gone, and her fate awaited. Years of fighting and resisting. Years of planning every day, planning every interaction, every life choice whilst this evil, unnatural curse got every consideration with each damned step of her life. Now the man that warmed her heart and made her dare to dream of a different way was condemned to suffer a fate worse than death. It was her fault. Her life, her heart, her love had sent him to something worse than hell. She straightened up. Water ran freely from her bleeding and battered body. This was of no concern. She had bled many times before… but now, where was it?

Only for a second, Kaylee saw the headlights of the car barrelling towards her. The decision was instantaneous. In the darkness of the night, in

5

the cover of the rain that car might not see her. She could step out in front of it. Maybe, God willing, maybe, it would not predict her move.

The harsh beam of the headlights stung her eyes. She glanced at the monster. This would take her away from it. This could save her. It was the only chance she had, no matter how remote. There was nothing to lose. She stepped into the path of the oncoming vehicle.

The collision forced air from her body as she slammed into the front of the car. There was the sound of screeching tyres as she became aware of something wrapped about her. There was no pain. There was no sensation of the impact, even as she heard the windscreen smash behind her. The creature held her tightly, wrapping its strong deformed body in a mesh of protection. All hope was lost.

The Doctor removed its grip as the woman hit the ground hard. It let her feel this. Why wouldn't it? Death could be painless, injury was painful. She lay gasping on the wet ground. The evening was now turning to black as she stared up at the sky. She wanted to look at it just a little longer. She knew she would not see it again. Not this sky. It was over. It was time. It had been a long battle and now she was defeated.

Lying on the road she was aware that people were approaching her. She could see their blurred silhouettes and hear their excited scared shouting. Even at this time, she was acutely aware of the danger they were in. They couldn't be here. They had to go and, as a young man leant down to her, she felt a rush of panic.

What have I done?

"Go… leave me… go," she gasped through the rain that covered her face, filling her nose and blurring her eyes. "Don't touch me, go, just go, don't touch me."

The man said something nice to her, something reassuring. He knelt beside her and held her head gently in his hands. He was in such danger. He didn't understand.

Oh Christ, please understand.

"Go… Go away! Go! Get away! Don't touch me! No! Don't touch me!"

He was joined by another as he carefully placed her head on his knee. Another young man leant over her and grasped her hands, comforting and gentle. Horrified, she tried to push them away. They had seconds, mere seconds to let go… she could feel it building in the air about her. If they were touching her during this moment, when the sky flashed and the ground rumbled, they would join her in the never-ending nightmare of its world.

What have I done?

"You can't touch me!!" she screamed furiously into the air, startling the two men and, for a moment, for a split second, she hoped they would listen and back away.

With a brilliant flash of lightning, the landscape was once again illuminated. The lightning paused, engulfing all of them in a brilliant other-worldly beam as a deep, rumbling THUD rippled through the ground. Exhausted and defeated, she turned her cradled head to the side to see the blue flames rushing to meet them. She could see the Doctor standing behind them watching with subtle conceit. It had won. Yes, a sick bonus.

The strangers began to make confused sounds, watching with confusion as the streets folded, fading gracefully away into the darkness. The screams of the hundreds taken before becoming louder, drowning out all else. They were all being taken to the Doctor's world, and there they would remain.

Marco was screaming for Mika's mercy as Chelamah walked past him and proceeded down the corridor. The others remained tight-lipped and masked. She ensured that no-one who walked with her, not Jason, Miya, or the other devotees, got the slightest hint of how horrified she was at what was occurring in the room they just left. As the elevator opened to allow them in, Chelamah noticed Crystal would not be joining them. She was going to wait, leaning against the wall, and watching the door they had just left. Marco's screaming suddenly stopped. They all knew what was happening at that very moment.

The elevator was an awful place to play this kind of game with these sorts of people. Not a word was spoken in what felt like the longest descent in history, but the communication was loud and clear. Jason smiled and Lucas, his devotee, smiled back. Miya picked up her phone and began typing. Was she faking this? Was Miya at all concerned? Chelamah stared straight ahead at the silver metal wall between Jason and Miya; expressionless, no emotion. She needed one of the others to speak, to say it.

"Mika just took one of us out, are you fucking kidding me?"

"Holy fuck, what just happened?"

or

"I can't believe what he just did."

But no-one did. A testament to the level the "Pantheon" had eventually reached. It's what Mika called them. There were dangerous complexities involved in playing this type of game. Whether they owned it or not, there was no trust anymore. Their small group had just become smaller. The cliques in the group made it even smaller still. It was more like a cold war than an alliance. No allegiance, no comradery, just a cold stalemate held in place by the guaranteed understanding of mutual destruction.

Jason, the Conduit, and Luka, his conceited devotee, made an awesome psychopathic duo. Standing together they exchanged mocking glances and knowing smiles. Miya stood alone, no devotee, and Chelamah suspected that she preferred it that way. There were many reasons for Miya to feel this way, but Chelamah chose not to speculate. Crystal was not with them. She had chosen to wait and enjoy Mika's display. God how she hated that woman. But in this army of monsters, Marco and herself were mere pawns. Handy yet eminently disposable and, when it came down to it, completely defenceless. The Ascendant conduits were more than comfortable that Mika had just taken a Devotee. She wondered how their attitude would change if they knew what she knew. If they knew that Will, a Conduit just like them, had been the first one targeted.

Noah, the Underling Conduit stood beside her. She felt him move closer as their arms touched ever so slightly. It scared her. Her craving for his closeness became fear, mistrusting and guarded. Now was not the time. Noah and Chelamah were complicated, dangerously entangled. She couldn't relax. But, as she felt Noah ever so subtly caress her hand with one finger she knew that he was vulnerable. He risked exposing them. Calmly she pulled her arm away and feigned rummaging in her bag.

When the elevator doors glided open, it took every ounce of her strength not to run. She wanted to scream. To run hysterically away from these people, however, she knew that she couldn't. She paced herself. In a careful and controlled walk she moved past the others, down the hall and through the doors onto the street.

The brutally cold wind, whipping through her clothing stinging her face, provided a sense of comfort. The city streets were dark and dim. The street-lights were only mildly effective at this time of year. Small yellow orbs sitting high above the dark, wet path. However, there was beauty in this normality. The monsters, for now, were behind her. She was alone. How she craved being alone. Tears sprung forth in her eyes like a cue, a sign that she was now away from them. The further she walked, the darker the streets be-came, and the more tears rolled down her cheeks. She could still hear Marco, his screaming and then that awful, awful silence as Mika's hell engulfed him.

It was midnight and it felt like it was the first time she had been alone for days. She walked along the footpath lined with tall elm trees. She began to focus on this moment, to be mindful and present. For now, it was over. She was exhausted and needed to sleep, but that wouldn't happen for a while. Every minute mattered. In the morning she would consider what to-night's bold move by Mika meant to her plans, but tonight it was not about her.

"I didn't know that was going to happen," a deep voice spoke beside her from out of the shadows.

Chelamah gasped in fright. Spinning around, she saw Noah step out from the tree line.

Large and solid, his silhouette in the dark would have scared anyone. Well over 6 feet with a strong, solid build, his shaved head covered by the hood of his thick, black coat. She was grateful for his broad American ac-cent, making him instantly recognisable even in the dark. Chelamah closed her eyes and composed herself. Quickly, he stepped out of the shadow and towards her.

"I d-d-didn't know," he repeated.

Chelamah had told Noah, more times than she could recall, that sneak-ing up and surprising her could end badly.

"Damnit Noah, I've told you not to do that," she shook her head. "You want to finish us both?"

"I needed to see you. I need you to know that wasn't me. I can't speak for the others, but I didn't fucking expect that. You have to believe me." He stepped closer, placing his hand on hers.

Defensively she pulled away. Not tonight, there was no place for affec-tion tonight. Not even from him. She felt so much shame and disgust. At Miya? Definitely. At Jason and Luka for giggling in the elevator? Absolutely.

But more so at herself. They had let it happen. She had let it happen. Though had she intervened, what could she have done? She was no match for an Ascendant. The curse she bore worked very effectively on normal people. But for Mika's type, with Noah's type, such a response would instantly trigger her own destruction.

Not one of the Conduits, neither Ascendant or Underling, tried to dissuade or placate Mika in any way. He was not stronger than Jason or Miya. That's not how it worked. If a Conduit or an Ascendant challenged him then, Mika would have had to decide - was damning Marco worth the risk of a confrontation with another Conduit? Was feeding Marco to his monster worth beginning a fight that he may very well lose? But no-one challenged him. Over the last few years, he had gradually asserted his psychopathic dominance over the others. Achieving this with the Devotees and Noah was not hard. However, the Ascendants? It was now to the point where they accepted his decisions as final. How did that happen?

"We did nothing," Chelamah choked.

"There was nothing we could do. What do you think I could do? I'm not Miya, I'm not Jason. Even they knew better. Fucking Jason called for it!"

"I know!" she shouted, backing away from him even further. "There was nothing we could do but do you believe me now? Marco was not the first."

"So they get to call people out? Jason, the little damn bitch? He gets to call it now?"

Noah dropped his eyes but not before Chelamah saw his tears, causing her to soften. His tears weren't for Marco, they were for his own shame, his own guilt. She understood this and knew that Noah, at heart, was a good man. He had integrity and a strong moral compass. This of course had been twisted, torn and damaged after years of living with his own horrors, but the foundation of Noah was strong. Her feelings for him were not unlike love.

"I... I believe you," Noah replied stoically, casting his eyes to the ground. "Something's going on. Will, then Marco? Did you see Jason's face?"

"And Luka's?" Chelamah replied. "They know more."

"They framed him for our benefit, not Mika's. Well I n-n-need to know more. Tell me what Will said to you. What has been going on?"

Chelamah shook her head defiantly and turned to leave, craving solitude. She wanted to be on her own and free from further chaos just for one night. Noah strode after her.

"No Chel, don't walk away, tell me what's happening. What do you know?"

"Please Noah, I don't know anything for sure yet. Give me tonight. I will find out."

"Tell me something… anything. Tell me what was it about your mothers Grimoires? Tell m-m-me what Will said… or how about you tell me who these other people are?"

"Some of the Grimoires are being used and they are being used well. I don't know how. I can't tell you any more than that yet"

"Why?"

"Because soon I could be Marco! Soon it could be me!" Chelamah lifted her hands to her head, exasperated. "They will hurt me. Everything I've said, everyone I've spoken to, they… will… know. And then it leads to you."

"You need me. You need to trust someone. I need to know so I can at least have a chance to protect you. It makes no sense. It's bullshit. What good would it serve them to get rid of us."

"We go. The beasts don't. I don't know why. You can't protect me anymore than we protected Marco. We don't have the power here. If they turn on me there's nothing you can do." Chelamah looked into the darkness. Her blood ran cold. With that statement, the risk to her very being was cruelly clear?

"And how is that supposed to sit with me? How am I supposed to f-f-feel about that?" Sincerity abounded in his voice. "I love…"

"No… no, no," Chelamah lifted her hand to him. Love? Intimacy? That word terrified her, and it should have scared him too. Fool. Their world twisted these things and made them into targets. Love and hate. Friends and enemies.

"Yes, I do," Noah breathed deeply. "I do. I couldn't let what just happened to him happen to you. I couldn't."

As if sensing her guard drop, Noah cautiously walked to her and put his arms around her. She resisted, weakly, before giving in. She needed this embrace, as terrifying and vulnerable as it made her feel. He gently placed his hand under her chin, bringing them face to face.

Noah stroked her face gently, "Do I believe in you? Yes. B-b-but you have to stop what you are doing. They will notice."

"Did Jason notice?" Chelamah quipped.

"That little bitch has a collection twenty d-d-deep and that's just this last year. He wouldn't have noticed the absence of one." Noah argued, looking Chelamah straight in the eyes. "Mika however… Mika will notice. Jason is numbers… Mika… Mika remembers. He knows what's his."

Without another word, Chelamah kissed him gently but quickly pulled away and walked away down the path. Noah watched as she walked away. Anxious, he called out to her "Just let this one go! Please!"

She didn't answer. Let this one go? One… like one was not enough? Marco was now just one of a faceless many. No, she could not afford to think that way. She would never let herself start thinking in numbers. One person, any person was *enough*. Just one was vile, obscene and an affront to God. But then again, so was she. Chelamah was cursed. This is what led her mother down this path in the first place. Aahna believed her daughter was haunted. She was, but it was not until Chelamah was eleven that Aahna became aware of how deep and twisted the curse was. Chelamah could walk in a world that others couldn't see. Painfully, sometimes excruciatingly so, she could move like a ghost within the realms of the Leviathans whilst remaining totally unseen and unnoticed. The creature she would become was hideous. Radiating revulsion and terror, as if hell itself oozed from its very pores. Though during these moments of metamorphosis, she noticed something else that she could do. This is what made her dangerous. A secret, a hidden talent that no-one but she herself, Noah and Will Mason knew she possessed.

Chapter 2

Chelamah arrived home after leaving Noah on the dark road behind her. Placing her coat and bag on the hook by the door, she slipped off her shoes and walked down the corridor in a daze. The normality of the surroundings seemed strange and weirdly irrelevant after the events of the evening. A kitchen to cook in. A bathroom to bathe in. A sitting room to watch TV in. Here she stopped and looked at the floor before taking a deep, cleansing breath. She glanced expectantly at the large painting that leant against the far wall. The air began to grow thick. A brewing unease and a sensation of dread overcome her. It would happen fast this time.

It was hard knowing the truth. Knowing that this was only one small, banal part of existence. Marco would have been at his home, not too much unlike this one, less than 24 hours ago. Now where was he? Being torn apart in a hell that weaved through this trite domain. She had been close enough to link quickly with this taking. She felt Marco in every dark impulse of her body. Completely unreachable to anyone but her. A shiver of cold ran up her spine. It was so close.

Slowly she walked down the hall to the door of her study. Upon the floor, resting up against the far wall, was the beginning of a piece of art. The work had been painted by her darkness, fuelled by visions and takings. She would draw what it would see. From across the room, it appeared as a collage of black and blue images and lines. Completely abstract. On closer inspection, however, its hideous representations became obvious. The amalgam of images haunted her every waking moment. Rooms within rooms, monsters dwelling within the dark recesses of their own sick playgrounds that she had crossed many times. Screaming faces and torn bodies calling out from their final oubliette. Most of these faces and scenes she had witnessed as a phantom in the shadows. Once again, the dread of where she was about to go grew within her as did the desire to go there. A want became a need. A part of her called to it. She prepared herself to take another step further into the nightmare that was her world. It was easy. She lived between both worlds at all times. It was simply a step to the side. The woman's mind's eye and the monster's hand would meet, and then, they would be one. Remaining unnoticed where controlling her monster's lust for darkness was the ultimate challenge.

"Marco," she muttered to herself, focusing on the target she wanted. She reached behind the canvas before her, gracefully pulling out a long thin blade identical to the weapon she had bestowed upon Sam. She wrapped her fingers about it and placed her closed hand on the floor. Touched by her, this weapon would be Marco's salvation.

Marco had to die. She had to kill him and the only way she could do this was to go to him. It would be quick. The human within her hoped he would not see her terrifying form or feel the horror that gripped anyone who saw it. The monster wanted him to fear it.

The soft screams of the taken began to waft about her. Louder screams linked with the soft beaten whimpers hypnotised as she watched the painting darken and groan. It was time to go. It happened quickly and she was grateful. She needed insight and, as truly terrifying as it was, this was the only way she could do it. She had to send her mind into that world and see what was left for her on this macabre canvas when she returned.

The monster erupted from Chelamah's body, rising from her as a grotesque, withered mass. Its white eyes sprung open, its long, muscled limbs began to stretch and contort. One body had become two as two minds slammed together as one. She would see what it saw, feel what it felt. The woman's thoughts, compassion and humanity were reduced to a whisper, locked in the back of a twisted and ancient mind. A mind, full of secrets, memories and desires from another wicked existence.

It lifted its hands to the blackened, moist fingers splayed twisting them in the air. It began to mutter maniacally. The screams of hundreds of tortured taken, heard through the gruesome canvas, were now echoed by its torn, gnarled mouth. It had no regard for the woman behind it.

Envy, need and starvation defined it. Chelamah would remain in her realm and the Wraith would return to its own. Body separated; minds entwined in an unstable truce. Chelamah felt this. As the joining became complete the sensations became less offensive, less intrusive. The thought

14

of a kill brought undeniable pleasure incapable of being ignored. Her small voice of conscience, locked in the back of its mind, was all that remained of Chelamah. This small presence would attempt to hone, harness and direct the monster's viciousness. Like steering a ship with a broken sail through an ocean of abhorrent evil. There never was any certainty of success for the human. For the Wraith, death of any nature was a win.

The inky darkness unfolded. The creature contorted. Flattening itself to the floor like a spider it moved across a moist, dank carpet. Its long arms and legs scuttling a thin body forward in complete silence. It moved in quick, certain bursts, only stopping for a moment to listen to the air around it. This domain belonged to another, and to this Leviathan, the Wraith was no more than an insect. A lesser annoyance that would be quickly dealt with.

The smell of rotting flesh and excrement filled the creature's skeletal nostrils. A smell of absolute revulsion to Chelamah was now utterly intoxicating. Whimpers and soft, beaten wailings brought a feeling of contentment and satisfaction. These suffering morsels that were once human. This was at least, its world, and this was where it belonged. A vulturous scavenger, feeding amongst the entrails and leftovers of a bigger, stronger predator.

As one being they heard the wailing, hysterical. Guttural screams mixed with the full-winded sounds of an injured body. This human was fresh, still trying to defend itself. The Wraith could feel its warmth and its raw, blood covered flesh. So fresh. Divine.

Upon the wall, lying flat against the red and black wallpaper, it observed the chamber. There were many here in this world of perverse flesh and blood. Some unrecognisable as ever being human. These mounds of meat and sinew were tied in macabre erotic positions designed for tortuous pleasure. Some wailed while others clawed pointlessly at the floor beneath them.

Some bodies, still recognisable as human, were adorned with leather collars and restraints. Their remaining limbs were interlaced with bright red tethers that wove in and out of pierced flesh. Some sobbed but most stared silently into the nightmare about them.

Beyond these tortured beasts, pushed to painful insanity, were the fresh cries of pain that captivated the Wraith's attention. At the far end of the room upon a bed of steel, under a canopy of lace, lay the bloodied, groaning form of the Lover's newest suitor. Long lengths of blood-red rope tied to four bloodied and broken limbs. The man groaned deeply, trying fruitlessly to move his freshly ripped and restrained body. His pain was so real, so beautifully crisp. There were no cries for mercy. No cries for help. This human knew neither of these virtues existed here. His fleshy lips torn from his face exposed gnashing teeth and ripped gums. Blood and body fluids saturated its pathetic form. Its throat torn from jagged bites that bled to no end, to no death. This victim was a Devotee and knew any fight was futile. Marco was owned by a creature complete in its stone-cold evil. No release.

The Lover admired her emaciated feminine silhouette in front of a full-length, ornate mirror. Her long, mottled hands played with glistening hair as she gracefully wiped blood-coated strands from her black and crimson face. White eyes blinked quickly as her head snapped to the side. The sound of gentle humming filled the air. Vain and completely mesmerised by her own bizarre, twisted beauty, she soaked in the sounds of despair and suffering that permeated the air.

The hidden Wraith didn't move. The Lover's unpredictability, its speed and its sudden explosive purpose was a predatory advantage. If it sensed the Wraith's breach of her world, it would be over. A Leviathan would know what a Wraith was seeking. And that which the Wraith sought was forbidden.

The Wraith allowed the sweet sounds of anguish to excite it. At home surrounded by pain and torment. The woman locked within the creature felt challenged by the sense of pleasure and peace this hellscape bought her. She stared through the creature's white eyes and thought through its contorted and perverted mind. Inhumane, perverse desires sat like a thick fog in front of her own thoughts.

The Lover rose seductively from her stool. With graceful, delicate steps she slowly made her way through her menagerie of collected "lovers." Long decaying legs appeared to end in high heeled stilettos by the protrusions of bone where feet should've been. Her thin hands were held coyly in front of her face. Razor-sharp nails covering her mouth as she gave a distorted smile of dalliance. Marco's weary but fresh reactions to pain, to torture were intriguing to the Lover. Every new addition for a Leviathan brought new flesh to explore and a million different possible responses to torture and torment to savour. Nothing died and rotted here. What was taken, remained taken. Death could not enter. Each sliver of flesh, each torn gnarled carcass lived here forever in full consciousness.

The Wraith moved into the shadows, spreadeagled upon the carpet coated with abandoned strips of wet shimmering skin. Its clawed hands pushed through the piles of innards and twisting bundles of human parts.

The Lover sauntered through the dimly lit crimson room towards Marco's damaged and writhing body. Chelamah knew that the bloodlust of the Wraith must be satisfied. Two motives, two desires working towards one outcome. The Wraith needed to kill... the woman needed to save. The most precarious moment had arrived. Chelamah would have to hand complete control to the creature. The Wraith's form began to change. Now becoming smoke-like and vaguely transparent. Unseeable by the dominant monster that now proceeded towards the bound man.

The pain had dulled in Marco's mouth to just barely below agony. She had torn at his chin with her jagged teeth. It was gone, replaced with the dual sensation of dried blood and thicken, congealed gums where once his lips and right cheek used to be.

She had lain beside him. Her dead white eyes had stared into his. She had whispered sweet and loving secrets into his ear as her long, vicious nails emasculated him - slowly, methodically. He was violated and defiled. Fixtures and apparatus of various forms were attached to his body that periodically clicked and twisted into life, penetrating further into him.

I love you. I will always love you.

Marco's eyes, wide and panicked, locked onto the graceful form that glided towards him. There was a moment of panic, a brief thrashing before exhaustion caused his muscles to spasm. The bound man closed his eyes, turning his head away from the monstrous woman as he braced himself for the attack.

The Lover looked down at him, her head swaying to the side in a swoon. She smiled, her mouth contorting into a mutated coy simper.

Lay with me

The Lover gently turned as she sat next to her victim. He felt her weight. He groaned and shuffled sideways, but his resignation was complete. His breathing increased. His eyes stared blankly into the scene around him. Slowly she placed her hand on his torn face. He flinched as the ripped skin began to seer and burn under her touch. What little movement was allowed, brought a change of quality to his pain which could be mistaken for relief as her hand wrapped around the bloodied mound that once were his genitals. She caressed the torn flesh, sweetly, tenderly as he began to thrash in new, unparalleled agony.

The Wraith moved like a wisp of smoke to the ceiling above them. The man screamed out in pain. A tormented sob bought the Wraith's murderous desires to the fore. It would be quick, sudden with certain death. There was no room for error. There must be no mistake.

If Marco had looked, he would have seen the white eyes of the spectre as it regained its physical form. It reached down toward him. Its legs attached to the ceiling above as it brought a long arm above the Leviathan's head. Marco writhed. His eyes opened and stared up. For a second he noticed the glint of solid metal above the Lover. The knife, real and uncloaked, brought recognition of the Wraith's true form. His eyes widened. He knew what it was and knew why it was there. It had to act.

The Wraith dropped onto the man's torn body. The knife slashed the man's throat bringing forth a spray of arterial blood. Accurate and fatal. It lowered its face, relishing Marco's guttural death gasp. Taking it deep into its body with a euphoric heave. Blood turned the Leviathan's arm red as the spent knife disintegrated to dust. It was done. He was dead. The pure bliss of satisfaction turned immediately to thoughts of survival. Now the Leviathan knew. Now the Leviathan could see it, and its rage would be unchecked.

The room erupted in screams and heat. The Lover's arm reached above her with lightning speed as the Wraith turned to shadow barely escaping her grasp. The room now lit by an alien, red glow as the Lover stood. Her eyes scanned her world looking for the intruder within. The one who had committed such an outrageous act.

Hunched like an insect, hidden amongst the humanesque forms on the floor, the Wraith lay still. Two things to be achieved: survival and escape. The Lover too, stood statue-like. Her white eyes blinked rapidly as the room was engulfed in the deep, crimson red. Human remains about the Wraith began to rise. Its gruesome hiding place amongst the tortured mutilated humans began to lift. It had experienced this before. The Leviathan knew what it was facing and was searching for it.

The Lover walked through the room, her hands slashing at the tortured forms rotating about her. The Wraith scuttled backwards, watching the Leviathan. The closer the Lover moved towards it, the more it retreated with supernatural stealth. It could feel the bare floor behind as it edged further and further into a darkness.

It was at this moment, when the Lover's domain faded into black, that Chelamah looked down at her arms in disbelief. She stood horrified to see her human hands. This was not supposed to happen. Not yet. Her heart began to pound... her human heart. The Wraith had gone but where was she?

Panic-stricken she glanced around her into nothing but darkness, an airless place. Horrified, the sound of heavy grinding forced her to spin to face a large, vibrating wooden door that was opening scarcely feet from her. From within came a gentle, flickering light. She was on the other side. The Lover and her domain were gone but the Wraith had not returned to Chelamah. Chelamah had returned to the Wraith.

There was nothing behind her but darkness. Before her, a door and arguably, the desirable path to take. Like a moth to a flame, she advanced.

oOo

A muscular blonde man in his 20s dragged on his last cigarette before stubbing it out on the wet ground. Frustrated, he wringed his gloved hands before once more peering into the foyer of the old building, watching his breath fog over the glass of the door. *I'm gonna die of fucking hypothermia out here.*

Still no sign of Jason. He had returned to Mika shortly after they had all walked away from the elevator and gone their separate ways. One text only, and Jason had turned back. Luka asked why, but Jason didn't know. He looked nervous and, given what had occurred to Marco minutes earlier, he should have been.

Jason asked Luka to wait for him and he agreed. Not out of any concern, but out of pure curiosity. Perhaps, though unlikely, Jason would tell him what Mika wanted. With the current unease in the group, information was power and that could mean survival. That was an hour ago. Jason hadn't reappeared. This was unsettling, but Luka knew Mika liked to take a very long time to say... anything. It wasn't unusual.

Eventually Jason's lanky, bespeckled figure left the elevator, stooped over with his hands in his pockets. He approached the door. It slid open as

19

he walked out past Luka and down the dark road. Luka put his hands out exasperated "and?" he called out.

Jason pivoted around in a circle, "and… what?" he sneered looking down on his Devotee while maintaining his stride.

"What did he say?" Luka jogged up to him. "What happened?"

"I can't tell you that," Jason snapped, impatiently pulling his hood down over his brow.

"Who was it about?"

"You. He hates you," Jason sighed facetiously. "He thinks you're a useless prick."

"Come on. I'm being serious. I was out here for an hour. Did you see the look on Chel's face? She was pissed. What was the go with Noah? He looked fucked up too. They wouldn't even look at us… bad vibes man… bad vibes."

Jason chuckled softly, "that's all they offer. Bad vibes and inconsequential talent. You saw their faces in there?"

"I saw the way Noah looked at you when you said what you would do to Marco."

"Noah is shit. I have no interest in talking about N-N-N-Noah," Jason parodied, waving a gloved hand in the air dismissively.

Luka laughed. "OK, speech impediment aside, he's a pretty big guy though. Would scare the shit out of me."

Jason didn't respond immediately. He thought that he would let that sit uncomfortably for a moment. Hopefully Luka would realise how stupid that statement was. After a pause, Jason just smiled to himself. For him, Noah was nothing, not when he had his constant companion. For him, no-one was a threat.

"Noah should scare the shit out of you. I agree." It was important that he let Luka know his place.

They walked quickly across the wet street. Jason pulled the hood from his coat, letting the rain hit his face, absorbing the moment. This was his favourite time. The Rising Fire completed; the Event was over for another year. He had now proven himself worthy to stay alive for another twelve months. A strange sense of calm washed over him. After all these years, the events of the night now seemed to retreat steadily like a dream. He enjoyed visiting his victims again. The sense of power it gave him. No-one should underestimate him. Just look at what he could do. He enjoyed seeing what had been done to them and, unexpectedly, he enjoyed the battle of wits that ensued between him and It. He was sure that his God found the process as fun as he did. He found it amusing that it tried to break him by throwing the pieces of shit from his past in his face. Like *that* would weaken him. It had not had that sort of effect on him for some time.

"Man, that was awkward!" Luka shouted, turning and looking at the building they had just left. "That will go down as the most uncomfortable elevator ride in history."

Jason laughed, "Yeah, the door couldn't open fast enough."

He descended the steep concrete steps to the city gardens, holding onto the ice-cold railing as the city skyline disappeared above them. With a joint sigh they began to slow as the steps provided a veneer of isolation. They were now alone, except for the occasional derelict bum that slept rough under the cover of the many large trees. They could speak freely.

Luka stopped walking. "Do you think I did the right thing? Telling Mika about the blood?"

"Yes!" Jason replied loudly. "Your other option would've been to not have told him. Which do you think Mika would've preferred?"

"Yeah… damn straight. I'm not lying to him." Luka chuckled. "You looked pissed too, in there with Mika. I thought you were gonna do it!" Perplexed, Jason stepped closer to Luka eyeing him curiously. "You thought I would do… what?"

Shuffling his feet uneasily. "Nah I mean, you know. You looked kind of… irate too," he replied cautiously.

Jason nodded. It was clear that anyone else but himself, or another Ascendant Conduit, could not understand how it worked.

"Irate doesn't cut it," Jason coldly replied with a thin smile. "If it did, you would've been gone when we first met."

Luka laughed but they both knew that this was fact. Their meeting and the following months had been full of frustrating adjustments. Luka pushed past him to the bottom of the staircase onto the gravel path.

"Mika doesn't have a list. Mika doesn't have a rule," Jason said, his voice getting quieter. Luka turned around to look at him, stood on the bottom step, illuminated eerily by the street light. They were both thinking the same thing, though it would go unsaid.

"Maybe Mika's list is more… flexible," Luka shrugged. "We could've just smashed the fuck out of Marco, would've been more fun for me."

"That would have been crude," Jason replied calmly, uncomfortable at the level of candour his companion was reaching. "That's what you would do, not what Mika or I would do."

"Marco was a fucking pussy anyway. Always had been since he arrived. Teaming him up with Will was a good match!" Luka sneered, which made Jason uncomfortable. The small smile left his face. He was not pleased with this comment, and Luka immediately wished he hadn't said it. It had been a long night and his tongue was loose.

"Luka... Will was an Ascendant," Jason said coolly.

Luka instantly looked to the ground chastised. His posture became rigid, nervous.

"I know. I'm sorry that's not what I meant," Luka was belittled, humbled. His voice quietened. His eyes cast down as he was admonished.

Jason straightened up, looking down on Luka again, dominant and threatening. "Respect, Luka. As an Ascendant, Will gets respect." He muttered quietly with a hint of regret, "that could've been anyone of us and Will made it a long time."

"Absolutely," Luka shook his head displaying a great performance of guilt. "I get it hey, I really get it."

"No, you don't." Jason leapt off the final step and walked to Luka who shrank before him. "You don't get it. You... Chelamah... fucking Noah... you don't get it." The whole thing made him anxious.

A sound that Jason had largely been ignoring up until now got his attention. His weariness increased as he became aware of the aching of his tired, battered body. He had hoped to sleep tonight but it seemed that that would be challenging now that his powerful friend had decided to return.

The sobbing, distraught speech came from the shadows of the trees before them. Jason knew that he was the only one who heard it. Luka wasn't *worthy* to hear it. The powerful being had returned to his side and was seeking his attention. The benediction by this awesome being was on him. Not for the unworthy. Not Luka.

A chanting and applause drifted over Jason's ears like distant rain, vague yet soothing. Happy, playful music brought a swell of strength in his throat. It had rested after their special night together.

The aura of happiness that surrounded his constant companion hid its lethal and vicious intent. At this moment it was performing a joyful, light and fragile dance. Its true nature, however, was violent and terrible. It was just how this "blessing" worked. That's what Mika called it. A blessing. A strength… a god-like ability. Jason meditated on this daily. He was blessed to be invincible. No-one could threaten him. He grimaced. Tonight he would fall asleep listening to the declarations of a God.

Jason felt the bluffed absurdity of his monster's presence descend on him, wrapping about him like a blanket of darkness. He silently faced Luka for a moment and then walked behind him, shaking his head as he stared into the black shadows with calm contemplation.

"It's here right now. I can hear it. I can feel it. It can hear me too and you bet it can feel me. It's everywhere, but nowhere at the same time. I see what it wants to do…" Jason added threateningly. He turned, watching Luka shuffle uncomfortably. "Its power… it's strength. My god… it's strong. Mika says it's a part of me! A part of me, but you know something? It's so much more powerful than me, and I don't always feel worthy of all that. It gives me power… it gives me its strength. Why? It cherishes the agony of those that hurt me. It places a wall around me… nothing can get through. It craves this. It stops death for me! I can't die. It won't let me. Do you know how many times I've tried? How many others have tried? It deems me worthy to be invincible. Me!" Jason put his hands up dramatically. "Because I matter to this god. I have been embraced by Him." He smirked. "Think about that… I matter to god…"

"I'm sorry" Luka said solemnly, "I didn't mean it."

"…I know what you meant. But remember: as much as it wants to hurt you - and it does want to hurt you - it wants to hurt you for me." Looking directly at Luka he continued. "It loves me, and not in a bullshit 'Jesus loves me' kinda way… this god pays out.". This god shows its love every fucking day. So much more so that every 365 days on the fucking line, it bends heaven and earth to get to me. It wants me with it. By its side." Jason lifted his hands again, smiling almost hysterically and leaving Luka confused.

Was he comparing his Leviathan to God? Luka had not thought of Jason as religious before, but this sounded something like Mika's strange sanctimonious doctrine. Luka became nervous. There was no God in their world. It was not allowed. Theism was banned, as was any reference to an actual religious deity. God had to be tangible, witnessed and real. God was the Leviathan.

"Such is the responsibility of an Ascendant Luka. Such is the beautiful burden of this awesome blessing! My life is not my own. It can be really

23

fuck… really challenging," he asserted loudly. The words 'beautiful' and 'blessing' were carefully chosen but still sounded forced. "But I see God, and more importantly, He sees me."

Sensibly, Luka remained quiet.

"That's my life, that's Miya's life, that is Mika's life… that was Will's life. He too, was worthy and loved by a god. Because of the immense love that was held for him, his god brought him home. What you… *you…* think of him is irrelevant." Jason's eyes blazed passionately. "William Mason was no pussy. Have more respect."

"I get that. My apologies," Luka nodded coldly.

The two stood in awkward silence. Jason was sure that Luka was looking into his eyes for weakness. Assessing his every nuance for a safe path out of a precarious situation. He must not show any. Luka was not his friend. None of these people were his friends. Any notion that perhaps they could have been was dashed tonight. Though tonight he too had called for Marco's destruction. Why? Firstly, it was appropriate. Marco had failed Will, therefore Marco had no use for the Pantheon. He knew too much to be set free. He had proven that he could not be trusted.

Secondly, if Marco failed Will, then Luka could fail Jason. Luka must never fail him. Before he met Mika he would never have thought that he needed someone to look out for him, to keep him safe. Before he became mixed up with these people, he had never felt the need for a chaperone or a companion. The Pantheon was supposed to make him stronger… so he made sure that they got the point. He needed to make sure that he kept Luka scared; made sure that they both knew that he was willing to condemn him should he need to.

The silence lasted way too long for either of their comfort. Luka smiled gently. Fake empathy, an attempt to disarm Jason perhaps. Jason would not respond to such manipulation. It didn't matter how Luka had interpreted the conversation. Luka did not know about Jason's new acquaintance. Mika wouldn't tell Luka that a new Ascendant was being introduced into an already dubious dynamic.

"Oh, fuck it, let's just go," Jason cursed flippantly. "I'm tired and I've got shit to do."

The rain started again but there was no hurry. At this time of year everyone in the damn city was used to living their lives wet and uncomfortable. Their conversation turned to plans and the list. Who was coming up. How it would be done, and how it would end. They would often repeat the list to each other, name after name. The list, of course, was neither written nor recorded. This would be foolish as these people would be gone, disappeared, completely and inexplicably vanished. During the process not a thread of their existence would come back. Therefore, it is impossible to link a Conduit to anyone taken. Jason was in awe of this. The beautifully crafted, miraculous alibi led to no denial to the gift bestowed upon them.

The list was memorised, and it became almost a competition. Who could remember them in exactly the right order? People they had been jaded by, hurt by, or those who had simply angered one of them. People who deserved the extraordinary wrath that Jason would place upon them. Happy Hands required this. Jason had no control over its appetite. He could, however, have at least some control over who was deserving. He was not the insignificant figure that so many were in the habit of ignoring. He had power and he would use it. Luka could also put forward a target, but the final decision was Jason's. This would often take time and for a reason he wasn't too sure of himself, he would make it difficult for Luka to choose a target. Asking questions, asking for descriptions, insisting Luka recant the event or the events repeatedly. Perhaps he deserved to know. It was, after all, *his* god, that Luka had prayed to.

Chapter 3

Noah walked through the evening darkness on the outskirts of the city. The sound of the bustling traffic and chorus of angry car horns faded making him more aware of the sound of his own, quelching footsteps. He knew this neighbourhood. There were very few trees here. Just row upon row of government housing. Stark, simple fibro domiciles without unique features. The only decorations that distinguished one dump from another was the extent of the mess in the front yard, a mixture of chain fences, broken gates and car parts.

The picture given to him sat in his pocket. It was not time to look at it yet, for as soon as he did, it would begin. Tonight was one of those nights. He could feel the rage wafting around him like a hot breeze. Memories born from a life of conflict were playing in his mind, fuelling this fire further. Every ember of this feeling fed the beast that walked with him. The footsteps behind got louder, heavier in his ears. The voices flowing from nowhere grew louder. Clearer. The eerie call of distant, distorted bugles. The calls of a hundred warring men joined the march beside him. Were they memory? Were they all brought forth from the monster beside him? He didn't know and really, it didn't matter. The outcome was the same. Let it rise within him until the moment. This saved time and numbed the unease of actively considering his actions.

Noah reached the shack which he called home. The fibro-cement home, box-like and stark, sat in the middle of yet another dark, cold block. This was his life. This isolated derelict house in the middle of a hopeless and miserable neighbourhood was the closest he had to a home.

The rain became heavier as he stepped towards the dark wooden door. He turned the handle and entered. As he did, he could hear the scurrying of thousands of tiny legs belonging to the cockroaches that shared his dwelling. They froze upon the dark walls, ready to hide the moment they saw light.

For days Noah would roam the streets. He kept this hovel to shower and to store odd things that held no meaning for him anymore. Token sentiment? An attempt to feel more human perhaps. Then he would leave, heading back into the world again. He remembered the nights he would stay with Chelamah. They were good times. Warm, dry, and loved. This had become an addiction that he knew he had to break. For her sake and for his. She knew very little of this act Mika had asked him to perform and he needed to keep it that way. Tonight, he knew what Chelamah would be doing. She wouldn't know what he had to do.

He shuffled forward into a large, bare room. No lights. He wouldn't need them. He preferred this moment to be in the dark. It seemed appropriate and he liked the darkness. As the door closed behind him he felt a sense of relief that was short lived. He had been joined by the other. The thing that always walked beside him was now watching from the shadow at the far side of the room.

Shielded from the streetlights against the greys and blacks that fell heavily on the walls, the tall figure was almost indistinguishable from the shadows. Statue-like, only its white eyes grew brighter and wider. It was looking at him. It was the only thing it could see. But it knew the drill. It knew what this place meant, and it could feel the impending moment as succinctly as Noah. They were after all, in this together.

An angry, warlike scream ripped forth rebounding off the walls about him. He watched curiously as the roaches retreated at the sound. Funny, he thought, that they could hear this while others couldn't. The high-pitched wail was followed by unmistakable sounds of war. Gunfire, mayhem and the one noise, above all others, that haunted his every waking moment. The sound of suffering and death. The figure in the shadow was pulling these nightmares from his mind. It moved suddenly. A sharp snap, from its large black boot hitting the ground, cut the air. In the dim light from the window, its large, mottled head became hideously clear. Noah felt a sense of urgency. He was not ready yet. But it was. He had to give it a target and soon. He turned and quickly walked through the doorway to his left.

The noises grew louder, becoming all-consuming as Noah aggressively pulled off his hood and walked to a strange, wooden structure that sat alone in the middle of the unlit room. This archaic seat was designed by others in the past to restrain the insane, the hysterical and now him. Above it, attached to the ceiling, was a thin dirty silver chain. It hung perpendicular to the centre of the chair. He had to focus. Releasing too soon would be bad. Very bad. If there was no target when triggered, the thing in the shadows would be free and it would head straight to the person in his mind's eye. Whomever that was.

Not her. Not her.

Without another thought, Noah threw off his heavy jacket. Wearing only a simple white t-shirt he sat on the old restraint chair. He winced uncomfortably as injuries, years old, met the well-worn, solid wood frame. Grimacing, he pushed his legs through two leather straps that fitted around his ankles. With a hard tug, he quickly pulled the straps. Reaching to his side he grabbed a broad waist strap which he left unfastened. Quickly, hands now shaking, he pulled the thigh straps tight across his hips, causing him to wince in pain.

Breathing shallowly, he looked up, staring at the door. It entered the room. Powerful but silent it stopped, watching Noah hastily pull the swinging chain before his face. It knew what this chair was for, and it knew what was about to happen. Noah could feel its excitement increasing, as was his. Their feelings, their desires were becoming one.

Its rotted, angular face stood unblinking and emotionless, yet it displayed within it an intensity, an anticipation. He had to control it, hold it back and not confuse his feelings with the murderous thoughts of the other. Their emotions were melding. Twisting and merging, finding the perfect pattern, the singular combination required to trigger the victim with chaos. Target in sight. Like the grinding of an old lock. Everything had to align and then the door would open.

His hands shook as he reached into his coat pocket and pulled it out. Holding the photo in front of him he looked. Here it was, here was the prescribed target.

He carefully studied the picture, every detail. Male. Young. Late twenties, with oily blonde hair. The picture was taken from a distance; not ideal. Obviously by a security device of some kind. Patchy with a pixelated background. He didn't know how but this guy had managed to piss Mika off. Not a smart move. Noah had to study it. Create an image. He knew that this is what he would have to keep in his mind as he snapped the picture onto the clip hanging above him. Fixating on the image. After that task, one face seemed to blur into another becoming a kaleidoscope of masks, emotionless and meaningless. But for now, he would focus and manifest this person into a tangible avatar that, if standing beside him, could not have been more real than they were already in his mind.

As predicted, his emotions approached the precipice. From the darkness of the corner, the Soldier moved quickly towards him with a ferocity that caused him to lurch quickly backwards, slamming his head against the frame. It leaned over him and their eyes met. The white eyes glared into his own expectantly, hungrily. Its body heaved. It didn't look alive. Its face, sunken and grey, searched Noah's eyes for the target. A memory, a thought, a focus.

Noah spasmed as a surge of rage ran through him, brutal and violent. The target had been seen.

The Leviathan towered high above him as Noah sunk back into his restraints. No longer was it just a sound or a shadow. A rancid stench filled the room that Noah knew would grow stronger and more overwhelming. Deathly sweet and sickly. Nearly seven foot tall it was dressed in a torn, weathered desert combat uniform. Its head, thick and wide, was oddly shaped with a large square jaw and a long, cruel nose. Its eyes white moved rapidly in its head, glancing about with an air of fascination and focus. Its head rolled in exaggerated and elaborate movements as if centring itself, orienting to the real world it had just joined.

The Soldier looked at him, a ghoulish smile stretched like plastic across its cadaverous face before it contorted into a resolute scowl. It looked up as if to sniff the air. Suddenly, it leapt through the room with bizarre agility. It was on its way. Noah didn't know where its target was, but he would know when it reached them. With that thought, he slowly placed his hands inside the leather straps tethering them to the barbaric seat. He leant back, steeling himself for what was about to come.

OOO

A wind blew through the void in which Chelamah stood. It prompted her to move forward, her legs weak and shaking as she approached the large, wooden door. This had never happened before, yet the unexpected change didn't surprise her. So much had changed. The unpredictability terrified her. Closer now to the door, the scene beyond was unveiled. It was a church, a place of worship. She could see the dark, wooden pews of the nave lit by candles above the altar at the far end of the aisle.

The stone walls, dirty and archaic, contained no stained glass or art. The flickering light revealed bloodied debris. Remnants of reddened flesh strewn about the stone were grimly obvious. The pseudo-night sky, so fake but elaborate, enabled the counterfeit moon to filter through the arched, empty windows of stone.

She didn't know where she was, but she knew what this place meant. It was another realm, another domain. She should not have been here. *Mika, what have you done?* There were no symbols of worship in this church. This place was created on assumptions, the inaccurate interpretations of a Leviathan. An attempt at authenticity made over millennia of seeing only through the eyes of another.

Upon the pews were men, women, and children, their hands raised in prayer, held together by wire that wove through their flesh. Hands forever in parody of what was real prayer and worship.

Chelamah stared at the cobblestone floor. She wouldn't look at the people. She could hear their quiet whimpers, the hushed mutterings of the damned. Without noticing, she began to walk the aisle. Accidently, a man's eyes met hers. His mouth was closed but his eyes stared ahead full of fear and hopelessness. She terrified him. As terrified as he would be by anything here. Every movement, every noise, every arrival would bring only pain.

She had not been bought here. She had entered on her own. What did it mean? Where was the Wraith? The Wraith had a chance of survival. A human had none. She was powerless in this world. Seeing her hands she stared at them in confusion. There were thick strips of dried blood upon her fingers. The blood of Marco. This should **not** have happened. No physical trace of these people could leave that world. Not a hair of their head, not dust and certainly not blood from those who were taken.

Eerie choir music blasted from the stone walls. Frantic, she spun around looking in all directions, hands raised covering her ears from the sickening noise. Horrified, Chelamah froze as the candles suddenly seared brighter into the darkness above. The unmistakable scent of incense filled the air. As one, the torn bodies within the pews launched violently forward. Forced to stand, propelled by metal scaffolding embedded in their legs.

Crude metal crosses now erupted from the walls, adorned with writhing victims. Each wore a crown of barbed wire as heavy metal bolts were pushed through the extremities of their bucking bodies. A sick, blasphemous interpretation of the deity. This was how it worked. Selected memories from its chosen conduit were contorted. Made tangible for the damned. A sick and depraved impression of reality. She stifled a scream as she covered her mouth. Forcing herself to remain silent and still amongst the groans of the damned. She had to leave, but how?

The door behind swung open. She twirled as a figure entered from the dark blue night, a tall, pale humanoid cloaked in a black robe. Around its neck was a simple white collar. Its skeletal face looked gangrenous, with a long-pointed nose. Waxy, thin lips gave the slightest, irreverent smile. Chelamah watched it moved regally down the aisle, the black robes strangely unmoving and immaterial.

She had not seen this Leviathan before, but she knew of it. The Minister, its last conduit was Will Mason. Her knees trembled. She steadied herself against a pew, nearly touching an incoherent, rambling mutation of a woman held upright by the vicious scaffolds. Quickly she pulled away. She could not let them touch her.

The Minister was not looking at her. Was this a hope or an observation? It didn't turn or react as it passed. Could it see her? She didn't know. She reminded herself that she had not been Lit. She had not been targeted. On that uneasy premise, the monster seemed to be unable to see her. Rules were rules.

Macabre, yet serene, the Minister ascended the altar. The surreal, nightmarish gospel music seeped from the walls of the nave. His bound parishioners gyrated with the music. Some struggled against the restraints, while others merely responded to the well-known pain with acceptance.

The Minister slowly pivoted to face its congregation. A Wraith could pass through these worlds of horror. A human could not. Not Lit but with no way out. What did this mean for her? Chelamah summoned her strength to stay calm as she slowly backed down the aisle. But… to where? No idea, but away from the evil in front.

The Minister surveyed the pews as its arms opened in imitation of a graceful welcome. Its mouth opened ever so slightly as words boomed forth,

And all the people answered and said, His blood be on us, and on our children and our children's children.

The sickly voice resonated throughout the hall accompanied by distant sounds of anguish. Chelamah gasped and covered her ears. The Minister's mouth opened but this was not where the deafening sound came from.

He reveals deep and secret things; He knows what is in the darkness. And light dwells within Him. In my distress I called upon the Lord. I cried out to my God; He heard my voice from His temple, and my cry came before Him, even to His ears. Then the earth shook and trembled; The foundations of the hills also quaked and were shaken because He was angry.

Chelamah had to leave. The calamitous noise caused her dizziness and nausea. This voice was guttural and vile. Without thought or control, her mouth opened and released a soft whimpering "no."

Instantly all sound ceased. Shaking as she swallowed hard and opened her eyes. She had spoken. Not a cry, not a scream but a whisper. The single recognisable word had been heard by the Minister. Its white eyes looked about, blinking rapidly. Had it really heard her? This was an offence? A voice, a word muttered during its twisted sermon. She fought hard to settle. She had to remain quiet, still. She couldn't be seen. Please God, don't let it see me. The irony that she was praying was not lost to her.

"The second death."

Without sound, the Minister moved down the altar steps. Stopping briefly, its head snapped to its left. The direction of her abhorrent interruption. It moved silently past its grim congregation. No murmurs, no groans. Even the insane mutterings had ceased. This was a rule. This was the Leviathan's world and it had complete control. The consequences of disturbing a sermon would bring suffering that even the insane knew to avoid. Yet someone had dared to speak.

Chelamah didn't move. She slowed her breathing. She focused on steadying her feet. It was in front of her. She could now see it in all its grotesque glory. The smell from its rotted, pus-covered flesh was acrid and foul. White, faintly speckled eyes rolled around in enlarged sockets. Searching but not seeing, it remained there. A tiny relief. Rules were rules. A Leviathan was granted its licence to see a human, via the Conduit. Chelamah for now was human. The only human in this arcade of the accursed. She prayed that she would stay that way.

She was human here, completely powerless but ever so desired. If it touched her, would it feel her? Would it move through her, like a ghost... like a wraith. She didn't know and wouldn't take that gamble. She stared at the tarnished cross that hung around its neck, hypnotising herself to stay calm. Her breath barely raised her chest.

It moved its head from side to side like an inquisitive dog. Sensing, feeling. Either way Chelamah feared it knew something different was in its midst. She drew quick and silent breaths. She had to get out.

Lifting its long arms, the corpse-eyed gaze lifted to the ceiling. It opened its grim and cavernous mouth. The noise that engulfed the chapel was ungodly. A chorus of screaming voices calling out accompanied by throbbing, distorted scripture. It pounded her ears. She closed her eyes, her head bursting with pain.

Without a sound, she gripped the sides of her head. The screaming of tortured souls was piercing. She clenched her mouth shut, lips held tight, throat locked and silent by willpower alone.

Oh god please, oh god please make it stop...

Mouth contorted, it lowered its head to hers. Chelamah dropped to all fours to escape the terrible sound. Hands held her head an inch above the stone. That was when the pain began. A searing almost electric burning engulfed her finger and then her hand. She had unknowingly touched one of those living cadavers. Wincing, she quickly rolled away. The ghoul's head, almost detached from its body, rolled almost euphorically, laughing maniacally at the joy of being touched by a human. Chelamah's hand, burning with pain, began to fade into mist. That was it. That was her way out. It was then that a distant, soft voice got her attention, "don't scream... don't scream."

She knew that voice. Daring to lift her head, she cast her eyes to the abomination that lay upon the altar before her. Surrounding it she could see the brightest of blue, the most extraordinary splash of colour in this world of grey. A cross, much larger than the others, had taken centre stage. Bolted upon it, with blood-soaked ribbons down his front, was Will. His macerated muscles and torn flesh trembling.

Will was here… completely unreachable. Mika, this was Mika's doing. His voice broke, calling through the pain and the broken fragments of his face.

"Chel don't scream… don't." Will's eyes were closed, his head twisted to the side straining not to look at her. Chelamah looked back at the stone ground as the Minister acknowledged Will's words with a slight turn of its head.

Will looked up, his bright, alive eyes locking with hers as she cowered on the floor. In that fleeting glance, she hoped he saw the regret and compassion in her eyes. She hoped he would know that she had recognised him. That he would know, that if it was ever possible, she would be back for him. Suddenly she yelped in pain as a violent, powerful tug on her left shoulder bought her up from the ground.

It had seen her because Will had seen her. Its long cruel hands clamped shut on her left arm as it pulled her up. Its face met hers as it looked at her curiously. It was confused that something, an entity that was not Lit, not targeted, was present. It was seeing her with Will's eyes, but not with Will's emotion.

Her scream muted through clasped lips was pitifully hidden as she was suspended by one arm. It lifted her, dagger-like fingers cutting into her flesh. White eyes rolled in its head, not looking at her but about her. What was it seeing? What could a Leviathan see of a person without that person being Lit by anger? She watched the skeletal face. Its waxy lips trembled ever so slightly. Curiosity? Without warning she was thrown.

Air was forced from her as she slammed against a hard wooden pew. The awful gospel music began again. It had heard her voice and it knew the beautiful melody of human pain. Its stance became menacing, like a performance, like a ritual. Arms opened wide as it moved forward. Despite the agony and confusion, she had a thought. One hope that gave her a chance. Fuelled by adrenalin she jumped to her feet.

The Minster came. She turned and looked at the tattered, disfigured creature restrained beside her. Hands shaking, she gasped before throwing herself upon it. Intense burning shot up both arms and through her chest as sickening rage filled her body. Screaming, Chelamah, threw her head back as her limbs lengthened and withered. Chelamah faded as the twisted Wraith replaced her. Once again, their minds melded.

In the echoes of its mind, in the joy of finding itself harnessing the torn flesh of a human, Chelamah pushed forth. She hoped that the smorgasbord of flesh would not distract it, tempting it to stay. Triggering the disgusting form to manifest was her only chance. The battle within her raged.

RUN... RUN

The Minister struck the Wraith hard. It in turn released an ungodly screech as it spun round, coming back and swiping at the Minister's face. Impudent and weak but distracting enough for the Wraith to move swiftly into the pews, backing away from the Leviathan that rapidly advanced. Weaving between the tortured parishioners, the Minister dragged its large nails like knives across the faces of those it passed.

The Wraith became smoky and its rigid frame wisplike. Only its eyes, shining bright like its pursuer, gave this ghostly apparition form. Without warning, it ran towards the Minister and then, to the Minister's fury, straight through it. The door Chelamah had entered slammed shut. The candles upon the altar burnt brighter.

RUN... RUN... RUN

The taken were wrenched painfully onto their knees as the room erupted once more into twisted, morbid prayer. The Wraith moving with incredible speed was matched by the long certain stride of its attacker.

Throwing itself from the wall, it twisted and landed on the ground. The door through which Chelamah had walked had closed but the door by which the Minister had entered stood open. Both Chelamah and the Wraith knew this could change at any moment. The Leviathan was in complete control of this world. It could contort reality. Change the very fabric of its realm to trick and confuse. With no other option, the Wraith scurried flat against the floor as it dashed between the pews for the door. The Minister made chase, swiping downwards towards the fast-moving intruder as it exploded past the wooden doors and into the enveloping darkness.

It was there, outside the Minister's realm and in the darkness, that she saw it. Falling into a pit of pure hatred and refined evil, her eyes were cleared. Her mind was wiped of all that was the Wraith. This let her humanity cruelly see what lay before her. Just for a moment. It was not a person, nor the place or an object, but incomprehensible, pure evil. A horror too obscene for words. Senses too vile for her to comprehend bombarded her. Then darkness.

Chapter 4

A young, hunched man scuffled across the street, a duffel bag cast over his shoulder. Reaching the footpath, he chucked the bag to the ground and knelt, flicking drenched hair off his face. Rummaging quickly through its contents, he pulled out a small hoard of watches - worthless. A DVD player – pointless. He looked at other minor electricals he had gathered during his evening's work. Phones and laptops. *Phones and Laptops.* That was all that would be of any value. Money was needed. He was beginning to hurt. Now he even felt the desire to sleep. It had been four days since his fix. His body had awoken, and every cell was starting to burn.

Yanking the bag back onto his shoulder, he turned, hoping to get some cover from the rain under the awnings of an empty alley. Panting, he leant clumsily against the wall. Fuck this area. This was not his area. Smash and grab through car windows was pointless when the vehicles were parked in an area as crap as this one. He angrily pulled a half-soaked cigarette out of his coat pocket. "Fucking shit" he hissed, lighting it with wet hands. Taking a drag, he thudded his head on the bricks of the wall behind him in frustration.

Sighing, he started moving back down the road. He had two choices: go to Macs to try and beg for an increase in his tab, or continue this collection of shit. All he needed was just one sucker to leave their laptop on the backseat or, the jackpot, a wallet in the centre console. Just one forgetful punter would do.

Dex made his way down the path alongside a school where he relieved himself on a tree while assessing the convenience store across the road. Just the usual comings and goings of various night-time characters. A shitbox of a white vehicle sat by the curb in front of him. He was tempted to peer inside before noticing the 'abandoned vehicle" label upon the cracked windscreen. He didn't immediately recognise anyone but had met Mac here twice before. If his acquaintance was here then he might be here for business. He hoped against all odds that perhaps a chance meeting might invoke pity.

A sudden chill crept up his already sensitive body. Thinking of the long night of withdrawals ahead, he walked toward the brightly lit store. His head began to feel heavy. He would have to use again soon. If not it would become obvious, and his group would notice. He had let them down, but what they didn't know wouldn't hurt them. There was always hope that this might be the last hit. His last and then, never again. No-one need ever know he had fallen off the wagon.

His pace slowed as a new feeling overtook him. His body was so sensitive. He felt every breeze, every footstep. Amidst this amalgam of feeling was he missing something? He looked up and down the road. Nothing but dark, wet streets. It was then that he realised how compromised he was. His senses dampened and his desires refocused. Would he even know if he was in danger? In danger from what? The possibilities were endless. Events had been playing out around him, but he had managed to keep a low profile during the turmoil. Surely the unease was unfounded paranoia.

He approached the store doors, entering. His hunger was returning too; fuck it. He shook his pockets. Only loose change. Hot dogs, one dollar. That one dollar could make the difference between a hit and spending the night jonezin. Pondering this, he noticed the door open behind as a familiar man walked in.

"Mac, mate" he boomed excitedly. "How you doin?"

The tall, dark youth smiled begrudgingly, noticing the bag on Dex's back. "Good mate and you?"

"Good mate, yeah good… what you doin up here?"

"I live two blocks away dude." Mac walked to the counter pointing to a packet of cigarettes. A feeling of desperation overcame Dex. He couldn't let the interlude end without at least trying.

The attendant turned as Dex awkwardly ambled up to Mac again. "Mate, I know it's not ideal but I'm fucking… hurting man. I was…"

"Get away from me dude," Mac glared at him, angrily shoving him back. "Don't bring that talk to me here, you fuckin goose."

Frustrated but desperate, Dex tried to turn away but doubled back. "Mate, come on, seriously come on. Just a bit of a chalk man." Dex was aware of how pathetic he was acting but he couldn't stop. He needed this hit.

Mac grabbed Dex's arm, pulling him through the shop. Dex walked with him, hopeful this was a good sign. His cooker might relent.

"You fuck. Christ, junkies, tell you fucking what." Stopping before the door, Mac turned Dex to face him. "I got no chalk here because I don't carry it in my fucking purse."

Dex looked pitiful. He was prepared to look this way. He was prepared to let Mac look down on him as much as he wanted, if it installed any sympathy, he would do it. He had done worse to score in the past.

"What the fuck's wrong with you man huh?" Mac leant in quietly, tapping Dex's face sharply. "You're not thinking bud."

"I'm sorry, I'm sorry I just... I'm outta coin till tomorrow mate. Been caught a day short is all. I swear."

"Yeah, yeah OK." Mac smiled arrogantly, giving a mocking nod. "Yeah, cashed up by tomorrow, yeah. The whole worlds cashed up tomorrow. You dogs think I'm fucking thick."

"I've never fucked you over Mac. I wouldn't do that. I've always come through, ay." He could see Mac thinking and his demeanour swaying. Mac sighed and Dex held his breath. This was a good sign.

"Follow me back in ten minutes. I'll see what I can do."

A sense of relief washed over Dex. He smiled. His jib sat in the crotch of his jeans. He was ready to go. But suddenly, a different sensation hit him. Even amongst his physical pandemonium this was unmistakable. The air became deep and heavy. Terrified, Dex turned from Mac who watched in confusion. Slowly he approached the window and peered out. It was coming. It was coming. Oh shit... it's me.

Beyond the scattered vehicles and vagrants, at the end of the access drive, loomed the Soldier. Its long, thick arms, black and mottled, ended in large torn gloves. It stared intently through the landscape to the only thing possible for it to see. Predator and prey regarded each other. Dex knew what it was and what it was here to do. He had seen these things before but there was only one way you could truly feel the visceral dread of its presence. When it saw you. And right now, it was looking straight at him.

It broke into a thumping sprint towards its target, its boots slamming the ground. It came to a stop outside the large glass panel. Dex stumbled back, as its head lurched to the side.

"Fuck!" dropping his bag, he turned and ran to the back of the store as it plunged in a supernatural twilight. Dex knew this would occur. The space they were now in was impenetrable. The smashing of glass followed by a startled scream from Mac only confirmed that it had entered.

Leaping through the window, the soldier landed heavily on the floor. Stunned, Mac looked at the glass on the floor and back at the gaping hole. There was nothing there. A veil seemed to have descended making the windows black and empty.

"Hey! Open the door!" Mac yelled angrily at the confused attendant, not noticing Dex crawling across the floor to the back of the store. Once there he sat against the wall as the Soldier began slowly, purposefully, striding down the aisles. Why him? What did he do? He wasn't privy to any of the shit that had gone on! Whatever was going on with the group he was a grunt, just a grunt! Completely worthless and not capable of defending himself in any way. Fuck them. FUCK them. The Soldier rounded the aisle and stared down at him. Fuelled by terror, Dex spun around to find his feet before the Soldier moved forward. Dex hardly had time to grasp a breath before a huge hand grabbed the back of his neck lifting him painfully.

○○○

Noah closed his eyes gritting his teeth as piercing pain wrapped the base of his skull. This was followed by a burning sensation in his upper back. He couldn't breathe. The wooden frame of the chair creaked and moaned as his body arched painfully. Every muscle responded to the cracking force in his spine. It had begun.

○○○

Hanging helplessly by his neck, Dex couldn't see the creature behind as it cocked its arm. The Soldier delivered a single bone crunching punch to the back of his ribs. His body jolted brutally in the air. A dead choke left his mouth. He tried to cry but was only capable of short breathless gasps. Another blow ensured the ribs were smashed. The soldier lifted him higher, watching the flailing legs turn limp. The world spun as Dex was sent hurling onto the shelves. He collapsed on the floor unable to breath, unable to move.

39

Mac turned from the window to the back of the store. Someone was in here with them. He couldn't see them, but someone was beating the shit out of Dex. He pounded on the security shield before the service desk. "Open the fuckin doors!" The attendant ignored him, desperately slapping the panic button on the countertop. Mac turned back, squinting into the darkness towards the sharp, pained breaths of Dex. Where was he?

OOO

Noah bucked forward, his body held in place by the straps. His chest sank as air was once again smacked from his lungs. The back spasms were accompanied by a new pain that shot down both legs. Fighting to take in air, he gasped. His skin bled as numerous lacerations appeared on his arms and face. Crimson blood soaked through the t-shirt.

Breath through the pain… breath through the pain…

OOO

"No… no… I didn't… no," Dex gasped, turning over as the monstrous humanoid stood over him. It smiled, a cruel thin smile its white eyes bulbous and crazed with excitement. Rolling onto his stomach, Dex tried to crawl. It crouched, forcing a knee into his back. Dex took only a single breath before he felt the vice-like grip on his head. The Soldier's large, black hands over his ears gripped him tightly. A sickening thud and a blinding light flashed before the young man's eyes as his head was slammed into the floor. His battered head was lifted again. It was going to kill him. He didn't have long. There was only one thing to try: anger. Only with anger did he have a hope of fighting back.

Forcing in a deep, painful breath, Dex pushed out a guttural scream through his bloodied face. This invocation brought forth his own entity. The Soldier stopped, remaining motionless with its hands still gripping Dex's head. Two mist-like arms shot from Dex's body, hooking themselves around the Soldier's shoulders. The shadow creature dragged itself out from Dex's body, pulling at the vastly more powerful monster on top of him.

The Soldier stood, letting Dex's head fall to the floor. The shadow creature slashed at the monster, tearing at the powerful body, inane but distracting. The Soldier looked down at the attacking creature. An insect,

40

something to crush, nothing more. Dex had to move. He had to get up. He tried his legs, pulling them under himself not daring to look up. The Soldier was distracted. He had to move.

Stumbling to his feet, blood dripping to the floor, he steadied himself as a blood-smeared hand clawed on the glass of the cooler. Turning, he faced the Soldier. It was amused by the weaker foe that still slashed at it. Dex's eyes rolled to a ghostly white as he took a step. Now he paused, a foot in one world and a foot in the other. His shaking hands steadied as an unseen force took over. His fingers now caressed his smeared blood into delicate patterns and shapes. The Soldier took a back step. A blanket of terror enveloped the room, plunging it into even deeper darkness. He heard those present scream. They wouldn't recover from this. Terror summoned by the stepping, enhanced by the panic of its Conduit, bought with it a supernatural and complete horror that would remain within them forever. Mac crumpled by the door, screaming as he clawed at his face.

000

"Shit, shit, shit," Noah grunted through clenched teeth as slash wounds appeared across his chest. His shirt was bloodied and red. These wounds would stay. This was a supernatural assault. It was a Devotee. Fuck it Mika. The little fucker was fighting back. This guy was a Devotee. He's a fucking Devotee. A terror so extreme hit Noah like a physical blow, subsiding only by the grace of the Soldier. As quick as it rose, the fear dropped. Silly Devotee… Leviathans live in horror. Just like *home*.

Just let it happen! Noah pleaded silently to himself, *just make it end, don't fight. You can't fight. just let it happen and it finishes for the both of us.*

000

Dex shook his head painfully. His hand resting on the bloody canvas began trembling again. He could feel the shadow slipping away. His eyes warmed to blue. He had two choices, flee or fight. He couldn't win but he had put up a fight. A grim sense of resignation overcame him. He was surrounded by traitors and hunted by cowards. He was so tired and cold. He looked down at the blood pooling on the floor. That would explain it. A

41

moment of silence descended. He felt a sudden, powerful calm wash over him. He had seen such hell. It was to this hell he would return.

The Soldier slammed him to the ground. With its victim pinned, it lowered its head and stared into Dex's eyes. Dex gasped and closed them. He knew this monster wanted to see this. See the fear in his eyes, the terror. He wouldn't give it that. He wouldn't let it see that he was broken. He knew it desired this… as had he. He would not give it the pleasure. The Soldier attacked with short, brutal strikes. Dex passed into merciful unconsciousness. His shattered body, useless under the assault.

OOO

Noah's body bucked and writhed. Limbs straining under the leather harnesses. He gritted his teeth, grunting loudly, never screaming. His body was savagely beaten, as he looked through the Soldier's eyes and felt through the victim's body. His target mustn't die. He was not to die. Noah's body turned limp, unable either to defend or react. His body slammed by invisible forces. His victim's consciousness was gone. He was close to death and the Soldier would kill him if let. It had to end now. Taking in an agonising breath, Noah forced a scream. That was the call to end.

OOO

The Soldier stopped. Standing over its battered victim, it listened intently, gazing into the destruction. Returning to the window from which it entered, it stood beside Mac, who was now catatonic with fear. The Soldier was unable to see him. There were others here, as destroyed as Mac. That was how they would remain.

It reared back, then leapt through the torn window frame. The damaged lights above the store flickered on, illuminating the wreckage. People gathered at the entrance, but none entered. The human casualties remained strewn about the floor, brought down by Dex's use of the shadow in a desperate, final effort to save himself.

Alone in the wreckage, brutally battered, Dex lay still, bloodied and beaten.

OOO

42

The lights of the room flickered as the Soldier strode back in, staring at Noah with alarm. Noah screamed and the Leviathan came to see why. Noah slowly, painfully turned his head to the side. "Stop now" he groaned. "Leave him." A moment of contemplation and the Leviathan stepped back into the shadows where the familiar distorted bugle play began again. The Soldier kneeled facing the wall.

Noah breathed as deeply as his pain filled body would allow. Tears of agony filled his eyes. Unlike his target, merciful unconsciousness had not found him, and it never did. He would endure the pain he caused others with absolute clarity. That pain would soon pass, but the wounds inflicted on the Soldier by the shadow would not. They were Noah's to keep.

○○○

The Wraith's blackened form lay on the carpet next to Chelamah, who didn't move. Her motionless body, palms covered in ink, were still placed upon the wet canvas, as if peering through a window. The Wraith let out a blood-curdling screech before falling back into her, returning to its dormant state within its human host. With a start, Chelamah fell to the floor where she lay unmoving, too spent for any thought other than *it had stopped*. She was back.

Slowly, she pulled her bruised arms and legs toward her body, curling into a ball. She gasped, grabbing her bloodied arm to her chest. She examined her hands, holding her quivering fingers in the poorly lit room. Marco's blood had gone, but the injuries on her body remained. She felt her chest and arms sting as burnt skin moved with breathing. She would have to tend to the wounds before they got worse.

Painfully, she staggered into the bathroom and turned on the light, squinting in the glare. Her clothes were tattered, her hair dishevelled and matted. Slowly, wincing in discomfort she began to peel clothes off her reddened, burnt skin. The victim she had embraced had scalded her like molten tar on her flesh. She was grateful she was still able to move her arm. Mercifully, her shoulder was also intact. She had feared it had been broken. She would have to shower and dress the burns. The physical discomfort was numbed by the visions that still swirled in her mind like a feverish dream. Will, the Minister, moving between multiple realms and then… *that*. Just before she had found herself on this floor, barely escaping a fate worse than death. But what had she seen beyond that door? What did she see when the Leviathan's facade of a world was removed? It made no sense, indescribable. Between two realms, between two sick, fabricated landscapes there was another. And it was monstrous.

Once showered, she looked at herself in the mirror. Her blood ran cold. She had seen those eyes before and with each visit, she had seen them changing. It would be more difficult to hide them now.

○○○

Noah opened his eyes and hazily stared at the stained plaster ceiling. His eyes were stinging; he had not been asleep long. He was still fully dressed, his boots resting on the floor a foot or more off the end of the makeshift bed. For a moment all was well, peaceful. But then the memory of the previous night pushed forth in his mind, knotting his stomach. Marco. Chelamah. The young man with no name and a bloodied, white t-shirt.

When the event ended, he had stumbled onto the mattress and fell asleep, hardly surprising after 48 hours of slumberless bullshit. Quickly, he rolled onto the floor and rummaged through the empty food containers and remnants of past tenants. He pulled out his phone... nothing. She had not made contact. A feeling of urgency overcame him. Clothes askew and dizzy from fatigue, he stumbled to his feet.

It was 7.30. Seven hours. Seven fucking hours of nothing. What had happened?

Snatching his beanie off the floor he shoved it onto his shaved head. Leaving the room he walked into what would have been, at some point, the kitchen. Phone to his ear, he willed her to answer. By the third attempt, he was making his way to the front door. Swinging it open, the morning cold hit him as he collided with Chelamah. He yelped, before grabbing her with startled relief.

"Damn!" He pulled her close to him. "Jesus what happened?"

The sounds of heavy, confident footsteps filled his ears, moving closer and closer. It felt his shock, sparked to life by his rush of adrenaline and now it waited for the anger. But this wasn't possible, not with her. Chelamah said nothing.

"W-w-what happened?" He began guiding her back into the house. She didn't reply, her head low and eyes cast down. There was a silence about her that was unsettling. Holding her, he looked around nervously. She could not enter any further. She couldn't know what was only metres away. The atmosphere grew dark and echoless. The air thickened; who was doing this? Him or her? He couldn't tell, but he could feel the dread seeping about them. This is how it started, and he knew from his side anyway, it would go no further. But what about her?

"Listen to me," he spoke softly, ever so slightly rocking her body with his. "Listen… just… listen… breathe. Let it go… breathe and let it go… you're with me… just with me… don't tell me what happened…not yet… just be with me."

To Noah's relief, Chelamah nodded. She spoke quietly, not lifting her head. "I'm seeing him again today."

"Who? Your m-m-mother's friend?" Noah asked. "Did he make it? He got through it?"

"Yes. There are others. I just don't know where, but he does. We don't have much time." Chelamah nodded again. "I need to see him. I have seen… It has me. I am still there." Her voice trailed. "I still see it. I'm not enough. You are not enough."

"Enough?" He asked confused, "enough for what?"

"Not enough pain. Not enough screaming. Not enough horror. Not enough loss or sadness. We are not enough," she muttered coldly. "It wants more. It will take more."

"Baby no… no. It won't take you…" Noah held her tight.

"It will. I need to talk to him. I need to know. There is no other hope. You have to walk… through the dark… you have to choose those to walk with," she replied.

"I choose you… I choose you to walk with. I'll be with you. Whatever this is, I walk with you, and we will fucking beat it. I swear to god."

"The gods I've seen are not worth swearing to." Chelamah shook her head.

"You and me, remember. You and me, we can see this through," Noah argued forcibly, holding her tighter.

"You can't walk with me." She shook her head once more.

"Why? OK, you're freaking me out now. Why? What happened?"

45

Chelamah gently pushed away from him and looked up at him with a sad smile of resignation. Noah pushed away; his nose turned up with a learned revulsion. He saw the whitening eyes that stared back at him. "Because I'm already there."

Chapter 5

The cold had no end. In the twilight of evening, on a wet park bench outside the library of a primary school, Ellie sat holding a hot beverage. The heat radiated through her gloves. This service station produced very ordinary coffee. Never busy, and the man behind the counter never attempted to engage in conversation.

The grey sky was fading to black. She yawned. The last two months had been very hard, and she was tired. First the events that turned her life upside down and now, her own mind ruminating over these same events with a mixture of confusion, fear and wonder.

The little boy sitting beside her echoed her yawn. Gloved hands wrapped tightly around a takeaway cup of hot chocolate. Together they stared at the empty school yard where so many things had begun. Joshua liked this bench and Ellie felt, given what was about to happen, this was a good place to reassure him.

The pain in her ribs from Bael's fist had nearly dissipated. Bastard. A few ribs had most likely fractured but she chose not to think too much about it. Josh's little body was still covered in yellowing bruises. She was grateful that, being winter, it was easy for them both to don many layers of clothing so no-one would ask why. During the period after the Circle it could be difficult to make up excuses.

It had been 6 weeks since she and a young boy called Josh cemented an unlikely friendship through a twisted kinship. A lot of decisions were made, and a lot of risks were taken. She didn't know why she had done it. A small person had entered her life. Almost from the outset she had felt an over-whelming urge to protect him. And she had. Dr Niles would have loved to pull this shit apart.

Though, in turn, this small person had also protected her. And then there was Sam. Without him, neither she nor Josh would have made it to the Circle. That was a win. No-one had ever survived being Lit until now. This was qualified by Sam and his own experience. No-one had ever made it back. However, with this child she had learnt things, important things. Mechanics that she had no idea existed until now.

Though now, it was time for the facade of normality to invade their space. Common-sense had to prevail. Ellie knew Josh couldn't stay with her. They would look for him, as Sam had warned. Not that he needed to. She wasn't stupid. Joshua was a child, only 8 years of age, and the absence of his mother wouldn't go unnoticed. Explaining it to him had been very hard. She liked to think that he understood.

He had sat there and listened, smiling softly when she did, nodding in the right places. The anxiety with each sentence built in his eyes, but he kept smiling - kept nodding.

It was three days since Ron's white car had been removed from the front of the school. It was also obvious, when returning to Josh's house of horrors, that people had been inside. That was Friday. Today was Sunday. School tomorrow. Sam and she knew that they would be waiting for Josh. Given how badly surprises often turned out for their kind, it was best she prepared Josh and beat them to it. Even though he didn't realise it at his young age, for people like them, having control was key. The unexpected, caused distress. Distress caused chaos.

"Is it because of bossy Sam?" he muttered, straw still sitting in his lips.

"No, no," Ellie replied. "It's not Sam. I can deal with Sam. Sam said it because he cares. You know that."

"Is it because I did something wrong, because I tried to change the toilet roll, but the spinney thing fell off?"

"No, not at all. The spinney thing always falls off." Ellie shook her head. "You have done nothing wrong. It's the way it works. People noticed your Mum isn't here. They will look for you. You're 8 years old. They will ask you questions."

"I'm nearly 9 but…" Josh replied, holding his gloved hand up first with four fingers, then with five. "You told me what to say about my Mum and Ron and never coming back and stuff. I remember it really well."

"They won't just let you stay with me. I wish they would, but they won't" Ellie sighed, shaking her head. "I know you think they will, but they won't. That's not the way it works. They will want to look after you."

A moment of excitement washed over Josh, like he had discovered secret, magic words. "You look after me! Really well all the time and give me stuff like they say a mum should! Let's just tell them that!"

Ellie tried not to look into his wide, pleading brown eyes. "You have to trust me. This is the right thing. The only thing we can do, OK?"

Quickly, as if startled, Josh clumsily slapped the pocket of his coat. With a sigh of relief, he tilted his paper cup and gulped the last drops of lukewarm chocolate.

Ellie smiled softly. "It's still in the same place it was five minutes ago?" Josh nodded "Mm hm."

She had purchased Josh a little phone from the shop. He was delighted and kept running his finger over it like it was the most amazing thing in the world. He put it in his coat pocket. He would then take it out again and wipe it with the cuff of his coat until it shined, admire it, then put it back in and… repeat. He was overjoyed at seeing the tightly wound black charger cable under the phone in the glossy new box. Like another gift. New things just for him.

Josh had her number, and she had his. This is what this phone was for, contact and a lifeline for Josh. She knew the chances of him being able to call for help before all hell broke loose was bleak, but at least he had someone he could vent his feelings to. Perhaps she could deescalate before things got dangerous. How effective she would be was doubtful. Sadly, it was only a matter of time before Josh would lose control. This would be his life now. He would have to learn some very cruel lessons.

Placing his cup down slowly on his lap, he stared at the path before them. That was where they stood when it happened. That was where the fighting and yelling turned into running and screaming. He had felt so safe the last few weeks. He had felt so cared for. The thought of leaving all of that was so deeply sad. He would miss being with Ellie, in the warm flat with the bottomless fridge and nice smelling soap. He would even miss loud Sam, who would sit on the kitchen bench and talk so much that Ellie would ask him to calm down all the time.

"So what happens then?"

"With what?"

"With everything… Will I come back?" Josh asked looking up at her "or… do I go to my aunt's house and never come back?"

"Your aunt lives here, yes? Close by?"

"Kinda," Josh muttered.

"Kinda? You said she went to the same shops sometimes and that when your Mum saw her, you left quickly."

"Yeah I think so. It looked like her I think, and Mum said *bitch*. Then I saw her going into the school on my way home Friday… it was the same lady I think."

Ellie hid her fear and nodded. That was obviously who had been at his house. She knew, therefore, everyone knew. With a reassuring nudge, Ellie stood and watched Josh grab his knapsack and stand in front of her. She could see the glint of tears in his eyes, his hands wringing furiously.

"It's OK. I am right here. And I will be, OK? We will still be best friends, yes?"

"B.F.F" Josh nodded softly. "Just don't let the scary man get you."

Ellie nodded, surprised once again of the tears slightly misting her own eyes.

"Never. Never Josh. Remember it's me and you, not…?"

"…us and them" Josh nodded strongly. "They are not our friends." His gaze drifted to the road beside them. "Like now… that stupid dog is on the road… if he was normal he would cause an accident or something… stupid."

"You do what we practiced, and it will be OK. If it's not OK you run… you run away so fast and call me."

Josh nodded. He wanted to run now, far away. But Ellie would have to come too, and he knew she couldn't. Ellie held out her hand, Josh bashfully but whole heartedly took it. Together they started down the path to the road.

There were so many things to be considered with Josh, and she was very aware of the risks. They barely had two weeks to work on the back story. What concerned Ellie was how quickly and tragically it could all go wrong. And it would go wrong. The thought of all hell breaking loose and her not being there for him, when he was scared and confused, was almost unbearable. Ellie knew she couldn't prevent it. Like herself, Sam and any other Conduit, there were nightmares coming for him that he would have to endure alone.

50

Rule number 1: "Don't mention the Dog. They won't believe you. No-one will believe you.

Rule number 2: "Don't mention me. They won't believe me either."

And rule number 3: the most important of all… "Don't get angry. If you feel like you are getting angry, run away."

The story which was rehearsed multiple times was simple in theory; Mum and Ron had simply not come home. They spoke about persistence and consistency. It was important to keep the story simple and solid. Sadly, Ellie realised that keeping secrets to protect other people was something Josh was very well-versed in. He had told this story before and tragically, Josh was not unknown to the system. She hated exploiting this. He would be safe, at least for another 10 months, but no one around him would be.

Ellie guided him to the path opposite the police station. Josh had some-one that cared enough to seek him out, and this made Ellie grateful. He would be with them and hopefully living not too far away. For now, all was well. She had chosen not to know too much about his family. It would only serve to worry her further. She was effectively delivering to them a small and chatty gateway to hell, with an insatiable appetite for chocolate milk. Ellie gently turned Josh to face her. "Now you remember, yes? The words?"

"Yes, I remember what to say because you asked me to say it like a mil-lion trillion times all the time," Josh sighed.

"It's important…"

"Super important!" Josh interrupted nodding, keen to show off his lis-tening skills. Suddenly he looked concerned, glaring with worry at the road beside them "… he's gonna cause a crash or something."

"It's important" Ellie repeated "… that you remember, and you will do it every day. You promised me, remember? You said you would do it every day? Remember? Everyday?"

Josh, eager to please, smiled and nodded quickly, his beanie flopping down over his eyes. "I promise, I will do it every day."

Light rain began to fall on them as they turned and faced the police sta-tion into which Josh would go alone. Now they had to function in the normal world again. A world that had no knowledge and no ability to un-derstand the world they were from. They would have to filter, manipulate and lie their way into this world.

"Will you call me? Will you still see me?"

"You know I will. Absolutely. Just be good and do what we spoke about. Remember what we spoke about. Remember all of it."

Josh nodded and once more tears sprung into his eyes. His hands played with each other once again. Before he lifted his arms, Ellie stepped forward and hugged him. He fell into her, warmly hugging her back.

"Now," Ellie said softly, "My friend. You go. I'm right here, OK, I'm right here." Josh nodded into her arm. Bravely he pulled his knapsack higher on his shoulder and pulled away. Ellie watched him make his way, slowly at first across the road toward the police station. He stopped, casting an eye behind him looking at something she couldn't see. He quickly rolled his eyes, muttered and pointed to the sidewalk. The Dog, he communicated with the Dog. An urge rose inside her to correct him, explain to him that no… we don't regard them as real. Sadly she knew, it was all out of Josh's child-like concern for rules and the safety of others. A gentle, thoughtful personality.

He's gonna cause a crash or something.

But there was nothing she could say right now. He would have to learn like she did. There were other ways to show concern for others now. Being nice wouldn't always do it, and it seemed so wrong that a child like Josh would become an adult like Ellie. Self-loathing 101, thanks Dr Niles.

With that sad thought, she turned and walked away. The rain was now heavier, and the cold wind cut through her coat like tissue. Although the art of being covert was abundant in Ellie, Josh was not as calculating as she. This scared her. They would not believe him, and they would, as they had her, slowly pick away at him until he was finally backed into a corner. That was her fear.

As Sam had said. "By saving him, you have condemned many more."

Self-righteous prick.

He will be OK. She repeated in her mind. He will be OK. Though she knew the truth. He would not be OK. She was not OK. Sam was not OK. There had been nothing about her life, since the age of eleven, that had been anything close to OK. And now, after a short reprieve, she was alone again.

ᴏᴏᴏ

Sam Morris stood on the side of the river, looking into the murky green-black water. A fatigue ran through his body. It was not being tired, not being weary, it was a type of exhaustion that he had felt only twice in his life. He was surrounded in the silence by torments and noises that only he could witness. He wanted to close his eyes and hear nothing. He wanted the noise and the voices to stop. If only for a moment.

I JUST LEFT HIM NOW, the message read.

It was Ellie. Joshua had been taken to the authorities. Poor little guy.

Tomorrow he would meet once more with his elusive acquaintance Chelamah. Things had been quiet, her responses guarded. Frustrated, this had fuelled him into a plan to be more assertive the next time they met. At their last conversation she was plotting to introduce him to others of his kind. Nervous, borderline terrified, but the curiosity was intoxicating.

The Child was behind him, her outstretched hands grasped a gruesome toy. A human head with the body of a bear. Her hand rose above her toy in anticipation, then came down in a tickling motion upon the brown fur.

Tickle, Tickle, Tickle

The giggling stopped suddenly.

You took it, Sam. A childlike voice said behind him. At his name, her voice dropped to a masculine, guttural tone. It was this that unnerved him the most. These changes to her voice during her ranting. Was this her true voice? Was this dominant, evil deep voice a glimpse of the thing behind the facade of the child?

"They are not yours." Sam spoke quietly but with complete conviction. "None of them are yours."

Was he saying this to her? To himself? To the universe? God only knew but he was sure of one thing. His tough guy act was slowly falling apart, week by week, day by day. She was determined to break and punish him. A high-pitched roar stung his ears and made him wince. He had become used to this sensory assault. It had not stopped since she had furiously returned after he dared take Martin from her.

He had been resilient, in one manner or another, since the Circle. But so had she. She had met his proud triumph of freeing Martin with absolute rage and insult. For this she was sure to make him suffer. The multi-pitched screech of a hundred voices swirled in the air. Each one fresh, visceral, as if experiencing their torture for the first time. In his darker moments he found himself wondering, was it worth it? Was he so titillated by the prospect of saving Martin that he didn't even think of the possible and inevitable consequences? Did he do it for Martin or... for himself. Mercy or revenge? A mix of both.

This question tore at him. Was he a self-sacrificing hero or a selfish, vindictive fool? Either way, from the moment he jammed that knife into Martin's living cadaver, his own torment had increased.

He watched the water as if in a trance. Pulling his phone out of his pocket, he typed a response on the wet screen.

R U GOING HOME NOW

He hit send. His trembling thumb, wet with rain, smeared the screen. In the short time they had known each other, Sam realised that Ellie was notorious for taking long pauses between messages. He wouldn't get a response, but if he left now perhaps he would get an invite by the time he was nearly there?

Since that night, when he used the knife, his whole life had become significantly more horrific. He didn't think that could have been possible but here he was. He knew why. In retrospect it made sense. He had insulted her before. He had screamed at her. He had said hideous things. She would merely watch his mocking with sinister delight, relishing the cause of the unpleasant emotion. She would then laugh at him, taunt and tease him with grotesque images and sounds.

Through his actions against her, on that night in her own hell, he had given a direct and forceful declaration of war. It worked and she lost that battle. He took something from her, and she was never going to accept such a blatant *fuck you*. Perhaps he should have chosen his approach more carefully. He had been so excited to have something to fight back with. He was impatient. Rash. Or perhaps just so consumed by the thought of taking from her that he didn't think it through.

The first time in his life he had the chance to fight back, and he jumped on it way too eagerly. Because once the knife had plunged into Martin's chest, once he had slumped into a merciful death, Sam had nothing else to fight with.

Mine, mine, mine, mine, mine, mine, mine, she repeated over and over. He walked towards her and gave her a passing glance. She stopped still and smirked. Her white eyes snapping open and closed in rapid succession. Her other hand clutched something on the front of her dirty white dress. She had been presenting this to him more and more lately. She had fashioned what had become her favourite new toy. A bulbous, round head screaming silent cries, the body of a brown teddy bear had been crudely attached to the base of its skull. Her long, mottled hands gently scratched at its light brown fur. He couldn't tell who the head belonged to. He didn't want to know. It didn't matter.

His damaged arms still hurt, and his legs were still weak and unsure. He had not showered for 3 days, and he stank. This was new for Sam and, weirdly, it fascinated him. The smell of stale body odour, the warm cuddly feeling of well-worn clothes. Unshaven and "scruffy." He finally looked on the outside how he felt on the inside; chaotic and dirty. The rain quickened. He wiped his brow, tasting the salt on his unwashed skin as the water ran over his lips.

He needed to see Ellie. He needed to get out of here. He needed peace. Ellie gave him a reprieve. The Child would maintain a distance of sorts when Ellie, or more so the monster that walked beside her, was present. He and Ellie had discussed this briefly, but right now, staring blankly, the thought of turning around and walking away with nothing but that thing beside him was unbearable.

ﾟ○ﾟ

"Come on Jason! One more! One more!" The voice spoke in his ear as the obvious lack of strength hit his triceps. How did this happen? How did your body suddenly decide to stop working?

"No, don't stop mate! Killing it!" The voice got louder and louder but as it did, Jason felt his arms collapse weak and lifeless to the side. A short

55

wrench in his wrists as the dumbbells hit the padded flooring underneath him. At least he hadn't dropped them on his face.

"That was awesome man, really well done… really." Jason lay on the gym bench, breathing deeply and quickly. His chest now burnt, but he knew that that was the point. He stared at the drop ceiling above him and the fluorescent lighting tubes, two in his field of vision. It was strange that he remembered this image in such detail. It proved how many times he had lain, beaten and exhausted in this very position over the past 6 weeks.

Tyler, his heavily tattooed yet quite short personal trainer buzzed about him talking about how well he had done. Tyler had applied the word *awesome* so many times but moments like these made Jason feel very, very far from anything like awesome.

"How much was that?" Jason asked wearily. "How much?"

"Six mate. You pulled out four sets of six." Tyler beamed over the top of him, his peroxided teeth shining almost menacingly. "It was…"

"Awesome, yeah I know… but the weight, how much weight?" Jason clarified impatiently.

"10kg mate, 10 big ones each side. Come on… sit yourself up." He reached behind Jason's shoulders and pulled him up to sit. Like a baby, like a child. Jason ran his hands through his short black hair. His glasses were covered in smears of sweat.

"Remember, not weight, effort yeah?" Jason slumped disappointedly. Last week it was 7.5kg and he had done 4 sets of 8. How could 2.5 kg each side make so much of a fucking difference? He stared briefly at his reflection in the mirror. Still as unimpressive as before. The first thing that he noticed, something that he always noticed, was the stark whiteness of his legs as he sat in these ridiculous black shorts. The second was his baggy oversized, white t-shirt. Deliberately chosen so this very view of his underwhelming physique wouldn't haunt him every moment in this brightly lit world of mirrors. It also had the advantage of hiding the deep slashes on his back. An accumulation over many years.

"Get your bearings matey, we're heading to your next favourite friend. Let's finish off with some body weight… push-up time champ." Tyler patted Jason on the back as he bounded away to the area of their next torture. Jason winced in silent agony, the light pat burning his skin. He paid a moment's regard to a familiar silhouette, standing tall in the shadows near the row of black, wooden lockers. Tyler walked right by it and as expected, he went completely unnoticed. Mika would believe this was why his constant companion cried so much. Mika would tell Jason that he needed to "gift" it. That it had been too long.

It hung in the far corner of the gym, a tall form wrapped in a cocoon of a multi-coloured shroud. Thick black strings fastened from the ceiling into the concealed being beneath the brilliant cloak. Feint applause seeped from the walls around Jason. It had been too long. It was desiring a gift and its constant intrusion into Jason's day were his own fault.

Jason sighed, pulled his towel out from beneath his legs and followed Tyler. He hated gym people. My god how he hated the smorgasbord of stereotypes that paraded around this building. All those young women with backsides so pert it looked like their anus was trying to kiss their lumbar spines. Young men who giggled like schoolgirls. He found this contradictory. The number of men who used the mocking phrase "Giggle like a girl." His recent hobby had enlightened him to the fact that men giggle, not women. This fuelled his disdain for them. He refused to admit that they intimidated him. How could they? He had his 'blessing'. But they could still lift more than him. They could still wear singlets, unlike him. They were still manly… unlike him.

His recent hobby had also been kept a secret from those around him. Mika would see this as an insult. He considered a focus on physical weaknesses as a failure to appreciate Jason's other… attributes. Mika believed these made them superior to all other people. Mika's amazing physical form didn't seem to have come out of nowhere, but Jason certainly wasn't going to quiz him on it. Dynamics had changed of late. Everyone was reassessing where they fell in the new world order that seemed to be emerging.

His Devotee, Luka, knew only because that was what was expected. "Going to the gym" would be considered a foolish concern for the physical. But not when under the guise that he was simply scouting for his next target, and he was not there solely for his own desire. As such it would be expected that his Devotee would know. It was Luka's responsibility to watch over him, assist him and when needed, protect him. So, he was making the most out of the opportunity, but ultimately, he would be expected to target. And for Jason, that was very, very easy.

What made Jason uncomfortable was that he realised that he wanted, even desired, more time in the "normality" of this place. Mika would've found that insulting.

Big, broad but short Tyler stood by the stretching area mirror, casting his eyes on the ground beneath him. He smiled encouragingly. My god, what did he use on those teeth?

"OK Jay-Jay!"

Jay-Jay… please not Jay-Jay. He had fantasised before, when Tyler had used this diminutive pet name, that he would just lean in and whisper into his ear, "you ever call me that again and I will finish you." But he never had and, over time to his complete surprise, he had come to like him. As far as people go, Tyler was not unbearable. He tried. He encouraged without mocking Jason's feeble efforts. He had never belittled the lack of physical prowess that Jason demonstrated. Tyler had shown him acceptance. It was something he looked forward to during their sessions This didn't make Tyler any less worthy of interest, but at present he was not on the list.

"The floor? I really hate the floor" Jason smiled and instantly noticed this. It didn't happen often. Good thoughts equalled good emotions, and these were rare. Tyler was safe, he was sure of it. A noise behind him caused sudden concern. Banter, loud and obnoxious. He had noticed these men moments before as he passed by them. More so the offensive brightness of their gym wear and the tan on their bodies that could not be naturally possible. One of them, a shorter Asian guy, was on the shoulder press. One darker, arm-sleeve tattoo guy, sat on the ground with his phone to the side recording. Seriously? The third was a synthetically muscled blonde dude looking like bad breath and date rape. He had the biggest mouth, making comments to others and had twice now been derogatory to Jason. Both times Tyler had managed to distract him, and he fell into that distraction with relief. Why? Why had he waited? Patience and planning.

"OK, down we go!" Tyler pointed enthusiastically to the floor. Jason's heart dropped as he realised how close he was, just a few metres away from these douches. How did Tyler not notice? Or was Tyler not bothered by it. A secret of the "normal" view of the world and how their inner aspects become fortified. He had not achieved this level of confidence, not yet and this… was weak.

The floor seemed so far away. Placing his hands in front of him Jason lowered himself to the mat, landing heavily on his knees.

"AH! He's broke them! They've cracked!" That same voice, followed by that recognisable snickering and giggling. Jason froze, hands and knees on the floor. A sudden jolt of embarrassment grabbed him.

Wake up … wake up… wake up, the voice spat, strangely androgenous and vicious.

Jason could feel it, reading his feelings and watching his irritation rise.

"Settle down ya clowns," Tyler laughed dismissively, crouching to Jason on the floor. "Just boofheads matey don't worry about them. Ignore them."

Jason dared not move. He had avoided this crowd, avoided these shit-heads, by coming at a different time. He felt invaded, attacked in what should've been his moment, his happiness? He felt emasculated and powerless.

"Just kidding! Just kidding! His legs are remarkable!" Mocking laughter. Another commented that at least his arms were bigger than his legs. The laughter continued.

Irritated, Tyler turned to engage but stopped as Jason muttered, staring at the floor beneath him "I thought those guys came at night."

"Yep. Only Monday mornings bud." Tyler gave a frustrated sigh. "Don't worry about them, hey, I'll talk to them. They're a bunch of wankers."

Jason had no time to ask Tyler not to. To demand he not be made to look as fragile as they thought he was. Tyler was already standing, striding over to the group, leaving Jason lying on the floor, pathetic, weak, and small. He was worthy of ridicule.

Wake Up!

The dark shadow hung in the corner, next to the entrance to the changing rooms. His eyes were closed but Jason knew this ruse. Its eyes were never closed. It was experiencing a scene it could not yet see but could feel through its Conduit's simmering temper. The air began to thicken, and the room had darkened ever so slightly but not enough, not yet. Jason's breaths became deeper, louder as he attempted to control this tipping point. Now was not the time. There were others here, including Tyler. There were no half measures with this process. He had no ability to control who came with him and who didn't. Mika would expect calculation and planning in the process, not rogue firings of "petty temper." Mika would expect self-control. And Tyler. He couldn't do it to Tyler.

The conversation between Tyler and the group of three douchebags became heated. He heard Tyler speak of suspension of membership and zero tolerance to bullying. He heard the blond-haired guy say, "Calm down mate, it was a joke." This man was tall, confident, and beautiful.

It confused Jason. Why do men like this, get bodies like that? It seemed an unjust advantage. Slowly he lowered his knees to the floor, turned and raised himself to a sitting position and pondered. There was no beauty in their flesh. It came off so easily. It tore like paper and slid off like well-cooked meat. This tough boy's stance, arms crossed with his head held high would break. He would dance like a fool, like a hysterical, powerless child. His perfect chiselled jaw would be ripped from his perfect face, again and again. He would be torn apart, mocked, berated, dehumanised. That voice so confident, so manly, would begin to scream and make horrific noises that would never have been thought possible.

Tyler, nor the group he was arguing with, noticed as Jason grabbed his towel and quickly left the gym floor, heading straight for the lockers. He would not look up. He had to ignore absolutely everyone, including Tyler who he was sure had called him as he rounded the corner. Swiftly he grabbed his bag and made for the exit.

Still in his gym wear, the outside air hit him hard, causing him to gasp in sobering cold. The rain was falling as he quickly, angrily, wrenched out his jacket and placed it on whilst still hurrying down the street. He had assumed that those three always came in the evening. That was why he stopped coming after work. He would be back. He would be back when Tyler wouldn't be there. That would be what Mika expected. A plot and a design. Your Leviathan deserved that regard. The list would be updated. It was, after all, his list to change. He was not one to be mocked. He had power and he knew how to use it.

Chapter 6

Sam sat in the warmth of his car, heater on and radio playing discreetly in the background. Exhausted, he was worn down and close to breaking point. The juxtaposition of having hope, new tools to work with, and new people, together with her constant assault was bizarre. He stared out the window at the wet streets. People moved like extras in his own miserable reality TV show. The resulting sense of detachment from reality was terrifying. This was now as miserable and bleak as the shit weather that surrounded him. Depression was gripping him and taking him down. Again.

The small figure was dressed in dirty white, that stupid bow still in her long, matted hair. White eyes burrowed into the side of his head, demanding that he look at her. Upon her lap sat 'teddyman', its flesh decomposed and ripped, mumbling incoherent words as she gently stroked its furry body. Looking down she smiled in delight as an eyeball slipped from its blackened socket, resting on the brown fur. She giggled, twisting her fingers around the long, yellowish optic nerve. Teddyman fell silent as she grasped the fleshy ball and squeezed, breaking it open with a silent pop. She began to giggle hysterically, her head thrashing around in frenzied enjoyment as white goo ran between her fingers.

The screaming of loved ones, the sounds of torture, were now with him 24-7. The wails, the pounding and the horror flowing around and through him never stopped. Coupled with that incessant childish music which surrounded her… it was absolutely *de-fucking-lightful!* And how, in the absolute bollocks, did she even hear the song about Baby Sharks?

Just to top it all off, just to destroy the final sinews of his self-esteem, here he was stalking Ellie once again. She hadn't responded to his text in the rapid-fire way he would have liked. In his desperation for company he had talked himself into believing that there was no harm in just turning up.

He needed to see her. Not call her. Why? Because he wanted to. Being with someone who understood his life was becoming more and more needed every day. And secondly, the Dark Child retreated from Ellie but more so from Ellie's... It.

Not Bael, not Bael... It... don't piss her off again.

He scanned the footpath in front of her building. He watched. It was so damn hard to identify anyone in this weather. Everyone looked like heavily wrapped Inuit's. No colour, no discerning features, just... people. He placed his hands on top of the steering wheel and lowered his face onto it. Closing his eyes, he took in the darkness. For a moment, he considered practicing 'deep breathing'. He had been led through the technique by many of his past psychologists. It made him feel silly. To his surprise the car fell silent. Had the deep breathing shit actually worked?

Slowly he lifted his head. Cautiously he glanced at the seat beside him. The Child was on her knees, hands pressed against the condensation of the windscreen. Her eyes large and bulbous as blue lips mouthed words Sam couldn't hear. He slowly faced forward, following her stare and noticed a fast moving, huddled figure making its way down the footpath. Her long black hair fell heavily from inside a beanie, and she was the only person on the street not carrying an umbrella.

Quickly turning off the ignition he swung open the door taking off down the path towards her. She stopped to cross the road. Sam noticed her earbud headphones as she looked one way, the other and then straight at him. Approaching, he tried to decipher how she felt about him just turning up. Ellie was always extremely hard to read. Smiling the biggest, friendliest smile he could muster, he jogged towards her.

"Hello!" he called and instantly knew it was way too enthusiastic. They had spoken only two days ago.

"Hi!" was her quick, cold greeting.

"Hey, how are you?" Sam responded, instantly feeling like an upbeat imposter. He didn't feel cheery at all.

"I'm OK, how did you know I was going home?"

"I didn't," he shrugged. Ellie noticed the tears in his eyes and unkempt appearance. "I just thought I would come. I thought, maybe you would need to talk about... ya know... Josh going home and everything... maybe?"

Ellie nodded slightly though neither she nor Sam believed she needed this. Sam's anxiety was palpable. "I'm… OK, but thanks. What have you been doing?"

Ellie noticed his defeated air. His voice was shaking. His eyes tried a little too hard to look vital. He was in trouble. His eyes closed briefly and for a moment took in the sounds of traffic, people, rain, and life. The Child's taunts were distant, comparatively inaudible to what they had been. He savoured this. Ellie watched him sway in exhaustion before embarrassingly steadying himself.

"Not much to be honest. Not much of… anything really."

"You look like crap," she stated matter-of-factly. Her voice was controlled, regulated and calm with just the slightest nuance of concern. He hoped it was concern and not annoyance.

Sam shrugged nonchalantly trying to ignore the sting of Ellie's remark on his personal appearance. For someone as vain as Sam, this was not easy. He smiled and guffawed as if it was merely witty banter. Ellie didn't qualify this by chuckling back. She meant it as a fact.

"So, he's gone?"

"No" Ellie answered bluntly, surprising Sam as the reference to Josh being *gone* seemed to offend her. "I took him to Marlin Street. He will let me know when all is OK."

Sam nodded, slightly embarrassed. "It was the right decision."

"The only decision." Ellie turned to face the road again. "It was the only choice we had."

Sam nodded in agreement. "It was."

Ellie smiled wearily. "We will see how things go won't we." Sarcastic. They stood in silence for a moment. The right decision? No. There was no right decision. The right decision would have been to lock Josh down before his unintentional reign of terror could begin. But then what? There was no out for Josh. However they handled it, they did not have the power to change anything. They were powerless to stop what would unfold.

"It doesn't seem like enough." Sam looked around nervously.

"It isn't," Ellie replied. "It's not going to be enough."

"Sweet…pessimism… what do we do now?" he shrugged. "What happens to us?"

"Now… you learn. It's the only chance he has. We need to learn what we can do. When are you meeting that person again?"

Sam was surprised. "You're interested? I thought you wanted no part in it?"

Ellie shifted awkwardly. She thought for a moment before answering. "I am interested. But you have to listen to me Sam. I need you to hear me. Be careful what you bring to me. What you bring to me… you bring to It. Filter what you say. Always. Like you, I'm never alone."

Puzzled but pleased by her interest, Sam nodded. "Sure thing."

Ellie watched Sam's eyes falter and roll with exhaustion.

"You need to sleep," she said softly. The calm tone of her voice seemed to enchant him. His eyelids fluttered briefly before opening once more. Staring into nothingness. Ellie knew this look. It had him. It was beating him into the ground. He half smiled, almost stumbling forward before he whispered. "I can't sleep. She… won't let me. She's trying to kill me. I'm coming a-fucking-part."

"What can I do?" Ellie asked apprehensively, unsure if there was anything that would make a difference.

"Let me stay with you. Near to you. Just for a while. She doesn't like you. Please… please Ellie, keep her away just for a while" he pleaded. "It's like the nights before the Circle but it's all the time now. I can't do it."

Why the Dark Child avoided Bael they didn't know, but that didn't matter. It could be pondered more closely at another time. For now it was something they could use. A new piece of information that in this situation gave them an edge.

"OK" Ellie murmured gently. "Come on."

"Just for a while, just…"

"Come on, let's go." Ellie grasped his arm. For a second Sam thought this was being caring or protective, though with a firm grasp on his upper arm, it quickly became evident it was authoritative. She didn't want him out here… in the street… amongst people.

"No wait! Wait!" Sam yelled loudly, startling Ellie, and causing her blood to run cold. "I've left my… my phone in the car. Just give me a sec."

Exasperated, Ellie turned to watch Sam as he ran back down the footpath. He threw open his car door and leant in. She watched as he rummaged around and then leant heavily, exhausted, and weary on the seat beneath him. His head hung from his shoulders. Suddenly he struck out. Half his body cloaked by the wind-screen, his body moved violently striking the passenger seat. The car rocked. Ellie took a step backwards. What was he doing? Quickly he leapt away from the car, slamming the door shut hard.

"Got it!" he called, holding it briefly in the air before shoving it into his hoodie pocket and running towards her. Ellie stared at the car, its interior light fading to black. She hadn't even noticed Sam re-joined her. He saw her staring and sighed heavily.

"Sometimes I just like to pretend, you know," he said, embarrassed and obviously unnerved.

"Pretend?"

"That I can actually hurt her."

Unsure what to say, Ellie simply nodded slowly. "Does it make you feel better?"

"No," Sam sighed. "But sometimes I think she really needs to know."

"Know what?"

"That she's a cunt." He turned and began walking up the footpath, leaving Ellie to stare at the empty car before uneasily following her increasingly unstable friend. She grabbed him firmly by the arm once again.

"OK weirdo. Look down and walk with me," she said firmly. "Don't look at anyone. Don't listen to anything. Just walk with me."

ooo

A small figure sat in the large waiting area with grubby, off-white walls. On a bench against the wall, Joshua Fielding looked like a ball of clumped fabric, wearing an assortment of clothes from his house that Ellie made him dress in. She told him that she would keep his other clothes special. She would wash them and put them in the machine with the nice smelling soap for when he came back. He looked at his hands, shyly lifting his fingers to his nose and giving them a sniff. They still smelt soapy and nice too.

He knew where he had to go. Past the loud man who shouted about the fence in front of his house. Then past the lady with black running down her face and hair of different colours, who seemed to be asleep on the shoulder of a big, tattooed man. Then to the bench by the wall which was out of the way and inconspicuous.

The other people were all different, but the same. Some were loudly talking, some were quiet, but none seemed happy to be there. Maybe they were

65

in trouble. Had got told off by the policeman behind the bench with the glass around it so high that people had to shout at him. Maybe the police noticed that some of them smelt like Ron's bucket and didn't like it. The memory made him sniff his fingers again.

The police people behind the window looked angry, but very neat. Josh hadn't seen them in a police building before. When they visited his house and drove away with Ron the second time, they had hats on and jackets with cool tools that shone and wiggled when they walked. That was what made Josh want to be one. He liked those tools very much. They looked tall and strong with blue outfits on, and Josh felt very, very small.

Feeling awkward and twitchy, Josh distracted himself by looking at a poster of people's faces hanging on a large white pin board; Josh supposed these people were missing, because the poster had a phone number asking for any information on where they could be. One picture was of a man and a woman. A pretty woman with nice hair and very white skin who was smiling. For a moment he stared at the picture of the auburn-haired stranger feeling sad. It said her name was Kaylee. That was a nice name. He hoped she would come home soon.

A man yelled. Josh jumped and looked at the floor again. You don't look at angry people because then they get angry with you. Even though it occurred to Josh that the very worst person in the room to get angry would be him. The Monster Dog was being an idiot. He couldn't see it properly, but its rasping and growling breaths suddenly got louder. Every now and then he would catch a glimpse of its massive wolf-like form moving about in the reflections of the window or the shiny doors. Only a flash of that familiar black shadow letting Josh know he was still there.

The woman with the black paint running down her face opened her eyes and looked at him. He smiled but quickly remembered not to and looked at the ground. She looked at Josh angrily, standing up and stomping to the desk.

He thought about going to the desk too, but Ellie didn't say that. Should he? He wasn't sure. Maybe he just waited there, and they would come and say "Joshua we were looking for you. Thank you for saving us time! Your new friend Ellie sounds nice. Why don't you go and live with her forever?" This fantasy triggered him to check his pocket for his phone. After all, if that did happen, he would have to call her to come and get him.

Another yell. This time from the lady who asked to use the phone with lots of swear words. The police officer got angry and told her, "Sit down, I won't tell you again." She looked ready to shout again but she must have noticed, as Josh had, that the police were really serious. He hoped they wouldn't yell at him like that. He felt scared again. He tried to remember Ellies' Josh; clean, with a full tummy and an illusion of safety. He scoffed at the police-station version, in the smelly clothes. That Josh was weak and scared.

This was all Ellie's plan. He had a friend. He put his hands in the huge pockets and pulled out his new phone, touching the screen and watching it spring to life with colours and shapes. New phone… new Josh. It was then that he heard a demanding voice

"Hey kid, let me use that for a second."

The angry woman had her hand out and Josh was instantly scared. The man with the tattoos looked at her, smiling. These people wanted his phone.

○○○

Ellie watched as Sam quietly lay himself down on her couch. That couch had been well used these last few weeks, she thought she could start charging rent. He looked exhausted and dishevelled. He had taken off his shoes a few minutes earlier and she was surprised by, but had remained quiet about, the odour emanating from the filthy socks.

"They stink!" Sam stated as if reading her mind. Ellie sat on the chair beside him, her long hair hanging over her face. She smiled awkwardly.

"They do," she nodded.

"Will you stay here with me?" Sam muttered, his eyes growing heavier with each breath.

I'm lost. Help me please. Help me, I want my mummy. The voice echoed in the distance. The Dark Child was not far away. But enough to grant him reprieve. *I cry now. I cry.*

"While you sleep? Yeah."

"And while I shower?" He opened his eyes and smiled cheekily at her. She shook her head.

"Judging by your feet, letting you shower would be a public service that you will perform very much alone." she replied smiling. Sam liked humour.

67

He used humour. Humour and silly banter kept him calm, and Ellie was exploiting this.

Out of nowhere, Sam suddenly put his hand up in the air as if about to say something extremely important. "Did you tell Josh the *'no looky, no touchy'* rule?"

Momentarily confused, Ellie shook her head. "What and what rule?

"You know… get pissed… don't look at anyone or touch anyone… that rule." He settled back down.

"Of course I did. But it's easier said than executed." Ellie sighed, *no looky, no touchy?... What on earth?* "But I would never use that phrase."

"Yeah, but he's eight."

"Yes but I'm not eight." She wiped the rain from her face. "Besides, has that worked for you?"

Sam sighed tiredly, eyes closed. "Like hell it has."

"It's unreliable at best." She grimaced. "You sleep first. Shower later."

Ellie stood and walked out of the room. Sam watched her with trepidation. He was scared she would leave, the fear palpable.

He lifted his head. "You OK? Are you going somewhere?"

"No" Ellie called, walking back into the sitting area with a blanket in her hands. She unwrapped it roughly and chucked it over his legs.

"No tuck in?" he smiled, opening his eyes, and gauging her reaction to his jibe. He was unsure if the look on her face was amusement or frustration. Perhaps a mixture of both.

"No, I don't tuck," she sighed, watching him wrestle the blanket over his legs.

Sam wriggled, pulling it higher around himself whilst Ellie watched.

"I should be alright you know, it's not cold in here" Sam yawned before closing his eyes.

Ellie gave a small smirk followed by a grimace, "It's about to be… I'm opening the window."

◯◯◯

The woman looked down at him, her hand still outstretched with ugly, red fake nails beckoning for Josh to hand her his most treasured possession. She couldn't touch it. Ellie said no, and if the phone disappeared, so did

Ellie. This thought was utterly inconceivable. Josh had simply replied "No", but this hadn't stopped her.

She simply flicked her ugly red nails and said "Come on, 2 seconds. Give it to me." Her cold, piercing blue eyes staring down at him. The tattooed man just watched on. She was in a very bad mood and Josh quickly realised that she may have been hungry. She was very, very skinny.

He glanced beyond her to the desk. The police weren't looking. The big dark man was now sitting where she had been. He was looking and smiled, but not in friendliness. He was enjoying watching Josh's eyes move uncomfortably around the room. This was entertaining to him. Josh was small and this woman was a bully. Without meaning to, his hand grew even tighter around his favourite possession.

"I'm not allowed to." Defiant but scared, his voice trailed into a whisper. He lifted it slightly with the plan of burying it deep in his pocket. Maybe then she would leave him alone. The adults in the room didn't seem to mind that she was being mean.

"You won't get in trouble. No-one here kid. Just let me use it" she hissed.

"No, I'm not allowed to" Josh repeated, his voice began to tremble.

Her eyes reminded him of something and someone. They were cold, unmoving, and vicious. They looked like Ron's. Vicious and spiteful. Her silly hair was all different colours but still looked like straw. Her teeth were yellow, and her make-up smeared. It all made sense. He had seen these types of people many times. All gathered in his house. Eating the meagre food from his Mum's fridge. Screaming with laughter with bad words on the porch while drinking from Ron's bucket. He knew these people.

Quickly, he shoved his hand in his pocket burying the phone deep inside. She wasn't going to touch it. She couldn't touch it. It wasn't hers. If ever it was held in those dirty, ugly hands it would never feel the same again. The phone was his link to the most important person in his life. She wasn't allowed to touch it. No-one was allowed to touch it.

OOO

Ellie acknowledged the large, tall shadow in the kitchen with a glance. He was looking at her with intrigue. There was, once again, someone with her. It had been listening to her speak and respond. This fascinated it. Noises echoed from the walls, faint but present. Why faint? It wanted to hear if she was to engage again with the mystery person sharing the same space as them. He would have known who it was. It was the same person as before. Sam's creature sensed hers and hers sensed his in return. At least it would have known the same person was there. This has only happened with Bael and Josh's' Dog. Bael and Sam's Dark child. Her monster had seen Josh that night in the junkyard and again on their *special* night. It had seen the Dark Child on the path outside her chosen location, but it had not seen Sam. However the dog and the child had never seen each other. This seemed to be a parlour trick of Bael alone. My god, that day seemed so long ago. The three of them in that car with no plan.

The sounds emanating from Bael were commonplace and routine. Its constant vigilance of her was not unusual, although now it was different. It had watched her before the Circle with an appetite. Now after the events of that night, and the arrival of Joshua and Sam into her life, she felt examined. What did this mean?

Unlike Sam, she hadn't had the pleasure of taking someone away from it. From what she had seen since that night, Sam's rebellious action carried consequences. Both Bael and Sam's Dark Child were responding to what occurred to each of them that night. Bael was intrigued, the Child enraged. Secretly, Ellie preferred enduring Bael's fascination about the happenings of that night, much more than its wrath.

The little one's coming home.

Ellie was gripped by the voice. She knew this sound. This was Bael's true voice. She had heard it that night two months ago when she challenged it. She steadied herself. Past the kitchen bench, beyond Sam on the couch, it stood in the darkness of the kitchen. All other sounds had stopped. It was waiting for a response.

Barely above a whisper, Ellie did respond "What did you say?"

There was silence. The human and Leviathan stared at each other. Both waiting for a reaction from the other. Ellie stepped back startled as Bael's deep voice continued.

The little one has an eternity to cry his tears. The Firewolf will feed upon burnt flesh. A forever of skin and meat. The child will be gone, as are the others before him. As like those yet to be. He will own this beautiful abomination, embracing the dark honour of our assemblage of Ascendancy. The little one is coming home.

Sam turned over and snored just once. Ellie couldn't move. Her mind whirled. The child - Josh. The wall... Josh was on the wall? The Firewolf? Josh was at the precipice, and Bael was letting her know. Mocking her. All her plans, redundant. Rushing to the kitchen counter she grabbed her phone. She pulled it up, scrolled with shaking hands and hit the screen.

Chapter 7

Josh could feel the phone vibrating in his pocket. He badly wanted to take it, but the woman was still there. She watched him wince uncomfortably, smiling the same mean smile as she looked down to the phone lighting up his pocket.

"There it is!" she exclaimed as, to Josh's horror, she moved forward grabbing his coat.

"It's mine!" Josh's voice broke, slamming his hand on top of hers, wedging it inside his pocket.

The woman chuckled. She found this funny. Funny how he would fight back. Funny how he thought he could stop her. She was like Ron. She was horrible and mean. Just like Ron. She smelt just like Ron. The room began to dim.

Her tattooed friend leant forward. Josh was scared. They were bullies. They were bullying him, and no-one cared.

"Come on buddy, let a lady use your phone. Be a gentleman" the man smiled. He had no teeth.

"No!" Josh called out. "It's not hers, it's mine!"

Her hand, with those ugly red nails, wrapped itself around his wrist. He clenched the phone tight. Her nasty hands were touching his gift and he could smell her rancid breath on his clean skin. It smelt like his old home. It smelt like that awful, awful house. It made him sick. It made him want to kick her, push her away. She was making him dirty again. He wanted to get as far away from her as possible.

"Come on," she giggled with surprise at his fight. "It won't take a second."

"Don't touch it!" he yelled as he jumped to his feet just moments before he heard the deep, thumping sound that rendered him frozen. A hideous, thundering howl echoed about him as the air caught in his throat. The darkness grew as the room began to fold away.

ＯＯＯ

Ellie barged through the open apartment door and sprinted into the corridor. Sam dazed, stumbled behind.

"Who? What did it say?" he called.

"Josh… now, it has him. We have to go. Now!" she called out running down the hallway.

"Who has him?" Sam exclaimed, following drowsily, shaking his head, attempting to make sense out of what he had woken up to.

Ellie pressed the elevator button repeatedly, muttering under her breath, "damn, damn, damn." She pushed past him and headed to the door of the stairwell.

Sam watched the complete change of her character with caution. Her hands shook and her voice was so uncharacteristically terse. He had to handle her carefully.

"Who has him?" he asked calmly. "Ellie… who has him?" But she was not listening. She grabbed his arm and dragged him towards the stairwell.

ＯＯＯ

In the waiting room, Josh had been sitting on a hard plastic seat tucked around a corner, out of the way of the main desk. It was clear that a few of the people here were accustomed to the tense and slightly impatient atmosphere of the place. Shielded behind Perspex glass, officers bantered amongst themselves, no sign that they had noticed that an unease had begun spreading through the room. An uncomfortable angst. The handful of people became restless, agitated by an unseen energy that sank upon the room like a fog. Two older men eyeballed the officers behind the desk with sudden, renewed impatience.

Nara, a young constable, first noticed the strange behaviour of the small child who stood still and alone as the chatter and chaos increased. She stopped mid-sentence watching the boy.

He hadn't moved. His brown eyes were barely visible below the rim of his beanie. He stared ahead, vacantly, unaware of what was happening

73

around him. His small body was wrapped in a very big jacket causing his arms to jut out to the sides. Only his finger twitched, ever so slightly. It was odd.

Nara excused herself from the heated conversation she was engaged in. She called out to the child.

"Are you OK?" Damn Perspex, she wasn't sure if anyone had heard a single thing she'd said all day.

The woman screamed, collapsing pathetically onto the sodden mud beneath her. The tattooed stranger, who only moments ago sat behind her in the waiting room of a police station, now bubbled and hissed upon a wall of scorching heat. The monster that had done that was now targeting her.

A small boy stood in front of the approaching dog-like creature yelling "Stop it! Stop it!" over and over. The woman looked about with utter confusion. She screamed again as Joshua stumbled towards her and the Dog advanced.

"Liam, Liam look." Nara gestured to the small boy, now ignoring the patron she had been speaking to. She grabbed the attention of the young officer behind her who joined her in observing the child.

"Is he OK?" her colleague asked.

Nara shook her head, reaching down and picking up a white swipe card, "I don't know."

"Hey kid! Kid!" The male officer called as, with a beep, Nara entered the waiting room and approached the boy, who gave no reaction.

She was going to kneel next to him as she asked if he was alright. That was what she had learnt. Come down to a child's level. Make them feel safe. However, his strange appearance stopped her in her tracks. His eyes fixed forward, his mouth moving ever so slightly... slowly she moved towards him.

"NO! NO! NO! PLEASE." The woman's cries were fragmented by the violent ripping and tugging on her upper thigh. Her head thrashed about with every powerful tear on her body. Josh reached for her hand. She grasped it squeezing desperately, painfully. Maybe if he held her long enough the dog would let go... give up. Maybe, because his Mum let go, she got taken away. He wouldn't let go... he would hold her. His legs buckled beneath him. He yelped in pain as the woman's death grip tightened on his outstretched arm. Her long nails cut his skin. His fingers became wet with blood.

74

The Dog shook her in its jaws, sending Josh slamming to the side.

"Stop it... stop it... stop it... stop it..." Nara heard the child mutter distantly, as if in a dream. His eyes blinked quickly. His fingers twitched on his left hand; his right was closed in a tight, white fist. Nara reached forward taking the fist in her hand, ignoring the gathering rabble about her. Others had noticed the event and were starting to pay attention. His hand was unexpectedly hot. For a moment, Nara ignored it, but the longer she held him the more she could feel an unnatural heat radiating from his skin.

"Can you hear me?" she looked down in disbelief at the small fist in her hand. Blazing hot but now covered by red blood that began to wash over her fingers "Shit..."

The more the woman screamed, the more the Dog shook her. Her eyes darted about, overcome by the brutality ravaging her body.

"STOP IT! YOU'RE AN IDIOT! STOP IT!" Josh screamed. With a muscle ripping thrust, the Dog threw her. Her torn limbs hit the dirt quivering, unrecognisable. Legs now chunks of flesh in blood-soaked denim. The chains upon the walls began slamming, twisting, grinding together. Walls throbbing with flesh-searing heat. Pleading, she looked at the child grasping her hand, his face filled with tears and her body trembled.

"Try to hold on..." he whimpered. "Just hold on...

Two more officers came from behind the partition to Nara's side. They lowered Joshua's small, stiff body to the cold floor. Nara put her hand to his face. No response.

Someone's voice broke through the buzz of the room, "call an ambulance."

"Can you hear me? Can you hear me?" Nara grabbed the shoulders of the coat, surprised at how deep she had to grip before feeling the little boy within. She squeezed hard. No response. His eyes stared at the ceiling while mouthing gibberish. The room was chaotic, but adequately controlled by the other staff.

"He's talking, he's talking," Nara said loudly to whomever might have asked. Blood continued to flow down his hand and drip onto the white floor below.

"Ambulance on its way!" a voice called.

75

"Is he breathing?" she heard her colleague ask as he knelt beside her scanning the child, trying to look helpful.

"Yes, he's talking so he must be breathing," she snapped back. She began to pat his coat, muttering to herself "Name, name…"

"What are you looking for?"

"His name!... anything! Did he come here alone?" she called out.

"I don't know, I didn't see him." Her hands quickly moved lower, patting the sides of the oversized coat until she felt something small and boxlike in his right pocket. Without thinking she thrust her hand into the fabric and pulled out a phone.

Automatically, she lifted the phone and hit the screen with a shaking thumb.

Locked, missed call.

No time to spend on this now.

The jaws of the Dog slammed on what remained of her left leg. Josh couldn't tell if she was crying or screaming.

"NO, NO!" she pleaded over and over, reaching back with one hand trying to scratch and pound the monstrous snout. With one violent wrench backwards, their hands were separated, sending Josh onto a rusted, metal frame with a hard thud. He couldn't hold her… he couldn't hold her, he wasn't strong enough. He stood, slipping on the oily ground. Torn scrap metal began spinning around him, lifted by an invisible force. He began to run. Screams echoed in his ears as metal collided about him as he fled. He was going to die. The Dog was going to kill him.

"Ellie! Ellie!" he screamed into the air before being slammed to the ground as he was struck by debris. Terrified beyond thought, he lay gasping on the ground. There was nothing he could do. Any thoughts of bravery or boldness were dashed. He was completely, utterly helpless.

"Jesus Christ!" Nara's colleague yelled, shuffling back as the child's body lurched violently backwards. His head flung forcefully to the side as blood now ran down his face. His right hand had multiple deep lacerations. His fist spasmed, before lying still beside him. It was then that Nara noticed that something black had begun to cover his body.

"What's happening?" she gasped, staring at the evolving injuries. "What happened? Mike, what happened?"

"Nothing happened... he moved, nothing *happened!*" Her colleague protested as if she had accused him of hurting the child. Turning back to Josh she noticed that the crimson blood which had dripped from his hands now smeared his arms and face, "What the hell is that?"

"Blood, he's bleeding? Where the hell did that come from?"

The muttering had stopped as the child lay completely silent.

He had to lie still. That's what Ellie said. She said he should cover his eyes, but he didn't... he just couldn't. Ellie had said that he couldn't help people and she had been right. Lying in the oil and dirt, his body covered with blood and muck, he made a decision. He would just do that. He turned on his side pulling his feet beneath him and closed his eyes tight as the onslaught continued. He could tell that the lady was on the wall. It wouldn't be long. It wouldn't be long now.

He opened his eyes, nauseous. The ground began to fade. Completely disoriented he tried to make sense of the people he was now seeing. A lady with short brown hair and blue eyes was above him. Beside him? He could no longer tell. He had been on his side, his face covered by his bloody, mucky hands. Now where was he?

The paramedics arrived in a flurry of activity. Nara, grateful and relieved, pushed herself backwards and let them do their thing.

"Do we have a name?" one barked forcefully, scanning the bystanders within the room.

"No, no name," Nara replied, backing away even further.

The lights above flickered slightly as, with surprise and relief, Nara heard the child scream, just once, before silence. She heard the paramedic say words like "seizure" and "febrile at 105, tachy on 140."

"Is he awake?" Nara asked as her colleague began helping her to her feet. There was no response. The waiting room had been cleared. Checking his neck and spine, the paramedic started removing his clothes after calling loudly "Blood here too. OK, let's look at him."

"He's losing blood... multiple points... let's move..." the paramedic said loudly, stepping to the side. Nara looked at the child's small, bruised and dirt-covered body, laying within a pool of blood. His eyes were closed. He must have woken for only a moment. Horrified, Nara looked at his little damaged body and felt ill. A long, blue scar snaked down his forearm.

The pandemonium outside the police station became obvious the moment Ellie rounded the corner. She skidded to a halt on the wet path and stared with dismay at the scene across the road. The blue and red lights lit the front of the building.

"Oh fuck." Sam slid to a stop behind her, echoing her thoughts, "that doesn't look good."

Breathless and dismayed, Ellie put her hands on her knees and lent forward.

"No, no." What could she do? Could she do anything? Was he in there? "I have to go in."

"No! We don't know yet. Ellie we don't know that it has anything to do with Josh just wait... just breathe. He may have left by now, just chill." Sam was nervous of this new, emotional Ellie before him. "Calm down yeah? Calm down."

Ellie straightened. The ambulance lights were flashing but she couldn't tell whether they were still inside the vehicle or in the building. "What happened? What? I only just left him there... *shit, shit, shit...* I don't..."

The doors of the building swung open as a stretcher was wheeled to the ramp on the side of the stairs. Ellie saw it first. She moved forward before Sam grabbed her arm holding her back. It was him. The small figure on the big white stretcher was Joshua. Without thought, she tried rushing forward as Sam tightened his grip on her arm.

"Let me go. We've got to help him." Ellie pulled at her arm, but Sam held tight. "He's been hurt."

"No, no... we can't just walk up there, you know that." Sam stood behind her. "No...no... don't do it."

She struggled to break Sam's grip. "We need to help him. We can't just... leave him..."

The child's sweet flesh was torn. He screamed for you.

It whispered into her ear as other sounds began to flow around her. Josh screaming. The night in the Circle. The fear and terror that fuelled the simmering coals of her temper.

"Shut up!" she muttered, putting her gloved hands over her face. "Shut up, shut up."

"Don't listen to it Ellie. Listen to me" Sam pleaded. "He's getting help! They are helping him… Think about what you're doing. There is nothing we can do that will improve this situation… nothing. It's waiting for a chance to make it worse. Don't listen."

He noticed a chink in the steel of Ellie's eyes. Her face softened very slightly. Putting both hands on her shoulders, he squeezed them gently. "He needs them to help him now… We will not help. You know that. He needs them more than he needs us right now. Come on Ellie… You're the thinker here."

Ellie watched from across the road as her little friend was loaded into the ambulance. Something had happened. He had been injured and she knew he wouldn't be the only casualty. What had she done? What could she do now?

"Fuck! Fuck!" she shouted in frustration.

"No! Stop it, Ellie no!" Sam glanced around them, the air turning dark. "Walk away now! Now!"

He will scream for eternity and wonder where… you… are.

Unthinkable. Absolutely unthinkable. She would not let this happen. She had to go to him. But the taunting seemed to calm her. This is what Bael wanted. This is where it wanted to push her. Had she become this sensitive to its manipulations? They were not clever or original. A new trigger had been identified and that was going to be used whenever the opportunity arose. Whether it had been Josh, Sam, or any other chink in her armour, it would be exploited. She couldn't let that happen.

Sam kept one hand resting, but ready, on her shoulder. He hoped that any moment now Ellie's common-sense, the logic and practicality she had shown time and time again, would kick in. She spun around with such speed that Sam imagined she may even strike him. But he could see her eyes pleading, almost begging for him to take control.

He spoke calmly, "You can't listen to it. Please don't listen to it. You've done this before. You know what it wants you to do. Don't do it."

This was true. Both Conduits knew what had happened. They had both made the same mistakes in the past. People were Lit, Josh tried to intervene, and this was the consequence. Sam sighed deeply, sadly "he didn't stand back Ellie."

Through the years, this is what they had learned that they had to do. Stand back, let it happen, don't intervene. Once that threshold was crossed, it no longer involved you. It was between Leviathan and the victim. The Conduit's role was complete. They were redundant. Ellie's eyes faltered, showing glistening tears and leaving Sam bewildered. This was a new aspect of Ellie to consider and observe. Vulnerability, a weakness. This served both as a comfort and a threat. Which way it ended up depended on her.

With one blast of the siren, the ambulance started down the road. Sam felt a wave of relief wash over him. They both watched as the vehicle rounded the corner. Both knew what this meant. They had been in the same situation themselves many times before. One or more had been Lit... your normal existence becomes a violent, hideous hell and you get taken away in an ambulance.

When you arrived there, you would be asked questions and the fucked up covert part of your life would begin.

"What do I do now?" Ellie muttered, staring blankly at the road in front of her. "I won't know where he is."

Sam bit his tongue, wanting to tell her she was being unrealistic. Wanting to tell her that promising Josh she would always be there was a stupid thing to do because she couldn't. She wouldn't be. But now was not the time.

"He won't be far. We'll find him. But now we have to go." Sam once again held her shoulders. She stared at him, desperately needing his judgment, his control. With a nod of resignation, she turned and began to walk past him. She stopped, just enough to regain her composure.

"We have to find out where he's going," she said with a sense of urgency. She walked by Sam and back down the path.

Sam nodded, amused by how she felt she was now the one back in control.

OOO

Joshua opened his eyes, finding himself in very white sheets. There were noises from people around him, out of sight beyond walls of blue, paper curtains. It reminded him of the walls in one of his classrooms. His head hurt and his belly felt sick. He moved his hand to his stomach. It felt heavy.

Lifting his hand, he discovered it was wrapped in a very white, clean bandage. It went almost up to his elbow. What was that for? He wriggled his fingers, and a sting ran up his arm.

Quietly, he sat himself up and looked about. There were so many sounds and voices. He knew that he was in hospital. He had seen curtains like this on a show he watched once. He didn't know how he got there. Perhaps he was in trouble, and he became scared. He remembered something bad. He remembered two people, a man with drawings on his face and a lady who kept trying to take his phone. His memory was a maze of violence and panic. Images of blood, screaming and helplessness. The Dog had been bad again. He could hear its roar echoing around him, unsure if it was a memory or in the space with him.

Two people were talking just outside the curtains. He couldn't see them, but they were right there. Quickly he lay himself down again. They were girls. He could tell by their voices. One sounded a bit upset. Maybe she was upset at him. Maybe it was the lady with the ugly hands telling on him. Telling the people that he had a dog that attacked her, and it was Josh's fault. He knew that they didn't come back though. Ellie told him this. They never came back. But what if this one time, she did?

He would have to say sorry, but that was OK. He truly was very sorry. He listened as someone said, "Just wait here. Just give me a moment," before the curtain rustled and opened. His plans of immediately saying he was sorry were forgotten when a lady he didn't recognise walked slowly in. He eyeballed her quietly from the bed. The lady had the same-coloured skin as Ellie, a lovely light brown. She was much older than Ellie though, with a round face and a big smile. Her black hair was up in a pretty bun with a little white clip. Ellie didn't put her hair up often and when she did, it meant that bad things were going to happen.

"Hello," she said gently. "I'm Sinead. How are you feeling?"

There was something extraordinarily warm about her voice. He felt compelled to answer, "I'm OK."

"I've been asked to see you by the police. You went there this afternoon, didn't you?" she asked, stepping closer to him, and putting her hands on the rails. Her nails looked nice. Not red and nasty like the other lady.

"Yes, I went to the police building to ask them something. Not to be bad or anything."

"Aw no, no-one thinks you've been bad. They were really worried about you." She shook her head gently, "Can you tell me your name?"

"I'm Joshua," he replied robotically.

Josh was startled when another woman walked in.

"It's Josh… it's him," she said loudly to Sinead. "Josh. Sweetheart."

The look of distress in this lady's face made him feel panicked, nervous. She was staring at him. Her eyes looked like she had been crying. He wriggled himself up the bed, ignoring the pain in his hand. The lady called Sinead put her hand up and the newcomer became quiet.

"Joshua, this is your aunt. You remember your Aunt Casey?"

"Not too much," Josh spoke quietly, glancing nervously towards her.

Joshua's mind whirled. Casey was his mother's sister. She looked like his Mum but was younger. She had the same red-blonde shiny hair that hung down to her shoulders on either side. His Mum's hair was much longer. She was pretty and had really nice eyes with a gentle smile and very white skin. There was a recognition of family that Josh didn't know how to put into words. But she was his aunt. She was the lady that his Mum ignored in the shops once and made them leave quickly. It was her.

"It's OK," Sinead spoke calmly, "Your aunt has been looking for you."

Josh nodded slowly, his eyes wide and studying the faces of these strangers. He focused on Casey.

"Hello" he muttered timidly, noticing the big blue bag on the chair beside him. He instantly recognised the buttons of his jacket. It was his clothes. In that bag was his phone. He needed that bag. He wanted and needed Ellie. She would be so worried and think he didn't like her anymore.

Sinead spoke quietly over her shoulder, "just be gentle with him. I told them they could speak to him after we had seen him. Just be gentle." Casey nodded in agreement.

"Now, I am going to speak to the police who sent you in. You relax and Aunt Casey will stay here with you." Sinead said with another kind smile. She then turned and left. Very quickly, Casey sat down next to the bed. Josh liked Sinead, she was kind and looked like Ellie. But his Aunty looked upset. Was she upset with him?

"Hey," she smiled, awkwardly placing her hand on his fingers that poked out of the end of the bandage. "It's OK, it's all OK. The doctors need to make sure you're alright. You were a bit banged up."

Josh nodded. He was a bit banged up and had been for weeks and weeks. His clothes had been taken off. He didn't know by who or why, but he knew they had seen all the bruises and cuts. The clothes were all in the blue plastic bag. He needed his coat. He imagined how many times Ellie had tried to ring him.

"I get hurt... sometimes," he said softly. "Sometimes I fall over and stuff. Mum said I was a clumsy clog."

Casey nodded, "mm hm" and held back her tears. Even a child could tell there were questions that were begging to be answered. The little boy's face was emotionless, but his eyes spoke volumes. Fear, suspicion, and paranoia. What did she want him to say? What would Ellie want him to say? Would they get mad?

Josh had seen those eyes before. His Mum's eyes looked like this. Before he did something terrible to her. Something so terrible that no-one could ever know. He hadn't meant to, and he was sorry, but today he did it again. He looked into Casey's familiar eyes and wished they belonged to someone else. They were making him feel safe, though he knew he wasn't. They were making him feel cared about, though he knew he wasn't.

"We don't have to talk now. We can talk later, you just rest. I'm not going anywhere I promise." She lifted her hand and brushed his hair tenderly from his forehead. "I'll stay here, and we can just... be here together," she smiled. Josh may have smiled back, he wasn't sure. He let his eyes close as his Aunt's voice and the stroking of his hair calmed him.

Chapter 8

Ellie sat on the floor against the wall of her living room and watched Sam sleep heavily on the couch. She had stopped pondering the various noises he made whilst sleeping. At 3AM it had become annoying, but Ellie let it go – he needed to sleep. The urge to go out during the night and find Josh had been crushing, but she knew that it would be fruitless. And besides, she had promised to stay. She felt frustrated more so because Sam was right. Joshua was with those that could, and would, help him. Let things calm down and then go back. Last night was not the time. Sam faded mid debate. Ellie was grateful she was the sort of person able to let an argument go. That could have driven some people nuts.

Overnight she had thought about things and at least knew where she was going. Josh's phone would turn on if he was able to get to it. Of that she was certain. She had to leave. Sam wouldn't be permitted to sleep for long after she left. He'd had a decent six hours. That would have to be enough. She had to find Josh and she could do that on her own. She would leave Sam to sleep, if by a miracle the Dark Child allowed him.

Did she have a plan? No. There were three major hospitals in the city. All of them could be taking ambulances at any time. Getting information would be impossible. She would have to be covert. Much easier done in a cafe when ordering coffee than in a hospital looking for a nameless child. God willing, he would find a way to his phone.

She put on her jacket. The large shadow watched silently from the chair opposite. It was strangely sedate and this itself was worrying. So much had changed for her and It in the last two months. Added players like Josh and Sam opened up a wealth of opportunities for It to explore. Evil fuck. There it was, studying her. Looking for weaknesses, searching for triggers.

She placed her keys in her pocket, checked her phone one more time - nothing - and headed for the door. A quick thought. She doubled back, darting into the bathroom and then into her bedroom. She emerged a moment later, trotting up to Sam who was still soundly sleeping on the couch. She carried her large, black headphones. Gently, she placed them over Sam's ears. Next, she placed a freshly rolled towel on his chest and a bottle of liquid soap. Not subtle, but damn necessary.

As she walked into the cold morning she began to feel foolish. Her presence would draw questions no matter where she went. What did she hope to achieve? As unreasonable and possibly risky as it was, she wanted Josh to know that she was doing something. She wanted him to know that she was there. Sam needed her. But Josh needed her more.

∘∘∘

One thing that Dr Niles Gardiner always noticed about Elenore Jameson's "homework" sheets was her incredibly immaculate handwriting. Meticulous and structured with every word written so very clearly. He also knew that her answers on the questionnaires were just as structured and as meticulously considered as the font in which they were penned. As frustrating as this was, he tried to read between the lines. It was just another attempt to evade exposure.

Her biggest challenge right now was, 'Dealing with issues from my past which may be contributing to my distrust of people.' A contrived answer that was both reductive and predictable. The next question asked how she could address these challenges. The answer, again crafted in that beautiful script, was composed of a well-rounded answer that one could read in a textbook entitled 'How To Reach Success with Crazy People 101.' This again was not unusual.

Only seven weeks earlier she had left his office with an ambiguous warning.

"You do want me to go to Niles, believe me you really do want me to go. Staying here would be so bad, so bad for you. You don't understand the danger and I can't stay here... I'm sorry."

The next scheduled session arrived and once again she returned. She walked into his office, sat down, and continued as if nothing had happened.

Did he address it? Yes. Her response was coldly apologetic and vaguely descriptive of challenges she had felt uncomfortable discussing. Although she had been sure to explain that she would be willing to discuss them 'in time'. They both agreed to this for their own reasons - Niles didn't want another storm out and Ellie didn't want to get in trouble for not abiding by her community treatment order.

Why did he not want another dramatic ending? He tried to convince himself that it was done in Ellie's best interest. It was best for her to continue with the program and for him not to get carried away with the semantics of her threatening statement. It was all due to this and not at all related to his attempt to find out more about the secret of something called Bael. All other links between Ellie and Will could be purely coincidental. But that name? No.

Will Mason had not been found. He had disappeared from the face of the earth, and no-one seemed to be looking for him. There was no family, no friends, no-one. That was tragically sad. Niles had believed that Will had friends. That he had been functioning well, but clearly that had not been the truth. Or at the least, Niles felt that Will had purposely given a different perception than how things really were for him. Had he really been fed that impression by Will, or was it of his own construction? Either way, it shook the confidence in his own judgement. Pretty harsh when objective judgement was supposed to be your speciality.

He adjusted his glasses. They slid down his nose slightly which caused him to sneeze. Rubbing his brow he looked at his watch. Next client was in two minutes. Just enough time to check one more thing. He had been tasked to follow up with the wedding caterers to investigate the provision of a vegan diet for his future brother-in-law's girlfriend. The one who really needed to gain weight. His fiancé knew that he was busy but when she had told him that her brother Michael was bringing his new girlfriend, Niles' response had been "Oh, I haven't met *herbivore*". With such a cringe worthy failure of a joke, Niles quickly volunteered that he would ensure the caterers were aware and that was it. The task was now his.

The call was undertaken leaving him slightly embarrassed. They already knew, having been given the information by his very involved future mother-in-law. Turning to the computer he eyed his schedule. New client, 75-minute session. The name was red. They were in the waiting area. Niles did like a punctual client.

Gathering his thoughts, he left the room. Not much more of Elenore Jameson's treatment order to go. He was still unsure what he would recommend, things being as they were. There was a lot more work required in their future time together. Distracted as he pondered this, he became aware of a lively conversation in the waiting room. His receptionist Kay was talking to a gentleman who leaned casually over her desk.

"Excuse me Dr Gardiner. Your client is here," she smiled bashfully.

The man was dressed in a striking charcoal black suit with the jacket opened revealing a white sweater. He was tall, fit and lean with a handsome face and an immaculately groomed, short beard. His piercing dark brown eyes sat heavily under a strong brow. The new client smiled confidently as he offered a large hand that Niles grasped. Niles was intrigued by his energy.

"Thank you Kay," Niles said as the two men shook hands.

"Mika. Mika Hexum. It's a pleasure." The gentleman spoke in a calm, confident voice.

Focusing his attention on the man before him, Niles smiled, "Niles Gardiner, please, come through."

"Thank you Kay, for your charming hospitality," Mika said smoothy, following Niles down the hall to his office. "Thank you for seeing me," Mika said warmly as they entered the office. "I understand my first referral was lost in e-space!"

"Yes," Niles chuckled whilst maintaining his professional demeanour. He gestured for Mika to sit, collected his iPad from the desk and sat down opposite him. "It does happen from time to time. I had a previous email address, and some referral sources still use the former unfortunately. My apologies."

Mika smiled and sat with his legs loosely crossed and hands relaxed as they rested calmly on the arms of the large leather chair.

Sensing his new client was ready, Niles smiled warmly, "So tell me, Mika, what brings you here today?"

Mika sat quietly for a moment. He shifted uncomfortably. Niles noticed his hands beginning to tap the arms of his chair.

"I would say it's overdue," he replied. "I am having problems and I am feeling a little in over my head. Possibly, more than a *little*."

Niles settled back and placed his notebook on his lap. His new client instantly reposed.

87

"So Mika, in these first sessions, I would like to find out a little more about you. A little broad perhaps and then we can, together…"

"I like your cat," Mika interrupted. "I've never had one."

Baffled, Niles opened his mouth to speak, giving an awkward yet friendly "Excuse me?"

Without a word, Mika gestured with his head over Niles' shoulder and with a quick glance, Niles understood. "Oh, that's my fiancé's cat."

The picture was at least three metres away. A small brown spot on the lap of his fiancé who was also quite small in the modest sized photo on the polished, wooden cabinet opposite Mika.

"I thought it would be," Mika smiled again. "The wedding is soon I imagine."

Niles noticed Mika delivered these grins with precision timing. They were disarming: friendly but purposeful. Mika's social graces were extremely charismatic and clever, serving well as tools of control. Niles mused that even though he considered himself immune to such manipulation, Mika had redirected him with ease.

"Yes," Niles replied. "Three months to be exact."

"My congratulations" Mika gave a small nod. "A big affair?"

Niles would usually not encourage this, however, he found himself responding. "Not as small as I would like. Not as grand as she would favour… so hopefully just the right size."

"Well played."

"Yes well, you have to control the grandeur of these events, don't you?" Niles quickly changed the subject. "Are you married Mika?"

"Me?"

"Yes you" Niles chuckled. "This is about you."

"Oh… no. No, no. Never been married. Never had the inkling and besides, then I would be expected to breed. The world is just not ready for more of… me," he grinned.

"Oh come now, I doubt that would be so bad?" Niles bantered. His new client was now self-effacing. The man was a social master.

"Not at all, perhaps just a social conscience" Mika jibed. "God forbid!"

"Doing your bit for humanity?"

"One can only try," Mika shrugged jokingly. "Perhaps I could find myself a partner… man or woman. If it came with a functioning womb, I would provide her cats to compensate and thereby attempt to quelch that maternal urge a little."

The last comment, as sarcastic as this was, came cloaked with the same warm smile. This potentially offensive jibe was incongruent with its delivery. Had he disclosed his bisexuality? Unsure. Niles knew the cat comment was aimed at him but chose not to acknowledge it. He had a feeling that that was what his new client was looking for.

"So back to you," Niles said with an air of authority, although he was surprised that this didn't come as naturally as it usually did. Was he intimidated by this man?

"You said lately that things haven't been going so well for you. Are there any aspects that you would feel comfortable talking about today?"

Mika lowered his head and for the first time since they met, he broke eye contact and sighed heavily. Waiting for a response, Niles remained quiet.

"I have lost a friend, Dr. Gardiner," Mika sighed deeply, his eyes meeting Niles once more. "It's been very hard."

Niles nodded empathetically, grateful he had something to discuss. "I'm sorry to hear that."

"Thank you" Mika nodded. His eyes drifted around the room with just the right amount of emotional wandering. A beautiful performance thought Niles to himself - a masterclass.

"It's been very hard. I find myself going over conversations… moments. The last time I spoke to him. All those thoughts. I don't know where to start, or how to feel."

"Do you mind if I ask what happened?"

Mika shook his head. Niles sensed a building tension. Tension in his clients he was used to, but no, this tension was building inside himself. He didn't know why, and it bothered him that he couldn't put a finger on a brewing suspicion. It had no discernible origin.

"No-one knows," Mika shrugged. "No-one knows what happened. It's a mystery and it makes no sense."

Placing his pen down, Niles leant back and nodded, giving the client room to speak. "That sounds very hard."

"It has been."

"Can I ask when your friend passed away?" Niles asked. To his surprise Mika looked amused. Without another word Niles felt embarrassed.

Mika shook his head smiling awkwardly, "Passed away? No. He didn't pass away. I said I lost him. He isn't *dead.*"

"Oh, beg your pardon. I assumed that you meant…"

"Dr Gardiner," Mika chuckled, rubbing his legs. "I'm surprised that someone like you would assume…"

There was no mistake, Mika had wanted Niles to fall into this trap. This handsome man, with social graces and charm, possessed an incredible ability to purposefully manipulate. Niles steeled himself. He would not show his discomfort no matter how much chagrin this banter caused him. He would shut it down. He would tell Mika that he didn't think they were suited and recommend another poor therapist.

"I apologise Dr," Mika replied as if reading the Nile's mind. "I have had a rough few weeks and I am being a bit of an ass. I apologise."

Niles straightened up in his chair, attempting to relax his posture for someone, he was sure, was watching him as closely as he was watching them.

"I understand that Mika, but for me to be able to help you this relationship cannot be combative. You need to be able to speak to me openly. So far, I feel that hasn't been easy for you. You should ask yourself two things. Firstly, am I the right one to give you help and secondly, are you ready to accept it."

Mika nodded enthusiastically, "yes and yes. No doubt."

They both fell silent. Mika looked for the moment to be subdued. However, Niles had witnessed this level of manipulation before. He would approach it with a cautious regard.

"So, shall we speak about your friend? Seems a good place to start."

"Please," Mika replied. "He was one of my best friends. Like a brother to me. You see, I don't have many friends. I blame myself for that. I can be a challenging character. But he was."

"When did you first meet… Sorry, I didn't get his name?" Niles settled back into his chair.

"I didn't say it," he smiled. "Will, his name is Will."

Niles was shocked into silence and froze. He knew that Mika, this stranger, would see past his game face to his absolute bewilderment. Coincidence? A friend called Will? Not Will Mason, just Will. Possible yet highly improbable. Was it calculated that Mika moved between past and present tense when referring to him? Given the complicated wordplay thus far - this was likely. The other scenario, that Will Mason's 'friend' was here for a reason. Now that was much more likely.

∞∞∞

Sam staggered into the bathroom. Ellie left? She had left him? He had been woken by the Child dancing idiotically with her human teddy bear in front of his face. This was followed by a panic attack as he felt something gripping his head. He had smacked the earphones onto the floor before jumping up and finding various toiletries raining down around him. The window was wide open, and it was freezing. He was so confused. His phone alarm then went off, startling him even further. By that point his adrenaline was so high that he could taste metal in his mouth.

"Jesus Ellie," he muttered.

The Child was now on the ceiling above him. Her *teddyman* hung from her arm like a sick pendulum raining down globules of saliva from the gaping, rasping hole in its face. Rubbing his eyes, he took a moment to steady himself. Today he would meet Chelamah again. Then he would meet others. He was a mess and he needed to shower. Gathering up the toiletries he staggered into the bathroom.

Chaos reigned in the bathroom. Voices, singing, screaming, all whilst he could see the ridiculous silhouette of a dancing child through the shower curtain. He scrubbed his body painfully hard. Cleaning *her* off himself. Clean up this dirty, depressed person into a semblance of something human before she tore him completely down. He needed *that* old Sam back.

Wrapped in a towel, he opened the bathroom door and ran into the still icy sitting room. His dirty, stained clothes were strewn about the floor. He wouldn't wear them. They smelt. With a quick thought, he remembered Ellie. She wore oversized clothes. She wore completely non-descript black garments that were neither stylish nor gender specific. They would have to do for now. He turned to her bedroom door but stopped short before opening it. Confused, he wiped the water from his eyes. Attached to the door, right at a well thought out eye level, was a piece of small yellow paper. Written on it, in clear capital letters was:

DO NOT WEAR MY CLOTHES.

E x

Joshua eyed the meal placed next to him. He woke up as the nurse and the doctor, with the funny teeth, entered. When they left, he thought he had time to reach for his coat, but then this man with brown skin came in carrying a tray. He placed it on the wheeled table next to the bed. The food was curiously covered with plastic lids and looked strange. The man took a long time to leave. Josh had one thing on his mind. He needed to get to his coat that sat beside him in the big plastic bag.

During the night, he tried to get it. He stretched the tube that came from his arm and leaned right over the rails of the bed. He had then been startled by movement and voices. Some were people, but the growling and the sudden sweeping movements that cast fleeting shadows on the curtains around him were the stupid dog. He tried, but sadly, he hadn't realised how short his arms really were. *Stupid dog and stupid short arms.* A nurse then came in and told him off. Well, kind of. He told him he would hurt himself and not to do it again.

With an effortless click, the man lowered the bedrail. He rolled the small table above the bed and tightly onto Josh's lap.

"There you go my small friend. Leave a jelly for you" he smiled. "You must eat, yes? Get better fast."

Joshua held his breath, willing the man to leave. "Thank you."

"If you do not eat you will not get big and strong." He shook his finger. "Look at me? You think I get this big without eating?"

Unsure what to say, Joshua shook his head, "No."

The man smiled kindly "If you do not like the horrible soup… you eat dessert, yes?" He winked as if it was a secret just between the two of them.

Joshua liked this man. He was kind and funny. He felt himself smile back before he felt a big hand being placed on his sore head and ruffle his hair.

The man left and Josh watched the swaying curtain. He was a nice man, friendly. He made jokes and liked dessert. More importantly, he had left the bedrail down. Josh pushed the table to the side. He looked down at the floor. Nothing would stop him now. The annoying tube was still gathered in his bed, but he had enough room. Pulling the sheets off, he was greeted with his very colourful legs. The bruises were still there but the cuts were all covered with special sticky bandages.

Wriggling his toes, he spun his legs off the mattress. With a small slide, his feet landed on the cold, hard floor. Steadying himself, he looked behind him. The tube was long enough. He could make it. He stumbled forward to the chair. He dove in hands first, pulling at the big jacket inside and into its pocket. His hands searched furiously. It wasn't there. His heart sank, tears sprung to his eyes as his searching became hopeless. He had waited all night.

Dismayed, he pulled his hands out and looked down at the ragged jacket in front of him. Where had it gone? It was then that he heard vibrating. It *was* there. Diving into the bag again his hands reached under the jacket, pulling the phone from the bottom of the bag. It was wrapped in a smaller bag, but it was back in his hands. Suddenly he became suspicious, darting back to the bed nearly tripping on his long white gown. Jumping back onto the mattress he kicked the table behind him. Sitting bolt upright he pulled the sheet up and held his phone between his thighs. He had it.

They would see him and take the phone. He couldn't let that happen. He would be patient and calm. He would wait until everyone was gone, though he felt that didn't happen here. The phone vibrated, just once before he tore the bag away. He threw the sheets over his head and lay down. They wouldn't see him now.

The phone still looked new. The long black charging cord would no doubt be in the special inside pocket. It made him so happy. Ignoring the nineteen missed calls he hit the call button. He had never had a phone before but knew, 3% battery was not good. He hit Ellie's name and waited.

◯◯◯

Headphones in, Ellie slinked down the stairs of the bus onto the footpath. Across the road was the second hospital of her scouting tour this morning. One more to go. The bus left quickly as Ellie pulled the hood of her jacket over her hair. Staring at the unfriendly, dull building in front she realised that, dressed as she was, she must have looked rather suspicious. Like Sam waiting conspicuously at her apartment door. Awkward and lost. Her phone rang

"Oh my god," she gasped in relief. She slammed it to her ear. "Where are you?"

"Ellie…" a small whisper replied. "Ellie it's me, Josh."

"I know. Where are you? I've been looking everywhere."

93

"I'm in a hospital."

"OK, do you know which one?"

There was a pause, she could almost hear Josh thinking.

"There's a big red ambulance sign when I came in."

"OK that doesn't help me," Ellie sighed. "Look around. Can you see anything? Any sign?"

She waited for a moment, listening to the rustling of sheets and Josh's 'thinking'.

"Hmmm..." he muttered, "Hmmm... they have jelly."

"OK. OK." She had an idea. "Look at your arm."

"I can't, they put a bandage on it!"

"The other arm, the hand. Is there a label on your hand?"

Josh was confused, what was she talking about, a label on his hand? Sure enough, pulling the phone from his ear he stared in amazement at the white band wrapped around his wrist. How did that get there?

"Josh?" Ellie called, "Josh?"

"Yeah there's a thing on me," he said surprised. "I don't know who put it there but..."

"Now look at it, what does it say?"

"Ummm," There was a rustling. "It says 09854 and then... Joshua Field-ing."

Fighting back frustration, Ellie sighed. She had worn these tags many times before, she knew what was on them. "Above that. It has a hospital name, above your name can you see it?"

Some more rustling followed by a confused sigh. "It says someone else's name too!"

"What name? What does it say?"

"Ummm...I can't read properly because it's dark. It says... oh," he stopped.

"Josh, I really need the name," Ellie begged. "Just read it."

Puzzled, Josh replied "Margaret McCull... something. I'm not sure. I don't know who she is."

Damn. The hospital Ellie had been at 25 minutes ago. Staring hopelessly at the wrong location in front of her she turned to scan the bus timetable.

"OK, I'm coming there. Might be a while, but I'm on my way, OK?" She scanned the road. The bus back would leave from the other side. "What's been going on?"

"I went to the police, and I was waiting to talk to them, just like you said, and while I was waiting someone tried to take my phone. Then the dog…" Josh said.

"What happened?"

"… The dog was an asshole."

Defeated, Ellie sat heavily on the metal bench, rubbing her face. He hadn't lasted an hour. She was not naive to what could go wrong, but she had been strangely optimistic. She hadn't imagined it would all go to shit so quickly. "So what's happening now?"

"My aunt was here and the doctors. The police are coming, I think, but I don't know when. They came to the hospital, but I was asleep… uncon-conk—sion."

"*Unconscious,*" Ellie closed her eyes wearily.

"Yeah that. Are you coming to get me? Are you coming?"

Ellie took a deep breath. She would try to see him. At least try to calm him. Perhaps she could quell his anxiety, if even for today. *Christ this is hopeless.*

"Yes, I'm coming," she replied. "Just please stay calm… say the words until I get there."

"Yes, I'm calm now you're coming! I'll get dressed. My clothes are here on the chair. Come quickly!"

The phone went dead.

No, no, no. This was not supposed to happen. Thinking for a moment, she turned and ran across the road. Once again, no plan. Chances were they wouldn't even let her in. That would mean talking to people. This was getting worse by the minute.

Chapter 9

As soon as the door opened the sickly odour of urine filled Jason's nostrils. Grimacing in disgust he entered the aged-care home. The smell made the corridor seem small and oppressive. He usually tried to avoid this visit until later in the day, when the residents had been sufficiently wiped down with oversized baby wipes. Then the stench was more bearable. As a candid doctor once said to him, when the man he had called grandfather was waitlisted for this place:

"Make no mistake, it's God's waiting room. Nothing more."

God had a tragic waiting room.

He walked down the short corridor to a long, oak desk lit by the sickly yellow glow of tube fluorescent lighting. There was one solitary nurse sitting behind the desk. She was an older, plump woman with small eyes and a tight little duck's ass mouth. She was relatively new. She had replaced the other fat cow who had sat here until a few weeks ago. That one had 'left' due to Jason's hangover and the terse morning greeting that she had delivered when he really wasn't in the mood. He remembered it briefly, wanting her destruction to end. His head had hurt badly and her screaming just made it worse.

He smiled softly at this memory, watching her silly fat frame running and bouncing about. He was sure he saw her body ripple when a huge fist had slammed into her massive belly. He even heard the fat in her throat as she screamed, muffled and croaky.

He rounded the corner and walked past the desk, down the wall-papered hall, giving a blunt "Hi" as the new nurse greeted him. He walked through the dining hall crowded with rows of fold-away tables, still adorned with cheap plastic flower arrangements and vinyl placemats. He had witnessed the worst of eating habits in this room; sloppy mouths and blended food.

Past the five identical doors to the left, all with little token laminated name tags upon them, to door number eleven. With a deep sigh of contempt, and without knocking, he opened the door to find the room in semi-darkness with only the dim, midmorning sunlight filtering through a curtained window. Taking a deep breath, he spoke to the lump in the bed that sat in the middle of the room.

"Good morning Grandpa Charlie."

There was a moment of silence. Maybe he's dead, mused Jason. He squinted into the darkness, and beyond the familiar silhouette of the bed where the old man lay, to the figure in the corner of the room. It was masked in complete darkness except for the whites of its eyes and the dense black shadow of its bulk.

"Hello, hello is that you Bill?" A hoarse voice called "I need to use the bathroom Bill."

"No. No, Bill doesn't call you Grandpa Charlie, does he?" The bed shuffled slightly, "and why are you still in bed?"

"Everyone calls me Grandpa Charlie," his voice grew aggressive, "so, to what do I owe this pleasure Master Jason?"

A bedside lamp suddenly illuminated the dark space revealing the old man in striped pyjamas. Tufts of white hair barely covered his head. His sunken cheeks revealed what Jason had suspected - he didn't have his teeth in. Slowly the old man pulled his withered hand back from the lamp, putting it back under the warm blanket. As aged and decrepit as he was, Jason was always intimidated by those strong, blue eyes. Piercing and cold. This was the man who never liked him and never trusted him. Never took him into the family and made it clear that he wasn't wanted.

However, the past had not been kind to old Grandpa Charlie. Charles Russo and his wife only had one son, Damian. The apple of their eye. Damian married Cynthia. Cynthia could not have children of her own and as luck would have it, Jason was brought to their home as a foster child. Due to Cynthia's desperation and Damian's desire for a son, it didn't take long for the Russo's to adopt Jason as their own. The barren Cynthia convinced her keen-to-please husband Damian that Jason should stay. But one day Damian and Cynthia vanished. They would never be seen again. Grandpa Charlie had nothing. Old fashioned and modest, Jason's adoptive father had called his parents. Poor, uneducated and cretinous is how Jason chose to see them. Damian had not come from money. He had come from dirt poor, white trash. Damian was a self-made man and Charlie was a testament to how sad and pathetic his life could have been. But Damian loved his father and his father loved him. In this turn of events, Charlie was left stripped of his only son, his daughter-in-law and, two months later, his wife.

Jason was 16 years old when he became the benefactor of his adopted father's estate with one, unfortunate proviso, that Jason must be financially responsible for the man he came to know as Grandpa Charlie. Charlie was thus left with a step-grandson who was spoilt and cold. Jason in turn was left with a burden he loathed. True to form, therefore, he provided only the most basic of essentials and nothing more.

"I was on my way to work… thought I would pop in." Jason crossed his arms and leaned heavily on the door frame.

The old man nodded, "at this early hour, I didn't think they would let anyone in."

"It's 10AM Grandpa. It's hardly early" Jason sighed, looking into the corridor behind him. "You seem to have been forgotten."

"Well, we seem to have lost some staff of late."

"Yes… yes I noticed."

"Yes… I'm sure you did" Charlie retorted quickly with a hint of sarcasm that momentarily stunned Jason.

An underlying level of suspicion had been there since the disappearance of his parents. It had increased over time and these kinds of subtle jibes were now commonplace. Years ago, Jason had been intimidated by them but, after years of inaction, he found Charlie's implied assumptions, or suspicions, were irrelevant and dull.

"What makes you say that?" Jason asked, smiling.

"Well, the whole place is talking about Nurse Carmichael. Just left work a few weeks ago and never came back. No-one can find her. Interesting… intriguing." Charlie laid back down onto the hard pillows.

"Which one was she?"

"She was an older girl. Sat at the front," he said waving, his finger.

"Aw ye… the really fat one… probably choked on a sandwich," Jason said dryly.

Charlie grimaced with disapproval, as he moved himself up to a clumsy slumped position on the bed "Jason you have a very dark sense of humour sometimes." Charlie chuckled, ignoring Jason's genuine viciousness. Observing Jason's triggers was important.

"Not dark, just observant. Lighten the fuck up for god's sake. Anyway, you needed to pee." Jason stepped away from the door, looking behind him, hoping for an interruption. "Or have you used your diaper since we've been talking?"

Charlie remained silent, not keen to give his grandson anything further to work with. He watched Jason standing by the door, unwilling to enter, and desperate to leave. Why did he do this? If he wanted to leave then why not just leave? Their interactions were asinine with the occasional sprinkling of politeness. Not enjoyable and, even in his old age, Jason's visits were not wanted.

There are worse things than being lonely, one of which was having this rude, cold-hearted young man visit him weekly to assess his health in hope of finding him at death's door. After all, every day he spent in this completely unglamorous facility, with its faux art and baby food, was costing Jason money. Charlie didn't know why he wasn't dead already but found it interesting how Jason regarded his living to be a passive aggressive act against him.

"Nah, I'm kidding Grandpa," Jason laughed. "Let me find someone for you. I pay them enough."

"No, no, Jason, leave them be. They will be on their way in good time." Charlie straightened himself up even further watching as Jason slouched with frustrated resignation against the door. He was so easy to read.

"So, as you can see, I'm still alive. Sadly, I continue to drain *my son's* bank account with this selfish habit of not dying. You may have to wait a bit longer. Perhaps better luck next week."

Jason feigned surprise, leaning his head forward and guffawing loudly "well that wasn't nice Grandpa Charlie. It's important that I keep an eye on my investments and this place is *very* expensive."

"Yes, well they do a very good job," carefully avoiding Jason's triggers. With a sigh, he reached to the side table and slid out a walking stick. Not that he walked anymore, since diabetes took his left leg, but he could use it to stand. *A standing stick* he would joke to his carers and enjoy a moment of false phoney chuckles.

"Well, it seems they are waylaid. Make yourself useful please Jason. Bring me that chair. Place it here." With the point of his stick Charlie swivelled himself to the edge of the bed and sat up.

Jason felt irksome and uncomfortable. It wasn't seeing the old man's body ravaged by the years and diabetes, but the idea that Charlie thought it appropriate to ask him for help. The look of disgust on his face was obvious. Charlie smiled gently "I can get myself into it. I just need you to push it over here... don't worry I can manage everything from there."

The old man slid himself into the wheelchair with great difficulty. He didn't ask the young man for help, and none was offered. Once on the chair, and with an exhausted sigh, he grasped a small yellow blanket from the bed and pulled it over himself. Turning the chair, he faced Jason who had returned to the doorway and was watching with amusement.

"Today is the day that the littlies come and pay us a visit. It's nice, you know. You see there is life in me yet. I can keep up with the young-uns" Charlie beamed contentiously as Jason slowly nodded.

"So there is," he said bluntly. "You're the Olympian of ragged old people."

Charlie started to wheel himself to the door. "So maybe you can start coming fortnightly now Jason. That way the wait won't seem so... laborious for you. Or maybe just wait for the call?" Before Jason had a chance to respond Charlie wheeled past him and into the wide, dark corridor. "Come along now, you really should be going. You've seen all you need to see."

With that, Charlie rolled down the hallway leaving Jason to follow grumpily in his wake. Charlie didn't allow further conversation with the boy. He had always been unpleasant and odd. Jason had gone from being a little oddball to a taller oddball. Charlie also knew that it was best Jason not be triggered. He greeted the nurses behind the desk, who waved back and waited for Jason to join him.

"So, call me if you need anything," Jason continued walking past without stopping.

"Yes, just like I always do," Charlie jibed. "Now leave, the school children arrive soon, and you'll scare them away."

"That's not what I meant, Grandpa..." Jason pulled his beanie back over his short black hair. "I mean if you need something, let me know OK?"

Charlie watched Jason with sadness. This was Jason's usual approach. Dark banter, venom but with the delivery of the slightest genuine sentiment a moment before he walked out the door. However, this was something Charlie had become immune to. This was a technique he had watched Jason use on many other occasions – mixing venom with honey. Confusing and controlling.

He continued to watch as Jason walked through the door and out into the cold morning air. He felt a heaviness lift. The weight that came from Jason's presence was a feeling of damage and loss. Charlie was a kind man. Loneliness was commonplace in his life now. Older and alone, it was something he had come to regard as a winding down of life. A half death that persisted before one faded into the darkness. He hated seeing the same loneliness in others. Maybe, he had pondered, when you feel lonely yourself you can justify this by remembering all the regrets you have had. That in some strange way made you feel that you deserve to end your life alone. As complicated as his step-grandson was, and as rare as he felt they shared moments of genuine, human intimacy, he was sure of one aspect of Jason's pained existence – Jason was never alone.

○○○

Checking the text several times, he was sure it was the place that Chelamah had asked to meet. Interesting. It had taken him forty minutes of driving up the narrow, winding roads of Mt. Marshblerie. He had begun to feel nauseous, but opening the window relieved the effects of the twists and turns. Then it started raining and the window went back up. The nausea commenced again.

The location surprised and then intrigued him. Why here? This was an unusual location for them to meet, though he did know today was different. Today he would meet with others. He didn't know who or where, but Chelamah had promised him that today, it would begin. He would start his introduction to the Pantheon. This, she declared, would be done incrementally. He knew there was a 'leader' and, it was clear, he would not be meeting them yet.

There was some kind of bullshit ranking within members. This concept seemed ridiculous and contrived. Some artificial hierarchy. He would love to meet the person who thought that would be a good idea in a situation such as theirs.

Checking his GPS, he turned towards Fort Splendour. The city's war memorial and 'listening' garden. He remembered being brought here by foster parents' number… six?… seven? One of them anyway. Rows of beautiful roses, each with a plaque of the fallen, led to the steps of the memorial. As a kid, he thought it was genius that they had placed the garden there. You had no choice but to walk through this devotion to the dead to reach their large marble shrine. Now though, he was just glad it seemed to have stopped raining.

Stepping out of the car, he looked around. There was only one other vehicle there with him. He was unsure if it was hers, but then who else would be up here? Wearily, he looked beyond the immaculate rows of flowerless rose shrubs to the structure above. He recognised Chelamah's slender frame and long coat. He waved but received nothing back.

He got closer. A list of rehearsed questions repeated in his mind. He was also charged with gathering information by Ellie. Suddenly he stopped. Chelamah was not alone. Behind her was a guy. A big guy. Excited but cautious, Sam reminded himself that this was the plan today. More people. More people like them.

"Good morning. I mean afternoon!" he corrected himself.

"Hi Sam, how are you?" Chelamah looked down at him.

"I am well. I actually slept last night. Why are we here?" He looked about, snapping back a yawn. "Seems a bit off the beaten track, doesn't it?"

Chelamah smiled "not for us. This place is very much on our beaten track. Sam, I would like you to meet Noah."

The big guy stepped forward, tall and intimidating. Noah moved past Chelamah, brushing comfortably against her. Sam noticed immediately. *These two are fucking.* Knowing his tendency to turn candid in possible awkward moments, he bit his tongue. That would be considered rude.

Don't be a dick.

Noah stared at him suspiciously. Sam wondered if Chelamah had talked him into this. Still eyeing him from beneath his baseball cap, Noah strode down the three stairs and to Sam's surprise, held out his hand.

"Noah." He said in a deep, American accent. This surprised Sam and he instantly wished he could pick its location. "Pleased to meet ya."

"Sam." Sam took his hand. "How are you?"

The child now stood beside Sam, staring at the marble stairs, past Noah and at Chelamah.

"Good. Cold but good." Following Sam's eye, Noah cast a glance to his side where Chelamah was slowly descending.

She watched the Child slowly approach her. There was no mistake when a Leviathan looked at you. A feeling of terror and weakness washed through your entire being at being prey to something so unnatural. But now she wasn't scared. She wasn't Lit. That wasn't needed anymore. Not since her last journey. She was already close enough, standing at the threshold.

Confused, Sam looked at Chelamah. Was the Child seeing her? If so, how?

"Are you OK?" Sam looked from the Child to Chelamah. She was distant, aloof. "What's been going on?"

The Child stood in front of Chelamah. She smiled at her, lifting her hands to her face, and gently wiggling her fingers.

"A lot. Come with us."

"And where are we going?" He was surprised at being led around the back of the monument, his shoes slipping on the muddy ground. Great, another pair of shoes ruined.

Walking up to the top of the hill, Chelamah turned to Noah and Sam. "I want to show you something. You can ask what you like but we should go there now."

"Good, I've got questions," Sam quipped.

Noah nodded "Hmmm… I hope so. W-w-we are counting on it."

"Well how many more am I meeting?"

"For now, one more." Chelamah replied walking down the path between the trees. "But this one's hard work. To meet Mika, you have to impress Jason."

"He's a bitch" Noah stated coldly as Sam chuckled nervously, following their lead into the trees. "I'm the asshole."

"Wow, I'm sold on Jason… Not you!" Sam looked at Noah smirking.

Chapter 10

Joshua's excitement was cut short by two talkative police officers walking through his curtain. He had only just pulled his track pants on when Aunt Casey led them in, sat down and started talking baby talk with him. Why did they do that? He wasn't five, he was nearly nine.

They asked him the same questions again. When did he last see his Mum?
She was being ripped apart in a big room with monsters crawling around.

What did she say to him the last time she saw him?
She told Ellie to take me away from the scary things.

And Ron?
He was being eaten alive on the floor of my house by a big dog. He begged me to make the dog stop chewing him.

They didn't ask about Jamie.
His eyes had popped, and he was cooking on the roof whilst smoke came out of him. He wasn't talking, just screaming, and making gurgling noises.

No-one ever seemed to like Jamie much. Maybe no-one missed him?

But Josh's answer remained the same. They went out in the evening after drinking a lot and didn't come home. The bucket was still there on the porch. Empty alcohol containers were strewn throughout the house. Most left by Mum and Ron, but some spread strategically by himself and Ellie. Ellie even left Jamie's little glass steaming pipe on the kitchen table.

Casey sat beside him watching him answer the questions. Josh thought she might be mad, maybe... worried? The police asked him about all his bruises and cuts. He replied simply that he was clumsy, and Mum called him a clumsy clog all the time. Casey took his hand, so perhaps she wasn't angry after all. He could tell she wanted to say something, and she was finding it hard not to. He was glad she wasn't asking him things. He would have felt really bad lying to Casey.

Every now and then he would startle. He felt silly. The police just kept talking but they noticed. First time it happened the man asked, "Are you OK?" He was OK. But the dog was making short snorty growling noises on the other side of the curtain. Sharp and loud. It made him jump. It did this often when people were around. The more Josh interacted, the closer it moved to him. Ellie had said that's because it could feel Josh getting emotional and he might feed it people. The dog was waiting for more people to put on the wall. These people had guns though... maybe if they did get all Lit up, they could shoot the dog?

"So young man, the doctor said you can go today. Your aunt is taking you home," the policeman said, distracting Josh from his thoughts.

"My house is too messy," Josh said, his eyes dropping, wringing his hands. Casey held his arm gently.

"No honey, you're coming to my house" she said softly.

This was not what he wanted. He wanted them all to go away, leave him alone. Ellie was coming. She was coming, and they were going to leave. He didn't want to go to his aunt's house or anywhere else. He wanted to go with his friend. A glob of vomit rose in his throat. His stomach hurt. This wasn't meant to happen. He didn't want to go anywhere but with Ellie. It was hopeless.

○○○

Sam looked ahead with trepidation. The path disappearing behind them and becoming less clear before them. His low-level tension had become low level fear. He told himself not to be stupid. He knew Chelamah... but did he really? They had met a handful of times, and each time she had been as cryptic as the last and now here he was, following her and some really big dude into the bushes. In past moments such as these, he'd told himself that he was protected, as much as this made him feel like a fucked-up person, it was true. And even though this man leading him through the bushes possessed, in some form or another, the same curse as he did, for the first time in his life the effectiveness of his dark child was unclear.

Suddenly, stepping through a curtain of wet foliage, Sam found himself walking into a small clearing. Between the banks of a crevice, stood an odd concrete structure. A large moss-covered dome sat impressively camouflaged within the growth. Covered with all that vegetation it was hard for Sam to know how far back it actually went. It appeared to be partially buried, or built, into the landscape, deeply hidden.

Sam had heard about the World War II bunkers scattered about Marshblerie. It made sense, being so close to the site of the old fort. First intrigued and then anxious, he stared at the heavy metal door to the underground chamber. His fear peaked when Noah grabbed the steel door. As the door opened, the sound of grinding metal echoed through the woods. Subtle.

"What's in there?" Sam asked, taking a step backwards.

"Come on in," Noah beckoned. "It's safe. Mostly… perhaps."

Sam looked at Chelamah who also stood back. She had noticed Sam's increasing anxiety. Sam had also noticed that Noah, for whatever reason, was being a lot more brazen than Chelamah had been up to this point. Perhaps he didn't have to worry so much about the consequences of pissing Sam off.

Glancing to the left he saw the Child beside him, her body bent over as if in a bow, her face stared dead ahead at the doorway before them.

Chelamah noticed his apprehension. "It's OK. I wouldn't have bought you here if you were in danger."

Sam nodded, "Yeah but that's what you *would* say if I was in danger."

With a blast of frustration, Noah sighed. "Bro, I don't wanna hurt you as much as you don't wanna hurt me. I'm not keen on creating some shit here because we don't know how it will end… and I simply can't be fucked right now. What are we going to do? Shoot you? Kill you? You know it's not that easy. We wouldn't be the first to have tried. Am I right? I could get pissed at you and really shoot myself in the ass. I'm tired and I slept on the floor so can we just go in?"

"Noah it's OK," Chelamah interrupted. Noah ignored her.

"You are a fucking Ascendant bro. Chel can sense it. She told me what is with you, or 'who', or whatever, and… I simply don't wanna go to war today."

Sam was taken aback, he turned to Chelamah. "You can see her?"

"I'm an Underling, but Chel's a Devotee. That's what HE calls me. Devotees can feel what you are… in their guts… right here." He put a fist to his stomach. "Chelamah couldn't hurt you even if she wanted to and I'd more than likely get my ass handed to me. So calm the f-f-fuck down and come through this door… I'm f-f-freezing." Noah gestured to the opening impatiently.

It shocked Sam. Noah's candour was refreshing. Brash, open with no bullshit agenda or cryptic rubbish. He was clear and in your face. Like Ellie, only more verbose. To his surprise it didn't make him angry. It made him calm. It made him want to trust the man. He knew exactly where he stood and for reasons that made him trustworthy.

"OK," Sam nodded slowly. "OK, let's go in."

With that, Noah strode through the open-door leaving Sam and Chelamah to stand quietly alone.

"Wow," Sam muttered in astonishment. "He's colourful."

Chelamah smiled wearily. "He doesn't know you… Give him time. He's scared of you."

"Scared? Why is *he* scared?" Sam mused at the six-foot seven guy, whose arms were bigger than Sam's neck, being scared of him.

"Because he should be. Ascendants are… risky for everyone including us. Come with me. He'll be OK." She followed Noah in. With an anxious exhale, Sam pulled out his phone and typed with millennial efficiently, before reluctantly walking through the door.

OOO

Joshua sat in the hospital toilet. Sadly, he looked at the door. They would be wanting him to come out in a minute. He couldn't stay in here for long, but it had been enough time to quickly read Ellie's message:

I AM HERE

His battery said 1%. He hadn't had the chance to search the bag for his charger. It didn't matter. He was surrounded by people now and couldn't do anything. He couldn't go with Ellie. He knew this. He was so scared. So many people in this place and so many questions he had answered with so many lies. His world seemed so strange. Only with Ellie did anything make any sense in this new life. He was going to go with his aunt and her husband, a man called Nate. He hadn't met him yet, but the thought terrified him. More people he didn't know.

He heard his name called through the door. "Josh, honey, are you OK?"

He was OK. OK-ish. Wistfully, he put his phone in his pocket and stood up. Flushing the toilet he hadn't used, he called out "coming," as he walked to the sink and turned the tap on. Josh watched the water run for three seconds and then turned it off. Lies, he thought, were not just words. Turning around, he opened the door.

His aunt was talking to him as she led him down the shiny floor of the hospital and out a big sliding door. This place had so many doors. It was like Ellie's spooky man. His big, horrible building had doors everywhere.

"Hey," Casey said to him, giving him a nudge. "It's OK, we're going home."

Josh faked a small smile. That was what she wanted. Walking across the foyer to the entrance where the ambulances were parked, he heard someone call out. Turning, Casey had noticed a doctor he had seen before trotting up to them. Casey and the doctor began to talk. He had papers in his hands, and they were talking about him going back to get his arms dressed.

He looked up at the talking adults, feeling very small. Casey placed a hand on his head and gently stroked his hair just once, before continuing the conversation. Josh looked about. So many strange looking people. Some looked really well. Others looked really sick. Some were in wheelchairs or walked with strange metal frames in front of them like his grandma used to. It was then that he noticed Ellie.

Dressed in her black coat and beanie she stood over on the other side of the room. She noticed him looking and smiled. He was overcome with relief and excitement. She was here. They were in the same place. It had seemed so long, and he had so much to tell her. His fingers fidgeted wildly, as he looked up at the two talking adults and then back to Ellie again who was gone. His heart sank. Where was she?

Slowly at first, he moved away from the talking adults. Merely two paces later, his legs broke into an unstoppable sprint. He rounded the corner and they collided.

"Ellie! Ellie!" he grabbed her coat, pulling her to him. "Ellie we got to go!"

Ellie held him back, dropping to one knee. "No, no, we can't. It's alright, you're alright."

"I'm not alright! The dog came and did stuff to people and then they saw me all weird," his eyes filled with tears. "They brought me here and called my aunt, but they keep asking me questions… they keep asking me things all the time about my cuts and stuff. I told them what you told me to say. We need to run away, now!"

Ellie looked into his eyes, eyes that contained such deep sadness and desperation. This was impossible. It would lead to devastation, something he didn't understand, not yet. In his mind he needed, and deserved, to be somewhere he felt safe – preferably with her – and yet he couldn't comprehend why that was just impossible.

"It's OK. They will take you home, remember? We spoke about this. I am here, I found you and I will find you again, but we can't…"

"We have to run now!" he shouted. The air turned thick. "They are taking me away Ellie!"

Josh was aware that the dog had arrived behind him. He heard a snarl in his ears. He heard the scraping of its knife-like claws on the hard floor, but he didn't care.

Ellie saw Bael slam his foot down beside her and lean forward menacingly. The two conduits looked into each other's eyes. She could see the defiance growing in Josh's stare with each passing second. She squeezed his hands tight.

"I don't want to go," Josh muttered, his eyes turned strangely cold and distant. "They *can't* make me go."

Quietly, Ellie held his hands, her eyes burning into his. Thinking, she cast her eyes to the floor, consciously relaxed her grip on his hands into a gentle grasp.

They can't make me go.

These words were adversarial and threatening. Ellie gripped his hands tighter, shaking her head slowly. What did this mean? No, they couldn't make him go. He could very well make them 'go'. She hoped it was purely semantics and not Josh legitimately recognising the power he had.

"No. You're right," Ellie nodded. "They can't. But you don't want to hurt anyone do you?"

She could see the wheels of Josh's brain turning. Fear and vulnerability were driving him towards self-protection.

"Calm down for me. Wiggle your fingers."

"I can't," he replied.

"Why?"

"You're holding them" he sighed then smiled.

Ellie gave a small chuckle of relief. She let his hands go as Josh began opening and closing them slowly.

"You have your phone. You tell me where you've gone, and I will be there. But we don't hurt people. It's not what we do. Remember... why don't we do it?"

"...because we are not like them." Josh gave a small nod. "Not like the stupid dog and the stinky tall man."

Ellie nodded. "Not at all like them."

"Or like the idiot little bitch troll," Josh whispered,

"Who said that?"

"Sam did. He said she was an idiot bitch troll from hell who deserved a pole up her ass."

Ellie gave a short titter. Sam, *seriously*.

"Of course he did. OK, yes. Or like the idiot little...."

"Bitch troll from hell" Josh finished her sentence.

"Bitch troll from hell...Yes, I got it." She nodded, hiding her chuckle.

"And... she deserves..."

"Yes, I know what it deserves, it's cool..." Ellie pulled him closer. "Go now. Relax and don't worry. I will see you soon."

"OK" Josh nodded. Hesitating for a second, he wrapped his arms around Ellie, squeezed tight and then ran back around the corner.

Ellie quickly stood back up and walked towards the entrance. Turning the corner, she passed Josh and his worried aunt. He told her he was in the toilet again. Ellie left the bright lights of the hospital and walked alone into the overcast morning. She would just keep walking and not look back. He was safe... for now. Perhaps she could rest. Her eyes were heavy, and her feet were burning. She needed to eat, shower and rest. A calmness overcame her. A feeling that, for now, all was OK. All was well. A feeling she had not had for quite some weeks.

Ellie placed her headphones over her ears and pulled out her phone, staring at what appeared to be a text notification. She sighed tiredly. It was from Sam. The screen lit up to a location pin. Underneath it was written:

IF I GO MISSING, I WAS HERE
SAM

Exhausted, Ellie rubbed her tired eyes and sighed, "You've got to be kidding me."

ooo

Sam descended the final step of the entrance. The dust stung his eyes. A disorientating wave ran through his body, a rush of nausea that caused him to gag. The childish squeal of the Dark Child resonated in his ears and then slowly faded to silence. The vertigo stopped. Nerves, he thought, pure anxiety. Taking a deep breath, he continued to follow Chelamah and Noah, peering into a large, murky hall with a curved dome roof. Ribbed steel supports eaten by rust stretched above him and ran the entire length of the roof. Archaic and interesting.

There was a flicker of light as Noah lit a candle at the far end of the bunker. "Is that for atmosphere?" Sam asked with nervous sarcasm.

"No, it's so we can see!" Noah snapped back, turning to Chelamah, rolling his eyes.

"Nothing electrical works here. No torches, batteries, anything," Chelamah explained, walking into the darkness. "Check your phone."

Intrigued, Sam took his phone from his pocket and tapped it. Sure enough, the screen was dead.

Chelamah reassured him, "Don't worry, once you go up those stairs it comes back. But not down here."

Sam found himself gravitating towards Noah and the candle. He noticed this with embarrassment. Like a moth to a flame. There was something unnerving about this place. Its darkness, its smell, but even more so the sense of something else you couldn't see. Even the slightest sound seemed exaggerated. Sam looked about with a sense of unease and the fear of possible danger. There were no windows and the large concrete dome felt like it was

111

burying them, closing in, weighing more heavily above them the further they ventured in.

"Why are we here?" he asked, attempting to hide the low-level panic in his voice. He glanced quickly behind him, noting the direction of the stairs he had just descended.

"Chel?" Noah gestured towards her. The rims of her glasses flickered in the candlelight.

"Why are we here? What is this place?" Sam repeated impatiently. "I don't understand. Why doesn't anything work?" He played with his phone again as he watched Chelamah.

She turned toward him. "That's not the only thing that doesn't work here. Notice something? Anything?"

What did she mean? He had bought nothing else with him but his phone. Sam was unsure of the point of the question. He cocked his head to the side. He was about to answer, and only then noticed the silence. Absolute silence. No strange reverberations, no echoes, no songs. No eerie, distorted nursery rhymes wafted around him. Just... silence. Agitated, he spun around on the spot, scanning the shadows and corners. The roof? He looked up, he looked down, behind him... he looked everywhere, and then turned, stunned, to his companions, eyes wide, mouth open in surprise, "What the hell... what the absolute hell. Where?"

"Calm down. It's a weird feeling but just... stay calm. Enjoy the moment." Noah turned to him, placing the candle before him, and watching him with interest.

"She's gone? but... how?" Sam spun to Chelamah. "How can she be gone? Where is she? What is this place?" Sam raised his voice as Chelamah stepped forward and gently placed a hand on his cheek. He was gripped by fear and confusion. Fear? Why would he feel fear? Why? She wasn't there... he could feel it deep in his soul... she wasn't there! How did this happen?

"It's just different that's all. You're OK," Chelamah soothed.

Sam's mind was awash with feelings. The most surprising to him was feeling fear. Like the lifting of a shroud, he was exposed and on his own without his constant companion. He never thought he would feel this way. "Where is she?"

"Not that far away bro" Noah said, moving deeper into the bunker, candle held in front of him.

Intrigued, Sam walked forward, scanning the concrete dome. Noah walked to his side, holding up the candle as it cast its dancing light across a strange display.

At first, they looked like faded, mouldy rags hanging from the wall. With his eyes still adjusting, he had no idea what he was looking at. There were ten in total. Each about two foot long, tatty and hanging randomly upon the grey background of the bunker. It reminded Sam of the coat rack at a child's school. Eclectic messy bundles of clothing. Then it dawned on him. These twisted and prosaic clumps of matter were the most horrendous entities that ever existed.

"Insane, isn't it?" Noah smiled.

"Oh my god," Sam gasped, rubbing his mouth, and stepping forward. "That's them?"

"It's a process called Stripping. It's not uncommon. The Grimoires taught some. To others, it was passed on, but we have not seen it outside our own group." Chelamah stood beside them, looking at the bizarre figures on the concrete. "This place has been 'Stripped'. There are three steps in the process; or I guess, three 'things' which are needed. You see that insignia up there?" she said, drawing Sam's attention to a small engraving, no bigger than a dollar note, that was hanging high on the wall above the discarded skins. "That's the insignia required. Item one. The box down there?" Chelamah pointed to a small, wooden box. Completely unremarkable, barely a foot squared and almost invisible in the darkness. "That's the second. That has been used as an Oubliette. A vessel. In this space, once you step over the threshold, the Leviathan is stripped, skin from monster. Skin hangs here, and monster... is now in there."

"And... the third?" Sam asked, intrigued.

"A Devotee. A Devotee activates the Stripping process." Chelamah looked back at the insignia and sighed, "once up, it takes a toll. We can't leave it up for long, but yes, here in this space it separates man from monster."

Sam followed her look. "I've never seen this one before."

Noah cast Sam a look which made him feel foolish, "This is pre-Aahna. She didn't show you everything. Aahna was a Scribe. A writer. Adept in the ancient act of Stripping."

Sam pondered the response before Chelamah stepped between them. "Stripping comes from a much earlier Grimoire than my mother's. Only

113

Devotees can activate the insignia and the Oubliette required for the stripping. As Noah said, Scribes draw them, Devotees activate them." She paused. "A Devotee like me."

"Why wouldn't you use them all the time?" Sam exclaimed.

Uncomfortable, Noah stammered, "Impossible. Once activated, that Devotee's trip down the hell lane speeds up… a lot. It takes from them, pulling them faster and faster towards-"

"Hell" Chelamah interjected, looking at Noah. "The darkness is inside us, like a disease, and it spreads. We reach a point of no return and then… we retreat to the hell side and stay there."

So, this was her inevitable fate. Just like himself, with the Dark Child, thought Sam? "So, you're just as screwed as I am," he stated.

"Yes," Chelamah shrugged, resignation in her eyes. "Mika calls it our purification. What a blessing huh?"

She stopped and looked at Sam. "Like the knife you used to kill the gift. The knife wasn't special. Me holding it made it special." Turning away from him she looked into the darkness and continued, "the Devotee who stripped this place never got the chance to take it down… she ended up with the others." Chelamah stared coldly. "I know that as a Devotee. I promise you. We would not have left that in place. It would have been a quick, cruel decline."

"Why are you showing me this?" Sam asked.

"Because they'll know when it's in play bro. You're about to meet Jason."

"Jason is a pure sociopath and full of ego. He'll tell you things that he has been instructed to and things that he shouldn't. You are an Ascendant. An Ace. You get a lot more information than we do. He'll see you as an equal. He's crazy, yes… but also desperate. Chelamah moved to the wall and pointed to the insignia. "He will think you don't know about this. Don't tell him. Give him the power trip of thinking he's teaching you something."

Barely understanding, Sam nodded, "So what happened to the group here?"

"We know what happened. We just don't know why." Noah looked at Chelamah, waiting for her to speak.

"This group of Conduits, right here in this bunker, used a Grimoire for separation. They had more than likely used it many times before and, let's face it, why wouldn't you?" She stopped and looked directly at Sam. "The

114

Devotee would have been here, ready to destroy the Oubliette - the vessel - as soon as the sun rose, when her colleagues had returned from their Event. It would've been torture for her, waiting for the time she could take it down. But, as I said, she never got the chance. The last Event something happened. Something arrived." She gestured with a nod of the head towards Noah who turned to face the far wall, opposite the strange mosaic of hanging skins.

Within the shadows of the bunker stood something else. It was a large, round opening. Dark and almost indistinguishable from the cracked concrete around it. It gave the perception of depth, jet black and endless. It reflected no light. The candles that lit the walls close by didn't illuminate it in any way.

"What is it?" Sam asked as he cautiously stepped forward. Noah put his arm in front of him, blocking his path.

"That, bro, is what showed up." Noah sighed, "and it tore them up."

Chelamah crossed her arms nervously. "The Event occurs on the same night every year. This group thought they had protection, and maybe it had worked before. But this time, on the last Event, something went wrong."

"More than one Ace near this and the things in there notice." Noah pointed to the ink black void, "It's a doorway, it's been referred to as an Oculus. An entrance and an exit. Most of the time it just…sits there. It needs a certain combination of players to work. Alone, we fly under the radar. Devotee, Underling. Ascendant, devotee. Nothing happens. But two Ascendants get noticed. Two or more Ascendants means trouble."

"What about us?" asked Sam worried.

"We're not Ascendants, you are. I don't know why but somewhere, something happened. Something turned.. It's not unusual for Aces to group for the Event. Probably happens more now than before. Whatever happened at the last Event bought this Oculus and others. They're still here. Something powerful happened that night and these doorways opened all over the city."

"The Circle?" Sam clarified. She had referred to it as the Event, as had Aahna.

"Ha," Noah sighed. "That night where we all get hunted down? It's called the Event. It's been called the Event for centuries."

"What comes through an Oculus?" Sam asked, ignoring Noah's patronising tone.

"Absolute carnage. For both Leviathan and Conduit, and everything nearby. There are 5 in the city we know of." Chelamah stared into the blackness with a desire that took Sam by surprise. "Horrific beauty. Raw, cruel power. So many Conduits were taken during the last Event. They wouldn't have seen it coming." Pausing briefly, she continued. "Remember. Jason and the others know nothing of this. I found them… don't ask how. They can't know Sam. You can't tell them. In the Grimoires, it states things will change. The boundary between theirs and ours becomes unclear when Bael begins to Ascend. Our group mustn't know. We can use an Oculus."

"How? If I go near them, I could be taken. Why would I want to do that?" Sam demanded. Chelamah reached inside her coat pocket, pulling out a folded piece of paper.

"You'll know where they are. The ones I know of. No, you won't be safe, but you're forewarned, which is more than I can say for the others." Chelamah, began to walk away, fighting an inner turmoil. Sam could sense it. Her monotonous tone, low and distant.

"What do they mean?"

"It means Bael is here. The others must follow Bael. Even if this means back to their prison. Bael will resist. Bael has jumped from Conduit to Conduit. He has held his gateway for millennia. Only one thing controls Bael: the Conduit. Like the others, Bael must follow the Conduit. But in the meantime, the armada of creatures in there - they are coming for their own."

Noah looked into the dark abyss, "We should go. Don't tell Jason any of this. He'll tell Mika, and then the shit will really hit the fan. Mika doesn't want Bael to return. Mika wants to replace Bael's Conduit with himself. In this hell there's only one trump card. Bael." Noah asserted. "A curse, but in the shitfest that's about to hit, a blessing. The rest of us are sitting ducks."

"We need to find Bael. We need to find Bael's Conduit. We need Bael's Conduit to send Bael back" Chelamah said ascending the staircase.

With that sentence, Sam wished he had never come. He knew this person. She was his friend. In that one statement, these people had now become an enemy of sorts, but he had an advantage. They didn't know about Ellie and her strength that had locked Bael down for so long.

Chapter 11

Ellie's world had become loud. Too loud and too bright. Walls of tension and unease were closing in on her and she didn't know how to push back. The interactions: The conversations: She had dared to enjoy them. The veil that isolated her was now less substantial, as was the shroud that covered the world. She found herself considering this new world as an enemy and, if the world knew what was best for it, it would do the same.

Walking the streets, wet and uncomfortable, she went to the pharmacy to 'restock'. She had planned to take the two full bags home, but her feet wouldn't stop walking. She traipsed forward on the wet paths through the city centre, hearing nothing but her music pounding in her ears. Hundreds of silent strangers passed unheeded. She wasn't sure why, but she had the need to hide in plain sight. No talking, no interacting, no scheming, just leaving her with her thoughts while cloaked by her loneliness.

Thoughts entered her mind unbidden - Joshua, Sam. She let them enter and then allowed them to fade away. 'Mindfulness', Niles had called it. She had actually paid attention and it was working. He would be thrilled.

As the rain became heavier, she manoeuvred to walk under the awnings above the shop entrances. Others did the same. Winter in this city was bleak and lasted so long. But there was something calming about the dreary dimness. No-one could see her. Not even the sun. She was in the dark no matter where she went. God, how she hated summer. It was bright, obvious, and glaring. But at this time of year she felt less like she was visiting this world and more like that this world was entering hers. The underpass to main street was approaching. It was time to go home. The rain was heavier and, as usual, she had left her umbrella sitting on the kitchen counter.

The noise started as a slow rumble. A commonplace sound. A passing truck or an ascending plane. Ellie paid it no attention. But her pace slowed as the vibration grew beyond her music's distraction. An odour hit her nostrils causing her to gag: a sweet, full-bodied smell. She had smelt this before. The smell of rotting flesh that provoked a metallic taste of blood to fill her mouth.

The dimness unexpectedly darkened further as a panic gripped her. She froze, staring straight ahead. The underpass was now encased in an inky darkness, the air morose. Fearful and curious, she dropped her bags, pulling out her earphones. Staring into the blackness, she gasped. There was Bael standing at the entrance, its back towards her.

What had its attention more than her?

Ellie felt dizzy as a lump grew in her throat. The sound crescendoed, growing clearer. It was roaring, screaming, pounding. It contained something created from pure malevolence, blended with a visceral rage. Bursting forth from the underpass it hit her like a canon of hatred and suffering, bringing her to her knees. Helpless before it she collapsed, the monstrous noise blasting over her with the force of a gale.

She saw a young man stumble from the darkness. She heard him screaming in rage. He then collapsed beside Bael. Bael didn't move, and scarcely glanced at the crumpled human. Beyond the man, looming out of the shadows, was something else. Without doubt, it was a Leviathan. Its movements erratic, its stance vicious. A macabre form of a man. Short, stocky and clothed in a white straight jacket. It approached the prostrate man, its target. To Ellie's surprise, on reaching him it paid him no attention. Instead, it watched immobile as four ethereal entities had emerged from the darkness after it.

Ellie lifted her head. She stared at Bael, who watched the scene with only the slightest of interest. The four figures appeared to be covered in a glistening, crimson oil. Their faces were twisted, contorted, with grotesque elongated noses and thin, wide mouths. Short and solid, they carried a variety of rusted weapons in their arms. With slow but certain strides they approached the Leviathan, who shuffled backwards leaving the man alone. "No!" The man bellowed at the advancing beings as he jumped to his feet. "What are you?"

Ellie watched in disbelief. This was a Conduit. That was his Leviathan. But what the hell *were they*? The Leviathan threw itself upon the man, encased him, wrapping itself spider-like around him as the figures launched themselves forward, bludgeoning him with their weapons. The Leviathan's

118

protection was of no use. The creature's blades passed through it as if it were a shadow, striking the man again and again, shredding him with their metal.

Get up, Ellie's mind screamed. *Move!* But she couldn't. She was immobile, as if the weight of gravity was forcing her down. Head heavy, she stared at Bael, who in turn, looked back. It was then, during a pause in the man's screaming, that she realised Bael was not the only one looking at her.

Shaking, the victim lifted his face and stared straight at Ellie. She couldn't hear but knew that he mouthed the word *"please"* through bloodied lips. How could she? She was powerless. She couldn't move or speak. The figures turned toward the underpass, weapons still embedded in their screaming captive. Slowly they began dragging him back into the void. The Leviathan peeled from its Conduit as it too was being hauled towards the void.

Four other figures now emerged from the dark and made their way past the impaled Conduit. Slowly they hobbled towards her. She had to get up, but the noise, the noise was numbing. She couldn't think through the chaos. *Get up!*

Suddenly she felt something beside her. Trembling, she braced herself for the worst. Glancing through the strands of hair plastered across her face, she saw Bael. It stood silently beside her, confident and statuesque. The advancing creatures stopped. They regarded It. Nothing was said, but the air was rife with communication. *Oh god please get up!*

As one, the beings turned. Ellie no longer saw the other Conduit. Only a trail of rags lay strewn where his body had been impaled. This was what had been left of his Leviathan. That path of debris had once been his monster. His screaming faded; he was now gone.

Impossibly a voice began to speak. A whisper, a gentle wafting chant normally impossible to hear. It was a language she didn't understand but she could feel its sinister intent. Ellie knew Bael heard it also.

Confused, she watched a soft, white glow emanate from her hands. Struggling to breathe, she screamed out in desperation "STOP!"

WILL YOU COME WITH ME?
Bael spoke. It was beside her, It's dead white eyes leaning into hers as she stared at the ground. Ellie turned her head defiantly glaring into its eyes. Its face had no expression as its long thick waxy lips moved.

119

WILL YOU DIE FOR HIM?

It spoke to her. It waited for a response. Amid the chaos it laid a large, cold hand on her head, caressing, almost affectionate. Hands that caused such carnage to others were now gently laid upon her. It could *touch* her. How dare It. She was outraged. How dare it touch her in such a way. Suddenly It moved even closer. She could smell its rancid breath on her face, feel its cold, mottled skin touching her own.

"Get away from me!" she hissed, cutting through the chaos. "Don't... touch... me."

TU ES IN LIBRO SECUNDO DE MORTE

With a final deafening blast, Ellie fell forward hitting the ground hard. As quickly as it had started, it was over. She lay on the pavement gasping. The stench of Bael still on her skin.

"Oh my god," she whimpered, trying to find her feet. She had to get up. She had to get out of there. She heard someone ask her if she was OK. No, no. No people. Not now. Summoning all her strength, she staggered to her feet. *Act crazy, act unhinged.* Without looking at them she screamed "FUCK OFF! GET AWAY! FUCK OFF!"

She just had to get away from here. She took off running. She wasn't fleeing Bael. She couldn't flee It, but she had to get away from people. All those targets. She could feel the beginning of their end; one step further and it would have been done.

In the middle of complete pandemonium, she ran. She heard cars screech to a stop, but tore through them anyway, ignoring the blast of horns that surrounded her.

It all happened so fast.

Ellie caught a glimpse of a car hitting a slide and hurtling towards her. No time to react, no time to move. Time slowed. Barely had her arms reached defensively forward when she rose into the air and was violently flung to the curb four metres away. The car slammed into the rear of another. That was where she should have been. Crushed between two vehicles. Her life would've been over. But Bael would not let that happen. Striding across the road towards her, It came. She pulled herself to her feet and fled down the path.

Ellie ran as fast as she could. She rounded a corner, listening to the sirens of emergency vehicles behind. Fuck, she had hurt people. But it could have been much worse. Hesitating for a moment, she ducked, crawling into the hollow under some large bushes.

Lying on her side, she drew breath into her burning lungs. What had happened? What the hell was going on? She had never experienced anything like that. Like a catalogue of horrors in her mind, she was certain that this particular event had never occurred before. It could touch her, yet she remained unharmed.

"Oh god, oh my god" she breathed hard. *Think, think.*

Painfully, she turned herself onto her side. Droplets of rain fell onto her face from the bushes above.

It was over for now. Or was it? She didn't know. Everything hurt from where she hit the pavement. It had stopped her from dying by tossing her. Thanks, she thought. As she struggled to gather her thoughts, panic washed over her again. Slowing her breathing, she closed her eyes. She had no answer for what happened. No explanation. But now she had to calm down.

The last Circle had been more than eight weeks ago. This kind of nonsense was expected then. Then she had been ready, prepared. This was not supposed to happen now. What were they, in the underpass? Who was that person? And why didn't Bael tear her apart? What the *actual fuck* happened?

○○○

Jason stood in the dark, dreary carpark staring at the bright building in front. He was hoping, practically of course, that the radiance of it wouldn't dampen his focus. It would be easier if he could take the bleak, dark chill in with him. He smiled softly to himself; it would be bright and 'merry' soon enough.

It was late and, as expected, the gym had all but emptied out in his 45 minutes of waiting outside in the miserable cold. His mind was cocked and ready. He had felt it building all day. Like a powerful compulsion that was close to the tipping point; all he would have to do was press one more button and it would be done.

Pulling his gym bag over his shoulder he slowly proceeded to the 24-hour exit. He saw the white SUV in the carpark knowing that more than one person had arrived in that vehicle. He had made a point of learning the routine of others. That was a rule. That was part of the process and tonight there was comfort in that. He was following the rules. He was doing what would be expected of him from Mika and the others.

He walked to the large glass door and peered inside. Quiet, but there was movement, he wouldn't be alone. He had counted on this. Opening the door he was met with the familiar energetic music. He heard them. The targets were there. The usual feeling of intimidation was not with him to-night. He had no desire to be "friendly" or have "approval." His curtain of fragility would drop, and they would see his awesome reality.

The Asian man noticed Jason enter and, for a brief second, noted the new poise in his previously diffident step. He made eye contact as a steely coldness washed over him. Hugging his bare arms uneasily, he turned back to his friends. Jason walked past them noting the placements of the small, round security cameras in the corners of the gym. He proceeded to the row of benches opposite the mirrored wall, watching the reflection of the men behind him. He smiled.

Jason watched the silhouette move in the darkness outside the window. A long, narrow form would descend like a spider from a web. Two narrow arms would lift clumsily into the air before it would rise again out of view. It could feel the anticipation.

Slowly, Jason let his bag slip down his arm and fall onto the floor. He removed his jacket, his scarf and beanie, placing them on top of his bag. He looked at himself in the mirror with the group of dirtbags reflected behind; tall… thin… weak. Their bodies were indeed amazing. It was unfair that such physical supremacy would be granted to people so obnoxious and ar-rogant. They hadn't said anything. But they would.

Looking to the roof, confirming the security cameras were above him, Jason sat on the bench. Any moment now he would begin the play.

OOO

Sam's phone went straight to message bank for the third time. Ellie pushed open her apartment door and stepped inside, slamming it quickly behind her. She desperately needed to speak to someone, and that someone was Sam. Her hands shook. She was scared and confused. After grappling with the events of the last hour, she came to the same conclusion every time. There was a Conduit and there was a Leviathan. Apart from that noth-ing else made sense.

She ran to her apartment window and looked out, scanning the land-scape below. Nothing was different. No-one was there; had he expected something else? She was acutely aware of how panicked she was. She was embarrassed. Ashamed of this vulnerability. Yet even though she didn't know what had just occurred, she was keenly aware that a Conduit, like her, had been taken by things she had never before experienced. And that those same things had come for her. Bael played a part in this, but not the part she would have expected.

She pulled off her coat, letting it fall on the floor. Hastily she switched off the lamp, pushing her hands onto the window and peering out again. Again, there was nothing to see, but she felt something. There was some-thing she had seen that she wasn't supposed to. Something she had survived that she shouldn't have. There was something in the dark streets, between the row of trees against the footbridge to her left and the closed shop on her right. There was *something* wrong. Her whole life had been full of some-thing wrong, but this was different. Her, Bael, Josh, the Dog, Sam, the Child. All scary revelations, but what she had seen that evening was alien to even these. This was different, a side she had never seen before and, she was sure, neither had Sam.

Running to the kitchen she swung open the pantry door. Dragging out two large bags from the bottom shelf, she spilled the contents onto the floor before kneeling down and rifling through them. Fire and oil. She had access to both. Then she needed to bleed; she could do that. She needed to be mindful not to set the entire building on fire. She paused for half a second to think. The garage! The parking garage. Large enough and quiet enough, hopefully at this hour, to pull it off. She pulled out the plastic bag of herbs last held by Joshua during the Circle. A few, pathetic remnants lay in the bottom. *Shit.* It would have to do.

Everything she needed, more or less. It would have to be enough. She would set up and hope she wouldn't need it. Roughly, she piled the contents back into the bags.

The phone rang. She seized it while staring at the contents on the floor. "Don't talk Sam… don't talk." There was no response. "Sam?" she said quietly.

"Make up your mind. You told me not to talk" Sam scoffed.

Ellie sighed in frustration, "OK, don't be irritating, just listen. Some-thing's happened. Something came for me. I don't know what it was. There were these things. They took someone right in front of me… I'm sure he was a Conduit, and I was next… it wasn't Bael. *It wasn't Bael.* It's the Circle Sam. It's happening now… to me. I can feel it. It's coming. Something's wrong…"

"Calm down Ellie. You OK?"

Ellie rapidly described the events to Sam. As she did the feelings of unease increased. He listened and she was impressed that he let her speak without interrupting. This restraint was rare, highlighting his concern. She displayed an uncertainty he had not seen until recently. More cracks had started to show, breaking through that facade of stoicism. First Josh and now, this.

"Are you safe now?"

"I don't know. I'm going to set up a Circle. I don't know what else to do."

"Don't," Sam said strongly. "I need to know exactly where it happened. Can you remember? You don't need to set up."

"Sam, how do you know that?"

"Just trust me. I need you to tell me where it happened."

"OK." She straightened up, hardly believing what she was about to say. "I'll show you. I'll meet you there… it's down near the-"

"No. No, you can't," Sam yelled, cutting her off. "Listen to me, you can't come, not with me. You have to stay away from there. You understand? Wait for me at yours alright?"

Confused, Ellie shook her head. "Sam, what's going on?"

"Promise me Ellie. When I hang up this phone, you will stay where you are."

Ellie turned to look out into the darkness once more. Today he met with the 'others' and the mystery woman called Chelamah. He knew more than she did and, as hard as it was, she had to trust him.

"OK…" she said quietly. "When we hang up, I will stay where I am. One condition though."

"Are we bargaining now?" Sam asked, surprised.

"Sam, I'm serious. When you get here you tell me exactly what's going on."

She was scared. This feeling was not nerves and, God knows, her life did not allow her to scare easily. She didn't have the 'jitters', nor had she succumbed to paranoia. It was a feeling she knew all too well: something was watching her. Ellie cautiously stepped out of the kitchen and walked slowly back to the window.

Bael was there with her, staring out the window into the night. She could hear the muttering again. Words that made no sense. An unknown language delivered in a tone she had never before heard. Walking towards It, the words grew no louder. It paid her no attention. It wasn't focusing on her, It was fixated on something else. She stood next to It and listened to the indecipherable words coming from Its vicious, oversized mouth.

"Sam… I…" her voice trailed off.

She looked out again. There were multiple humanoid shadows in the street below, scattered on the footpath, the road and beside the trees. Tall, featureless silhouettes. A dozen dimly glistening eyes stared motionless up at her. What was happening? What were they?

"I need to know what's happening," she finished, steadying her trembling voice. "*Everything.*"

Sam spoke, "I thought you didn't want to know *everything?*" He sounded smug.

"I didn't…" Ellie responded quietly, barely audible above a whisper, "… but that was before they were all looking at me through my window."

ᴑᴑᴑ

The three men were gathered together at the benches once more, the tall blonde sat flanked by the other two. This is where they normally completed their workout. Jason knew the time was approaching. From the cables, Jason half-heartedly performed an exercise that Tyler had shown him. He had to look at them to allow his disdain to swell like waves of contempt. There was a loud laugh, piercing the otherwise empty gym. Equally irritating and intimidating. Damn them. Fuelled by his increasing hatred, the familiar sounds of his rage began to echo from all around him, a distorted, childlike jingle of happiness - melodic but twisted. A soft, light giggling filled his ears. It was so close.

Jason eyeballed them from a comfortable distance away. What would they sound like when they screamed? What would those pretty faces look like when they were terrified? The creative possibilities were endless.

Once again, the young Asian man noticed Jason's attention. He glanced uneasily towards him and in turn Jason looked away. Jason wanted him to

125

notice this. He wanted engagement. Not that ignoring him would change anything. Not at this late stage. But it would certainly be more entertaining if triggered by a slight.

Blonde date-rape guy was now talking loudly. He pulled up his shorts, revealing well-defined quadriceps. His two lackeys paid attention as he explained his workout and protein regime. Sleazy short guy slapped the leg. This apparently called for outrageous laughter. Then, as they settled down, Jason noticed tall blonde guy's eyes dart over to him. There was a mutter. Here it was.

Jason, his towel tossed over his shoulder, left the frame and walked across the gym floor towards his chosen location. Placing the gym towel neatly upon the bench, he sat facing the wall mirrors, back to the crew of gaggling fools. He stroked his arm, running his finger down to his hand. Listening, the muttering continued, and he could see them glancing his way.

"Hey mate," the blond guy called, standing, "you wanna work in with us?"

There was a friendliness to his voice that caught Jason by surprise. He sat for a moment, not responding. He didn't look up. The blonde guy looked back at his mates, one of them pointed to his ears. Jason had his earphones in. Perhaps he hadn't heard them? But he had. The earphones had been silent since he walked in.

"Mate!" he repeated. "You wanna work in?"

"Colt, what're ya doin?" his smaller companion asked, turning to the young Asian man beside him. "Hey Tan, he's making friends!"

Tan reluctantly smirked. The feeling of unease had not shifted since Jason had entered. Something was off, wrong. Jason smiled to himself. There was another motive here?

Was it guilt? Being reprimanded by Tyler had made them realise the error of their douchebag ways? He had not expected this and, for a moment, was concerned it would derail him. Maybe they could be something like mates? A split second of contemplation. No. Too late for that. Slowly he turned himself around on the bench, facing them. Jason shook his head. "Christ no."

Colt turned to his mates, who were as baffled by Jason's response as he was. "You sure? It's OK, we'll show you some things. Come on man."

"You'll *show me* some things," Jason scoffed, void of emotion. "What could you show *me*?" Primed and ready. *What could you show me?* Jason had worded a question just begging for insult. Baiting a 'smart-ass.'

There was a moment of awkwardness. An act of grace being rudely rebuffed. Offended by Jason's candid, sarcastic responses, Colt gave a shrug. "We're just asking, hey. There's no need to be a dick about it. I was actually attempting to apologise dude."

"Rude prick," his mate added as he turned back to the bench. "Just being nice mate. You do you. No problem."

"Not man enough to accept an apology huh?" Colt jibed.

Jason gave a sigh. He hadn't actually heard an apology. He turned back around and faced the mirror. He looked at his reflection. His face dark with his eyes almost black in the shadow from the bright lighting above. Taking a deep breath, he took his glasses off and carefully placed them beside the towel in front of him.

"We asked so you wouldn't hurt yourself lifting big boy weights," Colt called. "They'll find you in the morning pinned under a 7-kilogram bar."

"Enough man come on, just let the guy work out," the young Asian guy groaned quietly, embarrassed by the behaviour of his friends. "How old are you dude, Jesus."

"Fuck it Tan, he's being a dick." The third guy, Landon, dismissed him, waving his hand flippantly in the air. "Ain't got Tyler here to have a go at us now have ya?"

Tan continued to watch cautiously. A feeling of foreboding in the air perhaps, sensing a darkness the moment Jason had walked in.

Chuckling, Jason ran his hands through his hair. Sluggishly turning himself about on the bench, he stood up. The men stopped and stared back, a confrontation? Would this puny, weak little twirp actually start something?

"Yes," Jason replied loudly. "Yes. It fascinates me how strong you are. Seriously, how does someone even start to become such fine examples of masculinity as the three of you?"

"Oh fuck off…" Colt yelled. "Seriously, shut this guy down or I'll deck him."

"Come on everyone, stop… this is ridi…." Tan started to speak.

"Can I ask you a question?" Jason interrupted, calm and cold. "Because I really need to learn. I need to know. What makes you think someone like you gets to insult someone like me? Is it because you're better than me?

Pharmaceutically enhanced body? Shiny, sparkly teeth and a fake orange tan? Is that all it takes? I noticed those pimple scars on your back. I've also heard what it does to your testicles. That's strange I mean… no matter how bad I have felt about my body… I never wanted to sacrifice my balls for it."

"What the fuck are you on mate?" The two men erupted into a mocking yet nervous laughter,

"Ignore him. Just let it go," Tan groaned anxiously. He looked at Jason. "Sorry man, they're being dicks. Guys stop yeah. We're pretty much done anyway."

Jason shrugged, rounding back to their question. "Me? Nothing. I like my testicles as they are."

Jason noticed movement behind him. He heard Tan plead again with the other two to leave it.

A tingle of adrenaline rippled up Jason's spine, just for a second; he was being approached from behind. They couldn't hurt him. It would just make things progress quicker. Turning slowly to face them, Colt now stood closer than the others.

"What are you going to do?" Jason raised his brow. "What now? What are… you… going to do?"

"He's not worth it man. Just walk away" Landon sighed. "Little twirp ain't worth our time."

"Aww" Jason mocked facetiously. "So still no apology then?"

"Fuck you man. Fuck you."

Chapter 12

There was nothing remarkable about the street Sam walked down. Ellie's recall of the happenings had creeped him out, particularly at the end of the phone call when she told him she was not alone. He would go to her, but first he had to see it for himself. There was no doubt, this was another Oculus, as described by Chelamah and her cheery boyfriend.

Jesus loves me this I know, for the bible tells me so.

Idiot. He had heard children singing this silly song on an ad for the Christian Association just hours earlier. It resonated in his mind for no more than two seconds, but that seemed to be enough time for her to pluck it out. So it had become her new favourite tune over the last hour, breezing about her as she skipped beside him clapping her hands.

Little ones to him belong. They are weak but he is strong.

Past the dark mall and then tunnelling under the main street was the underpass. This was where she was when it started. He needed to listen. Ellie had described a noise, but he couldn't hear anything over the little moron by his side. "Just shut up… for a second," Sam snapped.

He was alone. He hoped he was safe. The rules were still unclear, two Ascendant Conduits were required to trigger the happening, so all should be well. Glib, flippant… self-assuring. As long as Ellie didn't show up he'd be fine. *Surely not.* He couldn't have been clearer.

Walking down the ramp to the underpass, there was nothing of interest. Just a pedestrian tunnel lit by yellow, caged lighting full of dead bugs. He ventured further in. Although not a long underpass, he could see a turning and several alcoves that he assumed were maintenance doors leading to whatever utilities were required by the buildings above.

He decided to walk its length. At least then he could say that he had indeed seen nothing. However, he had a nagging suspicion. After further contemplation, he decided it was worth investigating. The first of the utility doors was to his right, a steel frame with a large heavy handle. Looking up and down the tunnel, he grabbed the handle and gave it a quick tug, then a push. Nothing.

Feeling slightly foolish and a bit like a naughty child, he went to the next. Placing his hand on the handle, he scanned the area once more before achieving the same result. He sighed in frustration. Random was not random. There must be a reason why an Oculus would appear, but what? In a bunker in the middle of nowhere and then in an underpass in the middle of an inner-city suburb. Why?

He continued to walk with the end of the tunnel in sight. He looked back the way he had come, the path still quiet. Then, just as he turned the corner, he noticed another maintenance door. He would try, but expected the same result. Thinking, he looked up. No CCTV. There was CCTV at the entrance and another in the middle. Here, however, he was lost to sight the moment he passed around the wide corner. If it was him going in one of these doors, he would choose one that was hidden.

Grasping the final handle he pulled, then pushed. His efforts caused the large steel door to open.

"*Shit!*" he gasped in surprise. His stomach in knots, he pushed the door further. Now what? Did he have to go in? He hadn't thought that far ahead. While standing thinking, screams of thousands burst forth and then just as suddenly stopped leaving him gasping, staring at the Child beside him.

"Jesus Christ!" he screamed. "Did you have to? Seriously?"

Unusually still, the Child stood by the open door. Her long, grey lips trembled slightly. Her open hand rose in the air so quickly that it startled him, making him take a step back. His hand still gripping the handle. He looked at her with morbid curiosity. She remained silent and still. Her blackened fingers twitching slowly just inches away from his body. He watched those fingers, those hideous, evil hands. What was she feeling? What was she doing? Her face remained putrid and unreadable, but there was something in her manner. Something different.

Against his better judgement he raised his hand, bringing it close to the blackened appendages. He recoiled the moment their fingers touched. He had felt her. *She can touch me.* Panicked, he fell back against the door, kicking out with his feet. "Shit! Get away from me! Get away!" he yelled furiously. She lowered her arm slowly, her long dagger fingers still gently twitching.

There was a second of regard, before she turned and skipped away, out of sight.

Taking in deep breaths, Sam wiggled his shaking fingers in front of him. Yep, all still there. She couldn't just *touch him*. She had never been able to just *touch him*. In the Event, once a year, or when he was in her realm, yes, but that was never an innocent, almost curious, caress. That was a full-frontal assault. Aimed to deliver the pain she delighted in. This touch was calculated, curious and innocuous.

Centring himself, he turned once again to the doorway and entered. As his eyes adjusted to the dark, he noticed a small stairwell leading down. Most likely down to storm drains or the like. Pulling out his phone to use the torch, he noted the black screen. Dead. Digging into his pocket, past his shameful pack of cigarettes, he pulled out his lighter. He flicked it to life. Holding it in front of him he descended three steps and he found himself in a large open area.

Copper piping of various sizes ran along the walls both to his side and above his head. Not much head room. He couldn't stand upright but the space expanded vastly about him. Then he looked down, holding his breath. His light illuminated a pattern he knew all too well. The burnt, ash remnants of a fire circle. Beyond this, at the far end of the room, was another all too familiar sight. Sam advanced nervously through the impotent protections to confirm his suspicions: a large, black void hidden within the shadows of the wall, as if it had always been there. Exactly like the Oculus he had seen earlier.

He moved the flame around the space. This was someone's Circle, and they hadn't been alone. So this is what happens, he thought. The answer was plausible. This is what could happen when two Ascendant Conduits were in the same place at that same time. He had seen it at the bunker. Inviting a second had ended them all. The Oculus was still there. He could see the evidence right here. Had the Circle failed? One thing struck him as odd but didn't surprise him: the more he learnt, the more he realised that certain rules didn't apply to all. There were some that were above this 'trap'. There had to be a loophole.

If two Ascendant Conduits in the same place on the night of the Event triggered an Oculus, then why not for Ellie and Joshua? As he was pondering this, Chelamah's voice replayed in his mind.

"In this hell there's only one trump card. Bael."

131

OOO

Facing the door that led out onto the street, Ellie rationalised her next move. Something had followed her here and it was a result of what she witnessed. They couldn't come too close, or they would have. The man who was taken by those things was just like her, a Conduit. They had come for her too, but something stopped them. They couldn't take her… or they didn't dare.

Bael is different Sam had said. Well, Ellie thought. Let's just see how different It is.

If they couldn't take her then there was nothing to lose by testing this theory. If she was wrong, they would take her anyway, regardless of the right time or circumstance. Leviathans make the time… they create the circumstance. They don't have to stand outside and stare like creepy stalkers. She had to know where she stood. Information was key.

She mustn't hesitate. She pressed the release button allowing the large glass door to swing open. The cold wind hit her, causing her to gasp. Steadily, she made her way down four small steps to the pavement below and looked about.

The wind was alive with sound, voices, singing, chanting and ghostly echoes that floated in the breeze. Various figures were scattered down the road, some hidden by shadow, some standing brazenly on the road in front of her. Different silhouettes, but all had a commonality: white eyes. Sharp, short bursts of movement of their deformed bodies also united them in their anticipation. These were not the things from the underpass. These were Leviathans.

Bael was not beside her, but It was with her. It was always with her. Even amongst the random voices, she could hear Its mutterings vibrating softly in her ears. It was bound to her. It would never leave, and she knew that they knew this.

"Hey!" she heard a voice shout. "What's going on?"

Ellie jumped, turning to see Sam jogging towards her. She hated to admit it, but the sight of him bought relief. He must have followed her path home. She turned again to survey the street, watching for any reaction from the creatures around her. Nothing. Not the slightest acknowledgement of another approaching Conduit.

Sam looked at Ellie standing almost trance like, staring into nothing. The Dark Child fell silent while quickly sprinting to the middle of the road. She was looking at something. Distracted, Sam watched her. Her hands hung by her sides, long black talons flicked like knives. A warning.

"What are you doing?" he asked, stopping next to Ellie.

Ellie continued watching the creatures before her. Her eyes landed on the grotesque form of a woman, large but short, taking a step backwards. Looking at something unseen on the ground before her. Sam watched too as the Dark Child lurched forward.

"Can you see them?" Ellie asked softly.

Sam looked up and down the empty street confused. "Who am I looking for?"

Her question answered, she closed her eyes. Make the noises go away, fade into nothing. Focusing on bringing herself into the moment.

Sam shook his head, joining Ellie staring into the street. There was a sense of unease, a threat he couldn't see. There was so much to know and so much depended on finding out. One wrong move and he would be finished.

"It won't let them near me," Ellie whispered.

"OK" Sam nodded. He would just accept that right now. "Promise me you will tell me everything and you'll tell me the truth. I promise you the same."

To Sam's surprise Ellie nodded. "I promise."

"Now come on. Let's go inside. We are gonna freeze to death out here." Sam tapped her on the arm and with one final look, she turned to follow. Her mind erratic as she turned the handle. She was so tired.

"We need each other; to be able to depend on each other. Things are happening. Things I don't understand yet."

Ellie nodded and pulled the handle. Sam walked past her, casting one more look outside.

"That's my scarf" Ellie observed, before closing the door.

ooo

Jason stood next to the bench, rolling his head, and loosening his neck. "Don't worry he can't hurt me. That's the problem with you dicks. You can't see real strength when it's right in front of you. So, I'll help you. I'll show you. And trust me... you will never... make... this mistake... again," Jason sneered.

The pressure dropped as Jason felt his ears pop and the hair on his arms rose. The men watched curiously, thinking about their next quip, their next insult. Jason sat back down facing the mirror, the security camera upon him. Pulling out his phone, he held it in both hands and stared at the screen. Tension built like a sneeze. He relaxed his shoulders and composed his face.

Now. It would happen now.

A crushing thump startled the three men, echoing into a distance that they could not yet see. It happened just before the room glided into darkness. Swirling fluorescent lights were replaced by growing shadows that reached towards them from all directions, as melodic, almost carnival-like music grew louder. The room contorted and changed. Gym equipment wafted lightly into the shadows like paper. From the darkness a new view emerged amidst a mosaic of colourful lights.

"Get down! Get down!" Colt shouted.

Even in his catatonic state, this amused Jason. The dick, did he think this was an earthquake? The mirror before him had slid back into darkness. It was suddenly replaced by a wall of red velvet, as he felt the bench beneath him become soft fabric.

Panicked, Tan dropped to the ground as the world dissolved and re-formed. In amazement he saw the floor change as it became worn, stained wood beneath his hands. They were all now upon a stage. Behind them was a large red curtain, in front rows of empty, velvet clad seating. Above was a large mezzanine gallery bearing the same barren dirty red seats. As things continued to emerge, each aspect of the realm appeared as if it had always been there. Rigid and real. Between the two blocks of seating, a long aisle stretched from the stage to large open wooden doors. These slammed violently shut in front of them, causing Landon to yell in fright.

The scene was set. The victims stared into the large, ramshackle auditorium. Dim lights revealed a battered gangway. Colourful patterns of light rolled around them from an unseen source, accompanied by the unsettling melody.

Colt stood and grabbed Tan by the shoulder. Both listened to distant and rambling voices in silence.

"What the hell happened?" he muttered.

"Where are we?" Tan responded, looking at Landon, who stood trembling. Tan felt it too, absolute morbid fear. BANG, BANG, BANG! more unseen doors slammed shut. "What the hell was that?"

"Can you feel it?" Landon whispered in disbelief. "Something's really wrong."

Tan placed a hand lightly on Landon's shoulder before striding to the edge of the stage, squinting into the darkened void of the dilapidated playhouse.

"We gotta get out of here," Landon hissed, gesturing from the stage to the aisle. There was something about the fear in his voice that made his companions turn. "This is fucked up."

"Ya think!" Colt snapped, turning again to face the front stage as the double doors now swung open and figures started to enter. "What the…"

People promenaded through the door in pairs and then down the aisle, both men and women. Semi-transparent male figures cloaked in black advanced down the aisle, all adorned with top hats and canes. Each was accompanied by the image of a woman in corseted dresses and large, wide-rim white hats. Two by two they moved, floating down the aisle. Their feet moved oddly, but gracefully in the air without ever touching the floor. Pale and lifeless faces were plastered with large toothless smiles as they threw their heads back in silent glee and unheard conversation. They had no eyes, only deep torn cavities that sat where eyes should have been. Row after row of seats were filled, from first to last, with the nightmarish, humanoid figures, all now ready and waiting for the show to begin.

The large doors slammed shut once again as the twisted audience turned and whispered excitedly to one another, their heads nodding in delight as their long, distended mouths twisted in silent laughter.

"Fuck!" Colt swore, shaken from the surreal scene before him. "We've got to go. Now."

"Those people… what's wrong with those people?" Landon muttered in disbelief, staring at the nightmarish crowd before him.

The three men looked at the seated audience of smiling, sinister faces that now stared at them expectantly.

"Yeah, we got to go."

"But where the hell are we? Colt! Listen to me! Where...?" Tan cried.

"It doesn't matter. Let's just get out of here!" Colt crossed the footlights and knelt down at the edge of the stage. "Move!"

The others didn't follow, rooted to the spot by surging fear of the phantom audience who, as one, suddenly stood, colourless eyes fixed on the 3 horrified men. Terrified, Colt took a trembling step backward. The audience then sat once more to continue their sinister banter.

"Christ what are they?" Colt hissed, turning around, "we can't just stay here."

"I don't wanna go down there," Landon muttered quietly, staring in horror at the aisle and the things that inhabited the space.

"Look," Tan grasped Landon's arm, pointing to the darkness of the wings, "this way, we'll try this way." Unhappy taking his eyes off their gruesome audience, Colt moved backwards. A sudden voice from the audience startled them and stopped them in their tracks

"Well, at least you all look fantastic up there."

All three men yelled in fright as they spun to face the front row seats. Jason lounged lazily in the middle of an aisle, hands in his lap looking up.

"Jesus Christ!" Tan screamed, bending over to catch his breath. "Where the hell did you come from?"

The three cautiously moved forward, careful not to pass the footlights. Jason quietly looked up at them and smiled. A cold shiver ran up Tan's spine. That was what he had felt. And now again looking at this person, that was the unease he had when Jason first entered the gym. His lack of fear, the incongruent smile. Was he insane?

Colt puffed. "What are you doing here?"

"Chillin," Jason scoffed coldly. "I'm just kicking back. Catching a show between sets."

Tan placed a calming arm on Colt's shoulder. "It doesn't matter, we have to go." Tan looked down at Jason, surrounded by the bizarre crowd. "Come with us?"

"Fuck him, we have to go!" Colt shouted.

"No!" Tan snapped in disgust, turning to Jason, pleading while careful not to move too close to the edge of the stage. "Mate, can you get up? Don't stay here... come with us."

Jason smiled gently. Tan frowned in confusion before loud, blaring music suddenly filled his ears and a spotlight lit him from the gangway.

"No!" Jason laughed and shook his head. "I don't wanna miss this. You guys look so amazing up there."

The large velvet curtain swung open. Behind it was revealed a wall of colour. In front of this things began to descend, suspended by long strings, landing on the stage around them. Ridiculous, small childish marionettes now lay on the stage. Slowly they began to rise and started to dance about. Simple yet chaotic, they all danced to the same cheerful melody while the crowd before them clapped in delight. A wooden cyclorama advanced from the back of the stage and began to change. Again and again, faster, and faster, each scene ground into another; water, mountains, buildings. All were simple, childish nonsensical representations of reality.

"What the hell's going on!" Colt roared, just before the crowd let out a large gasp.

The stage lights dimmed as the marionettes dropped lifeless to the wooden floor. Slowly, the backdrop changed to the familiar image of the gym they had only just left.

All three stared in astonishment at the cardboard weight machines and large glittering paper mirrors. Breathing rapidly, Tan glanced at the fallen puppet at his feet. He didn't quite comprehend what he was seeing as the image gradually became clear. The small, brightly coloured figure was grasping its tiny chest as it gulped in air. The breaths became shorter, shallower until they stopped altogether. Its small toy-like limbs lay still as the tiny hands spasmed and the twitching ceased. Snaking into its skin - for skin it was - were wires which tented and tore the flesh. Like a creature from a sick nightmare, these were humanesque toys made of flesh and blood. As Tan watched, its tiny mouth opened to release a blood curdling scream that was echoed by all the others around it. The audience burst into rapturous applause as the sound faded.

Before silence fully descended, a large figure began to lower itself from the gangway. It rotated slowly and smoothly in mid-air as it came down toward them. Arrayed in a garish cacophony of colours, with arms wrapped about its waist and legs crossed tightly at the ankles, it descended by the use of cables attached to its body.

The figure landed gently. Landon noticed its long, black pointed shoes, comical and clownlike. This was not a person, he thought. It appeared to be carved from old, mottled wood. Its nose was an absurdly sharp protrusion above large, carved lips. Its head hung slack, resting upon the filthy white frills on its chest. It was a marionette. As in the 'opening act,' strings extruded from each limb and from its head. Dressed in the colourful, ragged clothes of a clown, its grain-marked face had rose painted cheeks and two simple, black lines that mimicked closed eyes. What at first appeared to be long carved pieces of wood wrapped around its body could now be seen to be hands, attached to oversized arms.

The lights faded as a soft lullaby began to infiltrate the room. In perfect unison, the crowd let out a resounding "Awwwwww."

"The side!" Colt shouted with renewed urgency "The side, now!"

The other two followed Colt to the side stage, skidding to a stop as they were blocked by a black wall. Colt's hands frantically searched for a handle, anything, but were met with a solid and unyielding surface. There was no way out here. The lullaby stopped. It was followed by a high-pitched ringing bell that blasted the stage. Strobe lights now engulfed them all. Colt and Tan turned to face a massive, flashing sign that had appeared at the back of the stage

WAKE UP KNICKERNACK!

The audience that had been clapping and cheering in one accord, suddenly stopped. The men looked around in panic, the metallic chime urgent and startling.

"Jesus!" Colt ran past the marionette to the other side of the stage, but it too was blocked by the same thick wall. Distracted by efforts to find a way out, they hadn't noticed that something had begun to stir.

WAKE UP KNICKERNACK!

Again, the calamitous bell assaulted their ears while the crowd chanted in a short, sharp burst before falling silent once more.
"Fucking Stop!" Landon screamed, looking at Tan who shook his head in disbelief. "Stop! Stop!"

For a split second, Tan thought the marionette was rising back to the gangway. For within the shadows and the colourful, rotating lights, there was movement. Colt and Landon, noticing Tan slowly stepping forward. They watched. The ropes above the wooden man swung gently to the side, unfolding its arms from around it. At the end of each, long arm was a hand.

Massive fingers twitched while making loud, clacking sounds like fingernails on wood. The lights turned to ember red. Jason stood and walked to the front of the stage to get a better look. The men didn't notice, mesmerised by the waking creature.

With a jerk, the head lifted from its chest. Its eyes had changed. What had been painted lines of black had now opened, revealing two oversized white eyeballs, startlingly organic but embedded in the sharply carved face. Its legs sprung open as it lowered into a crouch. The audience clapped excitedly, as it peered from side to side.

Jason watched the men back away. He was waiting for the first one to test their luck and leap from the stage. That could be one of the many triggers. The soft melodic music began again but this time it contained the ominous beat of a distant drum. The marionette's head moved clumsily about on its wooden neck, tilting mechanically from one side to the other as its multi-jointed fingers snapped and creaked open and closed.

Landon ran first, spinning towards Jason he broke into a sprint. The marionette moved swiftly forward in smooth, sinuous movements. Its hands snapped around its victim's head encasing it in a mesh of wooden fingers. Landon couldn't move, immobilised by the crushing pressure that held his head. The marionette lifted him into the air. His cries were muffled as his face was crushed by the mounting pressure. Blood gushed from his nose as his jaw broke. Landon was brought backwards towards the creature, being slowly rotated to face his captor's macabre, red face. He could hear the hysterical screams of his friends. His eyes desperately tried to see something through the wall of wooden fingers that grasped him. He couldn't see anything. All senses were consumed by the slow crushing of his head. A glimpse, a sliver of light enabled him to see the round, white eyes of his attacker only inches from his own. Someone had his leg; he could feel the grasp and hear Tan yelling. They were helping him. His friends were there. Fuelled by this, he struck out blindly, throwing a punch into the air. He pulled his arm back again but was overcome by a blinding light that was followed by darkness and pain. The marionette had pushed its fingers into Landon's eyes, mincing the gelatinous balls into slush. He heard Tan cry out "Oh god!" before the grip around his mangled head released, causing him to fall to the ground.

Knickernack loomed above Landon, who lay screaming on his back. Bloodied hands grasped at his disfigured face. Tan was behind him, pulling him away from the wooden creature. He saw it pull its arms back to its chest while the long fingers went limp before it. It rose onto the tips of its over-sized shoes as its head lowered unnaturally to its chest. An elaborate performance that mimicked the sneaking of a child. The music changed. Now it was mischievous and cartoonish while the audience began to titter and giggle. The marionette trotted forward. It stared at the man who was aiding its last victim with pupilless white globes.

"Get up!" Tan screamed, pulling Landon's bloodied hands from his face. "Get up! Move!"

Tan fell suddenly silent. The thing was not coming for Landon. It was looking at him. Its hands shot forward as Tan threw up his arms in defence. He felt two violent pops in his arms. His shoulders raised involuntarily as his hands sprung into the air above him. Confused, unable to move, he looked up to see his bloodied palms pierced with thick, woven strings that descended from the darkness above. He screamed, throwing his body downwards in an attempt to break free. The pain was unbearable. Flesh and tendons were torn by the unbreakable restraints. He couldn't remove them, and the frantic writhing of his body only caused more damage and piercing agony. His hands were moved out to the side, causing him to hang like a tortured doll. The image was mimicked by the marionette, to the delight of the nightmarish crowd who gasped in awe. The marionette's large foot lifted from the floor into the air in time to a musical trump.

Immobilised, the creature beside Tan turned to look down before slowly lowering its foot.

"Help me! Help!" Tan began screaming.

Turning to the crowd, the marionette lifted its foot to the same musical parp and slowly looked once again at Tan. The audience giggled, as the marionette's head shook awkwardly from side to side as its foot slowly lowered once more.

Tan looked to Landon on the floor beside him. His eyes were gone. He lay on his back, his singlet so drenched in blood that it was alost black, and he was crying out the sound bubbled with clots of blood and thick saliva, choking him as he tried to breathe.

Raising a pointed finger in the air, the wooden head jolted upwards. An idea!

The crowd released a resounding "Oooooh."

140

Tan screamed in pain even before he knew from where it had come. His legs roared in agony. Horrified he looked down to see more thick string from the gangway above harpooned through both feet.

His felt as if it were on fire. Tan looked to the dim stalls as laughter and applause erupted. Nothing, no-one was there to help him. The marionette looked at his foot again, lifting it from the floor and then, its head turned to Tan. Ripping skin and tendons, the rope pulled Tan's foot effortlessly off the floor before releasing it to hit the floor once more. His other foot was then dragged upwards, following the marionette's bizarre dance to increasingly maniacal music.

Jason watched the show. He enjoyed the absolute humiliation of these people who made him feel so bad. But that was now past. Now they were gone, finished. They didn't know it yet but this torture, this pain, this terror would never end. Everything and everyone they had ever known no longer mattered. Game over. These three wisecracking fuckheads were removed from the world and no-one would ever have to suffer their arrogance again. But… there was one more. Jason smiled at the cowering figure that was curled into a ball, side stage. That wouldn't help. Knickernack knew where he was and no matter how pathetic and weak Colt looked, it would not inspire compassion or sympathy. The time for that had passed.

Colt's usual cocky-ass face was pale with terror, his lips trembled with the incomprehensible nightmare that confronted him. His big ol' muscles twitched with fear. He had no strength here: none of his jibes would work. This was Jason's world and Colt had earned his access to it by being a shallow, conceited piece of shit. The archetypal jock… nothing more. Uninteresting and common. One of many. A pointless person.

Tan began to ascend, screaming and writhing above the stage. Blood dripped down his body as he started to slowly spin. The strings wrenched his body into strange, contorted positions. Colt watched the scene, shaking his head in horror. His knees held tightly to him, he looked to the right. The door. That aisle running between those 'things' was the only possible way out. His body frozen, he would have to will himself to move. It was then when he noticed Jason standing at the front of the stage, considering him calmly.

Without a second thought, and wincing at the chaos about him, Colt scuttered forwards.

"Get help, get help" he hissed. "Mate you got to get help."

141

"You never apologised," Jason said coolly.

"Listen, listen go get help…" Colt grimaced as the screaming of his friends grew louder behind him.

"You said you'd apologised but you didn't."

He looked at Jason in amazement. "Dude, what? Mate you got to help us," he shuffled closer. "We can't get out of here. Please… please… fucking please!"

Jason nodded "I agree. It's kinda pointless to talk about apologies now. But… I want you to know that I didn't really want to do this. It had been quite a while since I had found a prize and I resisted. I really did. For what it's worth, I was going to grant you amnesty. But you just kept pushing it."

Colt shook his head in cold disbelief. Was this his doing? This little dweeb, had caused this? "What…" He shuffled backwards on the wooden floor. "What are you saying?"

The monster lunged forward, its long fingers slamming through Colt's leg. He threw his head back and screamed, trying to turn around. Painfully the stake-like daggers of fingers dragged him agonisingly to centre stage.

"You will never be seen again. Never. Not by anyone. You belong to me now. And you have a very long time to learn your lesson. The things you will learn here, my God…" Jason smiled in awe.

It released him, just long enough for him to roll over before its weapon-like hands slammed through his chest into the floor. His lung punctured, his ribs obliterated, he was unable to scream. Its other hand raised above Colt's gasping, breathless face, and hovered there. Knickerknack's way of ensuring that Colt really saw the implements that was tear his body apart before it happened. The long wooden claws sliced through his body with quick, sudden movements. Blood sprayed across the floor and on the face of his sightless friend, who crawled there in desperation. "For the record," Jason uttered piously. "I forgive you."

The phantom crowd stood in rapturous applause. The music became upbeat as the marionette's assault on Colt continued. Amongst the gurgling, screaming, and cheering, the room started to fade. It was over now for Jason. His part was done. Slowly he stepped back, staring at the dissipating stage. The colourful array of the stage lights melted into the bright fluorescent lights of the gym, causing him to squint. Looking up, the mirror appeared, reflecting him sitting on the bench where he would've always been, phone held before him. From tonight, those assholes would never be seen again. They would be reported to have been here, where Jason was right now, but simply sharing the same space was just circumstantial. There would not even be the slightest suggestion that anything untoward had happened, or that he knew a single thing. Wearily, he placed his phone down. He bowed his head in a sigh, stood up and took two dumbbells off the rack before him. Slowly he lifted them above his head.

The gym was such a nice space when he was alone like this; it gave him time to think, to ponder on his own.

Humming to himself and looking at his messages, he quickly decided to send a text. A nice text. A happy text. The gym would be so much more fun now for both him and his trainer.

HEY TYLER, AT GYM LATE WORKOUT. GO EASY ON ME TOMORROW OK?

He began to consider his next cautious steps around Mika. What should be the next move with Chelamah and Noah? And he pondered the new acquaintance he was scheduled to meet, all of which brought forth possibilities for his own, secret agenda. His phone pinged, he read the message smiling.

PROPS FOR EFFORT UR DOING AWESOME! BUT NOT ON YOUR LIFE J.J! CATCH YOU AT 3! LOOK FORWARD TO IT! TYLER

Chapter 13

Five bad dreams, Josh had counted. Five times he woke up in the night with nowhere to go. Each time he would wake staring at the white eyes of the nightmare that watched him in the dark. He wondered, was it feeding his mind these horrible thoughts whilst he slept? Or could it see them, just like he did? Was it watching for his reaction and enjoying his fear? The sun was now up, and he could hear the rain on the window. He moved his arms and legs under the crisp sheets. Still sore but a little better. His arm didn't hurt so much anymore, but bandage was annoying. His head still hurt too. He slowly turned onto his side and felt the side of his ribs grab him. They were getting better too.

The doctor at the hospital where Aunt Casey found him said they were 'old healing' fractures. That seemed to upset his aunt a lot. She made no noise as the doctor said they were traumatic injuries, but Josh could see her teary eyes. She lifted her hand and stroked his hair and he felt bad that he had made her cry. He felt bad that he seemed to make her sad all the time. Stupid Monster Dog.

Josh wanted to tell her that it wasn't her fault. It wasn't anyone's fault, not even his Mum's. It was Ron and... something else. He couldn't tell her though. Ellie made him promise that he wouldn't. These people, he was told, wouldn't believe him. Ellie believed him and Sam believed him. But these people wouldn't.

If it had been up to him, he would have stayed with Ellie. She even worked at his school, so she knew where it was. They could have eaten food, watched funny videos about animals and made chocolate milkshakes every day.

For a moment, Josh was calm. He sat up and looked around. This room was so bright. The walls were creamy and clean and blue, crisp blinds covered the windows. Like another world. Cautiously he pulled the blankets back, sat up and placed his feet on the fluffy carpet. Everything here felt very soft. Everything smelt nice - like coconuts. Quickly, he trotted to the door and looked back around this strange, clean room. No Monster Dog yet, but he quickly remembered what he had been told by Ellie.

Don't look for it. When you think you are alone, you are alone. Don't look for it.

Returning to the warmth of the blankets, he searched until he found his small phone. He checked it. It was still silent. Ellie had told him he wasn't allowed to turn the sound on, and she didn't show him how. He didn't want to tell her that he already knew. Scott at school had one just like it and he knew the tiny switch to turn on the ringing was on the side. But he wouldn't turn it on. Ellie said not to.

Last night he had told Ellie where he was. He found it on an envelope in the kitchen and told her his new address. Maybe she could visit sometime. Phone held tightly in his hand, he turned onto his back staring at the ceiling. The words. He had to say the words every morning and every night. He had promised. Although today there would be no reward of chocolate milk. Slowly, he lifted his hands into the air and began playing with his fingers. Quietly, barely a whisper, he started whilst lifting one finger at a time with each word, "Dark door… left, go, right, go, go, go, left, left, go, go, left, up 14, right, down 11, left, right, right… down, down, up 3 back to middle and again…"

Delighted, he smiled to himself. That was it! He had remembered it all. Last night he hadn't, but now he did. It was strange the way remembering things worked. But five times was needed, so he started again.

Ellie's challenge completed, he pulled back the blanket and let his bare feet touch the tickly carpet again. He looked nervously at the closed door. Last night, after he finished his chores, he nearly left it open. But Aunt Casey would have noticed that he had been up. She might get mad. He had wanted to ask her not to close it. Before everything started, Josh had always believed you would know what was on the other side of a door. This had all changed when he opened his door that night and the nightmare began.

145

He could hear talking. Happy talking, he thought. Taking a deep breath, he slowly opened the door. Down the hall a little was Uncle Nate, who he met last night, leaning up against the fridge drinking coffee in his running clothes. Josh timidly closed the door a little. Uncle Nate was a big man, tall and strong. His skin looked so clean, like Sam's... not like Ron's. He smelt good too. He was friendly, and very big. When he stood next to him, Josh felt like he had to look at the roof to see his uncle's face. So, Josh thought it safer if he didn't. He would just look at the floor.

"HEY! Good morning young man!" Nate's voice was deep like Ron's. It startled Josh, causing him to close the door a little further. "Sleep well?"

Josh's body trembled. His eyes wide like a startled rabbit. He looked awkwardly around him and then back down to the floor.

"Yes, thank you," the lightness in Josh's voice did not match the anxiety in his eyes.

His Aunt Casey suddenly poked her head around the corner of the kitchen door, smiling down the hall to him. Aunt Casey was pretty, friendly, and kind. Everything his mother used to be. She had the same long, reddish brown hair and big smile.

"Morning Sweetheart!" She smiled. "You hungry?"

Josh thought for the right answer. He was hungry. Was it OK to be hungry? Would Nate get mad if he said he was hungry? Maybe Nate wanted more food and Josh would eat it all.

"No, thank you."

"Honey, you have to eat something. You haven't had anything since dinner last night. How about something small?" Casey moved into the hallway. She bent her knees to come down to his level as if trying to tempt a scared animal out of hiding.

"Your aunt can make pancakes Josh!" Nate said loudly. Josh immediately froze. His aunt shook her head smiling.

"I think your Uncle Nate is saying he wants pancakes," she chuckled.

"No. No!" He turned around towards her. "I'm saying Josh does. Go on mate... please say you do, then she will make them... she won't make them just for me."

The banter, the casual jibing between two adults filled Joshua with dread. This is how it started with grown-ups. They laughed at first. They laugh and they joke. They would even start teasing each other but then, in a second, it would change. Like an explosion, they would start fighting. Then very bad things would happen, and it would be his fault.

"Yeah right," she teased, turning back to Josh just in time to watch the door close quickly. Her smile turned into a look of sadness and disappointment.

Casey slowly turned to face her husband, who even in this situation, had a comical, awkward frown to give her. He sipped from his mug and watched as Casey stood up.

"I think he's heard about your pancakes," he joked, coughing into his mug.

"Nate" Casey sighed, smiling softly. "This is serious, he needs to eat… he looks so thin."

"He will eat. Remember what the doctor said. His appetite will come back when he feels more secure here. I guess we just got to be kinda gentle with it."

Casey walked over to the sink. Leaning on the bench she looked out of the window to the rain falling in the backyard.

"I hate her for this… but I'm worried about her. Where is she?"

"Sharon? Mum of the year?" Nate scoffed. "Two years ago she did the same thing, remember?" Casey ignored the dig. Nate didn't like Sharon, and justifiably. He never had. Yes, she would have followed that piece of shit Ron to hell and back, but this was different. She didn't know why. Casey couldn't name the uneasiness she felt in her stomach, but something was wrong. Three years ago, Sharon, regardless of Ron, of her addiction issues and bad choices, had always fought for Josh. She turned up. She fought to get her son back from their parents. As reprehensible as her past choices had been, Casey couldn't say that Sharon didn't love her son. Josh appearing out of the blue, weeks after his mother went missing, and knowing nothing about her whereabouts made no sense at all.

From behind his bedroom door, Josh could hear them talking softly. No-one got mad at him. He was doing good. He sat down on the fluffy carpet and reached under the bed, carefully pulling out a crumpled parcel of aluminium foil. This was very nice food. Nate had cooked chicken last night and Josh had never smelt anything so wonderful. He had waited until they were both in bed and then quietly dragged the left-over chicken bones out from the bin. He wrapped them in a bit of old foil that had been used to roast the potato bake and squirrelled them back to his room for later. His Aunt Casey had left lots of chicken on the bone. She hadn't picked them clean like Nate had. Boys like to eat meat more than girls do.

He unwrapped his cache and slowly began prying small bits of flesh off the remaining two drumsticks. Not too much. Best to keep some for later.

Nate knew that although Casey and Sharon were complete contrasts, Casey was still quite naturally worried for her sister. He didn't like Sharon – never had - but he understood why Casey was concerned. Josh turned up in a mess and his mother and her piece-of-shit boyfriend were AWOL. It reasoned that wherever Sharon was, she could be in the same state as Josh, or even worse. As much as it pained him, even with his dislike for Sharon, he had to admit that the injuries Josh had were not caused by his mother. Irresponsible? Yes. A nutcase? Yes. A woman who would physically hurt her own child? No. But in Nate's mind, if Ron was responsible for this, and Sharon let it happen, she was as guilty as he was.

"OK" Nate conceded, "I'm sorry, that was too much." He walked behind Casey and put his head on the back of her neck.

"Two years ago Nate, Josh wasn't found like that."

Nate held her, but this was little comfort. There were so many things that didn't make sense. She took some reassurance that at least Josh was safe, but that brought many unanswered questions. His responses were robotic, rehearsed.

Where is your mother?
She went to the shops with Ron and didn't come back.

Who hurt you?
I don't know. I fell over a bit, and I cut my arm on the shed outside.

Who put the bandage on your arm?
I did it myself. I found one in the bathroom.

No matter where, no matter who asked, the answers were always the same. His haunted eyes and behaviour, however, told a different story. A story of fear and secrets. The more he was asked, the more he would repeat the same answers, like a mantra.

148

"When are we talking to those people again?" Nate asked gently.

"Thursday. Them and someone from the child protection unit." Casey sighed, taking a deep breath as if forcing herself out of her daydream. "It's better that he has a few days with no more questions."

Nate nodded in agreement. "Difficult though. Don't tell me you aren't tempted to shake the truth out of him."

"Something has happened. He's different… his eyes. He looks nervous all the time. Have you noticed that?"

"Yes. But it will come out in time. Not yet, he's not ready. We'll just be with him. He needs some sort of normal."

Nate saw his wife gasp and then sigh heavily as she stared out the window, squinting to see through the rain. He found this odd given the discussion they were having. Confused, he looked up.

"What?" Nate peered into the garden. "What is it?"

"Look under the gazebo Nate." She brought her hand up to her mouth and slowly shook her head in disbelief.

Nate leant forward and, sure enough, noticed a colourful display of various items of small clothing hung over the railings of the stairs leading to the gazebo in the middle of the yard. They blew in the wind like naval flags. It suddenly occurred to Nate what they were. He laughed nervously whilst hugging Casey tight. The two relaxed into each other and watched the colourful display.

"Josh appears to have done some midnight laundry" Nate smiled sadly.

"Yes, yes he has."

"You did show him the laundry basket, didn't you?"

"I did… but that explains the water all over the laundry floor. He used the sink" Casey said, holding Nate who stood behind her.

"Resourceful little blighter! Just a sink and some elbow grease." Nate smiled down at her. "Simple, so old school… civilisation could learn a lot from Josh."

◯◯◯

Two men unleashed themselves on one other in the ring. Luka launched a series of hard strikes on the man opposite him. Sweat plastered his golden hair to his brow beneath the head guard, his blue eyes gleaming with ferocity. Adrenaline coursed through his system, his body and mind now meshed together in a perfect natural harmony. This created the barrage of flawless and powerful flurries that pushed his competitor further back. A powerful direct punch to the face dazed him causing his guard to crumple. Luka then delivered a perfect knee to the face as he watched his opponent hit the mat. *Fuck yeah.*

"Back! Back!" his coach commanded as if calling off an attack dog. Shaking it off, Luka walked away from his sparring partner. His coach approached, water bottle in hand. Luka turned back to the fallen man in the corner, watching his own coach helping him to his feet. There was a look of dismay at his beaten face.

"Christ's sake Mitch. This is training. Call your mongrel off!" he yelled. "His attitude is shit mate."

"Yeah Cal, we'll talk." Mitch leant down to Luka who grinned spitefully. "Yeah, maybe we shouldn't damage them so much before they have a match."

Luka chuckled, slamming his gloves together as he spat out his wet mouthguard. "Maybe before a match his bitch coach shouldn't brag so hard."

Stifling a giggle, Mitch patted him on the back. "Go clean off. Get out of here early… I think Cal's about to burst a blood vessel."

"Again…" Luka giggled. Cal had already had two strokes in the last year. Luka was kind of looking forward to taking credit for the third.

Heading off into the showers, Luka unwrapped his tapes, flinging sweat-soaked equipment onto the bench as he passed. Walking into the locker room he pulled the last remnants of tape from his wrists. A sudden jibe made him jump.

"You do know that using shadows to intimidate someone is unfair."

Jason lay on the far bench, arms crossed over his chest staring at the ceiling. It reminded Luka of every movie he had ever watched that had the scene of someone in a coffin.

"I never do that. I don't have to do that." Turning to his locker, he slid his sweat-soaked singlet over his head. "What's going on with you Nosferatu?"

"Ha… you're funny" Jason sighed, his hands like a vampire on his chest. "It was a long night."

"I guess it was a lot longer for someone else, am I right?"

"Of course," Jason agreed. *Gym will be nice though.*

150

"So what's going on? I thought I wouldn't see you 'til tomorrow."

Jason sat up awkwardly, demonstrating no core strength whatsoever. Luka noticed. Thin, wiry, and always pale, an unfortunate beanpole of a man.

"Today I am meeting that guy. You set it up?"

"Oh, *that* guy? The 'Mika *asked me to meet'*, guy?"

"The same," Jason nodded. "Did you set it up?"

"Chel's *friend*!" Luka blustered sarcastically. "Yeah, it's ready to go."

"Well, I don't know if they're friends…" Jason shrugged. "I think he knew her mother or something."

Luka closed the locker and turned to face Jason, "Really? That woman? He knew what's-her-face?"

"Anna or some shit like that," Jason replied. "She saw him as… you know… the way you guys do and approached him. An amazing coincidence is it not?"

Luka chuckled, shaking his head. "And you believe that?"

"No" Jason stated pointedly, offended at the suggestion he was gullible. "But I will go along with it for now. Chel told Mika he's not that fucked up. Not like some of them. Apparently, I may be wrong, but I think he's a fag."

Luka nodded slowly, feeling suddenly annoyed. That word, *fag. Fucking queers*. It didn't seem fair. Such a power, such a strength in such weak hands. This guy whom Jason was meeting with was an Ascendant Conduit and a Fag!

"Really? Wow, that's *unexpected*. So, what's your angle? Gonna seduce him with your manly manliness? Get him to tell you all his secrets over iced frappes and rainbow-coloured tablecloths?"

Jason didn't laugh and Luka stopped the jibe. But something within him couldn't help but feel ripped off. *A queer… a goddamned queer… the Conduit of an Ascendant.*

"If it comes to that, I'll get you to do it." Jason stood and began to walk toward him. He reached in his pocket and pulled out a piece of paper, handing it to Luka who took it.

"OK." he nodded.

"Here is when and where. If you don't see me tomorrow, you know what to do." Jason pushed past him, leaving the room.

151

"Understood." Luka turned back to his locker, a growing contempt within him. He knew why. *A queer... a damned little queer.* He knew his growing resentment was the reason the room was beginning to chill. He knew his considerably weaker companion had been woken by his growing temper. But what the hell really... it was powerless. In this world he was strong. In the other world he was weak. In the middle of both he was a mere servant, irrelevant and obedient.

∞∞

Feeling the warmth of Noah holding her was juxtaposed to the coldness that enveloped her mind. She watched her existence slide further into the distance, every thought and feeling that once was hers becoming more like an echo with each passing day. Something was claiming its rights over her.

Looking at herself in the wall mirror, she looked ghoulish and dark. Long black hair framing pale eyes, which had once been a vibrant dark brown, so much like her mother's. Her soul, she knew, was being replaced with a cold, dead vessel that sought only one thing. Thoughts of rage, blood and anger constantly washed through her. Fantasies of violence and perversion swept over her like waves, again and again. Pass a man in the street and that man would become the centre of a torture fantasy. She would hear a child's laugh and it would be contorted into a screech of pain and suffering. Disgusting, abominable and absolutely desirable.

The night before Noah and she had made love. That's what she would have previously called it. Though now she would watch his body, see his muscles tense, smell his breath, feel the touch of his hands on her skin, and imagine how that skin and those muscles would look when torn from his body. How beautiful that breath would taste when its last gasp was breathed into her lungs. How those hands would writhe and grasp as he was relentlessly torn apart. Beautiful, awesome torture. *Make him want you.*

Noah lay behind her, his arm over her shoulder. She could feel every warm, bloody vessel in his body. She knew it could become beautiful again but not in the way it was before. It would be torn, stretched and wretched. Mutilated with such an intense longing so that they could enjoy these moments for all eternity. She could feel his loneliness. She could feel his desperation. *Your gift to him.*

No. Her voice within was still too strong to lose total control. No. Her time was coming, she knew this, but it was not here yet. The time was coming when she would become the creature she hated, but she wasn't quite gone. She wondered, would the choice be hers? Would she decide to give up. Choose to stand back into the shadows of her soul and let it take control? Or would the choice be taken from her? She didn't know.

"I love lying with you." Noah had woken. He held her tighter.

"We shouldn't have slept. We have to get up" she responded.

"Aww you say the sweetest things."

She smiled, biting her lip hard as she forced a fake giggle. It was required. Noah mustn't know how far she had faded. How far away she was from the woman he loved and how close she was to the birthing of the emerging beast.

He held her tighter, pulling her towards him and kissing the back of her neck. She didn't move, steadily watching her reflection in the mirror. His hand moved to her leg. She felt the warmth of his fingers and was overcome with an urge to deliver a brutal response. She would let him enjoy touching her, savour his thoughts and anticipation. Her eyes grew large. She began to smile. Watching her face darken and disfigure in the mirror before her into a twisted mask, a mix of disgust and jubilation. Her fists clenched: God, how she wanted to tear him apart. *Beautiful pain, beautiful suffering. forever.*

"No!" Chelamah pushed through, shoving her elbows into Noah's ribs who recoiled, confused. Clumsily, she slid off the edge of the bed landing on the floor.

"Hey! Sorry! I'm sorry! What's going on?" asked Noah in astonishment.

Chelamah stood, facing the mirror. He could see her reflection staring at him in the bed. "It's time for you to go."

Perplexed but amused, Noah mimicked her. "It's time for you to go. Come on, get back in here."

Without turning, Chelamah walked quickly into the bathroom and closed the door. She was losing her breath. She tried to stay calm. Oh god what was the point? This world was closing its doors on her. The other one was taking over. She looked at her reflection, dead and cold. She looked around… nothing had any meaning to her anymore. But something must, as a small inner drive still simmered. The man in the room. He was so big. He would tear so exquisitely.

Lurching forward, she placed her hands on the sink. Lifting her eyes to the mirror she saw the grotesque abomination staring back at her. "Please" she begged. "Ma... please help me."

Hesitating for a moment, Noah hovered before the closed door before knocking. "Chel? Are you OK?" He waited for a second before knocking again.

"Open the door," he said firmly. Chelamah was erratic. She was in trouble. He could sense it. About to knock again, he stopped, glancing around as the room grew dim.

Shit.

"OK, open the door now. Please, come on." He pounded. "Open it!"

As the room descended slowly into darkness, Noah stumbled back from the door hastily pulling up his jeans. The door opened slowly. Chelamah stood in her slip, eyes cast down and trembling. She approached him.

"I can't stop it," she said, trancelike. "It makes me want to hurt you. It speaks for me... in my mind. Pushing me to the edge of who I am. Of what I am. I was on the edge, looking over for so long, but now... now... I am over that edge looking up. I want the darkness to stop. I want the darkness to end but..." she spoke through tears. "A part of me wants that darkness to be infinite. To be everywhere with only the abundance of flesh and terror to lighten its walls. A small fragment of me feels sickened by what is in my mind. But another, feels absolutely wonderful. It's like poison, but you want more."

"Those thoughts, they are not you." Noah shook his head, refusing to accept the truth.

"Noah they -"

"No. No they're not you. It's the same for all of us... it makes you think that, but it's not."

"It's not the same. I am a Wraith Devotee. You know what will happen to me. I will become just like the creature that is attached to me. A monster. I'm starting to think like them! Right now I am imagining your intestines wrapped around me like a blanket. You'd scream." To Noah's horror, she smiled. "You'd scream and bleed. Every piece of your body would feel never ending punishment and your mind would be driven mad by despair and agony. It's sublime. I love you. So very much. Where that love comes from I don't know anymore." Chelamah's voice broke, her hands shaking as she raised them to her face.

"Then stop!" Noah roared in frustration, looking about him as the blackness began to lift. "Then stop going there! You know every fucking time you go there it gets worse. You know that, and yet you keep going. Look at your eyes! Look at your damn eyes! It's never lasted this long...you've got to stop!!"

Leaping forward, Noah grasped Chelamah's cold hands and pleaded. "You can't save anyone else. You have done enough. No going back for Will. No going back for anyone. You are not like us... you don't have to go there."

"I am not like you. I have been halfway there since I was 10. IT comes to you. I... go to IT" she muttered.

"Then don't go! Stay here with me!" Noah threw his hands in the air, stomping away from her. "Every time you go there it gets worse. You were told that. You know every time you go there it happens faster. Why did you do it? For Marco? For Will?"

"It will happen anyway."

"Not like this! Not this fast." Noah turned in despair "Give us time Chel... give us some more time."

"I plunged a knife into Marco's neck and breathed in his death like food" she uttered coolly. "The creature killed him and my God it enjoyed it; the human set him free. What happens when that human is gone? I become something so much worse. I will become like them."

He needed to know. He needed to know how she was feeling. What was rising to the surface.

"Why? Does it matter? One person out of how many?" Exasperated, Noah pulled on his T-Shirt.

"Yes it does." Chelamah walked to the window, opening the blinds, and letting in the light.

"Why?!"

"For what I have done and what I am. I am feeding the last bit of humanity left in me before I begin to feed on something else. When I am gone, the Wraith becomes uncontrollable. Now I can release those taken into death. As a Wraith, I will take them as my own. It's the least I can do... let me do this before I am gone."

Noah continued to talk as she made her way into the bathroom once more. She brushed her hair, listening to Noah throw around completely unreasonable plans that may save them both. Brainstorming with nonsensical speculation and bad judgement, driven by a desire to save her. She didn't affirm or agree to his plots and scheming. She let him continue and just listened silently. However, she did agree with one thing. She would not go back to the other place. She couldn't. Once more and she would be lost forever.

Chelamah had to keep her last damned journey for if, and when, it was absolutely needed. She would not return for Will today… but she would see him again. She would be in that world once more, that was certain, but it wouldn't remain a choice for much longer. The next time she chose to cross would be the suicide of her soul. She accepted this with grim resignation. She had been grieving her own existence for some time. And whether he liked it or not, she also knew that Noah was far closer to damnation than he knew. If he was taken, the last of her life would be his only hope. She couldn't waste that.

Chapter 14

Nate was funny. He told jokes that made Josh giggle. He talked to Josh like they were friends. Maybe Nate really did like him? Josh hoped so. He liked Nate and he imagined how wonderful it would be if someone who looked and acted like Nate, liked him too. Sitting in the car, driving to speak to stupid police and doctors, Nate would make jokes and tell Josh things. He pointed out the school he went to years and years ago. He told Josh the story of an off yogurt that he and his friends put in the drawer of his teacher's desk. Stunned, Josh laughed at how bad Nate behaved at school.

"So, from what the doctor said," Casey interrupted. "Do you think you would like to go back to school? That's your choice honey. When you feel you…"

Nate looked in the rear-view mirror surprised at the expression of complete elation on Josh's face.

"Yes. Yes please. It would be good because I had a project I had to do," Josh jumped in. School, friends, Ellie!

"Said NO CHILD EVER!" Nate laughed. "You're crazy. Hey babe, can I go back to work when I'd like to?"

"I can go back. I want to go back. It's good because there are things I left in my drawer," Josh pleaded.

"No, your uncle working is needed. Partly for money and partly for my sanity," Casey replied. "Seriously Joshy, you don't have to, but it's your choice."

Joshy. He felt sick.

"Josh," he corrected quickly.

He had not been called Joshy for the longest time. It stunned him. Memories of *Joshy*. His Mum called him *Joshy*. Ron called him *Joshy* when pretending to be nice, before he would get mad. Josh didn't like being called *Joshy*.

"OK," Casey chuckled light-heartedly. "Seriously *Josh*, it's your choice."

Josh was surprised. The instant relief of tension. He had spoken back, and yet, all was well.

"Nate, turn up here."

"Nathan," Nate replied facetiously. The couple laughed and Josh found himself smiling.

Casey slapped her husband on the thigh. "You boys are giving me a hard time. Shut up."

Nate smiled at Josh in the mirror. "I think that we are also kind of hungry and that makes us kind of angry. You hungry Josh?"

Happiness filled Josh's body. He was hungry and they probably wouldn't expect him to pay for it. Not willing to say it, Josh just gave a short, sharp nod.

"Settled, food first then... ugh... one and a half hours with this quack guy," Nate nodded. "We've got time, it's not too far."

Speaking quietly, Nate turned to Casey who had pulled a card from her handbag. "So, this is a child quack?"

"Psychiatrist, stop calling them quacks. That's so 2005," Casey sighed. "He's not a quack. I don't know. This guy works privately and with the department of child protection. Specialises in..." frowning, she examined the card she held before her. "PTSD and trauma. He comes highly recommended. Dr. Niles Gardiner."

Josh settled back in his seat listening half-heartedly to the conversation. Hypnotically he watched the large black creature ran beside them on the road, bounding through cars like a shadow, like splashes of black falling on the road beside him. He wished he would go away. Wistfully, he continued watching the darting shadow and began muttering quietly to himself, "dark door... left, go, right, go, go, go, left, left, go, go, left, up 14, right, down 11, left, right, right... down, down, up 3 back to middle and again..."

They were going to get food and, one thing was for sure, he would make sure the stupid dog got nothing.

ᗒᗑᗕ

158

Ellie and Sam both prepared to leave. They had spent hours sharing information about their lives, their experiences and current situation. Even though they felt better informed, they were none the wiser as to the current climate they found themselves in. Some information merely produced more questions than answers.

Sam had a theory that an Oculus would appear as a result of something unique happening at the last Circle. Ellie immediately thought it could've been due to themselves and Joshua all being there together as the realms opened, but this wasn't certain. As Chelamah had said, Ascendant Conduits were facing the Event together more and more frequently over the years. Yet, this had only occurred now.

Another idea was the location. If the result of two Conduits facing the last Circle together brought forth an Oculus, then there should be evidence of this. The issue of the timing could be addressed later, but the mechanism could be confirmed. The silo, the site of the last Event, when she and Josh were in the same space. Sam disagreed with this. After all, if this happened then how did Ellie and Josh not get taken by the Oculus? Ellie agreed, but one thing at a time. If the silo didn't have an Oculus, then it could be agreed that perhaps Ascendants together at a Circle didn't always result in one.

Of course, they couldn't visit this location together. Ellie would go alone. Anyway, Sam had some *new friends* to meet. The thought of meeting new people scared Ellie almost as much as finding a doorway to evil. New unknowns, new dynamics. Completely terrifying.

"Bus it? Seriously? I can drive you. I have the time," Sam sighed.

"No. It's not safe," Ellie replied, brushing her hair from her eyes. "It only takes 20 minutes… everywhere here only takes 20 minutes."

"I'll just drop you!" Sam exclaimed as if he'd discovered a genius solution.

"We don't know how close we can get before things turn to shit. That guy, on the road was 100 metres from me." Ellie led Sam to the door. "It's not safe.

Sam reluctantly nodded. "OK, then we meet up afterwards. I'll pin you on my phone in an hour."

Ellie grabbed her backpack and opened the door "Agreed."

"Then, you pin me your location, yeah?"

"Why?"

Sam shrugged. "What do you mean?"

159

"You know where I'm going. Why would I pin my location?"

Thinking for a moment Sam nodded. "Yeah, forget about that bit."

Sam trotted down the steps to the footpath. Ellie followed before turning to the bus stop and pulling out her headphones.

Sam opened the car door. "Go there. Have a look and leave. No point hanging around if there's nothing to see."

"Sam," Ellie called. Hands on the steering wheel, he turned to her. "Remember these people could be completely nuts. Be careful. You want information, but so will they. Don't tell them too much. You don't know them."

Sam smiled brashly "Oh yeah. I know. They *are* completely nuts. Absolutely, but that's half the fun."

She watched as Sam pulled into traffic, leaving her to her thoughts. Their goal was to find a way out. Their goal was to find a way to end all of this. She hoped Sam would stay focused, that he would be able to ignore the white noise that others brought with them.

Her headphones on, the music started drowning out the random voices of the dozens of the hidden monsters hovering about her. She sat down and waited for the bus to arrive.

OOO

Nate had pulled into the roadside cafe and Josh excitedly swung open the car door. He knew he was off to see something that Nate said quacked. He knew that this was some confusing adult word that even adults shouldn't say because his aunt told him to stop. But... he still didn't know what a quack was.

Joshua followed them into the bright cafe with shiny red seats. There were people already eating and the food looked nice. To Josh, 'nice' meant 'lots'. Peering round, he couldn't help but notice in big chalk writing on the menu board the word "Milkshake."

Nate went to the counter to get a menu. Casey gestured for Josh to get into one of the booths. Awkwardly he slid himself along the red vinyl. His multiple layers of clothes caused him to be all slippery. He nearly fell off. When he reached the far end, he propped himself up by the window and looked outside at the grey winter day. The streaks of rain ran down the window outside.

"So," Casey began carefully, placing her hands on the table and looking very serious. "Uncle Nate and I have talked, and we agreed. You can go back to your school for the rest of the year, but then we may have to think of somewhere a bit closer."

Immediately Josh started doing the math. How long? How long was the rest of the year? It was winter now so how long was that?

"Another school? I can't stay at my school?"

"I know it's a scary thought honey but it's quite far away from us" Casey smiled gently.

"I could get a bus," Josh stated.

"It's really far."

"Two buses?"

"It's OK," Casey reassured him, reaching across the table, and taking his hand. "We have plenty of time, so no need to worry about that now. Let's see how we go OK? We can talk about it later."

Nate arrived back at the table and the conversation quickly turned to the food. Josh happily chose the cheeseburger. He saw a lady with it on the way in. It had chips and little sauces with it. Nate also chose a burger while his aunt chose the chicken salad. Girls don't eat too much. He was sure that she wouldn't even finish it all.

Nate and Casey talked and laughed. They asked Josh silly, fun questions like his favourite thing to watch on TV. Nate liked documentaries on scary things, like killers and crimes. Bad people. Casey didn't seem to agree with this but just rolled her eyes, calling him a 'psycho'. A song played on the radio in the background, which Casey made a joke about. Nate laughed. Nate found a lot of things funny. He even laughed at Josh, and Josh never thought of himself as funny. Maybe he was?

When the food arrived, Josh's mouth was already watering. Not since Ellie's little kitchen had he felt such a compulsion to eat. It was incredible, with so many flavours.

Taking the last bite of the burger, his stomach rumbling, he noticed the creamy brown milkshake that sat on the counter, knowing it was his. Nate noticed his wide-eyed stare and glanced behind him. "Aw it's up… go grab it."

Josh smiled and pushed himself back along the slippery vinyl and off the seat.

"Don't run honey, you'll knock people!" Casey called behind him as he made his way to the counter. Watching his prize as he approached the bench, he was sure he would have to use both hands to pick it up. It was huge and had cream on the top with what looked like sprinkles of chocolate.

Carefully he reached up. He had to be sure and not drop it. He would have to walk slowly back to the table, so he didn't bump into anyone. Small hands clasped either side of the glass as he slid it off the counter and held it in front of him. He turned to make his way back to the table when a melody started innocently playing in the background.

That song. It was that song. His mother's favourite song. Moonlight Shadow. He stopped still. His heart began to race. He felt like he was going to be sick. A flood of terror washed through him. He froze. The glass fell from his hands smashing on the floor beneath.

A flurry of nightmare images suddenly filled his mind. The Dog in the house. Ron, eaten alive in front of him. Jamie screaming and writhing on the roof while engulfed in brilliant flames. His Mum… his Mum.

Eyes wide and terrified, he looked around him as he heard Casey call out. He wasn't here. He wasn't with them anymore. The bad thoughts, horrific memories of violence played with a soundtrack in his mind. The horrible little girl who suddenly appeared next to him in Sam's car and then the fiery place.

"Josh… Josh!" Casey cried running over to him with her hands out. He screamed, suddenly throwing himself backwards, slamming into the counter.

"Jesus! Josh calm down… calm down you're OK. We're here…" Casey's voice trailed off into nothingness. The calamity in his mind locked him within his horror.

Screaming, injured people. Monsters wanted to hurt him. They hated him. He could see them clearly in his mind creeping towards him past the flickering flames, their faces torn and bodies twisted. Blood everywhere and bits of people. Roaring, hideous sounds of a darkness he never could have imagined before that night. The smell, that awful smell. They wanted to get him. Ellie and him. They wanted to make him like them. They kept hurting him. Ellie hit them so hard, but they wouldn't stop coming. He heard her shout in his mind,

"No! Josh, no!"

Nate watched in panic, completely lost for words. The small child's eyes full of absolute terror. For a split second he looked at the woman in front.

"Mum," he muttered as tears began to run down his cheeks.

The Dog strode along the tables and the backs of the chairs. Its haunches high. Its head low. Its vicious white eyes staring through the people and straight to its Conduit. Lifting its massive head it released a deep, guttural howl. Josh's face dropped with dread. No. No more.

"No!" Josh wailed. "No! Stop it! Stop it!"

Following Josh's terrified stare, Nate looked behind him. Perhaps it was the chaos of the terrified child, or perhaps the winter sun had become even more obscured by dark, black clouds but he watched curiously. He was sure the cafe was getting darker. Almost as if a black mist was falling slowly from the ceiling. The room grew hot. He felt sweat forming on his brow.

Nate turned back to see a glass fly past his head. Missing him by inches, it smashed violently through the window. Josh bolted out the door and into the rain. He heard Casey calling him. He knew Nate was running behind. He had to run, had to go. The noises in his head, the things he saw. That song… that song pulsated through his petrified mind. He would run and not stop. Run as fast as he could, so fast that the Dog, the monsters, the screaming, nothing would catch him.

○○○

Sam waited at the location instructed by Chelamah. It was an intersection on a main street. *Strange*, thought Sam. He imagined it would be somewhere mysterious, but no. A hard wooden bench next to a half-frozen bush in front of a Computer Store. Hardly enigmatic or mystical.

The traffic noise drowned out the hymns of the Child. He was grateful for that.

He will wash away my sin,
let his little child come in.

She sat beside him with 'teddyman' on her lap, putting her hands in and out of its gaping mouth, intent on extracting its teeth. It bit her, which made her giggle and shake her head before squealing with delight and ramming

163

her fingers back into its bloodied, torn mouth. He was startled by the beeping of a car horn in front of him. Inside, the driver waved at him, before the window slid down.

"I've driven around the block three times, are you actually gonna get in?" Jason shouted out the window as Sam, stunned, quickly pulled open the passenger door and leapt in beside him.

"Three times I beeped!" Jason ranted.

"I'm sorry, everyone was beeping," Sam apologised, flustered. "I thought you'd be walking."

"In this weather? God no." Jason's hand darted to the side and Sam took it. "Jason."

"Sam." He replied just as abruptly, surprised as Jason laughed.

"Would be kind of awkward if you weren't. I just lured you into my car." Jason's hand was soft with long fingers but delivered a surprisingly firm shake. "Now I was told you and I were to be friends?"

Sam looked at the young man behind the steering wheel, staring intently into traffic. He was tall, thin and had very white skin. He wore very unstylish glasses, thick black frames, almost dorky. But his appearance didn't seem to match his voice, which was forceful, eloquent, and expressive. Sam was intrigued.

Jason noted Sam's bright eyes, handsome face, and air of masculinity. This was unusual. He didn't know what he had expected but he was sure that Sam would have been smaller, more... effeminate. You never can tell.

"So, you know Chel?"

"Yeah, I've kno-"

"Yeah for a while she said. Not to me of course, we don't speak much. She pretty much hates me, but she told Mika, who told me," Jason interrupted.

There were so many ways to direct the conversation from Jason's rant that Sam didn't know where to start.

"I knew her- ""

"Mother, yeah. I know. I never met her, but it's funny, a lot of us know *of* her. I haven't been here that long though. How old are you now?"

"35" Sam answered quickly, bemused at how quickly Jason just railroaded the conversation along.

"Yeah you're quite a lot older than me," Jason nodded. Sam was shocked. "Your goatee makes you look younger. I could never grow facial

164

hair myself, looks too wiry and messy you know. Probably genetic, but seeing as I have no real memory of what my parents looked like… you know… before. I can't tell. Best clean shaven. You go to the gym?"

Sam never regarded himself as a slow thinker, but this rapid-fire conversation was exhausting. Was this dude nervous? Excited?

Sam took a breath, his brain trying to catch up to the conversation. "Yes I do. Been going for years now. I mostly do- "

Jason butted in, nodded enthusiastically. "Yeah I go now too. I work with a trainer. His name is Tyler. Just wanna put on some weight you know. It's hard for me. What do you eat?"

Frustrated Sam looked out the window, eager for a break from this onslaught. This guy was hard work. He realised that introducing Ellie to this man would be an insane clash of polars. She would have a *fucking fit*. "Where are we going?"

"I tried this diet, but it didn't work too well. I just couldn't eat that much. It was impossible. Ended up feeling nauseous all the time- "

"Where" Sam repeated strongly, "are we *going*?"

Jason stared out past his misty windscreen, the rain began to pelt down once more. "Somewhere special," he quipped.

"Disneyland? The Eiffel Tower? What do you mean special?" Sam asked impatiently.

Jason chuckled. Sarcasm seemed to be appreciated.

"No," he turned his head, looking Sam square in the eye. "We're going to the Pantheon."

ooo

Ellie scanned the area, the five silos stood in the foreground of the old mill. There was nothing unusual that she could see or, more importantly, feel. Baron and isolated. This was why she had chosen the place six months ago.

She walked down the path where she had first set eyes on Sam to where it broke into two. Sam had run down one, and she and Josh the other. Casting her eyes to the building on the right she saw where Sam had retreated. No. He had been alone, and if things were as they thought, there would be nothing there to see. She continued down the other path where she and Josh had run, hand in hand, to the large, steel silo.

She felt uneasy but rationalised this. Of course she would. She was alone, the environment was creepy as hell and this place held some very bad memories. Bael stood before her in the darkness of silo one's shadow. It just watched as she approached. No strange behaviour other than It's *usual* strange behaviour.

Steadying herself on the slippery dirt path, she crossed over scuffs in the wet soil. She was sure they were the ones she and Josh had made whilst running for their lives two months earlier. The hatch doorway of silo number three came into view. Multiple torn holes and long rips decorated its frame. A testament to the ferocity with which she and Josh had been hunted that night. The door was slightly ajar. It didn't look like anyone had entered since. Why would they?

Ellie walked to the step, looking down at the concrete slab that Josh had tripped over. Cautiously she grasped the remains of the small door and pulled it open. It emitted a low creak.

Inside, the dim light radiating from the hatch above and the multiple busted holes of metal were barely creating enough light for her to see, but she could make out the ring of ash that had kept them safe. Bandage wrappers and empty water bottles were scattered about. She was sure she had collected them, but then that had been one hell of a night. Slowly, as she had so many times before, she bent over and began picking up the littered remnants of her last Circle. Wrenching a wrinkled, plastic bag from her backpack she began to fill it.

The last of the waste in the bag, she stood, gripping her aching ribs as she looked around. It was then that she noticed something amiss. Amongst the damaged steel, the punched holes and twisted metal of the silo wall was a hole of pure black. The void of black amongst the mosaic of dim sunlit rifts was barely noticeable at first, but it was definitely there. About 4 foot wide, elevated roughly 6 feet from the ground. Was this it? Was this an Oculus? Cautiously, she moved closer.

It had an ominous presence, chilling, causing her to step back. But no, it was harmless now. She was alone... as alone as she ever was. Without taking her eyes off it, she pulled out her phone; it was dead. She swiped the screen - nothing. Stepping back, she became aware of Bael behind her. The usual approach to ignore It was interrupted by a curious observation. It was peering beyond her, looking straight into the Oculus.

So, Josh and her… but if that was the case, why weren't they taken? If that was how Sam and his new group of friends thought this worked then yes… two Ascendants do summon an Oculus. However, unlike the bunker up on Marshblerie, unlike the underpass, they remained untouched, unaware, even, that this had formed right before them.

The explanation that sprung to mind was beside her muttering the same nonsensical language it had the night before. Was this why? Bael was why? But, she pondered, the mere presence of Bael didn't save the man in the underpass. Yes, It may have protected her, for God knows for what reason, but it made no difference for him. So even if Ellie was immune, why did Josh not come under attack? What made that night different?

Frustrated, she turned and stepped outside. She had taken only two steps before she stopped, clutching the bag tightly in her hand and looking up the path. The creatures that haunted her the night before had returned. A dozen or so twisted, contorted forms stood in the afternoon haze looking towards her with their white eyes. *Fuck.*

She looked at the wet dirt under her feet. They were not there for her. They were here for Bael, because It's ramblings had called them. The creatures shook and trembled but did not advance. What was this power It had over them?

Glancing up for a moment, she saw their deformed heads turn and begin to follow her. She became almost overwhelmed with panic. But no, Bael was now behind her and had their attention.

Making it to the road, she dared to turn around and look back. A dozen monstrous figures faced her, scattered about the grounds of the Old Mill. They seemed unaware of each other, fully fixated on Bael who stood in front of Ellie, looking on. Her phone vibrated to life in her pocket, causing her to gasp. Bael swung around in response, eyeballing it with contempt as she answered.

"Josh? I really can't talk right now". She heard the sound of running, and his voice calling.

"Josh? Josh, can you hear me?" No response, only static and distant sobbing. Her heart dropped. "Josh what's going on? Where are you?"

"He's gonna get everybody! He's gonna get everybody! I can't. I can't stop it! I can't stop thinking about it! I can't!"

"Stop!" Ellie shouted, "where are you?"

The phone went dead.

Chapter 15

Stepping into the elevator and swiping a card, Jason smiled at Sam. He hit the button for the penthouse suite. This was unexpected. Jason had mentioned a "Pantheon" which had cast expectations of archaic, old ruins or forbidden passages under old buildings. But no. Apparently Pantheons, in this day and age, were quite luxurious.

"Going up," Jason said loudly, awkwardly. Sam had noticed that he didn't seem to like moments of silence. He filled every possible space with words, no matter how trivial. Jason was not as comfortable with Jason as he would have people believe.

Sam nodded. Ignoring the vibration of his phone. *Now was not the time Ellie.* Perhaps she was merely responding to the location pin he had sent her moments before.

The doors slid open, and Sam found himself facing a large wall of windows giving a breathtaking view of their city. It was spectacular. The stylish furnishings, although minimalist, were set upon a floor of white marble. Two large columns ran from floor to ceiling, overlooked by a mezzanine landing. Sam stepped forward and was hit with a familiar feeling of nausea and dizziness. As it quickly subsided he couldn't help but smile to himself. He had been stripped. Intentionally or otherwise, the setup he had entered in the bunker was now in play. Did Jason know this? Was Jason stripped too? He noticed Jason looking at him, watching for any reaction. Jason has put this in place. Of that Sam was sure. Regardless, it didn't matter. It was done. He understood the precaution. After a moment of mild concern, he found it comforting. Equal footing, no risk. If he was Jason, he would have done the same

Walking into the foyer, he scanned the area around the elevator. Nothing obvious. Though as explained by Noah, it could be anywhere or anything.

Chelamah had not told him that this would happen but there was a good chance she didn't know. She was not the only Devotee. He was sure Jason had one also.

Jason seemed to take great joy from striding into the abode. He looked comfortable and confident, as if he owned it. Sam was sure that he didn't. He had seen Jason's car.

"It's pretty cool, yeah?" Jason gloated, stepping down into the sitting area.

"Is this what passes as a Pantheon now?" Sam asked sarcastically.

Jason frowned. "You were expecting a Monument? A mausoleum? Oh I know! Like Stonehenge?"

"No," Sam replied quickly. "But I wasn't expecting prime inner city real estate either. Whose place *is* this?"

"You can't meet him yet but don't worry, you might sometime. He doesn't live here. He stays here from time to time but not always. This is where we meet, well when I say *we,* I mean us," pointing his finger at himself. Jason continued, "him, me and one other. Used to be two but we lost one during the last Event. There were five of us four years ago!"

"What do you mean, Conduits?"

"Yes. Well, Ascendant Conduits to be specific. Underlings, Devotees have to be escorted by us."

Ascendants. Underlings. Devotees. Sam was astounded. What a weird little hierarchical existence they had forged for themselves.

"It's hard, you know. Because there ain't so many of us around. *Aces,*" Jason noticed Sam's look of confusion. Sam was concerned he had overacted. He had been informed of their strange, self-affirming vernacular but Jason couldn't know this. It sounded as conceited and pompous as the first time he heard it. "Ascendant Conduits. Aces. It's what we call ourselves."

Sam smiled cynically, "is it?"

"Yeah but don't worry. You may not have heard that yet. Come on through." Jason strode confidently to the other side of the hall, waiting at the entrance of a corridor for Sam to arrive. "Come on! My god you walk slow."

Sam followed Jason into the passage. He felt uncomfortable, like it was possibly something he would regret later. Not dissimilar to a hook-up app meet. The unease, however, quickly changed to fascination as Sam followed

Jason down three more steps into a dark brown room. He imagined this room once had windows, but not anymore.

Upon the walls were paintings. Arcane mosaics that all contained similar, scribbled, dark images. The images to his left were encased in protective glass coverings, the others weren't. Each canvas was a mish mash of many different shapes and sizes.

As unfamiliar with such things as Sam was, he was still able to deduce a few things Even though they all looked extremely similar in style, such that they could have all been created by the same artist, some were much older than others. This, he thought, was why the room's windows were covered.

The images encased by glass looked like they were painted on wood or plaster. The edges were ragged with fragments of material flaking off the ends. It was as if they had simply been ripped from a wall.

In the middle of the room was a dimly lit glass cabinet full of items that seemed eclectic and random. Above was a large spherical globe that shone an atmospheric light on the artwork surrounding them. Whoever collected this art had made sure it was well cared for.

"Fascinating, yes?"

Sam just nodded, walking up to the first glass-covered painting to his left. Shaped like a large anvil, it was an image of a woman. An old woman, wretched and bent against a background of faded reds, browns and black. She was facing forward, her head thrown back, as if looking at the artist.

"They look…" Sam began.

"Old… yes. Those ones, somewhere in the 1600's. They all are" Jason said pointing at the glass panels, "then it moves along."

Nodding Sam continued to examine the macabre art. The old woman's mouth was open as if torn into a scream. He noticed her arms seemed particularly large and strong. Her fingers were long, and her skin torn, as if the painter had attempted to scratch ink into her body giving her a diseased, mottled appearance. Hard to distinguish a lot of features. The lines behind her, angry streaks of dark colour formed something, but he couldn't make it out. A scratching, a word he couldn't immediately decipher was written in small almost invisible letters beneath her.

Bruja

Sam turned as Jason approached. "His name was Thiago Sanguesa. A Spanish beggar… or as we like to say now… a *Spanish person without housing*" Jason scoffed coldly. "These paintings date back to the 17th century. This is the Witch, or as our friend Thiago called it, Bruja."

Asshole. Sam took a deep breath, her eyes. "It's a Leviathan!"

"Yep," Jason nodded happily. "You see Thiago was a Devotee. This is what Devotees do. We call them Devotees, others call them 'painters', amongst other names but they are the same thing. You see there are three types of Devotees. Seers, Haunters and *fucking* Wraiths. All can release shadow either by force or by choice and when they do, this happens… They paint. And they can step."

"Step?"

"You and I have both felt that other place. It's not just how it looks… It's how it feels. A Devotee is technically between that world and ours all the time. By will only they can 'step' to the other side. One foot in both. 'Stepping' brings that fear here and it completely mind fucks people! People can lose their fucking minds."

"How did all this get here?"

"Mika. He's a *collector* of sorts. Found these in Europe and brought them here."

"Is that what he does? Like, collect art?

Jason laughed mockingly. "Mika does a lot of things. Let's just say Mika is… resourceful."

"Then who does the paintings?"

Jason sighed. "Devotees, it's just part of what they do. When they go there, a shadow is released, scaring the absolute shit out of everyone, but part of them remains, the human carcass, it paints what they see or what even has been. It's quite fascinating really, a glimpse into the other side. But Devotees are sad pricks. They start and end their journey at the door, stuck between both worlds. That's why they can be used to take things from ours to theirs and theirs to ours. *Handy.* But they are finally dragged into the realm of things so much more powerful than they are. They serve us and them. They become part of it. Short life spans for a Devotee… or a really long one, I suppose, depending on how you look at it. But all Devotees are bottom feeders in the other realm. Parasites, vermin. No more. But before this happens they can be really handy to have around. Then it's…" he raised a waving hand, smiling snidely "*bye-bye.*"

Sam thought about Chelamah. This bizarre group had obviously adopted the mantra… a Devotee was a bottom feeder, therefore was not worth as much even as a human. That was her fate. That could explain her strange behaviour, her odd, distant demeanour. It seemed unfair. Everything seemed unfair.

"But that happens to us as well," Sam observed. He was growing tired of Jason's arrogance. "When we die, we get taken."

"Uh uh," Jason shook his head. "Not necessarily."

"Oh, I'm sorry, unless we die a completely natural death but come on… how many of us make it that long?"

"Some do!" Jason exclaimed. "One of our Aces went home one night, BAM, heart attack. Gone! But come on… an eternity of oblivion? Or an eternity with these absolute fucking Gods. Sorry my friend but I know what I'd prefer. The Leviathan wants you with them. It's an absolute kick in the gut if their Conduit goes and has a heart attack on them."

Sam paused, unsure if Jason was one to speculate with. "What happens to the Leviathan then?"

"The same thing that happens if another Leviathan takes their Conduit. They go back. They really hate that. If they take one of us out, not only do we become part of them forever… BINGO… they get to move to another Conduit and another… and another. This has been going on for millennia. The more ancient the Leviathan, the stronger they are. The more Conduits collected, the stronger they are. In their world, being strong is really fucking important. They lose their Conduit by any other means and they are locked back up. Older, more practiced Leviathans eventually win. Why do you think every year they try so damn hard?" Jason ranted, shrugging. "Did you ever wonder why? Why does it do so much to protect you and then, all of a sudden, its hunting season? It's respect. You are their equal. You hold the key to the cage of the most awesome creatures imaginable. If they don't take you with them before you die… they have to go back. If they're successful, they get to bless another. The cycle continues."

Sam scoffed. "Until *what*? What's the point?"

Spinning energetically around, Jason strode to the first framed painting on the far wall. "That's the point!"

Curiously Sam approached the large frame. It was stark in contrast to the middle age scribbling he had just seen. It was a man, tall and thick, with large white eyes and a bizarre, elongated mouth. He was poised above a crack of light that emanated from the black ground beneath. Around him were figures, twisted scrawling of tormented, outstretched beings and symbols that Sam had never seen before.

"Bael," Jason said proudly. "Bael is the point. It's happened before. Bael destroys messed up civilizations. Bael changes worlds. Legend has it, he was the first. The monarch of the underworld. A supreme the others must follow. Must obey… loyalty to Bael grants them what they want."

"And that is?"

"Us! We grant them access to those most pathetic." Jason sighed as if the answer should have been obvious. "We feed them. Gift them with the suffering of the unworthy scum, cowards, and pointless people. The pain and fear of our 'gifts' go hand in hand. But Bael is not 'free'. Sadly, tragically even he has to adhere to the rules of the Conduit cycle. That's what we are doing here… find the Conduit of Bael… render them powerless. Feed him his well overdue reward."

"To what end?" Sam felt sick to the stomach. "Then he simply finds another. There's no point in doing it."

As if on the precipice of unleashing a great secret, Jason cast his eyes around the room.

"We have learnt how to separate a Leviathan from its Conduit and join it to another. The Conduit son of a bitch that controls Bael controls them all. The Alpha male… think of that power. That power needs to be with the worthy."

"And who would that *worthy* person be? You?"

Jason went quiet. His eyes glinted with suspicion, as if he had said too much. He then delivered what Sam thought was his first carefully considered response since they had met. "That… remains to be seen. But the Conduit of Bael is, ultimately, Conduit of all. It's happened before. Bael's hard to find. Seers, Grimoires, other Leviathans… Bael *chooses* who sees him and who doesn't."

Full of questions, his mind whirring, Sam noticed something else on the painting before him. A terrifying animal, a large black, decaying beast that stood in the foreground. He had seen this creature before. Quickly he scanned the bottom of the painting. The Devotee responsible for this one had written nothing. He had to ask, controlling his movements before he even spoke. He needed to appear innocent, simply curious, and not pointed.

Raising a hand casually to the painting and pointing to the animal "What's that?"

"Oh" Jason replied, thinking for a moment, "umm… yeah… Lobo de fuego… was also drawn by Thiago… over… ahhh… there!" he pointed. "Not as clear as this one though, a lot older."

"It's an animal. I haven't heard of an animal before," Sam probed deeper. He knew what this was, but he wanted to hear it.

"It's the Fire Wolf. Bael's right-hand man. Both Leviathans, both with Aces. Doing their thing. But in the past when Bael and his ally actually found each other, it has been pretty damn spectacular. There are no more powerful or ancient Leviathans than them. Together they form the perfect storm. Step one is to find Bael. Step two is to make sure these two don't come too close together… not yet anyway. Not until we find Bael."

"…and if they do?"

Jason shook his head, unable to find the right word for it. "Bael meets the Firewolf, then *others* begin to come forth, searching for their commander. They will follow him and hopefully… just the right Conduit will allow them to do it."

Bael, Ellie, The Firewolf, Joshua. They had already met. That was why they survived the Circle. That was why the Wolf could tolerate Bael's presence. They *wanted* to be together, just like Ellie and Josh.

OOO

Joshua collapsed on the wet grass of the oval. His lungs burning, his legs shaking with exhaustion as he looked up at the familiar sight of the school. Sobbing, he looked at the buildings. He missed it but he feared it. He missed his friends. He missed his classroom and he missed normal. Most of all he missed normal. Looking behind, he noticed the large dog slowly prowling towards him.

"Just stop!" He screamed, kicking his legs. "Just stop! Get away! You're not mine! You're not mine!"

The dog stopped its advance, watching Josh on the grass with interest. It lay heavily beside him.

"You killed my Mum! I hate you!" Josh screamed, getting to his exhausted feet. "You're an idiot!" He took a long deep breath, "f…f…fuck off!"

Immediately, guilt washed over him. He had used a swear word and what a swear word! The worst of all swear words. Hands brushing the tears from his face, he turned and stomped away.

"You don't have to be here! I don't want you to be here! You hurt my Mum! You hurt everyone! You tried to kill me, and my friend so why do you even wanna be here? Why?!" Furious he spun around to face the dog that now stood eye level with him. Enraged, he stepped closer to the dog, glaring into its white eyes. "You're chicken. You don't show yourself to anyone. You use me to hide in because you're a chicken. What are you? Big and strong and you pick on people so much smaller than you. You're just a bully!"

The dog reared back, a low growl resonated about them.

"You took my Mum. I didn't have anything else," Josh whispered, his voice breaking. "I had nothing else to take. You made me remember her and feel sad. Why can't you even let me remember her and feel happy? Why can't you let me do that? What did I do wrong? I was Josh. Just Josh."

○○○

Sam heard Jason ranting and tried to pay attention. However, his own agenda began to force itself to the front of his mind. He scanned the paintings, moving from one grisly parchment to another.

"Has anyone bothered to think about what these symbols mean?"

"Huh?"

"These." Sam carefully tapped his finger on the image before him to an elaborate motif scrawled amongst many others. "This. And the others, these symbols keep popping up. They mean something."

Jason nodded happily. "We know what some of them mean. Remember, this other realm is chaos. A world of violence and supreme brutality. Pretty much how ours would be if everyone wasn't so damn puny. As such, pride, division, and war is constant. We imagine that they represent different beings, different battles. The only one we are sure of is this one." Jason went back to the first of Thiago's paintings, humming as he moved.

"Bael, as feared as he is, also had enemies. As does anything powerful… it means you stood for something. I guess it would be hard to imagine how many he had, seeing as how ancient he is. Most of them were brought into order. 'Don't fuck with Bael' is the motto. There is, however, one that has

175

been fucking with Bael for years. This one right here. Ancient, powerful, and smart. Almost Bael's equal. This one really gives him a run for his money."

Sam looked at the image and felt the blood drain from his face. His mouth agape as he tried to contain the shock, but he found it near impossible. The painting, those eyes, that small, faded silhouette standing upon a mound of suffering, contorted bodies. Underneath it was scrawled:

El renegado

"This annoying thorn in his fucking side is the Heretic. Think like...Judas, but more of an asshole." Jason laughed loudly. "The Heretic has been around as long as Bael has."

Sam swallowed hard, wiping his mouth in a desperate attempt to look calm, hiding the turmoil he felt. The Heretic, that annoying little thorn in Bael's side. It seemed that Bael and he had a common problem. They both had the same pain in the ass... Bael's Heretic was Sam's Dark Child.

"But!" Jason blurted, startling him. "I'll show you something really cool. Come with me."

Casting a glance back at the eye-opening display, Sam followed Jason back up the stairs. Anxiety high, he wondered what Jason's, or indeed Chelamah's and Noah's response would be if they knew.

Yeah, I know the location of Bael, the Firewolf AND the Heretic!

What did it mean to be the Heretic? Jason had referred to this particular being with a certain venom. Did it put Sam at risk if he was identified as the Conduit of this villainous character? After all was said and done, the Dark Child was still formidable and still played by the rules. He was as secure as he could ever really be. His safety was always dubious at best.

The room they entered didn't have the windows blocked out like the other. Sam relaxed as the familiar skyline came into view, strangely beautiful, and for a moment it took his mind from the double gambit he was playing.

"What a view," he admired. "It's amazing."

"Meh, yeah," Jason shrugged from the other side of the room. "However, this is the view I think you'll appreciate a great deal more."

Standing next to a large, locked bookcase, Jason gestured allowing Sam to approach. One volume in particular caught his attention. It had the same leather binding as those held by Aahna, all those years ago. He remembered it well. Aahna's work had been a desperate attempt to save her own daughter from a fate worse than death. They have them.

"Grimoires. Years of study and information. Tricks, loopholes and 'get out of jail free' cards. We don't have them all. We used to have more."

"Where do they come from?"

"Well, pretty much the same five Scribes. Thiago being the first, if you discount folklore and fairy tales. The first *Scribe* Devotee. There are then the others. You could call it Mika's life's work, collecting this stuff. Not easy, all from different places, in different dialects. A Scribe does not have to be one of us," Jason concluded indicating Sam and himself. "The second and last Scribe were not blessed. Weird how they don't have to be. Devotees paint… sometimes Scribe but sometimes Scribes are just… people. They are 'Keepers of knowledge'. Witnesses to our world and gate keepers of secrets. Weird huh? Some recorded, many were probably lost as the ramblings of 'crazy' people."

Aahna. Aahna was the last. Sam was the subject of her study. He knew this. Her friendship however, her kindness was unforgettable. Did they have hers?

"Anna… Arna… or something like that. Chel's mother. They are key. We think they contain the most powerful of all the Grimoires, but half of them are gone."

"Gone?"

"Some fucker took them. We couldn't find them, but we believe of all the Grimoires, hers were the closest."

"Closest to what?"

"She called it immunity. Immunity from them. Can you imagine? Some think of that as freedom. Can you believe it?" Jason said, bowing his head with exaggerated sadness. "Ungrateful fucks. But these ones are still good though. Grimoires from the first one talk about gifting and shit. You know, how to keep them at a low simmer stage."

"Gifting?" Sam quizzed. "You mean, people?"

"Hell yeah!" Jason scoffed. "Can you imagine! That is what they need. That's what they crave. Like a child, man… you don't gift them often enough and they make your life a living hell! We have a certain amount a month or… so many weeks. It's your responsibility to know how often. Some more than others, apparently."

Offended, Sam bit back his words. Gifted? People were gifted? These were human beings: innocent men, women, and children. The word gifted meant condemning them to eternal suffering. He wanted to shout and scream, about the absolute amoral, disgusting practice of 'gifting' human beings to these creatures. But Jason had revealed so much to him already. There was still so much more to learn. It had been flowing forth unfettered. Jason's hesitation to share was decreasing with every passing minute. Why? Plotting? Testing Sam's resolve? Sam had a feeling. He had seen this before. Indeed, he had been this person. So desperate to be liked, so longing for a genuine connection that he was oversharing his *ass off*. What would Ellie do? She would watch. She would listen.

"People?" Sam swallowed hard. "So, you choose which people become a gift to them?" The word 'gift' caught in his throat.

"Yep. Like, no-one significant. Sometimes it happens, you know, when you don't mean it to. I'm sure you've been there, but usually we choose our gifts with consideration. Wankers, thugs, low life, bitches. I kinda feel bad when that happens… whoops!" Jason chuckled coldly.

How very fucking kind of you. Sam thought. If not for being stripped, the Dark Child would have been *gifted* roughly 50 seconds ago.

Chapter 16

The wind howled as Ellie approached the convenience store, only making it to the undercover awning seconds before the rain pelted onto the streets again. It was still in darkness. A brutal assault had occurred there a while ago, resulting in the death of a young man. The yellow tapes blew around the boarded hole in the window, creepy as hell. Poor guy… what a dump to die in.

She had decided that Josh would most likely be in one of three places. The school, her apartment or back at his family home. Although the thought of him being somewhere with his aunt would have provided some comfort, given his current state of mind she hoped he wasn't. No-one around him would be safe.

Looking at the school across the road, she could see Josh's bench. It looked empty but she couldn't be sure. It was growing dark, and Josh was quite small. She would have to search for him. With a deep sigh she pulled the hood over her head and jogged across the wet road.

Reaching the footpath, she turned back to the store noticing Bael had not moved. It sat on the bench; legs crossed like a gentleman watching her. Not paying It too much attention, Ellie continued into the grounds. Josh would be heading to where he felt safe. Scared, panicked, he had chosen flight, not fight. There was such a thin line between them, especially with an 8-year-old.

○○○

It was clear that the Pantheon was split, although when Jason spoke of Mika there was reverence and respect. Their goal was to find Bael and dispense of Its Conduit. Then, in what they perceived to be a rapidly worsening situation, they would be protected from whatever happened next. Bael was illusive it seemed, much like his Conduit.

However, there were fractures. Sam didn't truly believe Jason's intentions were the same as the others. A glint of vulnerability emerged when he disclosed beliefs about Aahna's Grimoires, showing that perhaps he didn't find his 'blessing' quite as magnificent as he was obligated to.

This, Sam could understand. What he would give to be rid of his 'blessing'. What would any of them give? More of a concern, however, was what they were not prepared to do.

"You admire them," Sam stated, holding his anger in check with everything he had. "But tell me, because I really want to understand. How does that strength, that power, belong to you?"

"How does it not?" Jason shrugged. "I choose who goes and who stays. I choose who has the exquisite honour of belonging to a real tangible fucking God. None of this shit!" To Sam's surprise, Jason crossed himself. "Hail Mary full of fucking grace! Did it ever work for you Sam? Tell me this, what does that God say about you? Sodomite? Abomination? Fucking homo!"

"Shut up dude," Sam straightened up.

"Yes! That's what their God tells them to do! Their god tells them to hate you, to be sickened by you. Their weak folklore tells them that you deserve to die." Jason laughed loudly. "But he works in mysterious ways doesn't he?"

"Firstly, I'm an atheist," Sam snapped. "And the insults? I've heard them all before and I seriously don't give a- "

"No! You're not getting it! Your God is right here! Your God is by your side! Your God has your back! Does theirs? Shit no! They beg for something that doesn't exist! They have never seen it and if they were honest, they *know it isn't* there! Us though… you and I… we know." Jason paused for a moment and gave a weird smile before bouncing up the stairs and out of the room. "Come on!"

Sam had to leave. This was getting crazy. If it wasn't for the stripping, one, if not both, would be gone right now. However, as he watched Jason open another door and head up a long narrow staircase, he couldn't help but follow.

"Where are you going?" he called, watching Jason vanish from view.

"Up!"

Impatiently, he followed Jason up the stairwell, barging through the door that Jason let close on him. The cold night air hit him at the same time as the dizziness arrived. So strong that he felt his eyes roll up in his head. She was back. *What was he doing?*

Sam panted, looking at him. "What are you doing?" Jason stood silently on the edge of the apartment building rooftop. The ice-cold wind caused Sam to gasp. What was his plan now?

"What's going on Jason?" Sam asked, preparing himself for the worst.

Jason stepped even closer to the edge. Without turning around he beckoned Sam. "Come here. I wanna show you something."

"I don't want to," Sam replied, wrapping his arms around himself.

"Don't be a baby. Come over here, look, it's incredible."

Reluctantly Sam walked towards Jason, who looked out over the city skyline. He felt nervous. It would be 20 stories up at least. He stood at Jason's side, looking over a small ledge, no more than one foot high. Looking down to the dark alley below, vertigo and fear grabbed him as he took a quick step back.

"Aw shit, no. I'm going inside."

"No! No wait and see. You see that there?" Jason gripped his arm. "It's OK. Look. I'll show you."

Cautiously Sam shuffled slightly closer. What was he meant to be looking at? He put his head next to Jason's, trying to find what it was he was supposed to see.

Jason turned his head, his mouth almost upon Sam's ear. "You know, in some countries their God tells them to chuck your kind off roofs… hail Mary full of grace…" Jason said in an almost seductive whisper. Sam froze as the danger of his situation became obvious. Jason's hand tightened around his arm as he brought the other to Sam's neck and pulled.

Sam screamed before stumbling to the side and then over the ledge. Jason was still holding onto him. He felt his grip as they both plummeted. Screaming hysterically, he fought against Jason's hold, fought against gravity. He was going to die.

An abrupt crushing sensation pushed the air from him. A feeling of being encapsulated, wrapped, and bound squeezed him a second before he and Jason landed hard on the wet ground. The air knocked out of his lungs, his mind frantically tried to process what had happened. His hip hurt. His body burnt and someone was laughing. Dazed and panting he lifted his shaking head to see Jason lying at his side, cackling as he gripped his shoulder in pain "Ow!"

Jason's laughter began to fade. Laying on his back, he turned his head to Sam, his eyes black and hypnotic.

"Our God, however," he panted, shaking a finger in the air. "Our God would never let that happen to us."

Jesus. He is insane.

Sam staggered to his feet. The Dark Child sat crossed legged on the ground beside him. She had her hand up in the air.

You got an Owie.

Shaking his head, Sam turned from Jason, who continued to laugh in between cries of pain. "Aw come on! Don't be like that! Ow! Jesus that hurts! Come back!"

Sam shook his head. "Uh uh… nope… nope." His stagger became a painful run. He needed to get away from here. He had thought he was going to die, and that was all done so that Jason could make a point. What was wrong with him?

"Sam! I'll call you! Ouch my fucking hand!" Jason's shout echoed from the alley.

Sam wandered down the increasingly quiet streets. His mind was full, his nerves shot. Looking about, he let himself fall heavily onto a concrete bench outside a closed department store. He had learnt so much, but until it was clear in his own mind, he didn't want to share any of it with Ellie. How would he tell her?

Yes, these people have Grimoires. Oh, and it's possible to separate monsters from people but - bad news - they're looking for you in particular so that they can kill you. At least I think It'll kill you, but I'm not sure. Remember, you told me what you were worried about? Other people making your life more complicated? It's actually happening. If they find out who you are, they will hunt you down because you have liberty to the only thing that will stop us all being taken! Oh, and let's not forget Josh! Bael and his Dog are like, best friends! …sorry.

Sam's phone began to vibrate. He sighed. It was Ellie. Grimacing as he reached inside his pocket, he answered "Yeah, yeah I know I was gonna call but I've had one hell of a night. I got thrown off a building."

"Josh rang and I can't find him. Where are you now?"

Sam shook his head in disbelief. "Are you listening to me? I just got thrown... *off a building.*"

The phone went quiet, before Ellie asked. "What, like literally off a building?"

"Yes! Why would I say *I just got thrown off a building*, as a metaphor?" Sam shook his head in amazement.

"Who threw you off a building?" Ellie was bewildered. "Why?"

Sam stood back up, gripping his painful hip. "This is me making new friends. I'll tell you when I see you. Where is he? What happened?"

"I don't know, I can't find him," Ellie spoke into the phone, turning her back to the horrific creatures that hovered silently about the school grounds. "I'm at the school, I thought he might be here, but I can't..." There were so many of them standing, motionless under the moonless sky. She could hear their voices, their weird sounds, mutters, and whispers.

"He'll be looking for you," Sam replied. Ellie turned around glancing at the beings about her.

"They're back," she said quietly; "Something's wrong... I don't know if either of you are safe around me. I've got to go. Find him Sam... somethings going on. I'm not sure what it means." Ignoring Sam's protests, she hung up, slowly placing her phone back in her pocket.

ᴑᴑᴑ

Before her was the darkness of the path that ran past the oval and to the other side of the dimly lit school. In her path were these mutated creatures. As disinterested as these things were in her, she would have to walk through the dozens of twisted monsters to get to the other side of the building. The scourge in her life was getting worse. She never thought that would've been possible, but here it was. She had the choice to avoid them, but what next? They would simply return elsewhere and cast this terrifying image on her again and again. Just like Bael did.

Slowly, she placed one foot in front of the other. They were never too close. She would not push their proximity, not bring them closer but she wouldn't avoid them either. The first creature was to her left. A large ball of fat holding a chain in its bulbous hand. It wore a simple pair of overalls, rudimentary. Whatever this creature tried to mimic would only make sense to the poor soul it had tormented. As she approached, she could see the tell-tale jerks and small twitches that she knew all too well. Its eyes, though embedded in puffy flesh, were white slits that stared unblinking towards the direction Ellie was walking.

Fear rose, Ellie's breathing became short. She would count her steps and keep moving forward.

The next Leviathan was lithe and short. Standing upright it was considerably smaller than the others she could see. Its small size meant nothing. Its lethality would be the same. Standing the same height as Ellie, she could see it wearing a simple, sickly yellow dress with small black flowers upon it. Its thick bobbed hair, the twisted ragged grin that ripped across its face from one ear to the other, reminded Ellie of a bad 1960s sitcom mother. Its hands, with inhumanly long fingers, were held in front of it. Pleasant, lady-like humming radiated around it. Its head cocked bizarrely to the right, its white eyes like golf balls rolling about in its head.

Ellie walked faster, fighting the urge to run. Strangely, as the freakshow of hell-like oddities passed her, the urge became significantly less. Bael was standing in front of her, watching her walk through the creatures. With every grunt, scream and sound, Ellie pushed back against the natural urge to react. She would not grant Bael the pleasure. She had dealt with It for many years. Her ability for fear had been exhausted quite some time ago. They were just like It. No different. Their intrusion into her life was not an improvement or a worsening. It was what it was.

She approached Bael and stood right in front of It. Her defiance, her stoicism strengthened. She looked up at It. It returned the gaze and looked down at her. With a lump in her throat, she pushed out the words "What now?"

Bael's head cocked to the side, It's mouth snapped back into that disgusting, evil smile. It gave her the slightest of nods. An almost indistinguishable nuance that if she hadn't watched that damned face for so many years, she never would have noticed. It was impressive. Pride? She wanted It to speak, It had before. The gig was up. She knew It could speak to her and now she had asked It a direct, straight-forward question. Would It take the bait? Ellie's mind whirled. This was about control. It had spoken

184

to her directly, but only at Its own choosing. If It answered now, it would have been at her demand. Perhaps Bael would consider that she had earned it.

"You won't make me," she muttered. "No matter how many of them you bring, you won't put me over the edge. They are no different to you and me... I know you."

Bael straightened up, lifted Its hands above Its head and opened them, as if greeting those behind her. A wretched bellowing caused her to spin around. They all staggered forward just one step and stopped. She held her breath.

"Elenore. Will you die for him?"

All of them were now looking straight at her; she could feel dozens of dead white eyes crawling on her skin. This was a threat. This was Bael; It could not attack her. It couldn't touch anyone unless she *lit* them. It stood to reason that neither could these others that now stood before her. They may have seen her, maybe Bael could grant them that, but the act of lighting someone was hers alone. If they set upon her, it would be against everything she understood, everything she had seen It do. No. Bael would not let her be taken. This was a ruse. Bael and these things were still bound by the rules, she was almost positive.... but she had to be sure, for all their sakes.

Hands trembling, she turned to face Bael who continued looking down at her. Its smile was gone leaving Its face flat and impenetrable.

"Do it," she prodded, feeling her stomach twist and her hands shake. "Do it. Give me to another. Go on." To her surprise, she felt a smile of mocking contempt spread across her face. "You can't do it can you? You can't give me to them anymore than you can touch me. *Fuck you.*"

It dropped Its face to hers. She met Its challenge. It would not give her up, and she knew it. These things were not here for her and Bael knew it. Piece of shit. Was this how desperate It had become? What was he trying to do? Threaten her into answering that single question?

"Would you die for him?"

No, she would not die for Bael. She would not die for anything It represented. But for another, that she didn't know. For the Conduit in from the underpass? She couldn't. This question was a riddle.

It moved, Its large, long hand came to her face. She flinched, heart thumping in her chest. Large, decaying white fingers ever so gently attempted to touch her forehead. Quickly, it pulled away. Unlike the underpass, unlike the times in the Circle, the barrier between them was fully in place. It was testing the boundary. It couldn't touch her and, she hoped to God, it was safe to assume the others couldn't either. She was overcome with an urge to push It. To see what It could do. It had done it before.

"If I hold you, I hold them as well. Remember that," she sneered, gesturing to the monsters behind her. "So tell me. Where is Josh?"

Its long mouth widened into a sickening smile, then It and its grotesque smile faded from in front of her. It had moved, standing in the shadows of a tree at the school gate. Glancing at the beings behind her, Ellie turned and began to follow.

OOO

"Find him Sam," she had said. As he hobbled towards the most obvious place that Josh would be, he couldn't help but marvel that the possibility of falling 20 stories was somehow lost on Ellie. The Pantheon ended up being closer to Ellie's apartment but further from his car. Walking across the street, he stopped to catch his breath. Taking in a huge gasp of air, he stared into the dark sky, letting the rain run down his face. This night had to end.

Wiping his brow, he could see Ellie's apartment building. He felt uneasy. It made sense that if Josh was not at the school then he would've come here. He would have been seeking Ellie just as she was seeking him. He wasn't sure what that all meant, with the most recent revelations in play. Civilisations ended when Bael and the Firewolf were reunited. That was what Jason had told him. What he didn't tell Jason, however, was that the meeting of these two old friends had already taken place.

Walking up the stairs to the entrance hall, he peered in through the glass door. Two dormant elevators and a few randomly chosen pot plants. No sign of Josh. He trotted back down the stairs, gazing up at the side of the building. He was sure her apartment was on the sixth floor. The lights were off. Sam was sure Josh would be here.

Rounding back, Sam had one last look through the glass doors. There he was. Sitting around the corner; visible only as two small shoes poking out from behind the wall. He must have the code to the main door. Well, why wouldn't he? He had stayed here long enough. Sam gave three sharp knocks. The feet were quickly pulled from sight.

"Josh!" he called. There was no reply. Sam thought for a moment. Josh wouldn't come to simply to anyone who called his name.

"It's Sam! Josh, open the door!" Sam leant his head, exhausted on the glass. "Come on… please. I would really like tonight to end on a positive," he laughed to himself.

A small head poke around the corner and quickly vanished from sight. Sam waited, cold, sore and with growing impatience. He knew the words to get Josh's attention.

"Ellies been looking for you," he said loudly.

Josh again glanced around the corner. Sam watched as his body followed excitedly, frowned, and then ducked back behind the corner. Relief washed over Josh, but so did frustration. He wasn't happy with Sam. If it wasn't for Sam, he wouldn't have had to leave. Ellie told him that it wasn't Sam's fault, but Josh wasn't sure if he believed her.

In the reflection of the chrome elevator door, Sam strained to see Josh standing up against the wall, his fingers rising one after the other in front of his face.

"What are you doing?"

Josh, embarrassed and annoyed, took a step to the side. "I'm counting to 10!" he shouted back.

Tired, beaten, and weary Sam knocked on the door again. "Come on Josh, cut that shit out now. I'm tired and I bet you're tired too. I really don't wanna end tonight running and screaming and I'm sure you don't either, so just open the door."

Josh and Sam's eyes met once more in the door's reflection. Sam could see Josh lowering his hands, a rapid change in a child's mood.

Hesitating for a moment, Josh ran out from behind the wall and hit the button next to the door, bringing it open. Sam stumbled in as Josh stepped back, looking at him in amazement. "Why do you look so bad?"

"I got thrown off a building, but that doesn't seem to concern anyone," Sam shrugged, crappy humour being his default. "What's going on? What happened?"

Fidgeting, Josh walked around Sam suspiciously. His eyes were fearful and anxious. "You told Ellie to make me go and everything went wrong. Everything was different. I don't like everything being different."

"What is different, tell me." Sam dropped his gaze, speaking soothingly which was very foreign to him.

"It's there all the time." Josh's eyes filled with tears. "I can't make it go away. I feel sick in my belly all the time. I can't go to sleep because I see bad things. I think bad things. It's like a blackness over me."

Sam nodded. Expressed through a child's words, but this was how it felt. He understood, and he needed Josh to know that. That as alone as Josh felt, there were others who knew this feeling and lived with the same burden.

"I know," Sam nodded. "I know."

"Why won't it stop?" Josh began to cry. "Did I do something bad?"

"No," Sam said sternly. "No. You did nothing bad."

Josh nodded. He needed to believe this. He needed to believe that he wasn't bad. "Why do things hate me, but not leave me alone? And things that like leave?"

Sam didn't know how to answer. He knew the reason. He knew the challenge but couldn't find the words to explain it to a child in a way that would make sense.

"Who went away?"

"Mum." Tears streamed down his face. "My friends. Ellie. You, you all went away. But Ron stayed, and Jamie stayed, and the dog… he stays. Why does that happen? I didn't want it. I just want to be Josh again!"

Sam stepped forward, placing his hands on the child's shoulders, leaning into him as the room began to dim. "You *are* Josh. Do you hear me? You are Josh. Josh is cool!"

Sam was surprised as Josh stepped forward sobbing, wrapping his arms around him. Slowly, Sam clasped Josh, patting him gently on his back. The two Conduits held each other, embracing in a rare moment of complete understanding.

"You are Josh. Josh is cool, and strong, and funny. We really like Josh!" Sam said softly, ruffing Josh's beanie.

He felt Josh nod into his shoulder, saying in a small, muffled voice. "And you are too."

Touched, Sam chuckled. Josh thought he was now making Sam feel better. Perhaps he was.

"Sam I am," he joked quietly, pretty sure Josh wouldn't get the reference.

The door behind them swung open as Ellie raced in. Seeing Josh, she breathed a sigh of relief as he ran to her.

"Where were you!" she cried.

"I was waiting for you!" Josh replied, as if it was obvious.

She shook her head, pulling him towards her and watched, concerned, as Sam painfully stood. "Are you OK?"

"Yeah I'm OK. It was a fun-filled night."

Taking Josh's hand, Ellie led them to the door. Noticing her agitation, Sam went to ask her why. Anxiously, she shook her head. *Not yet.* She would settle Josh and then take him home. Assuming, she hoped, there was one to go back to.

ᴼᴼᴼ

The elevator door opened to the Pantheon and Luka quickly entered. Message from Jason.

TAKE IT ALL DOWN NOW

Luka wasn't sure if the sense of urgency was embedded in the text or was being fed by his paranoia. Here, alone and at 1AM. Mika wouldn't be pleased. He wasn't allowed to have the code, let alone get the swipe card. Mika would kick both their asses. The securities he had put in place had to be removed. Now. He stepped back from the elevator door as it closed. Above it, on a barely visible stamp-sized piece of parchment, was a symbol. There, upon the hall table, sitting amongst expensive pieces of shit art that Mika had acquired, was the dollar shop vase Luka had used for the occasion. It had to be destroyed. The symbol had to be removed.

He would take the vase with him, destroy the symbol and he would do it quickly. He chuckled to himself. All the power that the Ascendants held, all that bravado, and they could be disarmed by a one-dollar piece of plastic.

This is where Jason bought the 'Queer'. In time, if things went to plan, the queer too would be using this place as a sanctum. An honour that Luka would never have. The injustice made his blood boil. In the normal world, this new guy was something to mock and shame. In the other… he would always be regarded as stronger than him. *A fag…* stronger than him! It was almost comical. Thoughts of his own actions behind the scenes calmed him. He would deal with it in his own way. He had been preparing that for some time now. But for now, it was the way things were.

Running to the windows, he looked over the city. There, he would hold it there. It would disperse and the strip he had placed would be gone. He

189

unlocked the door, grabbed the handle, and pulled. It slid open an inch. Jason had made sure it was unlocked when he left. He was to lock it before he left.

Startled, he heard the elevator door. He turned to see it slide open. Inside was a woman leaning heavily against the far wall. Short and petite with her blonde hair tied high up upon the top of her head. She wore a full-length coat while clutching a small red bag. Her face was obscured by a thick covering of makeup, giving her skin the appearance of a flawless porcelain doll. All the same beige except for her bright red lips that matched her bag. She gave him a small, surprised smile. Mika's Devotee. Her hard blue eyes lit up. He used to think those eyes were pretty. That was until he got to know her. Now they were some of the coldest eyes he had ever seen.

"Luka," Crystal simpered. She spoke slowly, mockingly. "Fancy seeing you here."

Luka's heart pounded. The cold air from the door behind sent a chill up his neck. Or maybe, it was finding himself alone in the company of one of the biggest certifiable bitches he had ever known.

"Crystal. What are you doing here?" he blustered. "Where's Mika?"

Crystal walked slowly toward him on her typically high heeled shoes. "I was out at a … but Mika asked me to drop by and collect something. He's not back until later today but, I think you already know that."

Luka glanced at the open door. Could she know? Would she sense it? *Oh shit.* He needed an excuse. Being in the Patheon, without Jason. *Shit, Shit, Shit.*

"And where…" she looked out the door, frowning. "Where is *Jason?* He should be here somewhere! Or are you here without him?"

Luka heard her words but remained fixated on the threshold of that elevator. This bitch was a Devotee, as was he. She was a Seer. She'd sense it.

Luka took a deep breath and nearly gagged as she stepped over the threshold into the foyer. She went to speak, but stopped, distracted by her own senses. Crystal had placed these before and although as useless as they were on her as they were on him, she could sense it in play. A hundred scenarios ran through his mind.

"Just like you aren't supposed to be here without Mika, but here you are," he blurted out thoughtlessly. Eager to argue rather than wait in silence for her to notice what was going on.

The tap, tap of Crystal's stilettos on the marble was unbearable as she made her way towards him. Her smile dropped as her cold eyes filled with satisfaction. "Well, you can take that up with Mika if you like?" She stood still, watching Luka's eyes drop, guiltily to the floor. "No?" she smiled. "I didn't think so."

Slowly, without taking her eyes off him, she let her bag slide off her shoulder and onto the couch while she turned around to face the elevator. She faked a gasp of surprise. "Oh dear, Luka… what on earth did you do?"

"Drop it Crystal. Nothing. I'm here now. I'll fix it and go home. Just drop it… please." Luka was embarrassed at his blatant begging.

She waved a finger in the air as she glanced at the walls around her. "Am I to believe… oh my God… you did!"

"Crystal please… please... I was told to."

"You stripped the Pantheon!" Crystal gasped dramatically. "You! Well, I have to admit, you are a lot braver than I would be. Maybe I haven't given you enough credit."

"For Jason, idiot, it was for Jason, not for me" he blustered.

"Idiot? Don't get cocky Rocky! Right now cocky is…" she continued speaking as she walked towards the hall stand, picking up the cheap plastic vase with disgust, "…the last thing you want to be. Wow Luka, Mika's taste certainly has changed of late. Look at this piece of shit. Oh! This is the vessel? Goodness me, Mika would be offended that this exquisite piece of crap even found its way into the Pantheon. But to think you stripped the Pantheon so Jason could show off to his new buddy… that would make Mika…" she lowered her voice as her smile vanished, "furious." She placed the vase back down.

Yes it would, he knew it. There was no way this would go unpunished, and he was an easier target than Jason. Would Jason let that happen? Would Jason have his back? Fuck… why did he agree to this in the first place.

"You know, when I found you all those years ago I thought wow… It was way too easy. It's not easy to find someone, but you seemed to lack something that all the others have."

"And what's that?"

"A spine, Luka. I thought you spineless. But now I'm thinking perhaps I was wrong! This is a ballsy act. It would have surprised me if it weren't for the fact that you lack any type of real intelligence. Something else that made you so easy to find. Jason? Jason's smart, but he's desperate. He so wants to impress. Poor thing. He doesn't appreciate the honour that was bestowed on him. Yet, we still have people that want to take us down. Look around you. The items in this place are pure gold to a certain select group of people. Guarded by a swipe card which you seem to have in your pocket. A pin code, which you also seem to have. And then there's Walter… the 100-year-old security guard downstairs. They are safe because of *who* comes here. Because of what the Ascendants bring with them! But you negated all that. You and that…" She stopped briefly as she swallowed the impending insult. "You and Jason bought a stranger into the Pantheon, showed him around."

"He wasn't supposed to do that?" Luka asked suspiciously. "He wasn't supposed to bring him here?"

"No! We don't know him. I have never *seen* him. How do you even know he's a Conduit? Fucking Chelamah? He could've been anyone."

Luka felt foolish and gullible. He didn't know that the newcomer wasn't allowed to be in here. Why? Jason seeking friends again? Jason trying to impress? Did this faggot mean so much to Jason that he would throw him under the bus?

"He wouldn't have known. It was just insurance for Jason, that's all."

"You're very cute, almost handsome. Good job too because you really are as thick as shit. You're assuming that he didn't. You don't know that," Crystal sneered. In a moment of genuine emotion, she added softly, almost sadly, "try to be smarter. Neither of us matter. We are nothing to them, remember that. *Nothing.*"

Luka took this moment to propose an amnesty. "It was for Jason. Let me take it down. I did what was asked. I had to, just like you have to. No more. Just let it go. I'll destroy it now anyway."

"Will you though?" she snapped. "I think you need a lesson on trust Rocky. I don't believe you."

"Of course I will, you think I'd leave it here? It was only up for a few hours with that new dude. An Ascendant, Crystal. You'd think with all these Ascendants, you and I would have each other's back a bit more."

Crystal bit her lip, turning her back to him as if in deep thought. He studied her, wondering how close he was to begging. If that's what it took, then he would.

"Do you trust me?" Crystal asked as she turned back. "No Marco. Jason sending you to look a fool. You're running out of people to trust. Chel is a pain in the ass. She's fucking Noah. Did you know that? Chel fucks home-less people?"

Luka shook his head, though of course he knew. Jason and he would often speculate at Chel's reaction if she knew the truth as they did. Chelamah was a halfway decent human being. Luka liked her. Crystal was a certified fucking sociopath. At this stage, however, it was important that this meeting was not disclosed to Mika. He would have agreed to anything she said. He barely nodded.

He watched as Crystal seemed to ponder the concept of not being a complete asshole. She cast him a sympathetic eye and nodded. "OK. I get you."

"You do?"

Crystal thought for a moment. "Yes, and I'm sick of talking to you any-way. Why don't you just go. I'll unstrip it." She sat down on the couch.

Luka gasped, stunned. Was this a joke? "Seriously?" he quizzed. "You'd do that?"

"Yeah, let's face it, I've got time. Mika won't be back until later in the morning and I'm gonna crash here anyway. You go home. One day, you'll pay me back… maybe." Crystal crossed her legs as Luka watched her care-fully. Had what he said worked? Had she taken his *all Devotees stick together* bullshit as legit?

"OK," Jason nodded, impressed. "Thanks Crystal. That's great. Seri-ously great."

He bounded back to the elevator, eager to leave. The atmosphere in the room was weird and hard to read. He was easily flummoxed by women. He just didn't *get* them and preferred to stay clear. In most circumstances any-way. Perhaps she understood his position?

"Just go," Crystal rubbed her eyes as if talking with him was exhausting, "and don't do anything like this again. Not here. Not ever. Be careful who you trust, Rocky."

"Sure," Luka entered the elevator as Crystal quickly called out.

"Luka!" she crooned. "Make sure you tell Jason that I'm taking care of it. I don't want him to worry. Just let him know, I've got it."

Smiling Luka nodded, "will do and, thanks."

The elevator door slid closed, and Luka leant upon the wall breathing a huge sigh of relief. Wow… just when you think you know someone. Maybe, this bitch wasn't so bad after all. The relief brought him sliding down the elevator walls to the floor. He sat, hands on his knees, breathing deeply. It was OK. Everything was OK.

He had done so many questionable things in the past. The most significant were his secret to keep. His impulsive actions years before were based solely on the need for survival, when his biggest fear was that he would slowly but surely mutate into a depraved freak. The final end for all Devotees.

He had been there the night Aahna died. Her death was due to the action of another, but he had seized the opportunity. He had taken Aahna's missing Grimoires. He had hidden them in the other world where no-one could reach them... no-one except him. The problem was, how to get them back. He had toyed with the idea of telling Jason but... things had changed. Everything had changed. He had told Jason a half truth and nothing more. Though for now, all was well. He could relax and breathe. Crystal would deal with the strip, and he could go home, take lots of medication and perhaps sleep. Moments before the door slid open, Luka sent the requested text. Crystal's generosity would surprise Jason as much as it did him. He could hardly believe the luck of his narrow escape.

Chapter 17

When Josh had arrived home it was 2AM. Sheepishly he entered the brightly lit house, staring in fright at the adults who rushed up to meet him before the front door had even closed. He thought he was in trouble. His aunt and uncle were there, as was another woman that he later found out was his aunt's friend. After the initial flurry, Nate called the police to tell them, "He's here." Josh's initial thought was that he was going to be arrested.

When all was calm, they sat him down and asked him what they thought was a simple question. "What happened?"

It wasn't simple. He answered quietly that he was scared and sad. "What scared you?" was the obvious response.

Josh couldn't answer that either. He had never felt so observed, so listened to in his entire life. Both Casey and Nate sat opposite him, on edge, waiting for every answer, watching every facial expression, watching for anything that could help them make sense of what had happened the afternoon before. All the while, the Dog prowled around the outside of the house. He could hear it. He could feel it.

Neither Casey nor Nate believed that he was merely 'sad.' Josh couldn't find words to explain what had gripped him. He hoped he would never, ever hear that song again. Eventually, noticing his exhaustion, Casey and Nate put him into bed. He lay there, staring at the walls and replaying the conversation with Sam in his mind.

He thought Josh was cool, strong and… something else. But he thought Josh was cool and Sam, Sam was very cool. So that was very good to hear. No-one had said he was "cool" before. With those words echoing in his mind, and the warmth of the bed soothing his body, sleep found him.

Casey watched the closed bedroom door from down the hall. Nate yawned, rubbing his eyes with exhaustion and concern. He had an inclination that they were both thinking the same thing. This kid was a mess, and maybe they simply weren't equipped to help him deal with it. It would be helpful if they knew exactly what Josh was dealing with. He wasn't sad, he was terrified. Nate remarked that he had never seen such raw horror in someone's face before.

"Tomorrow. We'll take him to the shr... psych guy" Nate stated. "We need help with this."

"He called me mum." Casey said quietly, turning from the hall. "He looked at me and he called for his mother."

Nate nodded. "I know, I heard him."

"Can I even help him?" Casey sat, arms crossed, next to Nate. "I don't know. I don't know how."

"We are helping him. That yesterday came out of *nowhere*. But to be honest, and I don't wanna make things worse but -"

"Where was he?" Casey stated, Nate nodded in agreement. "He was dry. It was torrential when he walked in that door, yet he was dry. Where was he?"

Nate had to admit, Casey's concern was justified. Joshua was traumatised and he had reason to be. There were many factors that could have, and would have, played into this. Instability, poverty, parents with addiction issues, verbal and physical abuse. The list of Sharon's failings was endless... not that Nate would mention them now, though this was key for Casey whether it came from curiosity, or even a concern, for her wayward sister. She was convinced that something had happened to Sharon, and that Josh had been there. Josh knew exactly where her sister was. But when did it happen? How many weeks was he alone if that were even the case?

Eight hours earlier, a traumatised child had run panicked from a cafe downtown. Ninety minutes ago, the same terrified child returned content and soothed. There was something in Josh's life that had sustained him since his mother left and that same something, when terrified, he had run to.

○○○

The 'Heretic' had slept on her couch, again. The 'Firewolf' had been fed chocolate milk to calm his nerves and then taken home. This, thought Ellie,

196

was absurd. In the early hours of the morning, Sam had told her what he knew. Doors opening, people being destroyed, leaving displaced Leviathans that were resisting returning to their hell-like state. Bael was first to leave, millennia ago, and then the others followed. Bael and the Firewolf signify the beginning of something, and that something isn't good.

An Oculus had ripped a gateway between them and us. Only Conduits could see it, existing as did the Leviathans. Out of the view of anyone else. An Oculus gets open when more than one "Ace" is in the same place during the "Event." It then remains there, ready for two or more Ascendant Conduits to jump start it into action. The reason for the Event was so that if the Leviathan gets to take you, then they simply get to move onto another. If not, if they lose you to another of their kind, or you die naturally (which would be nice), they must leave this world. The Conduit is their personal pipeline to this realm. The more Conduits they collect, the more powerful they become, hence Bael.

Ellie found it interesting that as powerful as Bael's legend was, he was still bound by the same rules as every other. He needed her to survive until he was able to take her. If she died, Bael would have to go back. Suicide seemed a noble option, however, she, like every other Conduit in history, had tried this. It didn't work. Hanging, drowning, gunshots, falling, even poisoning attempts were always thwarted by the Leviathan as it protected its gateway.

Bael and the Firewolf had already met, and although thought to be "bad", it had worked in their favour. It appeared that neither Bael nor the Wolf could resist attacking one when Lit. Their primal drives were unmistakable. Lit was paramount, Lit was desired more than anything. Bael and his Wolf had fought over them, allies turned to selfish, disloyal enemies.

Everything about their existence was focused on their unbridled longing for victims. It overrode anything else, even the victory of claiming their own Conduit. Bael had Ellie in its grasp. The Dog had Josh. Yet, the act of lighting Ellie triggered a response in the Dog to the detriment of both itself and Bael. But why? Was there something they needed more than their own Conduit? Perhaps, they didn't have a choice… maybe that was a process they must follow. It wasn't clear.

Ellie studied the large map on the cafe table before her, analysing the red dots that had been placed to indicate an Oculus. Simplistic, an almost kindergarten charm. Sam leaned on the chair before her, arms crossed tightly.

"This is them? All of them?" she asked.

"Yes, and of course - "

"The underpass" Ellie finished.

"Yep, the underpass."

They appeared scattered, no obvious pattern. Of course, that was kind of expected. These locations were chosen for their clandestine qualities, be that old wheat silo or in the basement of a disused inner city rat shack. They were chosen for their emptiness and isolation.

"So if we just say that they all opened two months ago, then it happened right at the last Circle," Ellie remarked, sitting back. "Can we also say that Josh and I caused this then?"

Sam leant forward, "No, no. We know that Josh and you survived it. We don't know if you started it. That's only one option."

"It makes no sense. From what you told me, Josh and I together could have done this, but Josh and I were safe. Yet no other Conduit who was with another could have stood a chance."

Sam reluctantly agreed, "it's a possibility. That could just be you know... your guy... like the underpass. But seriously, who knows?" Sam turned back to the map. "Including the underpass there are 6. The farthest being the Old Mill. Perhaps you didn't cause it. Josh didn't cause it. You survived it, but it doesn't make it the... epicentre? Remember most of us are gone anyway. Most of us don't make it past our first year. A vast majority of the rest end up nutcases. This past Event, many more were lost; anyone of them could have had something to do with that. I mean the bunker alone, 7 people gone. Aces, as they call us, were rare before - now we're officially an endangered species."

Ellie looked through the window to the cold streets outside. 'Her guy', sitting on the bench, legs crossed and watching her through the glass. "Would that be a bad thing?" she asked quietly before she had even thought about it.

Sam scoffed. "For us, yes!" Irritated, he leant forward. "Where do you fall in this Ellie? Are you that much of a fatalist?"

"Realist perhaps?"

"If that's the case then why are you even sitting here with me? We've both been to hell and back *multiple* times. I'm meeting dangerous people. I was thrown off a fucking roof, and I'm meeting that same guy again later this week for a drink! Hopefully a ground floor establishment, *but* I am keeping your secret because you my friend, like Josh, are being hunted."

"Josh is defenceless on his own," Ellie snapped. Why did Sam insist on injecting crappy humour into every single statement.

"Yes, and thank you for acknowledging that Ellie, but so am I." Sam raised a finger to his chest. "I am not you. If something comes for me, I have as much chance as that guy you saw in the underpass. Ain't no big scary dude protecting me. They want you because you are feared. They're terrified of you. I don't have that advantage. I'm doing it for all of us. You, me, and Josh." Sam lifted his coffee and continued. "We could get out of this. They're all talking about it. They're all looking for it. They know it's there. If anyone can find it Ellie, we can. Think of that, if not for you, think about it for Josh and all the other Joshs' who will be primed for hell in about 9 months from now."

"8 months, 3 days, 5 hours and 32 minutes to be exact" Ellie quickly replied. "But If I lead It into an Oculus, it's over."

"No it's not! This is not the first time! It happens again and again and again. I'm talking about ending it for good! But if you really feel hopeless about it, let me know now. If you really feel like we all deserve hell then tell me so that I can make the most of my absolutely shit life, instead of wasting my time." Sam calmly sat back, watching her. Surprised, he saw her soften. She dropped her stare as once again, that rare trickle of vulnerability made its way to the surface.

"I'm sorry" she muttered, as if it choked her. "So, this is what we do. We can't go to the Oculus sites together."

"Obviously," Sam nodded.

"Obviously," Ellie glanced out the window, "*my guy* is enjoying all the attention. Since my journey yesterday, he seems to have a lot more friends."

Sam quickly noticed her use of the forbidden pronoun 'he'. Before thinking, he asked "Since when has It became a He?"

Ellie sighed in resignation. "Since I realised that semantics are not going to help me now. You said they can't find me… you said he can remain hidden from these people?"

"Yes," Sam was impressed at such a straightforward question. "He is different. He's deeply hidden. I dunno, something about 'he *chooses* when he is seen'…not the other way around."

Ellie nodded, deep in thought. She knew she could regret what she was about to say but there was no way out now. She had been living in the shadows because she thought she had no choice. Before she met Josh and Sam, her life was effectively over: dark, bleak, and lonely. Now, however, a small flame burned within her. Hope? Strength? She had changed so much, she barely knew herself anymore. A little light in the dark changes everything.

"They want me. Vicariously that will lead them to Josh," she said.

"Or *vice versa*," Sam nodded. "Everyone around Josh is in trouble. If they can't find you, they'll look for him."

"How do you know that?"

"Because that's exactly what I would do" Sam replied. "I would simply look for the next best thing. Find the Firewolf... find Bael."

"How?"

"They have ways of finding people. You, like me, have just had our heads in the sand for too long. Hidden in plain sight. There are ways to find us. There's like... I don't know... a system. I think..." Sam paused for a moment pondering his words. Should he tell her? He had promised her the truth; he owed her that.

"They knew the Firewolf was here. They knew where. It was only a matter of time until Josh met you. Whether it be from the Dog or from them, if you hadn't met Josh when you did, he wouldn't be here now," he blurted out while stepping back to watch Ellie's response.

Ellie straightened in the chair. The coldness, defiance quickly masked her face.

"That can't happen. They can't have him," she muttered quietly, unnerving Sam. One thing he had learnt about Ellie was the more pissed off she was, the quieter her voice grew. "I need to see Josh and then I want to meet them."

Sam was stunned. "Are you serious? They are complete assholes. Trust me on that."

Nodding, Ellie began folding the map. "Yes, I'm serious. Let's just see how good at 'hiding in plain sight' he really is."

Ellie watched Sam's face turn from stunned to concerned. "You would do that?" he asked quickly.

"Yes. HE is coming for me. These people are coming for Josh and me. Josh can't deal with this, but I can. I want to know what it is and who they are. They won't know, I assure you."

"And if they do?" Once again, her default was to protect this child. Why him? Sam liked Josh; he was a sweet, funny little kid with big eyes and a gutsy but shy disposition. But Josh triggered something in Ellie, a weakness, a chink in her armour.

"If they see It… him… what happens then?"

"Then they do. Let's see what they have. You said they will find me regardless. Me being there will let me know if I have an advantage or not. Can you arrange it?"

Sam nodded, watching Ellie pick up her backpack. "And if they try to throw you from a roof?"

Ellie stood up. "It wouldn't go well for them, you can trust me on that one."

Impressed but stunned, Sam nodded. Wanting to ride on the momentum of her decisiveness, he grabbed his jacket and stood hastily, following her out into the street. He couldn't help but harbour a sense of unease – after all, it was clear that Ellie was willing to protect anyone she needed too, especially Josh, and would rather risk her own life than see anyone else suffer, and if that was her thought process then – in her mind – she couldn't lose. Tucking this thought into one of the dark corners of his mind, Sam scanned the streets quickly, saw Ellie do the same. His eyes met hers.

"More than one?" he asked quickly.

"No, not right now."

"Maybe they're all at the pub." Sam quipped, digging his hands in his pockets.

Ellie shook her head. She looked at Sam, and with a small, genuine smile that he had managed to force out of her she replied, "don't be a dick."

OOO

The room Josh sat in with Casey and Nate was very dark and 'woody'. There was a dark wood floor, a dark wood bench and dark wood chairs with dark cushions. It smelt sweet, like the perfume his art teacher used. She smelt nice sometimes, but then other times she used too much, and it made him feel a bit sick. Behind the desk sat a woman who looked like she'd be nice and friendly.

He felt nervous. He knew that it wasn't the woman he was here to see. He was here to see the man who must be very important to have this many nice things. It was even nicer than his aunt's house. This man was a doctor, Casey had said. Not a shrink, as Nate had called him.

Nate sat next to him, teasing him into play by kicking his foot. Josh would kick back and smile shyly. Nate would then tell him off for kicking him and they would quieten down. Then Nate would kick his foot again. Nate would make everything funny, and Aunt Casey would try to look annoyed but smile at the same time.

Niles walked through the door and cast his eyes at his receptionist. He was well briefed in this child's particular set of circumstances, interesting and complex. He had, in some strange way, been looking forward to this meeting.

"Joshua is here!" she smiled. "Dr. Niles this is Joshua Fielding," her usual announcement whenever there was a child in the waiting room was, as always, pleasant and warm.

Smiling, Niles looked over to the small boy seated next to an older man and flanked by a pretty woman who had stood up as he came in. Casey shook his hand and introduced herself, then Nate stood, and they shook hands. Josh, who has shrunk back into his seat, was not very good at shaking hands

The grown-ups, after exchanging pleasantries, all turned to Josh.

"Welcome," Niles smiled.

Summoning up all his courage, Josh stood and walked over to him and to his horror, the doctor held out a hand.

"You can call me Niles. What should I call you?" Josh had barely lifted an unsure hand before Niles held it, shook it, and let it go.

"I'm Josh" Josh said politely, feeling like such an adult. A real handshake. He hadn't been good at those before.

"Josh it is. Nice to meet you, young man. Tell you what…" Niles turned to Casey and Nate. "Let's get all of you together to begin with and then Josh and I will spend some time alone. Is that OK with you Josh? Your aunt and uncle can have coffee across the road while we talk?"

Unsure of the correct response, Josh just nodded. He was hardly going to disagree, and Nate gave him one of his big smiles showing that it was OK: he was safe and there was no need to worry.

Behind Josh's robotic voice was a desperate desire to please. Niles could see the haunted expression in his eyes, his fingers twitching by his side and that faraway look of a very traumatised child. One had to be careful with these little people. Gently, he held out his hand gesturing for Josh to follow him.

"Come on, friend," Niles smiled warmly. "Are you ready?"

Hesitating for a moment, Josh nodded and followed. He had another new friend. He had been making so many adult friends lately and all of them wore such nice clothes.

○○○

Jason's stomach was empty, which only added to the nausea he was feeling at the prospect of a visit with Mika. Lately their interactions had been civil; cordial, but uncomfortable. He put this down to recent changes and events: the suspicious taking of Will, made even more dubious by being asked to squeal on Marco and the introduction of Sam. He hoped he'd made a good impression and looked forward to catching up that evening. He pondered apologizing for the whole roof deal, but maybe Sam had appreciated the strong case he had made. That they were not normal; that they were indeed invincible. Anyway, it was too late now, it was done. Whether he came on too strong or not, didn't really matter

His hand still hurt like a motherfucker. Yes, it will protect you, but not perfectly. As usual, once the main impact was over, it was gone! Protects you from the *SLAM*, lets you feel the roll. Still, it was fun. He was sure that now, in the light of a new day, Sam would feel the same.

He had analysed himself in the bathroom mirror, naked and so pale. However, with a twinge of excitement he was sure he saw some form of definition in his chest. He toyed with the idea of taking a photo, not that anyone else would see it. But he could have a closer look later.

In the shower, he considered his day's plans. He would go to the Pantheon, then he would go to the gym. His gym bag was in the trunk of his car, ready for action. Mika wouldn't ask what his plans were, he would be looking for input about the previous night and their new acquaintance. He had already rehearsed what he would say. Nice guy, intelligent, possibly a little resistive to their ideology, but he would come around.

Sitting on the edge of his bed, he began pulling on his shoes, glancing at the phone sitting on the bedside table. Mika had called quite early and was only available for a couple of hours. Jason had to haul ass. Grabbing it quickly, it suddenly vibrated once in his hand. A message. He must have missed it with Mika's early call. Flicking the screen to life, he clumsily placed his glasses on and read the message from Luka. He expected it would say: *All done, no problems.*

As his eyes adjusted, he read the message before him. The first word to enter his mind was, No. He felt as if his stomach was in his throat. He forced a huge breath that turned into a scared quiver. No.

LEAVING NOW CRYSTAL DOIN IT SHE SAID DON'T WORRY SHE GOOD AY

Idiot. That fucking, *fucking* idiot.

The drive to the Pantheon seemed to take just minutes. Every green light, every quiet street seemed to convince him that the universe had decided he would not be granted time to think about his response to Mika. Crystal! Why would anyone trust Crystal? You couldn't turn your back on her. Even Mika had alluded to not trusting Crystal. *Fucking idiot.*

There seemed only a few options: firstly, Crystal did what she said she would, and Mika genuinely wants to speak about Sam. Completely unbelievable but a decent scenario. Second possibility, Mika targets him... but he wouldn't. Surely? That would be insane. There were no guarantees that Mika would prevail, after all, and therefore he wouldn't take the gamble. Mika could punish Luka for this. The most probable option, and Jason pondered how he would deal with this. Luka was a Devotee, pretty insignificant as a human being. Technically not a *complete* human. So Luka goes to hell... he would eventually end up there anyway! That was the best outcome. Luka would take the hit. A Devotee is useful, but it wasn't necessary to keep Luka around whilst Crystal and Chel were still hanging onto their humanity. Arguably though, Luka wasn't as far along the path as his peers. That could sway things in his favour. Why waste a good few years of Devotee ability and keep the older two who were circling the drain? Made no sense. But would he argue that? He was unsure.

Car parked, Jason made his way into the building, past the concierge and to the elevator. It was then he remembered, he hadn't received his card back; after all, he wasn't planning this – Luka still had it. Not a good sign.

Chapter 18

This man in nice clothes was very friendly. Josh looked around the office as Niles spoke gently, asking him about his family. On the walls there were pictures and a shiny clock. There was a desk that looked very heavy and expensive. He also made Josh sit in a big chair, so big that he was sure he looked silly on it. Maybe he would've fit better on the chair the adult was sitting on. It looked a bit smaller. This one caused his bum to slip around on the seat. Josh did what he was told. *Gone, did not come back. Don't know where.* Niles seemed to believe him too, which was easy because he didn't ask the same question dozens of times, like the police had.

Niles watched the distant stare in the young boy's eyes. The incongruence between the voice and expression. His language had been scripted. His simple responses were learnt through years of hiding things from other people in a desire to protect his mother, of whom he didn't speak of other than saying she had gone out. He had explained that his grandmother lived "really close", and when his Mum went out he was supposed to stay with her. This was untrue, but due to the ease by which it was said, Niles quickly identified this was not the first time he had said it. Josh's grandmother, and Casey's mother, Rhonda, had passed away 4 years ago from breast cancer.

There was no mention of Ron from Josh, not voluntarily. When goaded by Miles, he explained in the same rehearsed tone, that Ron was his Mum's friend sometimes. The same polite voice with the same 'deer in the headlights' stare. It didn't really matter, anyway - Niles was not here to investigate the circumstances around the disappearance of these people.

There was underlying trauma in this 8-year-old boy that was deeply embedded. Neglect, yes. Physical abuse? Check. Verbal and emotional abuse? Absolutely. All this with a big old dose of trauma. Nightmares and insomnia. Constant hypervigilance, monitoring his surroundings. Every single noise, no matter how small, seemed to grab his attention. His small clock, ticking almost silently upon the desk, kept pulling the boy's attention. The incident of yesterday, as described by his relatives, suggested a full-blown panic attack from a very scared, damaged little person.

"So you feel safe with your aunt and uncle. That's good. We like to feel safe, it's important."

Josh nodded enthusiastically, "yes they're nice. The house is nice, and they give me food."

"What's your favourite food?"

"They make this chicken that tastes so good, it's the best chicken I ever had..."

"Sounds great! So, you feel safe there. Where else do you feel safe? What makes Josh feel safe?"

Josh had never heard himself in the third person before and it confused him. "Who? Me?"

"Yes," Niles smiled, genuinely amused. "You... Josh."

"I like school because my friends are there." Josh shuffled in his seat. His eyes suddenly darted to the side as he slid forward, stopping on the edge of the seat, and looking at Niles.

"What are you thinking about Josh?"

The rasping, deep breaths of the Dog behind him were becoming hard to ignore. It growled as Josh let himself slide back into the seat again. "Nothing."

The signs of trauma were definitely there. However, how far had this gripped him? Hallucinations? Psychosis? Josh appeared to be reacting to something in the room.

"What are you hearing?" Niles said lightly, leaning forward and holding his hands in front of him.

"Nothing."

The distant grinding of metal was in the air, the Dog's growl, deep and threatening. Being asked to pay attention to these sounds made them louder. The man was asking him questions nicely; he really seemed to care. Josh wished with everything he had that he could tell him. He promised he wouldn't, but he wanted to. He told Josh when they came in that he wouldn't tell anybody anything. That with him, in this room, he could tell secrets. But did he really mean it?

Niles watched Josh's pleading eyes and quivering bottom lip. Too much. For now, this was too much. He wouldn't probe any further today. He would never push a child just out of curiosity.

"I said… nothing," the boy whimpered.

"I hear something," Niles gently smiled. "I think I hear your aunt and uncle coming back!"

Pulled from his daydream, it took a moment for Josh to register what Niles had said. He could hear someone had come in, very muffled but yes, they were back. Did that mean his time with the nice man was over?

"Can I go now?" Josh asked.

"Yes you can. We've learnt a lot about each other Josh. We can be friends, yes? Will we talk again?"

This was not what Joshua thought would happen. It was nice having someone to talk to. Especially someone as nice as doctor shrink Niles. Smiling he nodded "Mm hm."

Niles led Joshua out of the surgery with a joke about his fat, old cat. Joshua chuckled, and when Niles asked him if he liked cats, Joshua said yes. Niles asked if he liked dogs, Josh quickly replied "definitely not."

Josh was asked to sit in the waiting room while he spoke to Casey and Nate. He didn't worry. Niles had told him that he would talk with them for a little time afterwards, but that was about "boring grown-up stuff." Josh needn't worry about that. He leant back, his legs swinging under the chair, remembering the nice talk he had had with the man. He couldn't wait to tell Ellie about it. Maybe she could talk to him too. He was very friendly and clever. He had been meeting so many nice people lately.

OOO

As the door of the elevator slid open, Jason was surprised to find no-one there to greet him, considering all the possible precarious circumstances. A sign, perhaps, that this meeting was not going to be as ominous as he had speculated. Stepping into the Pantheon, he turned and looked behind. Gone. The insignia was gone. The plastic grandma vase was gone. The strip was down, but obviously not by Luka. Stepping into the living area, he listened carefully. There were people here. He could hear voices, though there was an unusual tone he didn't expect.

There was hearty banter coming from at least three different people outside on the terrace. Suspiciously, Jason stopped at the large window and peered out. The voices were coming from just around the corner at the north side of the large terrace, which was not visible from the door. Who was it? He could hear Mika. He was sure the woman was Crystal. The other voice he couldn't immediately place.

Taking a deep breath, he opened the door and stepped out. Taking a moment to gather himself he walked slowly on the wet travertine, towards the voices. He could see the corner of the terrace with three large terracotta pots, each containing a large palm that broke up the city skyline. Around the corner was where the company was. That was Mika's undercover entertaining area. He had seen it once before. For a brief moment, he began to relax. The banter he was hearing was light. No need for concern. That was until he moved a little closer and noticed the plastic vase sitting strategically amongst the three pots. The Oubliette was not destroyed.

Hearing a shuffling behind him, Jason spun around to see Luka, seated against the wall behind him. His coat hood covered his head, his knees pulled up before him like a scared child.

"What's going on?" Jason asked sharply, quietly.

Luka didn't speak or look up. He just shook his head quickly, staring at the floor before him. His skin ashen, his eyes dull and lifeless, filled with a profound hopelessness. The Oubliette. The Oubliette was not destroyed. The strip was indeed down but until that vessel was destroyed, Luka would "purify" quickly. He had obviously been told to sit there. Made to feel the darkness engulf him whilst looking at the cheap ass plastic vase metres away. Destined to watch the thing that was destroying him from the inside out. Jason was overcome with regret. Regret caused by guilt? No. Regret that Luka was so fucking stupid that he believed anything that bitch Crystal told him.

"*Luka,*" Jason hissed, "what's going on?"

What was he walking into? The jovial banter continued a few feet from him, around the corner and under the canopy. He had to go. He had to see. Centring himself, he glanced once again at Luka and then walked around the corner.

Mika was standing in conversation with a man who had his back to Jason, meaning he couldn't see his face. The man seemed to be explaining something to Mika, who was responding with his usual intense nod that

Jason had seen so many times before. Upon the soft seating was Crystal, legs crossed elegantly at the ankle, draped in a thick winter coat, holding a long-stemmed glass of wine. She seemed to be watching the conversation with enjoyment.

Feeling foolish and cowardly, Jason stepped forward, revealing himself. Mika saw him and a wide grin spread across his face.

"Ah here he is!" Mika swooned. "Come on over!"

Jason hesitated for a moment before remembering what would be expected of him. He smiled walking towards them, preparing to meet the stranger who turned around. Jason's stomach sank. His eyes widened as the faux smile from his face vanished.

"J.J!" Tyler beamed. "How are you doing mate?"

Jesus Christ, what was he doing here?

"Tyler..." Jason replied, catching his breath, "what..."

"I was just talking to Tyler about your recommendation concerning my wellness program," Mika said, up-beat with a smile, "great timing! I said to Jason- *JJ!* - I'd been considering a wellness program for my employees, you know, a perk of the job sort of situation - and I was looking for someone who knew what they were doing, and Jason said he knew just the guy!" Mika smiled, holding out a hand to Jason, beckoning him closer.

"Hi Jason!" Crystal beamed from her seat, gently swirling the glass in her hand.

Jason knew he was expected to lie. He also knew that how he played this was important not only to him, but to Tyler, who was in more danger in this upper-class penthouse than he had been anywhere else in his entire life.

"I appreciate it Jason, I really do." Tyler smiled, taking a sip from a small coffee mug. "As I said to Michael here."

"Mika."

"*Mika.* I've been looking to get into organisational training for a while now and this sounds amazing."

"Oh, it will be," Mika nodded, stepping back and sitting down next to Crystal, who seemed to delight in his proximity. Tyler sat opposite them. "We've been discussing the intricacies before you arrived. Take a seat."

Tyler was anxious, Jason could tell. But not for the reasons he should have been. Jason glared at Mika, willing him to stop.

"Jason, sit! Sit down for Pete's sake! It's the first few minutes without rain we've had for months. Enjoy the fresh air." There was an element of impatience in Mika's voice.

"So, Tyler," Crystal spoke, and Jason's blood ran cold. Her cold blue eyes smiled at Tyler like he was a new plaything. "Have you been working with Jason long?"

"Oh, about two months now, right Jason?" He looked at Jason for confirmation. Jason just nodded.

"Two months and look at all the good it's done you!" Crystal laughed with false amazement. "I said to him just last week, Jason, are you working out? You look amazing! And he does… you really do Jason."

Jason dropped his gaze to the floor, delivering a bashful nod of fake flattery. He couldn't look at her. He could hear it, the music around him, and feel the anger simmering inside. But this was Mika, and that would be very bad move. A move that, even now, he was unwilling to take. One thing he knew for sure, if it wasn't for Mika sitting there in all his narcissistic glory, he would take Crystal without hesitation. She would get strung up, torn apart, and ravaged again and again. She would dance for him. She would suffer for this. *Fuck her.*

"So, with all these glowing recommendations, I asked Jason… Do you think I could meet this 'Master Trainer', because I trust his opinion!" Mika gestured towards Jason, his smile said one thing, his eyes, full of bitter contempt, said another. "He hasn't done me wrong before. At least that I know of?"

Crystal and Mika began to laugh. Tyler laughed too, placing a hand on Jason's thigh, and squeezing. Friendly, grateful.

He couldn't remain silent. He had to start playing this stupid game. This is what would be expected and, God willing, it might make a difference.

"No, no. As I said, Tyler has been amazing, seriously. I really think you and him would be on the same page."

"Absolutely. We've agreed on that, haven't we Tyler?"

"Certainly" Tyler nodded, finishing the last of his drink. He went to put his empty mug down on the table beside him.

"More?" Mika reached for the jug on the small table before them and Jason's blood ran cold.

Put the mug down… put the mug down. Jason chanted in his head. *No. Don't hold it. If you hold it, you take it with you. He needs you to hold it. One more deletion of evidence you were ever here.*

Tyler hesitated, mug hovering between the table and his lap.

"Ahhh… it's strong," he laughed. "I'll be peeing for hours!"

"Yeah no more, Mika. He's due back at the gym at 2:30," Jason said, trying to hide the fear in his voice.

"Oh come on, enjoy the finer things. This is a pure mixed bean. Second only to Kopi. Come on… a small splash won't hurt." Mika was already filling the mug.

"What time is it now?" Jason sat forward. "You'd better get going yeah?"

Jason glared at Tyler and for a moment, he was sure there was a telling glint in his eyes that something was not quite right. "Yeah, yeah that's right. 2:30 I start."

"Jason. Let Tyler finish his coffee." Mika sat forward also. For a second his eyes met with Jason's. Competitive, cold, and clear. Jason was challenging him.

"Traffic sucks out there today hey. This rain… crazy roadworks. It's like, nearly two now," Jason stood, hoping for Tyler to follow. "And I don't want you running off to piss through our entire hour at three!"

"Why the rush Jason? It's seriously two blocks away." Crystal swooned. "Tyler rode here, anyway, don't you own a car Tyler?"

A little surprised by the direct question, Tyler shrugged. "I used to. Don't really need one here though. Got my bike, got my rain suit, all set." To Jason's relief, Tyler stood. "I really should go. But how about we meet Friday? I'll send you the proposal tonight and give you a chance to look over it."

"Yes, that would be great, thank you."

Mika and Jason continued glaring at each other, each waiting for the other to make their play. Would Mika light Tyler now? In the presence of Jason, knowing that Jason would very well be hit by it, and then what? Suddenly, Mika's gaze dropped to the floor.

Crystal smiled and walked past Jason, who eyed Mika with caution. Mika stood and extended a hand to Tyler who shook it with genuine appreciation.

"This means a lot to me mate. Thank you for the opportunity" he smiled.

"And thank you for giving me your time," Mika charmed back. "Oh! Don't forget your phone!"

Tyler smiled, picking up his phone that had fallen onto the seat beside him. Jason hurriedly turned to lead him away. He had to get him out of there. For a moment he remembered Luka and feared, once they turned the corner, that Tyler would see the weakened fool and engage further. But no, Tyler had to leave. He wouldn't overthink it. They just had to leave. He didn't know what he would say but he would say anything to get Tyler out of there. Turning the corner, he saw Luka. *Fuck.* He could hear Tyler behind him, and a range of stupid excuses came to mind for his presence. He turned, opened his mouth to speak and stopped dead in his tracks when faced with Crystal. Tyler, where was Tyler?

Seeing Jason's face drop, his mouth open in a silent miserable gasp, she leant forward and mocked, "You do look amazing. Seriously."

Pushing past her, Jason scuffled back around the corner where Mika stood, staring into nothingness. His eyes vacant, his breathing slow and rhythmic. Tyler was gone.

"Oh fuck…" Jason felt dizzy and ill. What had he done? "Oh fuck no… Mika no."

It was too late. Finding his footing, steadying himself he approached his fellow Ace, staring at his blank, empty eyes.

"What Jason? What? You're not going to light him?" Crystal remarked snidely.

The conflict raged within him. He could get involved. He could light them both, but then what? That wouldn't help Tyler, it would make a smorgasbord of him. He was gone. He hung his head in his hands.

A small cry of frustration pushed past his lips, delighting Crystal even further. "He's all gone now… *J.J.*"

Bitch, the absolute bitch. Jason reared up, turning to face her. This was it, he would finish her now. What could Mika do? No… Mika can take at will… so would he. *Congratulations bitch, you just made it to the top of the list.*

Crystal reached up, slapping a white piece of fabric down on the pot before the Oubliette as Jason's stomach cramped and turned, forcing him to his knees. Luka cried out painfully, pulling his knees further to his chest.

"No, no, no," she whispered, squatting down in front of him. "Not today Tiny. Not today."

"Why?" Jason lifted his head, his stomach twisting. "Why did you do that?"

Crystal placed a soothing hand on Jason's shoulder, "why? Jason, why? My god… Why would I *not*?"

It was hopeless. He was stripped and vulnerable. The Oubliette in play once more, Luka's vessel, Crystal's key. This had been planned, there was no way Tyler was leaving this building. Jason had been bought here to watch and his reaction had been prepared for.

"Control yourself," Mika said, turning the corner. Of course, he wouldn't approach yet. The strip was live. He would be vulnerable too. "Settle yourself down right now or I will take someone else. And trust me… it will be someone you will miss."

Jason steadied himself and glanced at Luka cowering, semiconscious, against the wall. He needed him. Without him, Jason was alone.

Mika gestured to Luka, shaking his head sadly, "make your choice my friend. You know he doesn't have much longer anyway. How do you want him to go out?"

"I did what you asked me to do," Jason replied, breathing deeply. "Exactly what you asked."

A few moments of silence passed, Mika watched Jason closely before looking at Crystal, giving her a nod of approval. Crystal smiled at him, reaching beside her, and picking up the small, white parchment. Then, adjusting her short skirt, she picked up the plastic vase and held it in front of her.

Crystal's eyes rolled over white as Luka screamed, throwing his head into the wall behind him. In Crystal's hands the vase and parchment suddenly disintegrated to ashes, falling from her fingers. Luka was released, but would he recover? How much of him would come back? Jason didn't know.

Jason stood, legs trembling and weak and his stomach still in his throat. He opened his hands, gently bringing air in and out of his lungs. Mika expected calm. Jason would give him calm… for now. He was not the "loose cannon" Mika thought he was. He would contain this, swallow the anger. He had more control than Mika ever gave him credit for. He would act grateful for the intervention. He looked at Mika, nodding understandingly. Fill that prick's mind with grandeur and the sense of control he so needed. Make him believe he was still the mentor and Jason the student. For now.

"You see what happens when you put us all at risk?" Mika spoke calmly, before hurtling Tyler's empty coffee mug off the balcony into the night sky. "It hurts everyone. It causes so much damage when one of us drops the bundle and forgets who we are. You brought a stranger into the Pantheon.

214

You exposed the very epicentre of our knowledge. You stripped our strength. But that man Tyler? Who, by the way, screamed like a little child, showed you are failing to appreciate the gift that has been given to you and that makes me very sad. Very disappointed. So now that man is gone. The gym is gone. We must talk, come with me."

Like a scolded child, Jason was led by Mika to the patio door. He glimpsed Luka looking dazed and confused, rubbing his face, and attempting to sit up. Idiot. Complete idiot.

Crystal remained a moment longer whilst the two Aces entered the Pantheon. She gazed at the city skyline against a sky of grey and dark blue. Looking down at her hands, she clapped them together, dusting off the ash of the Oubliette with disgust. Luka heard her walk towards him, the unmistakable sound of those stiletto heeled shoes. With what little strength he had left, he looked up and scowled at her.

"That, Cocky Rocky, was a master class in *trust.*' Crystal sneered, her face ugly and cruel. Luka looked away. He couldn't bare the coldness of her eyes. With a throaty laugh and a satisfied shrug, she turned and walked through the door. Behind her, the rain began to fall.

ᴏᴏᴏ

Tiredness from talking to the nice man with the comfy chair for an hour did not stifle Josh's excitement. He was going back to school! His aunt had mentioned next year he might change schools, but he chose not to think about that. He just imagined the wonderful comfort that normality would give him. His desk, his friends, his bench under the tree and the new lunchbox Nate had brought him from the shop – shiny blue plastic with a matching sports bottle, so much like the other kids- amazing. It would even match the new bag that he was allowed to choose himself. Not too bright, not too babyish. No superheroes. He was nearly 9 after all.

To Casey and Nate's surprise, as soon as they arrived home he gathered his new belongings that had been placed on the kitchen bench, and clumsily carried them off to his bedroom. Happily, he placed them on his bed. He would look at them some more and then put them somewhere safe. Casey came to his door and asked if he needed help.

"No, thank you," answered Josh as he continued to explain where he would keep all the things so they wouldn't get lost. Under his bed. Because then he could check where they were.

Casey assured him that the chances of them getting lost in the house was very low and perhaps, he could put them in the normal places that items such as these were kept. Like his bag could be kept beside Nate's gym gear, near the shoe rack? The lunchbox could be put in the kitchen pantry? No?

Casey quickly noticed the idea of letting them out of his sight bought anxiety. He began to bargain. Friday till Monday he would keep his new bag there perhaps? Smiling, she relented. If it made him feel better having his belongings close by, she would approach the situation again another time. She turned and walked from the door, feeling sad and troubled as Josh cheerily took his new items and began sliding them under his bed. Safe, she knew. He wanted to feel that he and his things were safe.

He stretched as far as he could, pushing the bag and the lunch box to the far end near the wall. Only his feet now poked out from under the bed as he hid his bounty. Satisfied that he could push them no further, he looked to the side and saw the black wire leading from the wall socket to his little phone. He listened carefully for a moment; quiet. No-one was there. He pulled out his phone, bumping his head on the wooden slats above him.

I WENT TO A SRINK AND I SAID NUFFIN TOO MUCH I GOT A NEW BAG AND I WILL GO TO SCHOOL TOMORROW WILL U B THERE

Chapter 19

"Please. Please help me" Luka had said before the line went dead.

Chelamah descended the rain drenched steps to the park opposite the building she hated so much. A phone call from Luka? Insane. They had not spoken for two years so why would he call her now? Why was he here? What the hell was going on?

Stopping on the middle step she scanned the large park for any sign of movement. "Luka!" she called impatiently, continuing down. "Luka!"

There was the slightest bit of concern. This was one of Chelamah's weaknesses. She had begun to hate the humanity still left in her, that reasonless concern for others. It had led her into bad situations. Noah didn't know she was here, and he wouldn't approve. Not that she would ever have requested his approval, but tonight she was even less willing to explain her movements or argue. Anger had started to engulf her. It drove her and filled her with confidence.

"Luka!" she shouted again. Nothing.

Reaching the bottom of the stairs, she hurried onto the path that wound around the park. He had sounded scared. He'd be hiding, but too weak to get further away from the place where obviously, something bad had happened.

Walking towards the tree line, with the park on one side and trees on the other, she continued to call.

"Fuck off!" A deep voice called from the dark of the trees.

"You fuck off!" she shouted into the dark. "Luka!"

"Hey, screw you lady!"

"Oh shut up!" Chelamah walked away from the trees. Nature's little homeless shelter in this counterfeit of pretty greenery smack in the middle of the dankest city on Earth. She stood still listening to the songs floating around her. She could find him easily, but she was so close to her end that that would be foolish. Finding him like a normal person was the best option.

The sunken park rose again at the far end into what? If she remembered correctly, it was a sports field. She could see the ascending stairs. Would he be there? Possibly. He had said the park, which was annoyingly vague, but could include these grounds.

Ascending another long staircase, she stopped at the top and looked about. She had been here only once, and that was during the day. At night, it was a lot more ominous. A large oval surrounded by more large, dark trees that hid the bustling city street behind. Clumps of bushes. Perfect.

She could feel him. God how she hated that. Devotee to Devotee. Another shadow was here. It was a warm feeling, an inexplicable sensation of kinship. She had hated Luka and avoided him, so much that she had forgotten how the presence of him, or indeed that bitch Crystal, made her feel. Her gaze was drawn to three large cricket nets over on her right. She didn't have to wonder: he was there. Jesus, how she hated knowing that.

Confidently she strode off the path and onto the grass, steadying her pace as her small heels stuck in the wet earth.

"Luka?" she called.

She heard a response, a barely audible call from within the black net. Fearlessly she walked in. There she saw a crouched silhouette, slumped against the back of the net. As she approached, he rose to meet her. Luka gripped his head and stumbled, nearly falling forward.

"Chel... Chel please," a soft voice pleaded, "please help me get home."

"What happened?" she asked, consciously smoothing her voice. "Why did you call me?"

"I didn't know who else to call."

"Jason perhaps?"

"No. I can't."

"Friends? Family? Anyone else but me?"

Luka stepped forward, the sparse light bounced off his pale skin. His wet, tear-streaked face was illuminated gently in the dim glow. "No-one else. I can't let them know of anyone else." Luka coughed one, deep sob. "No-one I know. No-one I like. No-one I care for."

Chelamah frowned. "Jeez Luka, thanks."

Intriguing, thought Chelamah, that Jason and Luka had been responsible for such sociopathic wickedness in the past and yet here he was, trying to protect the people he cared about. How unbelievably selfish of him.

"No you're cool! You're cool! It's OK."

"I don't care. Look, where's Jason?"

"He's still there, with them," Luka pointed to the building beyond the gardens. "I had to go."

Chelamah gasped "The Pantheon? He's in the Pantheon with Mika.... and *Crystal*! And you bring me here?"

"I just need help. I can't see... I can't think prop- "

"You know that she knows I'm here, now?" Chelamah spun around stepping out of the net. "Why did you drag me into this? You guys love this nonsense. I don't! Now, whatever bullshit you stirred up with them can so easily become my bullshit. I already have so much bullshit going on Luka."

Luka fell forward, hitting the cricket mat with a thud.

"Jesus," Chelamah rubbed her head. She couldn't just leave him.

Luka pushed himself to his knees. For a horrifying moment, Chelamah thought he might beg.

"They left me there, Chel. They made me stay there for so long. I came back but... I didn't come back. It's still in my head, in my eyes, in my ears. I can feel that place on my skin... you know the way that place feels? I feel it on my skin... it hasn't gone." He began to sob. "I want to come back. I can't wake up from it... it's stuck. I'm stuck."

Taking a deep breath, she looked down at the pathetic young man with regretful understanding. He was where she was a week ago. He would never truly come back and that commonality, that kinship, she hated. "Get up." she said, sighing heavily.

"I can't fucking see..."

"I'm not carrying you. Get up... now!" she ordered. This is what he needed. Direction, a pull back to their reality.

Luka nodded, his breath quivering as he stood. Chelamah walked towards him, stopping with her face inches from his. She could smell his body odour and his stale breath. He blinked at her through tears.

Quickly, without warning, she slapped him hard. He reeled backwards as her hand connected with his face. She raised her other hand, slapping him again.

"Fuck!" he screamed, grabbing his throbbing face.

"Feel it!" Chelamah ordered. "Feel it! It leads you back... feel it Luka. Follow the pain... follow it back. Look at me, *me*. Get angry with me. I am your danger now. I am standing where you want to be. See the danger... follow it."

The shock on Luka's face dissipated. Slowly he rubbed his face looking at Chelamah. A quiet understanding moved between them.

"Now. I'm *not* going to carry you. But we have to leave."

"And Jason?"

"I don't care about Jason! And Jason doesn't give a shit about you. Follow me. We have to get out of here right now before Crystal gets bored. Move." Reaching out her hand, Luka took it.

She would take him home. In a few days, if he was lucky, a portion of his torment would subside. Subside, but only for a time. After each return the scars grew deeper. The damage that remained increased. Remitting and relapsing, over and over again until there would be nothing left.

ooo

Even the cold outside could not stifle the excitement Joshua felt as he trotted through the house, hairbrush in one hand, socks in the other. This morning he was going back to school and his stomach was full of nervous, happy butterflies. Standing on tiptoe at the bathroom mirror, he parted his hair with precision. Fearful that the tuft at the back may, God forbid, stick up like a rooster and ruin the clean look of his new uniform, he brushed. Pushing the offending hair spike down into his crown, he held it firm for two seconds before releasing it. He watched as it popped back up again. More water, more stubborn pushing and then it stayed.

"Don't forget your bag!" Nate called from the kitchen. "I need it here! Got food, but no home for it!"

"OK," Josh called back happily, catching Nate by surprise.

There was a lightness in the kid he hadn't seen before. He couldn't help but smile at the misery he had felt at Josh's age of being told it was school time. Yet this kid acted like he was off to Disneyland. Normality perhaps, routine. It had been chaotic. Maybe the kid needed a dose of 'ordinary'. Whatever that meant.

He could hear Josh talking to himself as he rummaged around the bedroom. It was like he was telling himself off.

"No. No, you stay here" and "So stupid sometimes."

The Monster Dog stood upon his bed, saliva dripping from its jaws as its white eyes glaring excitedly at Josh.

"Uh uh. You're not coming. You just do dumb stuff all day and I don't want you there, because you ruin things."

Josh turned to see Nate standing in the doorway with a smile of confused curiosity. "Who are you talking to?"

Josh froze, jumper in his hand, one sock on and simply smiled. "No-one."

Nate nodded slowly, "OK my favourite little weirdo, grab your stuff it's time to go."

Swinging his bag up, Josh ran to the door holding it open as Nate put the lunchbox inside. "Is Aunt Casey coming?" he asked.

Nate scoffed lightly. "No, you got lucky. Aunt Casey really wanted to, but she's got to see someone today."

"Why's that lucky?" Josh asked innocently,

"She's a terrible driver." Nate put his finger to his lips. "Now come on. If you want us to have time to stop for that iced chocolate drink you like so much, we have to be leaving now. Bring your stuff out. I'll open the car."

Josh watched Nate leave. Lunch was heavier than he remembered. Turning to the door, he stopped as the Dog stood before him.

"What now?" Josh sighed in frustration. "Stop being stupid. You know you're just going to come there anyway so why are you being an idiot all the time."

The Dog quickly sniffed the air and then lowered its muzzle, menacingly. Its excitement, its agitation, even though confusing, couldn't damper Josh's mood. Not today. "Just stop. You're going to come but you're not going to hurt anyone. Not today."

Car running, Nate stood by the front door listening to the strange conversation inside. Kids have imaginary friends. His limited experience of kids, however, told him but Josh didn't seem to talk to it like a friend.

Unaware he was being listened to Josh continued staring down the huge monster.

"I'll just walk right through you anyway. You're just a stupid shadow like Ellie said. A stupid shadow that has to move." His bag slipped off his shoulder. Frustrated, he pulled it back up.

"Josh! Everything alright there?" Nate's voice called from the door as slowly, he entered and began walking quietly up the hall.

"Yes I'm coming," Josh called politely, turning back to his monster "Move." The Dog and Josh glared at each other. Josh simply had to walk through it. It would move. As big and scary as it was, it would move. However today Josh didn't want it to move simply because he approached, as it had before. He wanted it to move because he told it to. It wanted to make him look stupid. It wanted to make Nate think he was being bad by not coming outside. But Josh was in a good mood. He was going to school, and he had all his new things. He was getting chocolate milk. The Dog would move because he told it to. Fuelled by pleasant thoughts, Josh was not going to let it win today.

"Move out of the way," Josh goaded quietly.

A deep guttural rumbling emanated from the Dog's curling gums. It widened its stance, head lowered to the level of the small boy who challenged it.

"Move out of the way!" Josh yelled as he stepped forward.

Jolted by Josh's sudden shout, Nate was just about to turn into the bedroom when a terrifying, ungodly noise erupted about him. A roaring, visceral howl exploded as the door before him slammed shut with such force that the wood splintered and the frame shook. This was followed by a tremendous thump that dislodged the handle sending its spinning across the floor in front of him. Jumping back in shock, Nate called out to Josh before racing forward and slamming himself into the fractured door.

The door swung to the side as Nate, gasping, came face to face with Josh who stood quietly in the middle of the room with his bag over his shoulder looking back at him amongst the scattered debris of the drawers and his bedside table. He smiled. Nate looked about in disbelief. "Are you OK?"

Josh nodded eagerly, he didn't want Nate to worry "Yes, I'm OK."

"What...?" Nate stammered. "What happened?"

"I don't know. Something went bang and then everything fell off everywhere."

Nate nodded; Josh's face remained unchanged. He even looked... happy? He was as chipper as he was before the room had exploded. Nate couldn't understand.

Josh trotted out of the room and down the hall, leaving Nate to continue staring in wonder at the chaos before him.

"I'm going to the car now!" Josh called. He opened the car door and shoved his bag in before climbing into the seat, smiling to himself. The Dog moved. He did explode the bedroom, but at least he moved! The Dog had never done that to anything before. The last time that happened, was the first night the Dog found him in his room. That time it threw the bed across the room! Or at least he thought it has… Josh couldn't remember properly, but the Dog had not done anything like that since. He must've been really mad that Josh was being tough on him. Looking out the window he thought Nate needs to hurry up or they wouldn't have time to stop for chocolate milk.

OOO

As the gentleman took his seat, Niles settled back and hoped his anxiety wasn't obvious. Mika looked taller than he had the first time they met, dressed a little more formally in a dark leather trench coat with a tartan scarf wrapped around his neck. Very fashionable. Mika smiled, settling back and loosely crossing his legs. Niles immediately recognised the same demeanour of pre-eminence radiate from Mika that he had brought with him two weeks previously. This man would be unshakable in any situation.

"How have you been?" Niles began.

Mika nodded slowly before giving a reflective sigh, "I have been well doctor. And yourself?"

"Well also, thank you. Busy, but keeping out of trouble."

"Oh dear, that doesn't sound like much fun. Wedding plans all falling into place?" Mika smiled gently, goading an answer, forcing Niles to continue.

"Yes" Niles beamed. "All ready to go, not long now."

"No, it wouldn't be," Mika nodded. "You're a brave man. And your lovely fiancée? How is she?"

"Very well, thank you. Hopefully enjoying the short reprieve now that the logistics are finished with. It's her 'hens' night this weekend." Niles shook his pen tellingly in front of him.

Mika laughed. "My goodness, they still have them? And you? Do you get your… last hoorah?"

The play was the same. Mika was governing the session. He had taken control of the greeting after slowly lowering himself into the chair. He had ensured that the conversation quickly focused on Niles. He demonstrated his dominance by prompting a response and then forcing elaboration. Although a player in this otherwise extremely inappropriate therapy session, Niles was willing to allow it to continue. Curiosity, perhaps delving into a case study in sociopathy. Maybe let this go, filtered, and guarded of course but, would this bring more of Mika's intentions to the surface? Would it, either on purpose or by omission, expose more about *him*self? Niles feared Mika was too smart for that, but he would try. He also felt this pleasant play bought Mika some satisfaction. This could be what made Mika eventually open up.

"That is why your finger is bare," Mika observed. "I imagine your fiancée has an engagement ring. You don't. Men often don't, being granted just a bit more freedom before we end our lives, than they are. Her freedom ended with your proposal and the revealing of an expensive dowry in the form of a ring and… your freedom ends at the 'I do."

Niles cast a confused eye. "I have never thought about it like that."

"No?" Mika said, flippantly. "But she has. She will be a lot more concerned about your big night out than you are about hers."

His fiancée had indeed been questioning him about his upcoming stag night. She had read his guest list and made a few gentle remarks regarding the attendees. Mika's logic was sound, whether being amiable, charismatic, or inimical. Following Mika down any one of these interweaving paths would all lead to the same place. A concrete conclusion that he would deliver like it was obvious. One that you would have no choice but to agree with when he delivered it.

"No-one likes an imbalance of power, doctor. Women like to feel secure. We all do. A ring makes them feel safe. Branded. Life will no longer be unpredictable, terrifying, or exciting in any way. Never extraordinary again. Not much will happen to her, nor shall be expected from her, again. She shall be Mrs. Dr. Niles Gardiner. Safe. Labelled. Done."

Flabbergasted, Niles gave a slight bemused nod. The raw sting of an insult was creeping up in his throat, but he had to rethink the retort.

"If you say so Mika," he nodded while delivering a patronising smile. "Now let's talk about you. How have you been since our last session?"

Mika tightened his lips. "Hmm. I have been frustrated to tell you the truth Dr. Gardiner."

"OK" Niles replied. "Talk me through what's been happening."

Mika took in a long, drawn-out breath. Shuffling slightly in his seat he said "People. Just… people."

"Are we talking about a particular person, or people in general?"

"I would say both! I am feeling stuck in tedium. Trapped in mediocrity. Each conversation. Each interaction. Every life event I find myself either involved in or witnessing. All unrewarding and incapable of reaching my expectations. Funny though, some of that is my own doing. I know I have rather high expectations for something to be considered as 'significant' enough to keep me entertained." Mika lifted his hand, examining his finger-nails.

Niles nodded. Mika's arrogance was palpable. "So people bore you?"

"In certain manifestations yes. Most people do bore me. That is probably why I endeavour to make them more interesting. *Exceptional*. I do enjoy pushing people's limits."

"And your friend?" Niles feigned reading his notes. "Will? Did he bore you?"

Mika's eyes grew wide and intense. "No. He fascinated me. Absolutely intrigued me. Intelligent. Funny. And dare I say, kind? Yet, completely banal."

Niles was confused. "Yet in this relationship with this commonplace person, you found some value. Why do you think that is?"

"Commonplace? Oh no. No, no. Will was not commonplace, doctor. I also discovered that he contained traits that I even admired."

"Such as?" Niles prompted.

"Calculating. Manipulative. Deceptive."

"And these traits you find admirable?

Mika nodded enthusiastically. "More so I found them relatable. I understood them. It gave me a newfound respect for the man, but sadly I wondered how, given his innate prestige, he stayed within the status quo. To stay so, well, so… normal. But then the joke was on me because he wasn't normal at all. It was part of his play, part of a scheme. Looking for something I wanted and coming so close to it, and I had no idea. I admired that. You see, from some of my acquaintances I always expect the unexpected. Will, however, no. He hid so much so well and all in the guise of being unimpressive. I didn't have the chance to tell him this. I wanted to. But I ran out of time."

Niles counted his breaths, calming himself and pondering a response. "It helps, Mika, if these sessions are focused."

Mika didn't blink. He stared straight at Niles, his voice deadly certain. "Oh, they are focused, doctor. Believe me, these sessions are very, very focused."

Frustrated, Niles sighed and shook his head. "And as we discussed before, being adversarial is going to make it very difficult for me to help you."

"Am I being adversarial?" Mika looked puzzled. "To do that I would have to consider you a worthy adversary. The fact that I am entertaining this interaction, does not mean I accept you, in any way, as comparable."

Mika was a true narcissist. "I strongly believe that you know you are," Niles added quickly. "And I'm not playing this game. So why don't you tell me why you are here?"

"For therapy," Mika shrugged, feigning surprise.

"Tell me, how do I fit into that calculated and manipulating game that you admire so much? Tell me why you are here." It surprised Niles how quickly he had reached the end of his patience. This was a waste of time. Mika was here for a reason and Niles had called him out.

The room grew cold as Mika spoke slowly, staring at Niles with a deep contempt that instantly made him feel uneasy. "I want to know what Will *Mason* and you were talking about. Believe me doctor, this right here is the easy way."

The endgame emerged. Nile felt both panic and curiosity flood through him. This psychopath knew Will. This psychopath also knew what happened that night. Will was not dead. Had Mika just threatened him? How that threat would play out he didn't know, but against his better judgement, he pushed Mika further.

"What happened to him?" Niles heard himself asking before he had the chance to stop himself. "Where is he?"

"Tell me about the name…" Mika took in a big breath as an act of reverence "…Bael."

That name again. Images of Ellie Jameson flashed through his mind. Bael. Will's session, the eluded to a threat, Bael. What was this thing? What did it have to do with these people? Cult behaviours perhaps, a group psychosis of some sort. Whatever it was took second place right now. This man knew where Will was. "What do you know about Will Mason?"

Mika ignored the question. "Bael, Dr. Gardiner. I have a feeling you have heard that name before. Tell me where and from whom."

"Tell me where Will Mason is," Niles demanded, placing his hand on the phone beside him. Mika noticed this and gave a small smile.

The two men stared at each other across the airless room.

"I have to inform you that I have concerns about the safety of Will Mason, and therefore I will be informing the police about this conversation."

"Oh, but so do I!" Mika exclaimed mockingly. "He is my *friend* doctor. That is why I've been asking. I am looking for him as well. I am traumatised and distressed about my missing *friend*. He had spoken about you, and I thought, I may as well try to find something out that could help me find him. Ensure that he is well. It may have been under false pretences, I understand that, but given the circumstance, and the depth of concern... *as a friend...* I made a silly decision. I'm so sorry."

Niles kept still. This man was a complete psychopath. He would not play these games. It was entertaining Mika far too much.

"I am asking you to leave now Mika."

"Tell me about Bael Dr. Gardiner."

"I'm sorry, you will have to leave now, or I will call the police and have you removed."

"You initiate that process, Niles, and I become the endgame. Tell me now." Mika leaned forward, glaring at Niles.

A strange fear gripped him. He was being threatened. There were so many unknown motives that could have brought Mika here. But it was the way Mika's eyes suddenly looked black and sinister that disturbed him the most.

"Get out" Niles demanded pointing to the door, returning Mika's glare.

Mika sat back and sighed before rising to his feet. "So, it's the hard way then?"

Niles walked to the desk, under which was the duress button that would alert his staff to call security.

"Please leave Mr. Hexum. Our time together is over."

Mika pulled a disappointed face and casually walked to the door. "I'm sorry that it has come to this doctor. I really didn't want to be rude. I have had a challenging, frustrating week. And for that, I apologise." He opened the door. "But you will tell us, sooner or later. You will be begging to tell us. You can't win this, and that is not a threat. That is a fact. You know how to contact me. You will most certainly be contacting me. Good day to you Niles."

With that he left, calmly closing the door behind him. Niles sat down heavily on his chair, breathing hard. Us? Who is *Us*? His mind raced. Call the police? Of course, that was a given. If this guy knew something, the police had to be told. But also, he was now concerned for his own safety. Was it a genuine threat? Mika had said 'us'. Others were involved. He would not ponder that too much, the police he was sure, would advise him of the correct measures to follow.

"Could you please contact the police for me?" he asked his receptionist before hanging up and staring at the empty seat where Mika had sat.

In two days, he would be faced with a challenge. Ellie was due. She would come with her worksheets and her pleasant yet distant demeanour. Bael. She knew what this concept was. She knew its meaning. How the hell, given everything that had occurred with Will and since, was he going to successfully resist the urge to ask her. He had two days to think on this, to strategize. It had to be ethical, relevant, and not pointed. He would have to take her back to her past and not let it finish until she said the name 'Bael.'

Chapter 20

Sitting at his computer, Jason found himself listlessly staring at the screen in front of him. He glanced to the right, breaking the trance to look at the dreariness outside. The heavy dark sky and wet streets, full of ridiculous and pointless people. It seemed unfair that someone like him should be amongst people like this. Like the homeless man he could see through the rain-streaked glass, a cardboard sign held in his hands, asking for money. Every day he would sit on a milk crate, the lights would turn red and then off he'd go, parading in his own little march of patheticness. It made Jason sick.

He sat alone in the office room, a space he had rented for his own graphic design business. Perfect occupation. Alone, rarely ever meeting actual people. He was a lot friendlier in emails than in person. It worked out great. There was no gym this morning: he simply couldn't face it. Tyler wouldn't be there. Tyler would never be anywhere again. Try as he might, he found it hard accepting that the previous day's events were not his fault. Did he care about Tyler? In reality, no. Did he think Tyler deserved what happened? No. There was however, a very strong disconnect between the feeling of injustice and the ownership of guilt.

Three people were responsible for Mika's over-the-top display of power last night. Crystal, Mika, and Luka. The last one being the most disappointing of all. He knew what Mika was, of course he was capable of doing what he did. He knew what Crystal was, as did they all. But even though he knew Luka was no rocket scientist, he could still, in the light of this new day, not believe how fucking stupid he had been. This made Jason's dependence on his abilities as a Devotee sting. How he hated having to need anything from such a thoughtless fuckhead.

Looking out of the window, he noticed a man standing on the curb looking up at him. Luka. He knew it was him. That short, stocky stature, that long grey hooded jacket with the stupidly short scarf. Any doubt was re-moved when Luka lifted a hand and waved quickly, before placing it back in his pocket. Ignoring his calls for the last 4 hours had obviously made him a little desperate. But Jason was not in the mood. Leaning forward, he pulled the cord and the blinds quickly rolled down.

ooo

Sam arrived back at his apartment. It had felt like years since he had been home. He opened the door, pleasantly surprised that his key still worked. He noticed the lack of shine on the floor, on the counter and on his TV. Everything felt cold, dull, and deserted. The last time he had walked out of this place, his mind had not been good. Suddenly the memories of his des-pair hit him. God he was so sad and hopeless the day he left that door to walk by the river. What had changed? He didn't know but found it curious that now he felt hopeful. Maybe having a focus, having a vocation, had brought relief.

Holding a stash of envelopes in his hand, he flippantly cast them onto the hall stand as he passed. He had collected them on his way up and noticed they were all marked 'URGENT'. They would not be good news. Good news was never marked "URGENT". It was no surprise. He had no job. He had no money, and these envelopes were the material manifestations of everything he had been ignoring.

Being home now meant he could at least shower and change his clothes. Clothes and belongings that a small voice in his mind told him he really should take with him. It was likely the next time he came home, the locks would be changed.

He walked into the living room and looked at the blanket on the floor. Fuck that was a sad time.

"It's a big place" Ellie observed as she walked in, startling him.

"Jesus, how did you get up here?"

"I followed someone in. It's cold outside and your phone isn't working" she said.

Confused, Sam pulled his phone from his pocket. Shit. That would ex-plain one of his 'URGENT' pieces of mail at least. He wondered what else had, or was about to, stop working.

"Yeah," Sam sighed embarrassed, nodding his head towards the pile of enveloped misery on the side table. "That's about to start happening a lot."

Ellie felt bad for Sam. She had been curious, over the last few weeks, why home hadn't been an option for him. There was of course the Child which did keep its distance from Ellie but of course, he would be losing everything. If memory served, he had been fired just before they met. Or at least she was sure she had picked that out of one of his many rantings as he lay on her couch over the last two months.

"It's not fair is it?" Ellie said.

"I worked hard for all this, hey. I worked hard" Sam replied, running a finger along the screen of his TV and inspecting the dust. "I was so close. Nearly 'normal'. I don't know what will happen. I guess I just leave everything here. They, whoever they are, can just come and pick what they want. Sell it."

Ellie frowned and shook her head. "I don't think it's that easy."

Scoffing, Sam turned to his bedroom. "It's gonna have to be. I've got no money. I've got no job." He couldn't hide behind humour on this one. Resigned, he changed the topic. "What time are you going to school?"

"One. What are you doing?" she asked, hearing the rummaging coming from the bedroom. Sam emerged carrying what looked like a large, black case.

"Getting my stuff together. So you will see Josh? I hope he's OK, at least if he's at school, that's a good sign, right?"

"Yes. Sam what are you doing with your stuff?" Ellie watched as items of clothing began being tossed out of the bedroom and into the open case outside the door.

"Can you please grab... uhhhh... the headphones on the unit under the TV? I use them a lot."

Confused, Ellie walked across the room and picked the small case up before putting them in her pocket. She was still confused. What was he doing? Where was he going to go?

"I need ID, passport, birth certificate and laptop. How's the internet at your place?" he called. Ellie's blood froze.

Jesus Christ no.

"Why?" Ellie asked, dreading the reply.

"I got this modem thing I use, it's in the kitchen. If your signal isn't good we can just use that."

231

It seemed Sam assumed he was Ellie's new housemate. How on earth did he get that impression? She could not live with someone, and Sam was definitely not an easy person to be around.

"You're coming to mine?' she gasped. "Sam, you can't stay at mine."

"Why not? I've been there for weeks anyway!" he said, spoken like a true sales pitch before noticing the seriousness on Ellie's face. No. Ellie couldn't face it. She needed her space, her sanctuary, her couch! It was a one-bedroom apartment. What was he thinking? With everything going on, how could he possibly be serious?

"That's not a good idea. I can't. I simply… can't." Ellie hesitated, looking uncomfortably at Sam, deflated, as he rounded the corner.

"Oh" he said awkwardly. "I'm sorry. I just thought that…"

Ellie and Sam descended into quiet awkwardness. Sam nodded, tapping the door frame before heading back into the bedroom. He continued loading clothes into his case, less enthusiastically than before. Ellie was awash with guilt. This was not his fault. She also knew herself. It had been so hard since meeting him and Josh. A lifetime of isolation suddenly gone. She had spoken more in the last three months than she had in the last five years.

"Can I at least… stay till I find somewhere? I would sleep in my car but I'm not sure how much longer I'll have that either." Sam asked quietly, the chipper tone was gone.

Ellie nodded. "Go shower. Change. We'll talk when you come out."

Disappointed but grateful, Sam vanished into the bathroom and the door closed. Ellie watched the door for a moment. She couldn't let this happen to him. He deserved more, and he had always been there for her. She knew this. Slowly, making sure that the shower was still running she picked up the pile of envelopes from the hall table and carried them to the dining table and sat down. Bringing out her phone, she started opening one final demand after another. The least she could do was relieve this burden for him. Clear his life. At least give him rest and security. And, in the process… get her couch back.

ᏆᎧᎧ

Jason headed out the door, his stomach in knots. He needed to eat. His hands had stopped shaking for the moment. He wondered if that was because he was calmer or out of sheer weariness. Making his way down the

232

staircase, he stopped and let out a sigh. Luka had given up, leaving shortly after he had pulled the blind on him. He couldn't face him now. Making his way down the stairs, he turned into the long utility hallway that led to the back exit of the building.

Pushing the bar, he swung open the door and stepped outside into the cold. Tomorrow night he will meet Sam again. This made him happier than he had hoped. He needed validation in his beliefs. He needed Sam to qualify the strength they both shared. Perhaps, in hindsight, sending them both into a 20-storey fall was not the best approach, but it's what Mika would have done to prove a point. In fact, there was very little Mika would not do to prove a point.

With that unsettling thought, Jason became aware of someone approaching quickly from behind. He spun around to look into the faded hazel eyes of Luka. Skin ashen and dull, his face had sunk, aged ten years in one night.

"What do you want?" Jason sneered coldly, turning his back, and continuing forward.

"You didn't return my calls," Luka whined, trotting behind him. Luka's ignorance to what he caused yesterday was infuriating. As pitiful as he looked, as completely horrific as he more than likely felt, he deserved this.

"Luka not now."

Luka's shuffle slowed only for a second before he desperately scuttled up to Jason again. "I'm sorry. I'm sorry… come on. I'm sorry. I didn't know she would do that."

"You look like shit," Jason snapped viciously. He was sure, though he didn't look at him, he heard Luka muffle a sob. "You should sleep," was as kind a remark as he was capable of.

Suddenly Luka stopped walking, a look of sheer dread on his grey face, "no."

"Don't push it today. I mean it. Don't do it."

"I am asleep. I'm still asleep. I can't stop dreaming… I can't make it stop," Luka said, his voice beginning to sound way too much like begging to inspire any respect from Jason.

Rolling his eyes with embarrassment, he turned to face him. Luka continued, "it's a nightmare… everywhere. The rain, the air, the… the wind. All just… dark. It's moving in me, and I can't stop it. I can't wake up."

Jason didn't respond straight away. He didn't know what to say. This was the fate of all Devotees, but Luka had been fast tracked. What good was he to Jason now? He had only a few tricks left in him, at best. But those few tricks could make all the difference in the right situation. Luka had always been stupid, but now he would be stupid and desperate. Regardless, proximity to Jason would not help Luka. It would not stop the process of his descent into darkness, but he could still be useful until then. Jason would not let Luka off the hook, not yet. He needed to let him bathe in this a little bit longer.

"Just go home. Seriously, I've had it up to here with bullshit and I'm done. I'm that close…" Jason held up his thumb and index finger, pinching them together. "That close. So go away for now. Just leave."

Luka watched as Jason walked away. He felt overcome with loneliness and despair. It was known what would happen to him. He had seen it and he had felt similar foreboding shadows in the past. But nothing like this. His life, the life of Luka was nearly over, and he would become something else. Did he ever really believe that this would happen before now? Did it ever truly sink in, how temporary he was? His only hope was that the secret could be found. To do that he had to cross over, and he would only have one chance. Those Grimoires, those he had taken and hidden deep in the other hell, held the only chance for his salvation. To get there, someone had to be taken. They would have to be close. They would have to be accessible. He was sure this required more of him than he had left, but he had no choice.

Turning, he stared into the street, dazed, and panicked. He found himself beginning to run. He ran from his sickness, this disease. But the darkness that would not lift was the creature whose hunger for chaos and blood pulsed in his veins.

ooo

The classroom seemed different than before. It was as bright and noisy as always, but Josh felt that, somehow, he was watching the room rather than being a part of it. They had done some maths in the morning and then they had done news. The teacher had walked past Josh whilst another student was talking and gave him a caring squeeze on his shoulder. Maybe she knew his Mum was gone. Of course she knew; everyone knew.

Lunch had been nice, and he got to sit on the bench with his friends who, after a chilly beginning, were now acting happy to have him back. He looked different perhaps. His clothes were nicer, and his hair was done. Pulling out his lunchbox, he scanned their eyes looking for a reaction, an acknowledgement. Perhaps jealousy at how nice his lunch box was, and they would ask what was inside? They didn't.

They were going on an excursion in the afternoon to see some old people. His friends and the teacher had spoken about it. It had started the week before. He was told they made cakes, played games, and talked with the old people about all sorts of things. Josh was curious; he didn't know many old people, and he'd certainly never been somewhere where they all lived. He wondered what it might look like. He did know an old person once; she had eyes that were white, like the Dog. He hoped they didn't all have white eyes because he didn't like it.

Spelling complete, Josh could see the school bus pull up outside where Ron's car had sat for a long time. He was glad it was gone. They all put on their coats, hats and scarfs and headed out to the road where they were loaded two by two onto the large bus. Josh became nervous. He hoped old people were nice and didn't make him feel anything bad. He would be so angry if the Dog ate an old person.

Josh hated it when it rained so hard when he was in a car, or in this case, a bus. He couldn't see out of the windows properly. He couldn't watch the people and see the buildings. Just pellets of water, flashes of cars and, of course, the stupid large black Monster Dog running in the street. He wished that it couldn't run so fast. He had watched a movie once where a car went faster than a dinosaur. Dinosaurs could be very fast, but this Dog was even faster than a dinosaur.

The old people's place was not as Josh had expected. It looked old, but pretty, with big white windows and gardens that he was sure would be full of really nice flowers when the weather got better. He did know that old people liked flowers. He saw it on an advert once - they were in the garden doing things very slowly but looking really happy. He joined the other children leaving the school bus and waited whilst the teacher counted their heads. A "head count" she had called out. Josh always found this funny. Making sure no-one lost their head on the way there, made him giggle.

Inside, the building was just as nice. There was lots of wallpaper and nice pictures hanging on the walls. It did smell a bit funny, but then Josh thought that that was probably from the flowers in the vases that seemed to be upon every surface. The teacher walked them past three ladies at a desk. Only one called out "Aw, Hello!" Maybe the other two didn't see them.

They were then led through a large dining room with lots of tables and chairs. Josh noticed there were lots of placemats all with names on them. He thought this was kind of cool. At least they knew where they had to sit.

Through the dining room, they entered a large doorway where there were lots of old people. It was a very big room with lots of chairs and even more flowers and pictures on every single wall. Some of the kids waved hello and ran off to ones they had obviously met before. Two of the girls ran up to a big old lady with curly grey hair who was sitting in a wheelchair. She smiled and leant forward, giving them a little hug. She seemed friendly. So did the man in the armchair that his friend had run up to. Everyone seemed to be engaging in a conversation as Josh stood awkwardly in the middle of the room feeling increasingly alone.

He stared uneasily around the room, looking at the other children all of whom seemed so much happier to be there then he did. Some had taken games out of boxes. Others were showing pictures they had painted. He hadn't painted a picture and he didn't know any of these people. Turning around he looked at the door behind him. He saw his teacher approach. "Why don't you go and talk to someone?" she suggested gently as she crouched beside him.

"I don't know anyone," he replied shyly.

Sitting before the large, arched window in a big comfy chair was an old man. Josh thought that he looked like he'd be a nice person to talk to. He was dressed in a comfy red shirt which came too low on his chest so Josh could see his white singlet underneath. Maybe he had no hair, except for the grey hairs on his chest? His pants were very baggy, and he wore funny big shoes which looked like two big pillows on his feet.

The man stared at him warily. Josh looked back. Maybe he wasn't looking at him? No-one was talking to him. Josh felt sad about that. Poor old man. His teacher gave him a nudge. "You want to go and say Hello?" Josh panicked. Just because he felt sad for him didn't mean he wanted to be the one to talk to him. The way the old man looked at him was strange. Josh couldn't tell if it was nice or not but there was definitely something about it that had made him curious. Maybe, thought Josh, it's because I look friendly.

The child and the old man stared at each other for an awkward moment longer before Josh summoned up all his courage and started to walk towards him. The old man glanced back at the window, carefully ignoring the cautiously advancing child. Then, hesitantly, he looked back at Josh as his old, small eyes grew larger and then narrowed. He had a very big nose and, Josh noted, big ears. He looked like a cartoon character and so he was bound to be friendly.

Josh took the final step towards him as the old man rubbed his chin apprehensively. Summoning up all his courage, Josh spoke "Hi, I'm Josh."

The old man regarded him for a moment, taking a large, tired breath before forcing a reply. "Hello there young Josh. It's a pleasure." He held out his hand and Josh could tell that this was less a social grace than a lesson on proper introductions.

"Oh look," cooed a nurse, forcing the old man to roll his eyes. "Grandpa Charlie has a new friend!" In response, Josh was sure the old man muttered, "bloody imbecile."

The old man took Joshua's nervous hand in his, dwarfing it as he gave it a tight squeeze and a firm shake that nearly hurt.

"Are you Charlie?" Joshua asked.

"No young man. That's what people call me after a time. I have only just had the pleasure of making your acquaintance. You can call me Mr. Russo and I will call you Master Josh. Is that acceptable?" Charlie sat back as Josh thought about it for a moment before smiling and nodding. He had never been called a 'master' before.

ᴑᴑᴑ

Sam drove silently, unsure of what to say to Ellie who rummaged in her backpack beside him. So many questions. She was about to go to work for the afternoon, cleaning at the school. She lived in a small one-bedroom apartment in a suitable area. She didn't drive, although there were many sensible reasons for this. Her backpack looked ready to die, frayed and battered. Her clothes were simple, dark and had no style whatsoever. However, she had just paid over thirty thousand dollars in debt in ten minutes… all for him. Every card, every bill, every car payment, and all the late mortgage payments were taken care of. His relief and gratitude were overwhelming.

As was his curiosity. She sat there with the same demeanour. No big deal. It hadn't bothered her. Who was she?

"Can I make you dinner?" he asked sheepishly.

"Why?" Ellie asked, placing her bag on the floor.

"Because you just saved my ass."

"You saved mine first, to be honest." Ellie looked at him, "it's no big deal. Seriously."

"That was a hell of a lot of money."

"Yes," she agreed. "Now you've got time."

"To what?"

"To get a job. To be in a good place again," Ellie said in an uncharacteristically upbeat voice. "Perhaps with everything else we've got going on, we can at least relax that money will never be a problem. Whatever we decide to do."

Sam tapped the steering wheel in frustration. He loved the optimism, he really did. And he probably needed a good dose of it right now, but perhaps being in 'a good place' wasn't ever going to be realistic. Not for any of them. Ellie gazed out the window.

Ellie had money to run, yet she wouldn't. Why? As soon as he thought of this he wanted to ask. Why are you still here? Why don't you just go, run, get as far away from here as you can? Find somewhere quiet, somewhere far away where no-one would ever find you. Where no-one has ever heard the name Bael. He was worried. Where was her head at? What was she thinking? Where did she see herself in all of this? All these players. Josh, him, and now all the others emerging into the light: Bael, the Heretic, the Firewolf. But where amongst them all, did she see herself? Did she even consider herself a person worthy of being saved at all?

Chapter 21

Sitting at the bar, Noah quickly threw back another whiskey. He felt his throat burn and his head spin as he placed the glass down, giving it a tap for a refill. He liked this bar. Even after his sixth shot, the bartender didn't shoot him a look of disapproval like so many others. He wouldn't be here much longer. Only long enough to calm the nerves, dull the pain, before washing down the oxy and then… to the shed! Over the years this had increased his tolerance for all things intoxicating, which made nights like tonight much more expensive than they used to be.

There were times in the past when he was a little too eager, too keen, to nullify the upcoming events, but that never ended well. Can't drink to excess, pass out and piss himself when he got 'home' or become so out of it that he lost control. As Mika had said, an Ace had two modes: on and off. An Underling however, had some form of control. Taking the small sheet of tablets out from his pocket he turned it over. Four left, only four! One for before and three to get him through the night until the phantom pain subsided. Too early yet, a few more shots should do it.

Turning his chair, he looked at the TV on the wall behind him. The bar was empty. Most people were still at work. This thought used to embarrass him, but not anymore. Being on the fringes made life so much easier. As far as Chelamah knew, he was still employed at the metal works. His stomach sank. The list of things Chelamah didn't know had grown so much. Heartbreakingly, there were many things she would never know before her end. His biggest guilt was taking advantage of that.

This was his role now. He was an on-call henchman, unleashing himself on anyone without question. He had access to the Pantheon. He had been granted a Devotee. This had not sat comfortably with some of the Aces and he understood why. He was not an Ace. He was not a Devotee. An Underling was caught between. At first it appeared that Mika simply didn't know what to do with him or how to use him. But he knew.

Mika paid a retainer that enabled him to sit here, drink and have accommodation to prevent Chelamah getting suspicious. That was all that mattered. He had already received the picture via his phone. The target was fixed. Chelamah had messaged him. He had responded that he was working late. Although she had not, until recently, turned up at his 'dwelling', he couldn't take that risk tonight.

Spinning back around to face the bar, he knocked back the latest glass, repeating his request for more to the bartender who had begun to give him 'the look.' It was OK. This guy still had at least three more shots to offer before he would say anything.

◠◠◠

Charlie spun his chair around at the top of the indoor ramp, watching Josh wheel a badly behaved trolley of seedlings in front of him. "Come on young man," he called impatiently. "It'll be winter again before we put those in pots."

"The wheel keeps going the other way," Josh complained, fighting his way up the carpeted incline.

"Don't blame your equipment Master Josh. Put your back into it, come on."

Josh didn't understand the phrase. Put his back into it? Did he mean, push it backwards? He wasn't sure. He was about to ask when Mr. Russo wheeled himself away down the corridor, "this way Master Josh!"

Holding the trolley steady on the incline, Josh looked back at the dining room. He was pretty sure he should be with his classmates, but the teacher had told them that it was OK to be helpful on their visits here. He thought that he was being very helpful, so that should be OK. Taking a deep breath, he threw his weight behind the skewed wheels and continued up to the corridor that Charlie had rolled down.

"You, my boy, are very, very strong," Charlie beamed watching Joshua fight his way towards him. Josh grunted. Charlie couldn't be sure what he said. Wheeling himself back into his room, he turned the chair to face the door and waited as first the trolley then the red-faced boy entered.

240

"Ah wonderful. Wonderful." Charlie cast a sneaky look over Josh's shoulder. "Now, we must get them in the pots! I think four will do it, then we must get the trolley back."

Four?! Joshua couldn't believe it. He could have carried four. He didn't have to bring up the whole trolley!

"Why did we have to bring everything then?" Josh asked in astonishment. Charlie rolled his eyes. "Because we need to choose the best ones. As soon as Doris - Did you see Doris?"

Josh shook his head, no.

"Doris, the highland cow of a woman from room 9? No? Well, she would have told Sister Landsdale that we were rummaging, and then right after tea she would've been straight at them! No sir! Not on my watch. We need to see them all and claim the best ones. Last year, that grey heifer managed to steal all the begonias and she only had one leg then! Now she's got wheels, so we must be quick."

Josh felt a sense of urgency, even though he didn't quite understand what Charlie was going on about. The old man gestured to the confused boy who quickly closed the door.

Charlie examined his bounty, picking up the small seedlings and looking intently at their leaves. Josh looked about. The room was very strange and smelt like old clothes. There was a simple dresser with a few pictures on it. They would be his family. He must love these people very much; they were the only pictures he had.

"Hmmm" Charlie pondered. "A little too wet but never bother. Begonias need little care Master Josh. Not too wet, mind, not too much water."

"They're very small." Josh spoke quietly, watching Charlie turn one over, before placing it back on the trolley and picking up another.

"Yes, but they grow big in nice, fluffy dirt. We look after small things. It's what we do when you are as big as you and I."

Josh wondered what fluffy dirt looked like. He stepped closer to try and see whatever was so interesting to the old man. He peered over his shoulder. "Do they grow inside?"

"Yes, yes they do. With a bit of sun," Charlie smiled, admiring the little green leaves. "Keep them out of the cold. They like it better here."

Josh nodded. He wouldn't like to be outside now either. He'd never thought of plants 'liking' anything before. He had also never looked at them this closely.

Charlie smiled and placed a second seedling onto his bed. "Now, two more shouldn't be missed, but…" he lifted a finger. Joshua waited in anticipation. "We must be discerning. Find one for me Master Josh… have a look on the bottom there."

Eagerly, Josh bent down and scanned the seedlings on the bottom shelf. They all looked the same, all green, all… planty. What was he looking for? What did *diskerned* mean? Just when he thought this, he noticed a little seedling in between two larger ones. It was small, the leaves of the others almost completely covered it. Josh put his finger in and ever so gently, touched the dirt. Soft. Not too wet. Concentrating, he wrapped his hand around the tube and pulled it out.

"Ah" Charlie nodded. "Yes, that one is lovely isn't it?"

Josh smiled; he had chosen a good one! "Is it diskerned?"

Confused for a second, Charlie turned to Josh and chuckled, "Oh yes Master Josh. This is indeed… *diskerned*. When you return tomorrow, you can help me find the best place for their new pots."

Joshua nodded happily. That would be great. He wondered, how much would they have grown by then? He would go home and perhaps ask Nate. Nate had a garden, or he said he did. "Under the mud" he had told him, "There is a great garden."

Charlie and Josh both looked up, hearing Josh's name being called down the corridor.

"Oh now, you must go." Charlie quickly turned his chair to face the door, guiding Josh with his hand on his back. "Remember, be good until tomorrow and don't tell heifer Doris what you saw here today."

Heifer Doris. Josh laughed. That was a strange name. "I won't tell her."

"You are my favourite partner in crime," Charlie teased. "It has been a pleasure, Master Joshua. Until we meet again, my friend."

With a big, happy smile Joshua opened the door and trotted out, leaving it open behind him. Charlie smiled. What a nice boy, with a good and kind heart. There was something unique about him, honest and innocent. Wanting to be involved, wanting to learn and wanting to please. It brought Charlie great sadness to see that this boy, like his own grandson, was not alone.

Perhaps Jason would not have been that dissimilar to this child all those years ago. This is what they were before they were taken apart and turned into something else.

Jason had always been highly intelligent. He was funny and he could be sweet. But Jason had never been kind and sadly had quickly lost his innocence, wrapping evil around himself like a shield. The ancient monster that had curled up with that lost child had produced a comfortable coupling.

The boy Josh was different. He carried a genuine warmth that emanated from him. There was no bitterness or anger. He was an undamaged, new soul. Unlike his grandson, Joshua, and the parasitical beast that dwelled within him, would never comfortably co-exist. His monster was awesome, strong and primal as it must be. But it was being kept at bay by a worthy human like Josh. It was a fitting retribution for such a despicable thing.

ooo

Ellie peered out of the windows of the library. The school day only had half an hour left. She imagined Josh would not have that much time to see her. He would be picked up, and after last week's events she was sure he would be kept close by his well-meaning relatives. They would be watching his every movement until they weren't there anymore. This would be only a matter of time. A scolding, a minor disappointment and for a single moment Josh would forget that he wasn't human. It would force him into being alone again. Fuck. Why did she feel so powerless, and why did she care so much?

Could she take Josh with her? No. Children don't just vanish, and both their lives would become unbearable. Could she approach his family and plead for understanding? That would result in a direct path to the mental health ward at the Boronia Heights, either due to insanity or via being arrested for stalking a child. Wow, that sounded creepy. Stalking a child. She wasn't stalking a child. Josh tragically was not a child any longer. What was she going to do?

"Hi," a light-hearted voice said quietly behind her. Mildly startled she turned to see Josh standing by the door, bag over his shoulder smiling at her. Jesus. He looked like a different kid. Happy, bright, the complete polar opposite of the pale little human she had met months ago.

"Hi, you!" she cried a bit too enthusiastically as he ran forward, wrapping his arms around her. "How are you?"

"I'm good! I went to an old person's place, and I met an old person, and we stole plants together!" Josh gushed.

"Why are you here? You should be in class."

"I said I needed the toilet. We just got off the bus and I said I was busting. I knew you'd be here. The Dog knew too." He cast a glance behind him. "He's sitting over there in the corner now. He's been weird today. He busted my bedroom up."

Of course the Dog was here, and she imagined it sitting right next to Bael who stood in the shadows watching with interest.

"What's been happening?" Ellie asked as the information flowed towards her at an incredible rate. Nate and Casey were nice, and Nate makes good chicken. He had a bedroom where Casey said he could put posters up if he wanted, but he had to use white tack, not the other one that stains the walls.

"Yeah, don't stain the walls," Ellie smiled whilst walking to the small, round chairs in the middle of the library. The "Book Nook."

"No, no I won't because Uncle Nate said he will show me how. He's really funny and makes jokes all the time and makes Aunty Casey crazy! Like Sam makes you crazy too!"

Ellie gave a short chuckle, that was true. He really did.

"Are you OK?" Joshua asked out of nowhere. Ellie felt a lump rise in her throat. Why did this question trigger such a reaction? Was she... OK?

"I am..." Ellie began, horrified as she felt tears well in her eyes. "OK. I'm OK."

Josh was happy. He was happy, but it wouldn't last. It was so grossly unfair.

"Hey," she changed the subject. "Did you stay not angry?" Speaking in 'Josh language' made her blush with her solecism. Wording in a gentle 8-year-old language was, however, important.

"Yeah I've been good and not got angry at all. Sometimes I get angry with the Dog, but that's OK because we hate him, and he can't eat himself. If he did, I would get angry with him all the time."

Josh described the Dog wrecking his bedroom and this intrigued Ellie. Like Bael before the Oculus. Like the Dark Child in the underpass. The dog could interact with the physical. There had only been two situations where she had seen Bael do something like this. First, in the event of an imminent risk to her existence either by herself or by something else. Secondly, as the Circle approached he would become more aggressive. He would bring things forth, change the environment around her but still, even then, it never 'touched' anything. Never had it directly interfered with the real world. With the arrival of the Oculus and the growing hoard of creatures that surrounded Bael at various times, this strange phenomenon had been increasing.

"Then I saw a shrink doctor? He was really nice and friendly. His name was Dr. Gardens. He asked me all sorts of questions- "

"Josh, no." What the absolute hell. Of course. Of course, it would be Niles. "What did you tell him?"

"Nothing," Josh gasped defensively. "Nothing, I told him nothing and he didn't ask about anything too much."

Niles didn't need to. She knew him. He was skilled at prying out information whilst disguising it as conversation, polite, caring and sometimes even inane.

"You can't see him," Ellie muttered, knowing they were powerless to stop it.

"I have to. That's what the grown-ups said. I have to see him." Josh answered, confused. He had just told Ellie he liked him, and Ellie looked upset. Maybe she thought he would be Josh's new friend and he wouldn't like her anymore? He felt sad. He knew this feeling. "It's OK." He leant forward, "you're still my best friend."

"No, I mean yes… that's not what I…" the school bell rang. Josh would have to go.

Picking up his bag, he looked sadly at Ellie. He hoped he hadn't upset her by liking someone else.

"OK just remember…" Ellie grasped both his hands. "Not too much. They won't understand, and it puts them in danger. Dr. Gardiner won't know it, but it puts him in danger, so we must look after him. Remember, we don't speak of it."

Joshua was confused. Gardiner? That was his name. Did Ellie know him? And danger? Why would he be in danger, unless Josh got mad, which he wouldn't. So why was Dr. Gardiner in danger? He trusted Ellie. He would do what she asked.

"OK," Josh nodded. "I won't."

Ellie nodded, forcing a smile.

"I'll message you after. See you tomorrow?" Josh asked.

"Yep" Ellie nodded, fighting back the anxiety in her voice. "Be good and I'll see you tomorrow."

Josh nodded happily and ran awkwardly out the door, his large bag slipping off his shoulder. Niles. Goddammit. Something was brewing. Something was wrong. The feeling of impending bullshit grew inside her. She had no control over this. Watching the door quietly, Bael moved beside her, leant down in front of her and gave a small nod.

"Go fuck yourself" Ellie sneered.

OOO

Casey arrived home and noticed the absence of Nate's car. Of course, he would be picking Joshua up. She pulled into the driveway and exited the car with a sense of urgency that she knew wasn't actually required. She had at least another half hour before Nate and Joshua would return. Harmless, she thought. Searching Josh's room was completely innocuous. Perhaps she would find something, anything, that may give her a hint as to the strange circumstances surrounding her nephew. There was something he had been, and still was, very scared of. On the way home she had convinced herself. It made no sense that Joshua didn't know where her sister was.

On entering the house, Casey dumped her handbag on the hall stand and rushed down the hallway. She stopped at the empty frame that used to contain a door. Nate had told her what had happened, but she had not been expecting this. He had removed it and left it leaning up against the wall. The wood was split and buckled. The handle had completely come off. Inside the room was as Nate had left it. A cold shiver ran up her spine. This was bizarre, absolutely crazy. How does a child do this much damage at all… let alone in less than 10 seconds, as described by Nate. This scared her. She hated to admit it, but Josh scared her. The faraway eyes, the rehearsed responses, the secrets.

Gathering herself, she entered the room and glanced around. Where to start? The cupboard and the drawers were nothing but shattered wood strewn upon the floor. He had so few belongings and whatever belongings he did have he preferred to keep under the bed.

Brushing the fragments of plywood from under her, she knelt down and looked beneath the bed. There were numerous silver food packages. A box of chicken biscuits and two bottles of water. Pulling her phone out, she turned on the torch and awkwardly angled the light back into Josh's secret hoard. Food packets, water containers and bundled up balls of clothing.

246

Something grabbed her attention at the very back of the bed, against the wall. A black cord ran from the power socket, disappearing below a box of prawn crackers. Reluctantly she flattened herself against the carpet and leaned in, hitting the box to the side. With surprise, she wrapped her hand around a small phone.

Quickly, phone in hand, she backed out from under the bed. What was this? Now at least, they knew where Nate's spare charger had disappeared to. She sat up, in the middle of the floor and pressed the screen. It was on silent, no password, no protections. How did he hide this for so long? Scrolling through the phone she noticed multiple messages. The messages commenced weeks ago at the hospital, continuing to as recent as yesterday, at 11PM. All sent and received by the same two people. Who the hell were ELLIE and BOSSY?

Chapter 22

It had not been the first time that Niles had been threatened during the course of his work; it hadn't even been the first time this year. This time, however, the unease planted within him was not subsiding. He stood on the crowded train, ignoring the occasional free seat. For some reason this evening he found it more comfortable to stand. His short twelve-minute train trip seemed to go very quickly, lost in thought as time raced by. He had considered calling the police again. That was still very possible, and he felt he needed to. Will Mason was still missing, and never mind his own curiosity, he constantly reminded himself that this was about the welfare of a patient. He would ponder it further and plan his next action in safety from home. The office today felt very unsafe.

Ellie was tomorrow. Ellie was there for Ellie... not for Will. Not for Mika and not for him. When his mind began playing conversations over in his mind, tricks of semantics to be able to bring up her bogeyman, he got angry with himself. This was not what Ellie was there for. It was hard to draw the line.

Moving through the other passengers, he disembarked at his station. The train pulled away and Niles started up the stairs to the overpass. Jessica would be home already, and they would discuss wedding plans... again. This thought would usually frustrate him, but tonight he would be keen for the distraction.

Walking into his tree-lined street, the rain began to bucket down. He lifted his umbrella and proceeded down the quiet row of townhouses. Jessica had parked out the front again. She hated reverse parking into the garage. Although he had never told her this, he found it strange that someone as accomplished as her was so bad at driving. He looked up at the house. The lights were on downstairs, shining through the windows. Fear and anxiety overcame him, why? The thought of not moving, of being in that building, filled him with dread. He had not had a panic attack for many years. Taking a deep breath, he pulled himself together. Where was this foreboding coming from? What was it that had unsettled him so much, that as night grew closer, he felt like running?

◯◯◯

The darkness in the room drifted over Noah's restrained body. With the picture of the target firmly in his mind, his nose began to bleed. This had happened before - not every time - but often. The usual sounds of war ripped through the air. The pounding footsteps of the Soldier echoed in the house seconds before its large, solid frame marched heavily into the room. Standing before him, it was powerful tonight. The blood that dripped off Noah's lips was testament to the energy that it had brought. He focused on the target, thinking hard. His face, his blue eyes, his skin. The thought projected into the monster before him. The switch was hit.

◯◯◯

Niles greeted Jessica with a hug as he entered. Taking off his jacket and scarf, he decided he would change before dinner. Shredding the skin of his professional facade may assist him in calming down. To feel like Niles again, instead of this neurotic mess. Changing into his jeans and t-shirt, he made his way back down the stairs to the smell of cooking coming from the kitchen.

Pasta. He knew it was pasta because with Jessica, it always was pasta. Wholemeal pasta, of course. He walked into the kitchen, saying a quick hello to Winston, the large cat that ran around his ankles.

"Coffee?" she asked, turning from the stove.

"No. No, thank you" Niles replied. Caffeine just didn't feel appropriate right now.

"So, the menu is sorted. RSVPs returned and so far, all are coming." Jessica turned back to the stove. "We need to go over the hymns…"

"Have we not?"

"Yes we did but there were two you didn't seem quite as keen on. Let's have another look." Jessica replied, adding more sauce to a bubbling concoction.

As per routine, Niles fetched two wine glasses to place on the table. Along with serviettes, water, and parmesan. For a split second there was foreboding of a boring future that came over him.

"Your freedom ends at the 'I do.'" Mika's voice played in his mind. The damn psychopath was stuck in his head.

Niles ignored it. He had faced others like Mika before and knew the residual garbage of their interactions didn't last long. It was merely a bad day at work.

Distracting himself from these thoughts, he engaged in conversation regarding the upcoming nuptials. Jessica, though pleasantly surprised at his enthusiasm, didn't notice his anxious pacing between the cutlery drawer and the table. Will... Ellie... Mika... What was he missing? They were all the same. All the same. There was something significant he wasn't seeing, and he had the feeling he was a mere pawn in all of it. A bystander, not quite seeing the situation of something he had no control over.

"No, I preferred the first set" Niles continued the conversation through multiple thoughts. Jessica began talking again.

Bael. Will, Bael... Ellie, Bael. Mika... Bael. What else? History, backgrounds... all the same. Joshua... Joshua?

"And then possibly, that other one? The one your mother liked. Keep her happy." Deep in thought, he made his way to the sink and stared out into the dark backyard.

"Yes... so many allowances to keep my mother happy," Jessica sighed, moving some plates to the bench. "I appreciate that Niles. I really do."

Nile faked a chuckle. "It's essential, she terrifies..." he stopped. In the darkness outside, something - someone - was walking, striding towards the house. Niles watched the tall figure approach the back porch before, fuelled by adrenaline, he darted to his right and locked the door. Ignoring Jessica's confusion, he wiggled the handle. Locked. Staring up through the condensation on the glass it took a moment for the image, that was literally inches from him, to make itself clear. It was right there, right in front of him. He could see its white eyes.

He barely had time to cry out before he was grasped through smashing glass and pulled violently through the gaping hole to the cold outside. The soldier spun him around, sending debris scattering across the porch. It then threw him violently onto the muddy earth. The air left his body as he raised his head in shock. He heard Jessica scream.

Orienting himself, he tried to push himself up. Tried to yell at her to call for help, but the soldier sent his boot into the side of his head. Stunned and dazed, blood ran down his brow. He was then lifted, effortlessly, and held in front of this man. This man with white eyes and rotted skin. The urge to fight kicked in. He swung his fist into the stranger's deformed face, without phasing him. His closed fist recoiled painfully.

Jessica was screaming his name. She was inside the house.

Please god… call for help.

"Jess! Call the Police! NOW! NOW!" Niles screamed desperately.

The Soldier dropped him. He placed an arm behind his back and pulled out a large, long blade. Fighting through the pain, Niles turned to run, but slipped on the wet earth as the weapon was dragged across his back in one, smooth swing. Niles collapsed as his back spasmed. *My god, he's going to kill me.* Crouching over his victim, the Soldier grabbed Niles's hair and wrenched his head back as he brought the blade to his victim's throat. This was it. He couldn't move. He was completely incapacitated. This man was strong. He was useless against him. Pathetic.

Niles waited for the final strike. He could feel the cold blade on his exposed, extended neck.

"Please. No," he gasped through rain, tears, and blood.

The Soldier grasped Niles's forearm, bringing it up with a gut-wrenching *SNAP!* Niles cried out as the Soldier slowly stood, releasing his arm for it to fall painfully beside him. With a jolt, the Soldier left, running into the darkness, and leaping over the fence with unnatural skill.

Niles squirmed in the dirt. He couldn't breathe. He couldn't think. Who was that man? He had never seen anyone like that. What happened? Jessica was beside him. She was sobbing. She told him, "They're coming, they're coming" He tried to roll over. The pain in his arm stopped him. He screamed before vomiting on the ground. His head fell forward into the mud, tasting dirt and vomit. They were coming, he would be OK. They were coming.

○○○

Noah had screamed. It was coming back. His right arm was throbbing and spasming painfully. A searing, burning pain radiated across his back. The Soldier entered, loudly slamming its boots before stopping in front of him.

"Enough," Noah grunted. To the sounds of the bugle, the Soldier dipped to one knee, hanging its head. Filled with alcohol and opioids, Noah finally fell into an unconsciousness that even the pain couldn't break.

OOO

Joshua spooned the last of the chocolate mousse into his mouth with absolute delight. Absolutely amazing. He was worried that maybe he would never taste such an amazing thing ever again. Nate had picked him up and the ride home had been a bit strange. Nate asked him lots of questions about school, but he seemed nervous about something. His laughter on the way home seemed less relaxed than usual. He made three jokes about Joshua's bedroom and then waited before laughing, like he wanted Josh to say something. Josh just agreed: yes, it was a mess. Yes, they could use the whole room as firewood if civilization collapsed.

When they arrived home. Casey was nervous too. She sent Josh to get changed in the spare room where she had moved all his clothes. She and Nate then spoke quietly in their bedroom for a while. Grown up stuff. Josh put his clothes on, put his bag under the bed in the spare room and quietly took his phone from its usual hiding place. Carefully moving it to the other room. After dinner he would message Ellie and say Hi.

Casey played with her spoon, turning it over and over in her hands. Nate, folded his arms and sat back looking awkwardly at Josh, smiling when Josh looked back at him.

"It's good huh?"

"It's really good," Josh mumbled through the food.

"So, Mr. Russo? Sounds like a nice man."

Josh nodded happily, "Yeah, he is nice and very old. He has grey hair and wrinkles everywhere, but he's really good at wheelchairs and flowers. He likes flowers and knows lots about them. He taught me about Begonias."

"Oh, Begonias? They're lovely" Casey nodded. "You know your grandma, she loved Begonias."

"No," Josh shook his head.

"No?"

"No, I don't know her much. Mum said she was a crazy bitch, but I didn't know her." Josh sighed, causing Nate to scoff in surprise.

"Josh!" Casey was shocked, her eyes smiled though her voice tried to sound cross. "We don't use that word! My goodness."

Josh nodded, he understood. He learnt that word was not nice today because sometimes old people forget things and it's not their fault. "Sorry. Mum said she was a bitch, I meant."

"Whoa!" Nate recoiled, bursting into laughter. He looked at Casey, shaking his head, who smiled anxiously back. Josh wondered what he had said again. "Josh, Josh, Josh. No bitch... no."

Slowly removing the spoon from his mouth, he stared at Nate and slowly nodded. Maybe Mum was wrong? Maybe grandma wasn't a bitch.

Through the laughter and the lightning of the atmosphere, Casey folded her hands in front of her. She thought for a moment and then asked, "So sweetheart, who is Ellie?"

Silence fell. Josh froze, staring at Nate who was now frowning uneasily at Casey. "Subtle" he remarked.

Josh didn't move. His spoon hovering over his bowl, completely still as if scared to respond.

"I don't know," he said quietly. His eyes darted from Nate to Casey and back again.

"OK," Nate interrupted, surprised that Casey seemed to have nowhere else to go with this question. "Is Ellie a friend? Someone you know from school?"

Josh didn't know what to say. How could something so unsettling come out of nowhere? "Ellie is my friend."

Casey nodded, holding back a mass of questions. "Did you see her today?"

"No," Josh snapped. Why were they asking? What were they going to do? This is what they were speaking about in the bedroom. The grown-up talk was about him and Ellie. A growling rose from the wall behind him. "She's my best friend. You don't know her."

"Oh nice. Where did you meet her?" Casey asked.

"I don't want to talk about it now," Josh said. The smile had gone from his face. He placed the spoon down and looked up. His eyes became wide and distant as they were the day he first arrived. Nate could see him preparing, fortifying himself for evading the questions. But over the child's shoulder, Nate noticed the kitchen walls begin to dim… what was this? In the diner he had seen the same thing. Was he imagining it? Sitting forward, he stared over Josh as the room grew warmer. "Wait…" Nate muttered, sitting forward and blinking.

"Honey it's not that you can't have friends but…"

"She's my best friend. I told you that."

"Yes and that's great. We need friends!" Casey smiled as Nate continued to watch the room around them. It was subtle, gentle but he had seen this before…

"I need to go to my room now," Josh said, kicking himself back from the table. He stumbled off the chair with a sense of urgency that stunned Casey. "I'm tired. Very tired, and I have to go to bed and stuff." His hand flexed open and closed. Casey went to speak. Nate interjected, "yeah you go mate, you go. Brush your teeth, OK?"

Casey shot Nate a look. Nate watched Josh's face, those eyes. What was he thinking? What was he hearing? Josh nodded, turning from the table, and scurrying away into the hallway. He could hear them talking in adult secret voices. Casey seemed angry. Nate sounded calm, but they both sounded serious. How did Casey know about Ellie? Had he told them by accident? He felt like such an idiot. Maybe he forgot and said something. He didn't think he did, but he had done that before. He closed the door behind him and looked at this different room. He hoped this one didn't explode. He wouldn't know what to say.

◯◯◯

This was Mika's doing. The bastard sent someone for him. Niles lay in the hospital bed, eyes closed but very much awake. Jessica was beside him. He could hear her. She had been on the phone multiple times to various relatives and friends. The police had left. All Mika's details were provided via his very distressed office assistant who Jessica convinced not to come to the hospital. After they had left, to get a moment of silence, Niles feigned sleep. He was aware it was later than he had thought. His arm was cast. He didn't remember them doing that and rationalised that he must have been

254

under anaesthetic. His back was numb and tight. Opening his eyes hurt. His cheek bone felt like hot rock, swollen, and grazed.

He heard a sniffle. Jessica was crying. Opening his eyes, she immediately looked up.

"Hey," she soothed, moving to his bedside, and stroking his face. She took his hand in hers. "Oh my God. You're OK. You're OK. "

Niles swallowed hard, giving her hand a squeeze. "I'm drowsy, my mouth is dry." He slapped his lips uncomfortably.

"You were under. They had to set your arm, but it's all done." She lifted a plastic cup with a straw to his lips. A few sips, before Niles groggily shook his head.

"Did they find Mika?"

"I don't know. Kay gave them the info. I guess we just have to wait." She continued to gently stroke his head.

Niles nodded. "This guy was sent by him. I know it. He told me. He threatened me."

Jessica nodded. "They'll find him, don't worry."

The memory of the attack was seared into his mind. It was a brutal, bold assault by someone who had done that many times before. Even in his pharmaceutically induced semi-euphoria, the memory of his attacker sent shivers up his spine. That wasn't a normal guy. His attacker was a pro, a confident, hardened assailant. His eyes though. Why couldn't he remember his eyes? He wished he could describe him better, clearer. He couldn't remember. The face was odd, strange but he couldn't describe it in a way that didn't sound completely absurd.

"Baby," Niles squeezed Jessica's hand. "Did you speak to them?"

"Yes, yes I did, it's OK."

"Did you describe him? I can't remember... I can't... I can't see it properly, that's all..." Niles stuttered. "I can't remember it clearly right now."

"I couldn't," Jessica cried, shrugging in disbelief. "I couldn't."

Perplexed, Niles looked at her, "Why?" he asked

"It was raining so heavily, it was dark... I..."

"*Why*?" Niles repeated.

"Niles, I didn't see anyone. Something was happening, I could hear it, I could see you, but I didn't see anyone." Shaking her head, flabbergasted.

Stunned, Niles let his head fall back onto the pillow. He had been pulled through a door. He had been beaten and slashed. How could she not have seen someone... anyone. Trembling, he exhaled. This was not enough. How could he not remember? How could this have gone completely unseen? Feeling the sedatives slowly lifting, the pain began to gently radiate through his arm and shoulder. They had to find Mika and the man responsible for this. This person, whoever it was, came to kill him.

OOO

Luka took the bottle of water from Chelamah's hand as she stood over him. "You have to drink. No matter how sick it makes you feel. You still need water."

Sitting on the floor, Luka lifted the bottle to his lips "You didn't have to come back." He took a sip before gagging.

"I know" Chelamah agreed. "Swallow it. Just a bit."

Luka grimaced, forcing the water down. It tasted metallic. "It tastes bad."

"It won't for long. The worst will wear off soon."

"I still can't see in the light properly."

"No," Chelamah replied, "that won't wear off I'm afraid."

Chelamah moved to the back of the basement. She could hear movement above them. She was surprised that Luka, of all people, lived with his grandmother. Who would've thought. A simple room, a double bed, a large TV but a very impressive computer setup. Luka's home made her feel sad. Lonely, unexciting, and temporary. She wondered when he realised there was no point in thriving. No point in studying, working, or learning. When had he accepted that his human life was not worth paying much attention to? That he wouldn't be a player in this world for very long so why bother? What a cruel tease. Born human, grow and get a taste of what that really means just before you become a monster.

"Why are you doing this?" Luka asked suspiciously.

Chelamah sat on the floor, leaning against his bed, and facing him. "I honestly don't know."

"Devotees looking out for each other?" Luka held his bottle up as if about to give her a 'cheers'. "That's what Crystal said. Salut' you fucking bitch."

256

Yes, she was. Chelamah smiled. "Yeah, she's pretty damn awful."

Luka looked embarrassed. "Aren't you going to ask me?"

"No" Chelamah replied. She knew why he had done it. She didn't think him stupid. Gullible yes, stupid no.

"Why?" Luka asked, looking at her quizzically.

Chelamah sighed, staring into space. "Because I know why."

"You do?"

"The same reason why I'm sitting here spooning water into you. Maybe we give a shit about each other because no-one else does. But we aren't the stupid ones. We aren't the weak ones. We know what we are. Crystal doesn't. She plays the game so hard that Mika actually lets her think she's won. He knows this. But she's the same as us, nothing more. I'm here because at the end of the day we're fodder to these people. We're disposable. I know that, you know that. Crystal, however, doesn't see it. The more she fools herself the closer and closer she creeps to her end, and it *will* happen. Crystal seriously believes in the lie she has constructed for herself. She's a lot further along than she thinks. And when she falls, and she *will* fall, it will be at a much higher price than ours. That's the definition of stupid."

Luka nodded slowly. It made sense to him. He liked Chelamah. He always had, as had Jason. In fact, most people did. It was such a shame she was wasted on a two-faced prick like Noah. She was right. Crystal tried to bring about his end and for what? There was nothing she would gain from him not being in the picture. It was all just a cruel and nasty game. That was all, nothing more. There was no other thought, no planning. It was just entertainment for a petty, nasty mind. The least that they could do was be there for each other.

He stared at Chelamah. He wanted her to know. Why did he want her to know? Because she was right. They were disposable.

"Noah killed your mother," Luka declared coldly. "Noah killed your mother because Mika needed her out of the way so he could get her Grimoires. They were protected. The protection broke with her death."

Chelamah jumped to her feet. "That's not true."

"Yes, it is. It is true, I swear to you, and right now I have nothing to lose by telling you. She didn't kill herself. I know it. Jason knows it. Mika and Crystal know it. She didn't jump. She was attacked and thrown."

"No," the room span. Chelamah gasped, trying to catch her breath. "*No.*"

"Why do you think Noah went from just a curiosity to a place at the table?" Luka took no pleasure from Chelamah's pain, but he did take satisfaction that he would no longer have to hold their secret. "He was a good boy Chel… he did what he was told."

Chapter 23

Noah's head lulled to one side. Drool dripped from his mouth. He swallowed, shaking his head uncomfortably as he heard the familiar creak of the restraints beneath him. He opened his eyes and felt nauseous. Jesus, how much had he taken last night? He couldn't feel his hands. His legs were stiff and cold.

"Fuck" he muttered, banging his head on the rest behind him. He wriggled his fingers, warming them up before uncomfortably dragging his right hand out of the restraint. He extended his frozen fingers, gently and painfully opening and closing them. What an idiot. He had been in this thing all night. At least the pain from the last venture had gone, but he was gonna be sore after at least 12 hours harnessed to a wooden chair.

"Ow, ow, ow" he grunted, pulling painfully on the second restraint. It was tight. The left always was. Loosely restrained right hand but everything else gets battened down. Only usually, he would then release the restraints and collapse painfully onto the bed. But thanks to the whiskey and oxy, that wasn't the case last night.

"What are you doing?" A voice asked accusingly.

Startled, Noah stared through the haze to a familiar silhouette standing in the doorway.

"What?" Chelamah repeated, her face hard, her voice stern, "…are you doing?"

Speechless, Noah quickly turned his attention back to the strap.

"Chel… no… wait." He panicked, releasing his arm, and turning his attention to the legs. "Please just listen."

Chelamah walked in, glaring in disgust at the structure around him. So, this was why she was never allowed here. All of this was why he had looked so damn nervous when she arrived the last time. That chair once sat in the

Pantheon. That chair had once been used by another, and she knew exactly what its purpose was.

His face contorted with pain. He slid from the seat and stood, steadying himself on the wall beside him.

"My mother?" shaking her head in disbelief and grief, she cried. "Damn you Noah!"

Christ, she knew. "Please just… just wait, just… listen." Frantically he chased her into the front room.

Reaching the front door, Chelamah turned to face him, furious "Why? How could you do that? She was all I had. I have nothing left. Who was it last night? Who? How many have there been? And why? Let me take a guess… Mika!"

The room plummeted into darkness. Noah shook his head in panic. "N-n-no, no, no, Chel no. It w-w-wasn't that simple."

"My mother was the only hope I had! So who else did Mika tell you to destroy? Kill? Huh? Or did we just maim last night? Or perhaps, we just beat the shit out of them and threw them off a roof! God damnit Noah! I knew this about Jason. I knew Miya but you're in bed with him too."

"You know I'm n-n-not! It's not like that, there was nothing I could do, it's what…"

"What he wanted!" Chelamah interjected. "Christ! Complete disclosure? I have been dealing with what's left of Luka. Mika has all but finished him. Like he finished Will. Like he finished Jennifer and Cameron and Liam. But not my mother Noah, not her. That's on YOU. Do you understand? Do you?! Why do you all listen to him? You all let him inside your head already knowing what he is, what he'll do to you. Why?"

"Stop," Noah yelled. Chelamah was primed. He could see her eyes beginning to shine, her voice began to deepen.

"For what Noah? What did my mother do? What did any of these *people* do?" She screamed.

If she attacked him, the Soldier would attack her. It was a certainty. It wouldn't matter how calm he was, he wouldn't be able to stop it.

Noah straightened himself, looking at Chelamah in defiance. His voice calmed. "I am an Underling. I do what I am created to do. No more and no less. You are *my* Devotee."

Chelamah nodded before scoffing in sad resignation. "Yes, I am. But you are merely a lapdog. You're no better than *them*."

"Neither of us are," Noah scoffed back.

Chelamah shook her head. How dare he. "Stay away from me. Because I'm going to hell. And you will be coming with me I swear to God."

She marched out the front door slamming it hard behind, leaving Noah alone. Staggering back in shock, he fell onto the decrepit couch and placed his shaking hands over his face. She knew and she was gone.

ᴑᴑᴑ

Ellie received the call early in the morning. Her appointment with Dr. Gardiner had been rescheduled for a week's time. As odd as this was, it was more so a relief. With so many things happening, it was harder to regulate her emotions. Harder than usual. She was close, so close to being signed off. Community Treatment Order over and done. No more weekly visits. No more playing with Niles once a week. Though now it had come to light, he had another toy to play with: Joshua. It didn't seem unreasonable in a city as small as theirs. There wasn't an endless supply of child psychs, and he was at the top of his game. She hoped, and was quietly confident, that Josh wouldn't say her name.

Ellie sat in the bank, waiting to be called. She had an appointment, and since she had arrived they had been extremely pleasant to her. Of course they had been. They were making lots of money from her and had been for quite some time. She had written a list of things she needed to discuss. Planning was required, as always. The blood money of her family needed to be used wisely. She would not use it to benefit herself, that was not how she lived.

The tellers sat behind the counters, customers all lined up, waiting their turn. One very made-up woman sat behind the centre desk she had just approached. The automatic doors opened, and she heard sounds from the shopping centre beyond them. So normal. So, so normal. What did that even mean? She would never know this normal. She heard the sounds of children, laughing and carefree. That had been taken from Josh. That had been taken from all of them.

Sam still laughed. How she envied his ability to laugh. He laughed when he was happy. He laughed when he was in danger. He laughed when he was terrified. He even laughed when he was crying. Josh saw wonder in things, so many things. He watched an old man pot plants and it filled him with

261

delight and curiosity. Something she could never feel. It drove her crazy. It made her so *displeased* with them. It was something that she just could not do. Bael? Yes. Emotions were dangerous? Absolutely. But Sam had the same burden. How did he laugh? How did Josh still see goodness and joy? What was wrong with her? The upcoming events could finish her. More than likely, they would. She would meet these people and all it would take was for Bael to reveal itself to them. She didn't know if he would or not. Ellie knew his goal, but she didn't know his game plan. She didn't know how he planned to achieve a goal. How he would it, or would not, benefit by being revealed? Only Bael knew. She had no idea.

"Miss Jameson?" A voice said as a gentleman in a suit came out to meet her, hand outstretched. They shook hands. Formalities over, she followed him as he graciously led her into an office.

OOO

Nate knew this conversation was coming. He had dropped Joshua at school knowing that the moment he left the house Casey would start studying the phone again. He understood this. Of course she would. She wanted to know where Sharon was, and she knew that Josh knew. Nate knew this too. He stood tentatively in the doorway, waiting to enter the house. He also knew that he had to talk his wife into adopting a more subtle approach. He could not change her mind.

Walking into the house, he glanced in the sitting room and for a moment thought it empty. But Casey was there, sitting around the corner on the floor like a teenager, phone in hand, scrolling intently.

"Case, I ..." Nate sighed. Casey immediately raised her finger.

"No, listen to this! Listen! They are talking about something... something bad. Josh keeps referring to it as being *bad*. This person, this Ellie, is not a kid, Nate. I'm telling you now, this is an adult. This other one? *Bossy*? Their name is Sam, I think. Josh calls them Sam. They know this person. That day, that day in the police station..." Casey quickly pulled up the report beside her, the hospital discharge plan and pointed to the date. "Yes! This person tried to call him 8 times! At exactly the same time we were told he collapsed. Where were they? What was going on? Then they messaged."

"What did they say?"

"They said to RUN. Just RUN." Casey looked up, shrugging in frustration. "Then… then he was in the hospital. They saw each other there."

Nate moved towards her. The desperation in her voice was heartbreaking. No, he didn't understand, and yes, he was intrigued, but they had to be careful. He was no psychiatrist, no shrink, but Joshua was an absolute prince of evasion.

"Yes! I agree with you! I agree! but…" Nate ran threw his hands up in frustration as he sat down in front of her. "We have to let him tell us when he's ready."

"We don't know who these people are!" Casey shouted, shaking a finger in the air. "Nate, we don't know. They are talking in codes, riddles. I don't understand it. Something happened, something *is* happening. Listen to this… listen, OK? Josh said something called… 'Fatty' took a lady and a man at the police station. What the hell is Fatty? Nate, there's more to this. Josh asks this Sam person a few days later that, if this Fatty gets a policeman, can the policeman shoot him, and then Josh can save his mum."

"Jesus," Nate gasped, taking the phone from Casey's hand. Reading the response intently.

NO CHAMP THAT'S NOT HOW IT WORKS. TRY NOT TO THINK ABOUT IT. IS THERE ANYWAY YOU CAN FIND URSELF SOME CAKE?

Completely at a loss as to what to do, Nate sighed and continued reading. Casey was right to be scared. Who were they? What mind games had they been playing with a child? These people could be dangerous. A whole other life was going on right under their noses. Discussions, speaking of past events, upcoming meets, and warnings. So many warnings. Nate found himself holding his breath. He breathed out heavily, leaning back on both arms and staring at the ceiling above him.

He shook his head. "Something's not right. Not just this. Josh is a great kid. A great kid! But he scares me."

"Why? He isn't scary. It's these people… this is what…"

"You weren't there!" Nate leapt to his feet, shouting. "You weren't there when the fucking house blew up. It was crazy. Did you not see what happened last night? Didn't you feel it? The cafe? There is something wrong with him."

Casey stared at him, defiantly at first, but he watched her resolve crumble. Yes, she had felt it too. Like Nate she could not explain it and it made her feel foolish and paranoid.

"He saw this Ellie yesterday, you know," she said quietly, calming herself.

"Huh? When? He was at school," Nate snapped.

"Yes and so was she. That's where they met. The library." Jumping to her feet and grabbing the phone, Casey cried "Take the phone away. Hide it."

"Can we at least talk to him first?"

"We will. We will talk to him, but I need that phone gone. I want to know who these people are. We need to know now," she demanded as she raced from the room. "If Josh is in trouble we need to know."

Nate followed his wife as she hurried down the hall. "Where are you going?"

"They are at the school. Whoever this is, that's where they are. You stay here. Hide the phone. I'm going to find this Ellie person."

OOO

Niles could feel the acid rising in his stomach. Those damn pills had made him feel like vomiting all night. It was either that or suffer the orchestra of pain in his arm. God damn, it hurt. He lifted his head slightly off the bed as he waited for the pharmacist to bring the medications he would be taking home, or rather to his in-laws' place. With the attack and then the 'punishment' of staying with his in-laws, his anxiety was understandably peaking. Thankfully, the gut churning medication had a sedating effect that he wholeheartedly embraced.

They had found no evidence of his attacker. None. Jessica not seeing a thing only fuelled his frustration. She sat next to him, guilt ridden as he protested again and again. Mika had been spoken to. Allegedly and predictably, he was horrified at Niles's misfortune. They knew where he was and with whom he was at the time it happened. There was no evidence that he had any involvement at all. Why would there be?

Niles had ignored the multiple well-wishing calls from colleagues during the day. His attack would not go under the radar in their small, professional circle. It was the extreme risk of his occupation and something that all of them had feared at one point or other. There was, however, nothing saying that this attack wasn't random. Niles had to accept that, even though his gut told him otherwise. A freak occurrence, an unlucky, unfortunate run in with a mad man.

"How are you feeling?" Jessica asked.

Niles smiled but said nothing. He felt terrible.

Jessica held his hand. "A few days out of the house. Let the police do their job. Get security reviewed, then we go home."

"I want to go home today," Niles replied quickly.

Jessica turned her head from him, her voice breaking. "Please, please. Just two nights. I can't be there right now."

"Winston?"

"He's with Mary-Beth. I'm not too worried the cat at the moment, Niles, please."

Niles thought to argue but instead smiled as he squeezed her hand and nodded. For her piece of mind, he would. The back door he was dragged through was currently plastic sheeting.

"Yes," Niles agreed. "Let's go to your folks."

Jessica smiled, her eyes red from little sleep and crying. He noticed her hand tremble in his. She had seen nothing yet that also seemed to fan the flames of her fear. He understood this, deciding that he would watch her tonight to ensure that she slept. If he was concerned, he would prescribe her something to help her settle. Then, he would most likely pop a pill himself. He could tolerate Tom and Judy for a few nights, he was sure. They were pleasant enough, if a bit overbearing, but certainly his well-being would be a priority. They were a good family.

He had managed to shower in spite of the plastic bag wrapped around the cast. Now dressed in clean clothes - he didn't ask Jessica where his original clothing was, they had, no doubt, been disposed of - an enthusiastic orderly bought him a wheelchair to take him down to the main entrance. Niles didn't need or want one, but the orderly argued robustly.

Jessica wrapped his scarf around his neck like a child, tucking it in and placing a sports cap on his head. He blushed with embarrassment before taking a seat on a hard plastic chair that caused the sutures on his back to sting and ache. He sat, waiting for Jessica to bring the car around to the front of the building. Awkwardly he pulled out his phone. Emails confirmed that all appointments were rescheduled. Kay was on it. He would call her tonight if no-one else. She would worry.

He looked through the windows to the outside world. God it looked cold and miserable out there. His mood was low, very low. He scanned the room for something to keep him preoccupied, and more importantly, awake. Calmly, he found himself locking eyes with a complete stranger who stood on the other side of the window.

His first thought was how beautiful she was. Slender and elegant, her hair was wavy, shiny black cascading to her shoulders, her skin flawless with large, brown eyes. She was staring at him, and a feeling of recognition moved within him. He had seen this exquisite woman before. He was sure of it. If he hadn't been so sedated, perhaps he could have remembered where, or at least when. He started to feel embarrassed at how long they'd been regarding each other, but a part of him wanted to just lose himself in her peaceful allure. *Allure*. Good god. He hadn't ever regarded that as a word with any substance. Yet here he was. These drugs were something else.

Jessica entered, taking his attention for a split second, and when he looked again the woman was gone. He went to stand as his fiancé placed her arm under his elbow like an old man. If only she understood. It wasn't the injuries that made him shaky, it was the drugs. He looked through the window expectantly. She was gone. Perhaps she hadn't been there to begin with?

Once securely strapped into the passenger seat of the warm car, Jessica sat down next to him. Slowly she reached over to him, and he took her hand.

"It's OK," he soothed. "It's over."

Smiling through tears she nodded as the car pulled away.

Chapter 24

"And then it came out again, and I said, 'don't let it out!', but they did!" Joshua continued to explain as he pushed Charlie through the dining hall to the ramp. "They never listen when they're in year two because they're only small. I was small last year too, but the rabbits got out and then they couldn't find them again, so we had to look as well."

Charlie sat quietly, smiling to himself. He had forgotten how much children could talk. The exciting saga of the accidental release of the rabbits from the classroom next door had caused quite the scandal.

"Absolutely Master Josh. It's criminal, but could you please remember I am in this chair that is currently…"

There was a loud crash as a footplate collided with the leg of a side table sending a big bunch of fake flowers onto the floor. Josh peeped out from behind Charlie to the mess on the carpet.

"Don't worry about them. They are as fake as Nurse Morgan's mammoth bosoms," Charlie waved dismissively. "Now come along, escaping rabbits aside, I have something even more exciting to show you."

Josh pulled the chair backwards. Charlie looked past his feet as the faux plant was crushed beneath the front wheels as Josh propelled him up the ramp.

"OK" Josh agreed, pausing for a moment to ponder Nurse Morgan and her mammoth, before adding. "Did I tell you that they escaped before that one time, and that they had three rabbits, but they only found two, but then they said they only had two, but we knew they had three?"

Cynically Charlie shook his head. "Oh Master Josh. That's criminal."

"I know!" Josh continued his story as he shoved Charlie up the ramp and down the hall towards his room. Charlie tuned out as Josh's tale continued. Using his foot he opened the door as Josh, caught in the excitement of his own story, pushed him through.

"SHHHHH!" Charlie hissed softly, as the chair came to a stop. "We must be quiet. Look."

Josh fell silent and stepped from behind the chair, looking about the room curiously. What was he supposed to be seeing? The curtains were open. He could now see the layer of dust on the table with the pictures. Surely that wasn't what Charlie wanted him to see? It was then he noticed three little pots lined up along the window frame in a perfect row. Each bathed in the gentle, afternoon light.

"You planted them," Josh smiled.

"Yes, but we have to be quiet around them. You see, they are still a little scared."

"Why?"

"Aren't you a little scared when you go to a new home?"

Surprised that he had never thought about plants being scared before, Josh quietly stepped to the window. "Will they grow here?"

"Not too much sun. Nice, soft soil. And *quiet*. Yes I think it will suit them nicely, don't you?" Charlie gestured for Josh to have a closer look.

Josh nodded and looked at the little green leaves that Charlie cared about so much. It was a strange thing, he thought, that these plants didn't demand Charlie to care for them. Charlie just wanted to. Such a small thing, such a gentle desire to care about something that you didn't need to. It made Charlie happy, and it made Josh feel happy too.

"They look happy already," Josh smiled, remembering that there were four. "Where did the other one go?"

Charlie pointed to the table with the pictures. "It's over there! I did three but I didn't have the energy to do another. You chose that one. You can tuck it in."

Josh trotted to the table. The seedling tube and a little clap pot filled, no doubt with 'fluffy dirt', sat beside it with a small plastic spoon. Touching the spoon, he looked down at the small stack of rough paper beside the pot and noticed the beautiful handwriting. He couldn't read the joined-up words, but he had never seen anything like it. A line of delicate, elegant squiggles.

"What are these words?" Josh placed his finger upon the textured paper. "They look really nice."

A trance gripped him. The words seemed to flow like a journey across the old paper and somewhere, without even being able to read them, they made sense. They were telling Josh an unspoken story. Charlie watched Josh as he gazed upon the writings. It stood to reason that these would make sense to the boy. This writing came from his hand but not from his will. Penning secrets, riddles and statements that flowed from him without any need to ponder or for thought.

"Oh yes. They are very nice. Can you read them?" Charlie asked quietly.

Josh began to shake his head and then stopped. Could he? The writing told a tale. It was telling him a story, but not through its words. It told it through its beauty, its dancing flow and blooms.

"It…" Josh stopped, as the words flowed into his mind. "The Heretic betrayed the commander. Bael, the scourge of men and beast of many faces. God had prepared for this. Imperfection was created to condemn and control that which was intractable and lawless. There are no mistakes. There is always reason. Perfection is locked inside the flawed."

Smiling, Charlie nodded while Josh blinked his eyes as the daydream lifted and he looked back, "or something like that… kinda. I can't read too good."

Wheeling himself over to the bench, Charlie stopped beside Josh and ruffled the child's hair. Leaning back, he let out a large sigh. "Oh my boy. For so many years I have penned words just like these. It seems that you can read them a lot better than you think you can."

"Why do you do it?" Josh asked, picking up the seedling whilst still staring at the magic words.

"I don't seem to have a choice. I think you can understand. Sometimes we don't get a choice about what comes to us."

"Can I have one?"

Charlie gave Josh a stern, certain look. "As much as I would love to give my new friend a gift such as these, I am afraid I cannot. Giving them away would be akin to giving you my own arm."

Josh nodded. He understood. Charlie, however, pulled something out of the pocket of his old, chequered shirt. It looked like black string. He looked at it for a moment before holding it out to Josh, who stared at it in fascination. The old worn string looked like it was fashioned from an old boot lace.

Fastened to it was a small piece of paper with the most beautifully drawn squiggle that Josh had ever seen.

"But this one," he held up, placing it over Josh's head. "This one belongs to you."

Josh turned the little symbol around to look at it. It was drawn in the same wonderful hand as the pages he just read. "It's awesome."

"It is indeed. It will keep you safe. Scare the bad away." Charlie smiled and nodded. "Do you know when I wrote this one?"

Josh shook his head.

Charlie looked behind him as if he was about to tell a big secret. "Right after you left yesterday. That's what happened. Some people, some special people, make me want to write and write. I will keep these here, keep them safe... but they do belong to you. And this special one belongs around your neck. Does that make sense Master Josh?"

It didn't make sense at all, but Josh still smiled and nodded. Josh wanted to take it home and put it under his bed. The normal bed, not the broken one. He wanted to promise that it would be safe, but slowly it became clear that Mr. Russo was protecting them. Maybe better than Josh could.

"Listen Master Josh. It must stay around your neck. Never take it off, you hear?"

Josh nodded. "Why did you write them for me?"

"Who knows! But maybe because you are a very brave boy."

Immediately Josh blushed, turned and walked away with the little clay pot. A hundred memories of him being 'not brave' played like painful clips in his mind. "I'm not brave; I cry sometimes. Sometimes I wasn't brave at all."

"No," Charlie said sternly, making Josh feel for a moment he was in trouble. "That thing with you, that darkness, I see it. It's a very bad thing young man. A very bad thing that causes a lot of hurt."

Josh frowned. What was he supposed to say? What was the old man talking about? His new shoes? The small pot in his hands? Or the monstrous beast prowling the corridor with its grunting and growling ebbing and flowing as it paced eagerly outside the door.

"That thing is your enemy. That thing would devour the world if you allowed it. It is so very strong, so big and powerful. And who could hold back such a thing as that? You. You lock away an evil that, if the world had on its shoulders, it would quiver and collapse. It is your bravery, your heart.

You are its worst enemy. Remember that Master Josh. And that takes a man of such courage. A man of great bravery." Mr. Russo's eyes, though old and wrinkly, looked tearful. Mr. Russo was talking about the Monster Dog. How did he know? Could he see it? People with good eyes couldn't see it. Mr. Russo needed glasses and yet, he could?

"You can see him?"

Hesitating for a moment, Charlie turned his chair and pointed impatiently at the windowsill. "Onwards Master Josh, that small plant is getting dizzy just hovering in the air. Take your spoon."

Giving a small "Oh" Josh trotted back to the counter, grabbed the spoon and ran back to the windowsill. This had always amused Charlie about children. So easily distracted, trains of thought jumping over each other like crickets in a field.

"Mr. Russo, is this fluffy dirt... fluffy enough?"

"It's plenty fluffed. Now are you happy with where you will home him?"

Josh nodded, turning around and focusing on the little pot and spoon. He had to get the little plant home.

Charlie smiled as he watched the child ponder such a simple task that carried so much weight. Josh felt responsible. That little thing, powerless in even Josh's hands, needed him to care for it. To nurture it.

"And call me Grandpa Charlie, boy, everybody else does."

∞∞∞

Ellie arrived late to work but no-one would notice. She would be in the library at school finishing time. If Josh had an opportunity, he would come to her. He knew she was there every day and that was enough. She would speak to him, listen to him, look for cues on how things were going at home. Putting the vacuum on her back, she knelt down and plugged it in. The librarian had already left for the day, and she would lock up before she left and headed to the administration block.

Tonight was the night. She was unsure of the exact mechanics of it yet, but she would soon know. Ellie had to be close to these people without being identified. This depended entirely on Bael, of course. They would not be able to see it, but their monsters might. It seemed so strange, other creatures such as hers. It also seemed strange that Sam's original idea – '*we could tell them you're my girlfriend!*' - had seemed a good one to him. He was gay and

271

35. She had only just turned 18. Creepy on so many levels. When she pointed this out, he quickly agreed that it wasn't a good idea after all. Thank God.

Music in her ears and the vibrating vacuum in her hand, Ellie didn't so much hear a sound behind her, but felt it. Always tuned in, slightly on edge, she turned around and was startled. A person. A real person was in the room with her. The woman's mouth was forming words that Ellie couldn't hear above the music in her ears. Quickly she pulled her headphones down.

"I'm sorry, the library is closed. Admin is still open though." Without waiting for a reply, Ellie slid her headphones back over her head, only stopping when she heard her name.

"Ellie?" Casey said firmly. "Are you Ellie?"

Panicked, Ellie stood still and turned to face the stranger. She was older than her, with strawberry blonde hair. She looked uncomfortable and weary. There were a few options as to who this woman was but, in her gut, she already knew.

"Who are you?" Ellie asked coldly. Casey cautiously moved forward.

"Are you Ellie?" Casey asked staunchly.

"I asked," Ellie replied, shit. *Shit, shit, shit.* "Who are you?"

Ellie slid the vacuum off her back and placed it beside her. This could be anyone. There were people looking for her and, right now, her worst paranoid fears were becoming a reality.

"I've been waiting for you. Joshua," Casey replied. "You can either tell me or tell the police, it's your choice."

Ellie took a deep breath. How could she possibly warn this person that being aggressive with her could be a fatal mistake? She took another breath as the stranger's eyes looked deep into hers. She was terrified, not of this person but of direct confrontation.

Ellie could hear the rattling of chains and tortured screaming. It grew louder as Bael sat patiently on an unseen chair, hidden in the shadows of a dark aisle to her side. In her peripheral visions were others, shadows that began to emerge carrying with them their own demented tunes and echoes.

She had to calm this down. She couldn't let this tip over. For this, she needed the women to calm the fuck down.

"I know Josh," she stated, aware that Bael was slowly striding towards her. Josh, her weakness, her kryptonite. "He goes to this school."

272

Casey nodded sternly. "I know you've been talking to him. I know who you are."

"Do you?" Ellie replied lightly, engaging a sense of curiosity to subdue her rising anger. "If you know then why you are asking?"

Don't challenge her. De-escalate.

Casey opened her mouth to speak. Ellie interjected, "I am Ellie. I know Josh. Who are you?"

"I'm his family. I'm his mother's sister," Casey snapped, brushing her hair back with her hand. Uncomfortable, Casey didn't like confrontation anymore then Ellie did. Perhaps, she could sense the evil that eagerly waited in every shadow of the room.

"OK," Ellie nodded calmly. "Now we know who each other are. Why are you here?"

"I want you to stop messaging him. I found his phone. I know the conversations you and this other person have been having with him. I read it all."

"Then why haven't you contacted the police already?" Ellie remained stone-faced. Casey looked taken aback by such a direct challenge. Ellie could feel, however, that there was another reason that Casey was here. That reason was more important than merely keeping Ellie away from Josh. If she had read Josh's phone, of which she made him promise that he would keep with him always (nice one Josh), keeping her away would be merely incidental. What did she want to know?

"Oh I will," Casey stated. Maybe she would, thought Ellie. But right now, she was bluffing. "And I'll tell the school too."

"OK," Ellie nodded. The thought of losing her job was not a sad one. But the police, the police would be bad.

Casey raised a finger at Ellie. "We have the messages and the numbers. They would know who this other person is. They would find out. So I want…"

"What? What do you want? Me to stay away?" Ellie snapped. "We've done this already. What do you want to know?"

"I don't want to know…"

"Yes you do. You're here, you didn't have to be, but you are. I also know that you are a good person. You and your husband. Josh thinks you're both great." Ellie shrugged, smiling softly as tears welled in Casey's eyes. "He wanted to stay with me, you know. I wanted him to, but he couldn't't."

"Who are you?!" Casey shouted through sad frustration. "I don't understand! What happened to him?! What happened to Sharon?!"

Ellie nodded, thinking two steps ahead. Feed her information, bring her down. Enough to placate her for now. Give her time to think. Casey and her husband had sensed something was peculiar with their nephew. Nothing too bad yet. Tragically nothing as bad as it was about to become, or else Casey wouldn't be standing in front of her.

"I gave him that phone to talk him into going to you. He wouldn't have otherwise, believe me. I tried, but you can't really *make* Josh do anything. You probably have a feeling that Josh isn't quite like other children. You're right. He isn't. There's something with him that is awful." Ellie shook her head. She needed to convince this woman to handle the situation differently. "It really is awful what happened and what continues to happen to him. Josh and I met by accident, seriously. Pure accident. But let me tell you this, to give perspective. If Josh and I had not met, neither one of us would be here now."

There was no mistake, what Ellie was telling Casey was scaring her. It confirmed to Ellie that Casey had noticed something but couldn't quite put her finger on it.

"What do you mean?" Casey gasped anxiously.

"Don't make him angry. He's a great kid, but he's still a kid. He's going to get angry." Ellie's voice choked with pent up emotion, sadness and regret. "You won't see it coming. Neither will he. You have no idea what it is. The little you know about it keeps you safe, but not for long. He won't want to. He'll try so hard not to, but he won't be able to stop it. Please, just don't make him angry."

"My sister," Casey replied, wiping tears from her eyes. "What happened?"

"Just stop asking him. She's not coming back. It was a horrible, horrible accident. He couldn't have stopped it. Please don't ever make him feel that he could. Just look after him, make him feel safe. I can't. I can't tell you anymore. I can't help you." *I can't help you.* Never had that phrase been applied so literally yet disguised in words so dismissive. It was as if she was sending someone to their death.

Fortifying herself, Casey nodded angrily. "Fine, then I go to the police, and they sort this out."

"No, no wait!" Ellie blurted as Casey turned heading for the door.

"Don't contact him, the phone is gone. He will not be here tomorrow. I imagine you'll be hearing from the police very soon. Stay away from him." Casey stormed away.

"No!" Ellie stated fearfully. "Don't take it away. Don't. He likes it, we calm him, that's all. Please don't take it away, he'll... Goddammit... something will happen. Do you understand? Something *will happen*."

Rolling her eyes in feigned fortitude, Casey headed to the door.

"Stay away. You hear me? Stay away."

She left, leaving Ellie to watch the door swing closed behind her. Christ. Oh Christ. She was going to take his phone. She would, no doubt, challenge Josh about it and then... oh Christ. She was powerless. There was nothing she could do.

There was a sudden boom! The room turned to chaos. Books flew from their shelves as furniture smashed against the walls. Ellie fell to the floor covering her head. Biting back a scream, she waited for the ruckus to end. Again... it was changing again. This was her, this was Bael... this was them. The room fell silent. Slowly she lifted her head and looked at the wreckage about her. Her hands trembled as she pushed herself up from the floor with debris still falling to the ground. The fire alarms started. Of course they would. People would come. Shaking, she ran to the counter and grabbed her backpack before manoeuvring her way through the debris to the door.

The siren continued as parents and children scattered from the school yard. The teachers had their yellow vests on. This had only been a drill before, but Ellie was grateful. Happening now meant that half the school had left already. She could leave and hopefully, go unnoticed. There was Josh, Casey was loading him into the car, quickly. He was talking, he was delaying but she was adamant.

Walking from the school gates, she noticed with deep self-hatred that her mind was playing out the likely scenario. They would challenge Josh. There would be no police. There would be no calling anybody. He would destroy them and then he would come to her. It would be awful but necessary, perhaps. A gruesome, selfish yet beneficial solution. Casey and her husband's fate was sealed.

Chapter 25

The shroud of darkness had ever so slightly begun to lift from Luka's mind. The voices and slick black cloud that covered everything was fading. Chel said this would happen, though he would never return to what he was before he was made to sit in the abyss. His mind was now molested by absurdly cruel and equally delightful thoughts. As he emerged from this dark cocoon he wondered, did he return enough to endure one more journey?

Taking a drag of his cigarette, he desperately craved the smell he previously despised. Senses were dulled, tastes were lifeless. His palate was craving something that was not of this world. Death. He craved the sickly scent of rot. The hunger was all consuming.

So he would have to try. In that place was the only thing that could help him and, even though he didn't remember in his organic human mind, the monster in him would know exactly where it was. But to go there was risky. He may not be able, or want, to come back, thus serving to only expedite his descent from man to monster. A descent which was going to happen anyway. He could feel it edging ever closer; at this point he had nothing to lose.

To reclaim the Grimoires he needed his friend back. He would have to tell him what he had done. Sadly, he reflected, he had given up his advantage. He had, in an act of contemptuous revenge, told Chelamah about Noah; about her mother. It was the only advantage that he had over Noah. He could have used it as leverage against the Underling, to force him to take him back there. But he had been stupid and impulsive, and now he was furious at himself and his stupidity.

The day he had watched Aahna take her plunge he had seen the Soldier savagely attack her. It was during this chaos that the shadow inside him simply glanced to the left and laid hands upon the Grimoires, before disappearing into the dark rip left by the Underling and his monster. Now, sitting in the alley of the old apartment building where Aahna met her end, Luka stared up at its dark facade. He remembered entering, remembered the bullshit that followed, but then… the memories belonged to something else.

This was the time before Chel. This was a time when Noah served The Pantheon in a role barely above Luka's. The Grimoires Noah delivered to Mika were not complete. Adequate to placate him, but not complete.

The Grimoires of Aahna had been taken by Luka into the realm of the Soldier while it was at the end of a leash held by Noah. Though Luka would not be told who, or even if, Noah was currently taking someone down, Jason would. Even after the last indiscretion, Jason would know. He had to follow the Soldier again and, to do that, he had to know what Noah was doing.

☉☉☉

Joshua had watched from the back window of the car as the school siren blasted out across the grounds. He was glad he had left. The teachers were wearing their yellow tops. They wore them sometimes when they had a drill and they all had to go outside and sit on the oval. It seemed silly doing a drill thing when the school was emptying anyway. Maybe they were just testing the sirens.

Relaxing against the car window, with the Dog pounding the road beside them, he sighed and thought about his day. Mr. Russo - Grandpa Charlie - saw the Dog. This was crazy because he was told that couldn't happen. The only person who had seen the Dog was Ellie. Well, others had but that was very bad. Why would some people see his secret? He would have to ask Ellie about it at school tomorrow. He would message her tonight, after dinner, but wouldn't ask her that question. That question would be better when they were together.

Casey seemed a little upset. She was smiling, asking him about his day, but he could sense the unease in the car. She mentioned his bedroom again. She said that it was very strange, and then she looked at him as if expecting him to say something. He just nodded and agreed. There was nothing else he could say. It was strange. They both knew that. The only difference was he knew the reason why it happened, and she didn't.

As they pulled into the driveway, he looked at the house and a strange feeling overcame him. He felt uncomfortable. Not by anything that was happening, but at what he felt was going to happen? The young boy didn't understand the feeling of foreboding. To him it was just a sensation of dread and sadness.

Casey gave his knee a squeeze and got out of the car. Josh opened the door and walked to the front of the car. He stopped and watched Casey smile at him before walking up the three small steps to the front door. As she turned her key, Josh felt unwell. He didn't want to go inside.

○○○

Her damn phone wouldn't stop ringing. It was work, of course. Today was the day they'd chosen to notice her. Had Casey spoken to them? Most likely not. It felt as if the rules had suddenly changed. Now, Bael and this whole nightmare was invading her physical world, touching it, destroying. Previously only triggered by rage, was it now triggered by conflict? She didn't know if this was just her or others, but she did remember Josh's text: THE DOG ECPLODED THE ROOM.

And Sam? Was this happening for him too?

There was little chance that in the chaos surrounding the school Casey had had the chance to speak to anyone. If it was going to happen, it'd happen tomorrow. If the police were going to be involved, it would be tonight. If Casey and Nate get put on the wall, that would also be tonight. Why? What part of her sick psyche made that thought able to bring her relief? Was she merely considering it a possibility, or was she actually hoping for it? No. This level of introspection was not helpful right now. Now, she had to roll with whatever happened.

The phone rang again. She couldn't turn it off, that would be suspicious. They were checking, merely checking. The fire drills in the past had required the staffing roster to be collected. Her name would have been on it. She had to answer, or things would complicate further.

It was indeed the school principal. Thinking quickly, Ellie responded that she hadn't been there today as she was sick, and she did call. Someone took the message, but it seemed they had not passed it on. Ellie went with that and sighed a "sorry". The principal said nothing more. She was in the clear, from that ton of bullshit anyway. It would not matter. She would not

278

be returning anyway. Tonight, she would wait for Josh. Then they would run. They would go anywhere they wanted. Away from these people. Away from the increasing shit storm around them. Sooner or later, everything that was building between Sam and these people, the monsters and themselves, would hit them all in the face. They had to go. Let it play out without them.

As Ellie was planning her next move, a nagging thought kept making itself heard. Without them, it couldn't play out. And everyone involved knew that Bael and the Firewolf were needed. It was only a matter of time before they were found out.

Ellie would meet Jason tonight. She had to know. She had to see what Bael would do. Would Bael let himself be seen, or not? This would give her an indication of not whether he was intending on winning or losing; about how Bael was going to play the game.

ɔɔɔ

Sam would once again meet his new acquaintance at 8pm. He sat lazily on his couch, TV on in the background as he pondered what the night ahead may bring. He had messaged Chelamah… no response. This was strange. He expected long gaps between Ellie's messages, but not Chel's. He wasn't worried, exactly, but found it curious. She knew he had met Jason and still, nothing. Reminding himself it wasn't all about him, he checked the time on his phone once more.

They were meeting in a very public place this time, which was a relief. Jason had revealed an impulsiveness at their first meet that was unsettling. He wasn't sure how far Jason was prepared to go, or for what reason, but his body still hurt. He glanced beside him to the green mottled torso upon the lap of the small girl. She smiled down at it. Slowly she wound her long fingers around the intestines that had already been twisted many, many times before. The chest muscles twitched. The shoulder stump of the left arm lifted up and down, almost to a beat. This poor soul would be so used to the pain that it knew nothing else. Small, purulent streams of body fluid trickled down its torn, sagging stomach and pooled on the couch beneath. In his own mind, as it always was.

The *teddyman* sat beside her on the couch, the head back on the mangy fur tonight. Sam didn't know if the flayed body once belonged to the head of this tormented toy. He had learned over years not to ponder such things.

279

The torso he had seen before, and they looked at different stages of decomposition. The head looked fresher than the trunk on her lap. Snapping himself out of these thoughts, he stood and headed into the bathroom to brush his teeth and quickly spray some cheap catalogue-special cologne that he'd found in the cupboard. It's not like this was a date – the very thought of intimacy with Jason made his skin crawl.

Making his way to the front door, he stopped to don his scarf and coat. What was the agenda tonight? What was his goal? Last time he didn't have one. He let Jason do the talking and a floodgate opened. He would see where tonight's adventures would lead him. Play it by ear. The Child joined him at the door, *teddyman* in hand, mouth gaping again like a goldfish.

Sam left, turning the light off and slamming the door behind him. The room was now in darkness but was not silent. There was the slow, dripping sound of sanguineous, purulent fluid as it continued to run from the couch onto the carpet below. It was something visceral and real.

ooo

Ellie had never constructed a list for running away before. She had no time. Methodically, quickly, yet with hands still trembling, she filled her case that lay on the floor. Kneeling beside it, she began to place the sort items she required. Clothes - not too many - ID, passport, bank details. They had money, and lots of it. Once they started moving they could go anywhere they wanted. She would be free; Josh would be happy. But what of Sam? Would she tell him? Would Josh and she take him with them? Every new thought bought knew dilemmas. Yes, yes they would. He was out there doing his best to protect them. He deserved nothing less than them to help him. But that would mean three Ascendants together. Two was bad enough, and if this was becoming worse for her, then she was sure it was for the boys also.

It was not too late. She had time for Josh to come to her and then they would get Sam. She had little doubt that he would agree. A drastic move like this was something he would thrive on. Tonight, she and Josh might stay somewhere on the outskirts of the city, they could find Sam tomorrow morning and leave. She didn't know the schedule of the people with him. How soon until they would be missed? It was OK. Find Josh, get the *fucking phone* and go. The only people aware of that damn phone's existence were

Sam, Casey and Nate. If her predictions were correct, two out of three would not be an issue for much longer. Not be… an issue. Her stomach turned as she leant heavily forward, hands on head.

Not an issue.

My God. How callous had she become. These were good people. They had looked after Josh so well and she was willing to consider them disposable and inconvenient. She had defended herself for so long, and by doing this she had protected others. Why was she ready for others to suffer a fate as horrific as it would be, as long as the horror didn't come from her?

None of them were immune to the danger, but they knew it existed and, dare she believe it, were less vulnerable. They had some protection, defences they could try. Normal people had nothing. These people who cared for Josh had no chance. Did Josh want that? No. He would never forgive himself. She had never been granted a day without reliving shame of that first night.

Pulling the suitcase lid down, she stared at it in contemplation. She had no choice. She would have to make them listen. They would have to see and understand. If it didn't work, if she couldn't convince them, then the outcome would not be her fault. But she had to try.

OOO

Joshua spooned another mouthful of mashed potato into his mouth. Nate smiled at him from across the table. He had never before seen someone pay so much attention to the sensation of taste. Josh's face showed intent concentration on what his taste buds were telling him. Josh looked up and caught the smile. It was funny, Josh thought, how sometimes even when adults smile they still look sad. Like Casey on the drive home. Her face smiled, her voice sounded happy, but… she was sad at the same time. He couldn't quite explain it but then he reminded himself that he had smiled sometimes when he didn't feel like it. Maybe that was what they were doing. He hoped he hadn't done anything wrong. He'd been very good and had stopped doing anything he thought might make them upset with him. They weren't shouting or hitting him, so that was a good sign.

Joshua had told them about his day and about Mr. Russo, who was now letting him call him Grandpa Charlie. He told them of the little begonia and the tiny pot that the seedling now called home. He was happy the plant got to see out the window and hoped it wouldn't look back into Grandpa Charlie's old, dusty room too much.

"So how often do you get to go to the home?" Nate asked.

Josh pulled a thinking face. "Um… we go for two days in a week, for four weeks. It's nice, but sometimes it smells a bit but that's because the flowers are old and die. Grandpa Charlie said that the ones that don't die aren't real anyway." Josh stopped in thought. "That's why he wanted to take some real flowers into his room because otherwise this lady with no legs - heifer Doris - takes them all."

Nate laughed. "Josh, do you know what heifer means?"

Confused, with his mouth full of the last remnants from his plate, Josh shook his head.

"It means a calf-less cow," Casey shook her head tiredly. "It's not a nice thing to call a person."

Josh was shocked. Wow. He thought it just meant an old *lady* or something. He stopped himself from smiling. *Heifer.*

"OK," Casey smiled. "All done? Do you have any homework?"

Josh nodded without a second thought. Time alone, time to message Ellie and tell her about Grandpa Charlie and the Dog.

"Alright sweetheart, go finish that up and then we'll talk."

Talk about what? thought Josh. That was a strange thing to say, of course they would talk. They had been talking since he got in the car. Did that just mean she wanted to talk about some more? He wasn't sure what else he would have to say but he would try.

Collecting his plate, he carefully lifted it from the table and walked to the dishwasher. He noticed the glance that Casey gave Nate. Maybe Nate was in trouble? It was weird, but he was sure he hadn't done anything.

Jogging through the kitchen to the room down the corridor, he thought about how good he had become at texting. Ellie and Sam would be very interested to know about Grandpa Charlie and Josh couldn't help but think, though he didn't know why, it would be important that they knew.

In the dining room, Nate pushed his chair out and leaned back heavily. Casey stared at him silently for a moment before saying, "I told you I won't go to the police until we speak to him. Just let him settle a bit first."

"And I told *you* that we really should have that doctor's input before we do," Nate stressed. "He's been through enough. Can we at least keep him out of the firing line for the- "

"What firing line?" Casey snapped, insulted. "He is not in any firing line, and we've got to make sure he's safe. I told you that the woman - *girl* - at his school was not right. It was weird."

"All of this," Nate leant forward angrily, straining to keep his voice down, "it's weird. I don't want to fuck him up even more than..."

The two adults quickly stopped talking as Josh skidded around the corner to the room. His face pale, his eyes panicked, he was wringing his hands anxiously.

"Honey," Casey got up. "Sweetheart, what's wrong?"

"I need to call the police" Josh gasped, tears filling his eyes as he choked back a cry.

"The police? Josh... what..." Nate jumped up, alarmed.

"Someone stole something from my room." Josh sobbed just once before looking at Nate and Casey with desperation.

The adults fell quiet. Casey could feel Nate glaring accusingly at the side of her face as she took a deep breath. Obviously, they would talk now.

Chapter 26

The room was spinning. Joshua could hear them talking to him, but the words just didn't matter. He felt sick and scared. Ellie. Casey had spoken to Ellie. Casey said she was worried because she read his phone. She explained that she told Ellie not to come near him anymore. Standing in the kitchen, Josh pleaded, no. He could hear the words, but the words didn't matter. His phone, his phone was gone, and Ellie was told to stay away. No, that couldn't happen.

"No. She's not bad. She's not bad. She's my friend. She stops things. Please don't," he begged. "I'll be good! I'll be good! Don't make her go away. It will be bad."

"Honey no. I know she's your friend, I know, but you need time to get better. You need time to settle sweetheart, please!" Casey knelt in front of Josh, taking his trembling hands in hers. He pulled them away. "Joshua, listen… just listen to me…"

"Just let him go. Let him go," Nate turned to Josh, speaking gently. "Mate I know. I know it's hard, but we need to make sure you're safe. Your aunt and I are so worried about you. We want to make …"

"No!" Josh cried. Why didn't they understand? Safe? He wasn't safe anymore. They weren't safe. No-one was safe. "She made me safe! Things will happen if she's gone, bad things. You've got to give me my phone. It's bad. It's really, really bad…"

His eyes darted about the room. He was looking for something, somewhere to run to, to get away. He grasped the small trinket around his neck. They would take that away too.

"I told you." Nate muttered into Casey's ear. To Josh, calmly, he said, "are you going to come and talk to us? Come and talk to us. Sit down and talk to us."

A look of pure dread washed over Josh. He turned to run. Nate clasped his arm.

"I can't talk to you!" Josh shouted. "Don't make it… don't make it please… don't…"

The home began to darken. Inexplicable shadows of black and red crept over the room as the streetlights outside the windows became dark. Wisps of smoke drifted up the walls beside them.

"Joshua!" Casey shouted sternly. "Calm down!"

Taking a deep breath, Joshua stopped pulling away and turned to face them. "You can't just take other people's stuff! It's not yours! You're just taking stuff and I've been good! I've been good!"

What had he done? Being shouted at again, for nothing. He had just come home from school, nothing more. He had done everything they wanted him to. He had never argued, never been bad. Yet they had taken away his friend, his phone and they were sending him to a school where he didn't know anyone.

His voice shaking, his eyes gleaming, he knew it was beyond the point of return.

"No, no, no," he muttered. Josh glared at them, managing to catch a large, ragged breath before the house shook with a violent, shuddering thud. The monstrous howl of the Firewolf echoed through the house. His breathing stopped, held tight in his chest as his body froze. Nate grabbed Josh pulling him closer "Hey, hey Josh… Casey, call someone! Call someone!"

Casey watched the room around her turn a seething red. The walls melted away, replaced by rust-stained steel. The floor turned to rancid mud beneath their feet as hallways became sinister dark corridors. The ceiling moved away with a violent *crash!* Casey cried out, quickly covering her head as she felt Nate fall beside her.

They watched in bewilderment as their home mutated around them, pulsating with a growing, penetrating heat. Nate tried to pull Joshua closer to them. He stood, completely motionless as large, swinging chains slammed onto the walls, rasping and screeching as they swung back and forth on the glowing metal.

Josh shuddered as he fell forward onto his hands and knees. Taking a large gulp of air he cried out "No!"

Nate glanced about. Had there been an explosion? There was fire and immense heat, but there was no smoke. They had to get out. Jumping to his feet he grabbed Casey's arm, who screamed in fright. He then turned to grab the boy, who remained crouched in the mud, his hands covering his ears.

No. They hadn't done anything that wrong. He didn't mean to. Josh was pulled to his feet. "We've gotta get out," Nate looked about, trying to sound calmer than he was. "The door... Casey *move*... the door!"

Dragging his wife together with Josh, Nate stumbled into the hallway where the front door would have been. He stopped, dumbstruck as he was faced with a long, steaming corridor that seemed to go forever. Nate shook his head. This was crazy. This made no sense. A primal howl vibrated from the walls. Nate froze. Casey covered her mouth, muffling a scream.

"What was that?" Nate gasped. "What..."

Shaking, Josh looked about. This place looked different. This wasn't the junkyard. This was their house. The walls had changed, the ground had changed, but now they were inside a rabbit warren of hot steel walls. The Dog was here, and that only meant one thing. The howl bounced off the walls again, directionless and ubiquitous.

"Don't run," Josh hissed quietly. "It knows where we are."

"What?" Nate whispered, turning to look behind him.

"Just stay quiet... maybe," Josh replied hopelessly. He knew it would make no difference. He knew that any moment now the running, the snarling and that horrible high-pitched screaming would start. What had he done?

Nate looked down at Josh. He didn't see what he expected. Josh wasn't scared. There was sadness, a resignation, but no fear. It dawned on him. Josh had been here before. Josh looked up. Their eyes met for a moment. Nate saw guilt and regret, like he was saying a sad goodbye.

Casey was crying, grasping Nate's arm tightly. Josh couldn't help but think when the Dog came, she would scream the worst. It started as a low vibration that crescendoed to sounds of a wild animal growling... snarling. They could hear its rasping, wet breaths but couldn't place it. It seemed to be coming from everywhere and nowhere, from every dark corridor, from every wall.

○○○

Sam had answered. The signal got lost. He hadn't heard her at all. The address was only minutes away, and she hoped she was not too late. Her

286

plan? Nothing… she had nothing. Convince them, she had to convince them. They might call the police. They might tell her to fuck off, but she had to try. If she could just get them to listen to some of what she had to say. Just enough to warn them. They needed to know Joshua was dangerous. They needed to know what could happen at any moment.

Rounding the corner in the rain, Ellie spotted the house. Walking closer she recognised the car parked in the driveway. The house was quiet. Dim lights shone from the front windows. *It* was here, standing in the shadow of a tree in the front yard. It nodded, smiling at her, while raising a hand in a gesture to approach, welcoming her. She found herself starting to run. She knew what it meant. *Bastard, the absolute mocking bastard.* Running to the front door she pounded on it as she listened for movement. Thumping it again and hearing nothing she jumped off the front step. Grasping the window frame she pulled herself up to look inside. There he was.

Josh, she saw him. Standing in the entrance of the kitchen looking back at her.

Hesitating for a moment she called to him. "Josh! Josh it's me!" He didn't respond. She called again. "Josh! It's Ellie!"

She sighed in frustration. Why couldn't he hear her? Where were the other people?

"Oh no," she murmured as realisation dawned. Letting herself fall clumsily to the ground. Jumping to her feet she ran back to the front door pulling the handle. Locked.

Not wasting time, she ran across the front lawn and down the driveway. She had to get in.

♢♢♢

"It wants us to walk around," Josh whispered, his voice trembling. "It won't make a difference. It knows where we are."

Profuse sweat ran from Nate's brow. The heat was incredible and getting hotter.

"Who? Josh? Who?" Nate hissed, still holding Josh's hand tightly. "Who is here?"

Unsure how to answer, Josh was about to say, "the monster," but stopped as he heard the clicking sounds of razor-sharp claws on the floor behind them. He turned, dreading seeing the familiar, growling shape as it emerged from the dark corridor. Silently it approached them. For a second Josh thought to just duck, just cover his ears and hide it all. Soon Nate's hand would be wrenched from his. Casey would be torn from his arm. He just had to let it happen. If he covered his ears like he was supposed to, maybe he wouldn't remember it so well, as Ellie said. He didn't want to remember this.

Nate and Casey spun around, looking in disbelief as the Firewolf became visible in the red-hued light that radiating from the walls. They both recoiled in horror. Josh jumped backwards.

"Run! Run away! He's really fast!" he screamed. He couldn't just let them get eaten. He couldn't let them go on the wall. He would try. He would do anything he could. He wouldn't let the Dog win easily. Not again.

The Dog leaped forward as Josh sprinted to the left. He could still feel Nate's hand grasping his arm. Josh could see the end of the corridor in front of them. A way out? Most likely not, but somewhere to run. Josh, Nate, and Casey raced into a large metal dome-like chamber. The only entrance was the one they had just used. It was a dead end.

"We can't get out!" Casey screamed, turning back to the entrance. "Where is this?"

"Josh!" Nate shouted. "Josh, where are we?"

Walls towered above them, each one an intricate arcade of metal arches that were separated by large expanses of raw, searing metal. Human screaming and pounding reverberated around them in a vortex of gruesome echoes and sharp, spiralling screeches. The walls flashed white hot as *the Taken* emerged, all chained against the arcade walls. Men, women and children all held in place by the gruesome restraints, their flesh sizzled in individual horrific frames of iron.

Josh recognised the sound behind him. Casey had vomited.

"They can't hurt us today!" Josh said, a bad attempt at reassurance.

"Oh God," Nate's legs went limp beneath him. He stared in horror at the people around them. "Oh God what are they?"

Joshua looked at them. A cold yet soothing numbness overcame him. The heat blasted his face. He removed his jumper, dropped it at his feet as he stood looking at the wall of victims in his t-shirt. He heard the adults scream and watched as they ran past. The growling behind confirmed the Dog was here. But that feeling… something was strangely calm. For a reason he couldn't explain, he reached up and placed his fingers on the little

288

piece of parchment that sat on his chest. It felt nice, cool, and calm, not hot like this place. The chains began to twist and clank. It was time. They were to go on the wall.

ooo

Ellie slammed through the back door, sliding into the kitchen and almost immediately saw Josh before her staring blankly into the sitting room. She ran up to him, putting one hand on his arm as his jumper slowly, impossibly melted away to dust.

"Fuck," Ellie gasped. There was no more she could do. She couldn't help him. It had already started. But it had started once before, and they had been able to make it stop. How far had it gone? Every second she waited gave his family less of a chance.

Sitting in an armchair in the corner of the room, Bael lifted one leg and placed it across the other. His hands lay folded in his lap. His rotted, gaunt face was emotionless. Ellie took a breath, stood up and stared into those dead white eyes. "Get me in."

Bael's head cocked quickly to the side as a smile snapped across his face. He bought his hand up and delivered a contemptuous shrug.

"Get me in!" she yelled furiously. His smile vanished and hands lowered. The Leviathan continued staring at her with banal amusement. He knew. He fucking *knew* what she planned to do. Pit Bael against the Firewolf, end it. They had done it twice before. He wasn't going to allow that a third time. A horrific, horrible idea entered her mind. An idea so outrageous, so completely abhorrent, that he would never expect it. It was perfect. She quickly ran around the corner into the kitchen, gathering her hair on top of her head.

Ellie's hands trembled as re-entered the room, standing behind Josh. Bael watched her with that awful look of amusement on his grotesque face. She could feel the disdain, the mockery. That was until she placed her arm around Josh, pulling him close to her and bringing the point of a razor-sharp knife to the child's throat.

"Fuck you" she spat. Praying to God, she pierced the boy's skin. The jugular, she had to miss the jugular. Not too deep. Deep enough to mean business but not deep enough to kill him.

Bael immediately towered before them, bellowing with rage. It would happen now, whether he wanted it to or not.

OOO

Nate put himself between Casey and the Firewolf as it leapt forward. Nate was slammed to the ground as the creature sank its massive teeth into his arm. He yelled as it began shaking him from side to side, serrated teeth sawed at his shoulder. Casey screeched hysterically, running towards them. Nate was dropped to the ground. He tried to move but the monster leapt on him. This time its shovel jaw slamming shut on his upper leg. Without warning, the Firewolf stopped and released him, turning its huge head to Josh who curiously lifted a hand to his neck and pulled it away red with blood. *Where did that come from?*

OOO

Holding the knife steady to her friend's neck, Ellie looked above her and smiled. The room changed. It worked. She was threatening the life of its Conduit. The Firewolf would not let this happen. Its attack on her would be immediate; she knew this, and so did Bael. As the unnatural change took place, Bael did not care, glaring at Ellie as she smiled up at him, blood dripping down Josh's shirt. She had dared to play Bael, dared to play the Wolf. Forcing them into conflict. Forcing this to end. The scene began to make itself clear. She looked at the arcade above her as Josh moved under her arm. People, victims. Why were they here? Like a Circle, like the Event?

Stunned, Josh turned around to see Ellie looking over him at Nate on the ground.

"Ellie? What are…" Ellie pushed Josh to the side as the Firewolf lunged forward. She closed her eyes. Would Bael let her perish? Play the ultimate "fuck you" card straight back?

Bael stopped beside her, grasping the Wolf by the throat, casting it aside, slamming it onto the hot wall. Forced into the process, fuelled by the threat to its Conduit, the Dog lunged for Ellie again. Bael slammed his fist into the dog's muzzle with absolute outrage. Ellie could feel the pure rage behind the attack. The Wolf was getting pummelled for Ellie's noncompliance.

Opening her eyes, Ellie quickly stared at Josh and gasped.

290

"Josh?" she called. "What are you doing?" Grasping her head, she was brought to the ground by a sudden, brutal pain. She couldn't see, everything went dark and cold. A small trail of glinting light left her body, syphoning into Josh.

Josh, confused, bought his hands up to his face. Whisps of light, like little rivers, began coming through the walls towards him. Faster and faster, brighter and brighter, with a strange metallic screech.

"Ell…" he began before the same brilliant, white light that encompassed them during the Circle, burst forth from him with a resounding and electrifying *boom!* He threw his arms out, his head cast upwards as the remnants of every soul of any remaining earthbound Ascendant exploded forth from him.

ΟΟΟ

Sam screamed, falling forward onto the table, fists clenched. "Jesus Christ!" he roared. His drink flew from the table, smashing onto the floor beside him. The Dark Child screamed in a thousand voices. In agony, he kicked himself off the bench seat, falling onto the floor, gasping in pain. Was this an aneurysm? Would he actually be able to die? If it wasn't for the pain, he'd be OK with that.

ΟΟΟ

Jason writhed on the wet ground of the car park, his car keys still grasped in his hand. The car alarm was sounding. He couldn't see. His legs wouldn't work. The pain, oh God the pain. He could hear the bellowing of his Leviathan, its twisted, marionette form spinning in and out of reality above him.

ΟΟΟ

"Miya! Miya!" She could hear them calling. She had fallen onto the floor. Her sight was gone, her eyes simply switched off as an incredible pain crashed through her skull, bringing with it a profound weakness.

"Get her some water!" her assistant screamed, forcing a cushion under her head. She believed she was going to die. Surely such pain was impossible to come back from. Would death really be so bad?

291

All was calm. Josh hovered in the air as a wonderful sensation of tranquillity flowed over him in waves. People were screaming. The Dog was shaking and roaring. The man, Ellie's big scary man, was right beside him. It didn't matter. Ellie would be OK and now, the light was starting to shine through the darkness, making everything bright and normal again.

The pain in Ellie's head began to ease. Vision started to return. The black walls of the arcade were melting away as the heat faded. What was this? This was insane. What did Josh do? It was ending and Bael was indignant and humiliated. *No control you sick fuck.* No control.

Sound closed in on them as the walls returned and reality was amended. The pain dissipated. Ellie let herself fall backwards as Josh, stiff and unconscious, fell on top of her. Before them were Nate and Casey. Casey held him in her arms. He was awake and torn between the fear of the changing space and the pain in his limbs.

Slowly, Josh opened his eyes and became aware that he was lying on someone. He turned his head and heard Ellie's voice tickle his ear. "Can you get off me please."

Surprised, Josh quickly rolled onto the floor as Ellie grimaced and sat up.

"You're here?" Josh's eyes filled with delight. Ellie went to answer but before she could, Josh threw his arms around her and held on tight. Ellie hugged him back. He was trembling. She placed her glove over the wound on his neck and sat on the ground holding him. It was OK. It would be OK. Looking up, she made eye contact with Casey. She was a wreck. Ellie was surprised she could talk at all. "What are you doing here?"

Ellie thought for a moment, as Nate called out in pain again. "He's gonna need an ambulance" she stated matter-of-factly, gesturing to Nate.

Getting to her feet, Josh stood beside Ellie, arms now wrapped around her waist, burying his face in her side.

"This is Ellie?" Nate yelled accusingly. "What do you want?"

Ellie was calm. There was no need to get upset. It had already been shown to them. Josh murmured something into Ellie's coat where his face remained buried.

"Josh," Casey leant across Nate. "Josh, come here."

Josh didn't move. Both he and Ellie knew he wouldn't have to.

"*Josh*" Casey repeated, her voice shaking with fear.

"We will be leaving now," Ellie said. "Now you understand why he can't stay. It's what we do to people we care about. It's awful... unthinkable. He doesn't mean to, none of us do. We have no choice. There's nothing we can do. It's where we take people. It's where my family are. It's where your sister is."

Casey slowly shook her head, breaking into tears. "I don't know what just happened?"

"You both just had the luckiest night of your lives. I don't know how," Ellie shrugged, smiling nervously. "But neither of you were supposed to come back. You were supposed to stay there. No-one ever comes back."

"I don't know what to do," Casey pleaded. "What do we do?"

"Nothing," Ellie replied quickly. "Absolutely nothing. This did not happen. Josh comes with me. Me, and people like me, stand a chance. If this happens again - and it will happen again – you won't come back from that. Cover for us. Make excuses for us. But he can't stay here with you, and now you know why."

"No," Nate painfully pushed himself up on his elbows, spitting "No. You can't just take him."

"I'm not taking him," Ellie sighed tiredly. "He's coming with me, and if you want to stay alive you won't stand in our way; not now, and not in the future. And that's not a threat, we're just trying to protect you. The safest thing for you to do is pretend we don't exist."

Ellie turned awkwardly, Josh still wrapped around her, holding tight.

"Wait!" Casey called, "Josh... I can't... please"

Ellie turned back for a moment and looked down at Nate on the floor. "Call an ambulance," she said, before looking directly at Casey and continuing. "Let us go. I swear to you, no-one else has ever had the chance you just had. It won't happen again."

"Please... look after him. You must promise," Casey cried as she backed towards Nate.

Ellie felt Josh slide from under her arm, quickly leaning over and picked up his little phone from the couch, sliding it into his pocket.

"I will," Ellie nodded. It was time for them to leave.

Ellie and Josh left the house, walking towards the road. She looked down at his small, white face as he peered up at hers and smiled. "I made the Dog go *bang*!"

"Yes, you did."

"And there was light and stuff." Josh reached in, pulling the tattered bootlace from around his neck. "Where's the paper gone?"

"I really don't know." Ellie held him close as they continued down the dark street. Gently she slid off her coat and gave it to Josh telling him to put it on. She had never seen that before, and she was quietly confident that Sam and his new acquaintances wouldn't have either, because one thing had held true until now. Once a person was Lit, there was no return. Ellie had just forced Bael's hand. Josh had just broken all the rules. There would be repercussions.

Chapter 27

The blood from Luka's nose had pooled on his lap. In stupefied silence, he tried to make sense of all he'd just seen. The ability to see hadn't come to him for quite some time. He had forgotten what it was like to feel that omnipresent. Seeing everything with no history or context, almost all of it like a vivid dream that would quickly fade the moment his nose gushed with blood.

A sudden, overwhelming memory hit him. He had seen a boy in a world of fire and ash. There was screaming. There was a 'gifting'. But something went wrong, something had interrupted the process in a way he never knew was possible. Such a brutal force had been released that he was sure it had been felt by every Devotee in the city. An image that would remain embedded in his mind, able to steer him towards this child whenever he chose. This was how Devotees found others, to varying degrees. Himself? Not so much. It had only ever happened to him once before. He couldn't be sure, but he felt that if he had had this clear vision with his admittedly mediocre ability to see, then surely the others would have seen it too? Crystal, especially - the one with the ability as a Seer - would know exactly what she had to do. *Damnit.*

This boy was an Ace. He knew it. He saw the Wolf. The Wolf of fire. This, though he couldn't remember exactly why, was important. The Wolf... he had heard and seen the Wolf. What had they said about it? What was the significance? Fuck, he wished he could remember. He'd been thinking about Grimoires for so long now that he had forgotten anything else. Why was he so shit with these things? Right now he needed anything to use as leverage. The Wolf Leviathan.

The Wolf and Bael.

Red-faced, Sam stumbled out the door of the bar. He ignored the call from the nice barman behind him with the offer of an ambulance. He was fine. The pain had completely gone. It had now been replaced by a strange warmth. All was well. How could something that unpleasant end so quickly? He had thought that he would die. Having just faced possible death, his biggest concern right now, however, was the warm wet patch emanating from his crotch. What a Goddamned mess... but God, the pain had been excruciating.

First thought was to get away. Second was to call Jason. He would reschedule, as frustrating as that was. He looked around him and noted that the Dark Child wasn't following. She would eventually, of course, but for some reason she wasn't here. It made him nervous.

Hearing someone vomit onto the street, he turned. It was a little too early for someone to be power chucking on a Wednesday evening. Sam stared at the hunched figure across the road, leaning with one arm on a streetlight and the other on his knee. It was him. It was Jason. "Hey!" Sam called impatiently. "Jason!"

Jason looked up, shaking his head with a mixture of embarrassment and annoyance.

"Christ, stop shouting," he muttered as Sam ran across the road to him. "You OK?"

Straightening himself up, Jason looked at Sam as if offended. How dare Sam ask if he was OK?

"Yes. Jesus." He started walking in a slow circle. "Just felt a bit shit for a moment, ya know. Like bad food or something. I need a minute."

Sam reluctantly gave Jason a moment, glancing behind him, then beside him. No, nothing. "I felt it too," he said quickly.

Jason glared at him in disbelief. "What? No! Oh come on. So this was the both of us? What did you do?!"

Sam put his hands up. "I didn't do anything buddy. I was waiting for your late ass."

"In your head? Then everywhere else?"

"Yeah, the same and... shit... it was just *shit.*"

Jason reeled back in sadistic delight. "Ha! And you pissed your pants!"

This was not important right now. The joy it seemed to bring Jason was disconcerting.

"Three drinks in! Three! I was just about to go and… shit happened…" Sam replied, regretting it half a second later.

"Oh God!" Jason mocked him. "Not that as well!!!"

"Fuck off. I thought I was having a stroke. What's wrong with you?" Sam began to walk away. *Little twerp.*

"No, no I'm sorry!" Jason trotted behind him laughing. "It's not funny! You're right."

"No, it's not, because something just happened, and it happened to both of us. You ever noticed that that never means anything good in our world?" His mind instantly turned to Ellie and Josh. "I think we should call it a night."

Jason stopped following. Sam was reluctant to look back, however, he turned with a sigh. "It's just been a bad few days. I just need to rest, sort my shit out."

"We had plans," Jason said coldly, looking profoundly disappointed. "A bad few days? You want to hear about mine?"

Unnerved by Jason's sudden mood change, Sam thought quickly. He hadn't considered the big picture. He needed Jason to trust him, to confide in him. If he hadn't been so horrified by the pain, and then humiliated by the surprise pissing, he would have played it cool.

"I know. I'm sorry, just…"

Jason watched him closely. Sam felt particularly analysed, like he was being assessed for any possible delivery of offense. Jason looked genuinely hurt. Was that the word? Or, God forbid, rejected? *Jason is very, very fragile.*

"It was a bad few days Sam," Jason said coolly. "I've been looking forward to tonight, you know. I'm here. Took me a while to get here too."

Sam nodded uncomfortably. Relief washed over him as his phone rang. He answered the phone without a greeting, turning evasively from Jason saying, "you know people would be more likely to answer if you didn't have your phone number hidden."

Jason watched as Sam spoke on the phone in short, sharp responses. Who was he talking to? He didn't have a Devotee. He didn't have a Pantheon… could it be that Sam had a friend?

Sam buried his head in his hand. "What? Jesus Christ, you're kidding me."

Brazenly, Jason walked up to him, making no attempt to hide the fact that he was interested in the conversation.

"I can't. What do you mean?" Sam sighed for the tenth time in two minutes. *My God, people were hard work.* "Can you tell him to stop talking for a second? Just tell him to hold up, I can't hear you."

Sam listened, nodding and grunting. "Where are you now? Mm hmm."

Obviously frustrated, Sam began walking briskly away, pulling his car keys out of his pocket as he went. "OK. Just remember this though. If I decide to sell my car it's *your* fault. You guys are going to get us into so much damn trouble."

He hung up. How the hell was he going to explain this to Jason? What happened? Ellie and Josh were together, *again*. That meant that chaos was the outcome… again. Though not as he would have expected. He had at least confirmed that during the conversation.

Jason strode beside him. "Where are we going?"

"To pick up my sister."

"You have a sister? Getting you in trouble?"

"Don't worry about it. My sister and her kid." Sam cringed hearing such bullshit come from his own mouth.

"Wow, like a sister and… what's it called? Like a nephew?"

"Yes. Just like that. Sister, nephew." Sam hit the button on his car. He would play this by ear on the way there. If Jason's Leviathan could sense Bael, now was its chance. "Look, it's not far from here. Twenty minutes round trip tops."

As he spoke he imagined Ellie's face, horrified and confused probably. Hopefully not angry. And Josh… *shit.*

"How old is the nephew?"

Jesus, just stop talking about it.

"He's… 8 or so. And he asks just as many questions as you do." Sam pulled into the dark street. Jason sat next to him in the car like a child eager for entertainment. The number of ways things could go very wrong over twenty minutes was ridiculous. This was not how Sam had imagined the night, but he was intrigued. It had also happened to Ellie, and she had a lot to tell him. She wouldn't of course, at least not with a stranger beside him. However, that was just par for the course.

◯◯◯

Luka sat in the darkness of the basement once again, alone. He had managed to drink something. Enough water to wet his lips and calm his stinging, dry gums. He would have to eat eventually, whether he felt like it or not. The last 12 hours had bought some relief. His vision seemed to be 'lifting' slightly. The shadows of other realms around him were not as stark as they had been. The gruesome images of the place just a step to the left of his existence had faded.

He rubbed his head. The sensation of his hand on his shaved head felt good. Relieved, he was beginning to feel things again. To what extent the symptoms of this 'illness' would continue to fade was still unclear. He would never be the same again, but he hoped against hope that he wasn't as far gone as he feared. His mind was full of conversations, scenarios of survival and outwitting play. He had never been that smart and he knew the truth. Devotees much smarter than him were not able to escape their fate. His level of stupidity had been made painfully clear to him only two nights ago.

If he got out of this it would be by luck and, maybe, with a bit of scheming. He had none of the former and sucked at the latter.

A sudden noise scared him to his feet as Noah, flanked by Luka's grandmother, opened the basement door. Noah descended the stairs. Grandma would have been happy that Luka had someone come to visit. Noah was being polite. He thanked her for letting him in and proceeded down the stairs. He stopped, glaring at Luka with an intense questioning gaze.

"Noah! What…" Luka shifted uncomfortably, "are you doing here?"

"Just came to check on ya. Heard from Chel that you ain't feeling too good." Noah turned, rubbing his chin, casting a glance at the staircase as Luka's grandmother ascended, closing the door behind her.

"I've felt better," Luka replied carefully. Noah had an intimidating presence; a quiet confidence that was carried by only the seasoned of their kind. "Why do you care?"

Noah smiled, as if hiding a secret, lowering his voice, "I don't care. I'm not going to pretend I do. I came to see you to ask why you d-d-did… what you did."

Chel told him? Was this a ruse? He was the only one who knew, besides Mika and Jason. Possibly that beast Crystal. No, of course she did. And in his fucked-up state that night, he didn't care if she had. Now he cared. He forgot how intimidating Noah was. The intensity and his damage could be felt as soon as he entered a room.

"Did what?" he gulped hard.

"At first, I thought it was Crystal but it makes sense it was you. I know she came to you the other night. I know you spoke to her. And you told her what happened to her mother... you miserable little fucker." Noah shook his head. "She was all I had, you know. I didn't have her for much longer and I knew that. But for you to drive her away from me now was low, even for you."

Luka clenched his jaw so hard it hurt. What he would give to be able to punch Noah in his head right now. He desired this so much, he could feel the darkness stirring within him. It was like feeding them both poison. Yet Luka stood no chance. There was no point in attacking Noah. As human or as a monster, Noah would demolish him.

"Fuck you Noah! Jesus... Do you know what they did to me? Look at me! I'm fucking edging mate... I'm hanging over the side. Yes, I told her, and I'm not sorry. You should be sorry. You should want to say sorry."

Noah raised his hand to silence him. "You took away my chance to say sorry."

"Bullshit. Chel is a good person..." Luka dropped his voice. Bizarre and strange that amongst this band of homicidal maniacs they all agreed on one thing: Chelamah deserved better than her fate, and better than Noah. "She is the only one of you wankers that hasn't fucked me over. She was there for me when no-one else was. She was there for you too. And all she got was fucked over time and time again. The least I could do before I turn into that *thing* was give her the truth about who she was *really* fucking!"

Noah remained quiet. This couldn't escalate, not now. Luka waited for a response as Noah nodded, considering his next move, his next words. Slowly he replied. "You're right. She deserved to know. Does she know you were there too? Or did you leave that bit out?"

"Asshole," Luka spat.

"Bro. Don't insult me. Don't *insult*. Because if I was you, I'd remind myself who you're talking to. I don't need a picture of your busted Devotee face Luka. I've got everything I need right..." he tapped the side of his head hard, "*here*."

Now was the time. Luka had nothing to lose. He had to reveal what he knew, what he did, and then he could bargain. Bargaining remained an option. "OK, Soldier," he smiled facetiously. "But I wouldn't do that if I were you."

"You threatening me? Interesting. I don't make a habit of making prey out of my own, but for you I'd make an exception. You know it could happen anytime Luka. You wouldn't see it coming… few do." Noah turned and began to walk to the staircase.

If he left, Luka knew his time was up. He had to show his cards now… there was no other choice. Fearful, desperate Luka jumped forward.

"The first Grimoires of Aahna," he spat excitedly, "I know where they are. The Wolf? I know where that is too."

Shocked, Noah slowly turned back, his eyes wide in disbelief. "Bullshit."

"It's true," Luka shrugged. "It's true. I took the Grimoires. I put them where no-one could find them but me. I saw the Ace with the Wolf. You know it's possible! But I need your help. I need you to help me or we're all fucked, including Chelamah."

"You… it was you." Noah's eyes shone brightly. The first Grimoires of Aahna Sina Tambi. What they were reputed hold… what they could do.

"But I swear. If I get visited by your fucking goon, I will go to *hell* before I tell you a fucking thing… I swear it man." Luka stepped back nervously as Noah took a step toward him. "You push me one step further and I'm gone. You'll never know what those Grimoires could do. So, let's talk. You and me. There's not much for us to lose anymore."

Noah listened intently. If this dumbass was right, if the Wolf was present, then so was something else. This could be big. This could be a game changer. As thick as Luka was, he was essential for the time being. He would be safe for now.

ooo

It was impossible to come up with any kind of polite conversation with Ellie glaring at him in disbelief via his rear-view mirror. Her black hair was hastily tied up. This was how she looked after the Circle. He could only see the top of Josh's head, thankfully, or he would have had two pairs of eyes demanding his attention. They had picked them up where they stood, dripping and haggard, on the side of the road. Their dishevelled appearance surprised Jason. Why were they there? Flat tyre, Sam had stated. Bullshit. Sam was not under any false perception that Jason would buy this. Neither was Ellie. As she climbed into the back seat she stopped and looked at the stranger like a spider. This was echoed by Josh, who only stopped talking when he climbed in behind her, making eye contact with Jason before suddenly falling silent.

Sam introduced them as sister and her son. Ellie looked flummoxed. She was barely 18 and yet this seemed plausible to Sam. She rationalised that she was covered in the usual crap that nights with Josh often ended with. Maybe this was for the best. Josh, however, looked completely surprised, smiling at Sam with confusion and started to correct him. *Silly Sam, that's crazy!* He was silenced only by Ellie grabbing him firmly and pulling him back into the seat with her. There were adult things going on… again! Josh thought it best he just stayed quiet.

For two blocks nothing was said. Jason looked uneasy, as did they all. But why? That was the question. Why did he look uneasy? Was it the strange behaviour of the ragged pair that they had just dragged up from the side of the road? Or was it something else? Sam kept calm. Jason was prone to blustering. If he had sensed something, he doubted Jason could be discrete.

"What were they doing there?" Jason asked quietly, but not discretely.

"Car tyre blown. I said to her - didn't I say to you El? - that tyre is on its way out." Sam laughed a little too heartedly. Ellie turned her head to look out the dark window.

"I didn't see a car. Did you walk?" Jason turned uncomfortably around. Sam took a deep breath. He was talking straight to her. Josh looked at him and smiled. This was becoming lots of fun.

"Yes we walked," Ellie explained in a voice, a normal relaxed tone that took Sam completely by surprise. Then, as if donning a mask, she turned to face Jason with a smile. *A smile?* "He did tell me. I never listen."

"She never listens!" Sam exclaimed, *my God she's playing along.*

"No. No I don't." Ellie jibed back. "Sometimes I can be a complete *dick*," her shot was well fired and hit its mark.

"Oh my God," Josh gasped quietly, covering his mouth. She just swore, and in front of a stranger!

Nodding, smiling, Sam sighed. "Don't be too hard on yourself. It happens to everyone. So, am I taking you home?"

"Yes, that would be great. Thanks." She smiled but she didn't blink.

"And your car? I can take you out to get it in the morning?" Sam asked, feigning nonchalance.

"That would be great. I'd appreciate it."

"No problem. No plans in the morning. Should be fine. I'll come around at about 9?"

"Please. I seriously don't know how you put up with me. I am a complete pain in the ass." Ellie shook her head in self-deprecation. She was wading deep into the murky depths of passive aggression. Safer, thought Sam. She was doing it well. Even Josh looked visibly uncomfortable at this awkward exchange, glancing from the back seat to the front seat and back again. This wasn't how Sam and Ellie usually talked to each other. It was because of this man. Why was Sam looking so weirdly happy? Why was Ellie *smiling* like that?

"Hi, I'm Josh." He said politely to the stranger.

Jason turned around briefly in his seat, "Hi," he replied curtly. Josh had the feeling he had annoyed this strange skinny man in some way, so he let himself slide down in the seat, wrapped in Ellie's big coat. He would continue to stay out of it.

The car ride quickly came to an end with Sam pulling up to the curb next to Ellie's building, breaking hard.

"Jesus!" Jason exclaimed as his hands hit the dashboard, "you're gonna kill us!"

"Just one moment!" Sam jumped out and went to open the back door. Ellie's door was already open. She was out and pulling Josh along with her. Following her to the door, Sam could feel Jason watching their interaction from the car. He was curious, of course. He wasn't stupid. Well, not as stupid as Sam had hoped.

"Hey, hey... I had no choice, he was already with me," Sam muttered quietly. Ellie sighed, taking her keys out of her pocket. "Are you guys OK?"

"Yes" Ellie nodded, "we're OK. I guess that answers that." Jason had not reacted. Bael had not made himself seen.

"It's good to know new things," Sam agreed with a hint of condescension. "He couldn't sense you."

"I know new things," Josh wholeheartedly agreed. "Tonight something new happened, but Ellie got a headache and then Nate got bit and stuff... so that's kind of bad."

"Christ." Sam frowned, casting Josh a double take.

Sam looked at Ellie who smiled at him. "I'm not a complete social cripple Sam. I can talk to people. I can pretend very well. I just don't like to," the smile vanished. "We're kin now, apparently. Say goodnight to Uncle Sam, Josh."

"Goodnight Uncle Sam" Josh responded with not much thought before looking and then grimacing with confusion "He's not really my..."

Sam rolled his eyes and interrupted. "I know. I know and that's great but... tonight? What happened?"

"Not now." Ellie swung the glass door open, shaking her head. "Not now. Deal with him. Don't talk too much about what happened tonight." She glanced at the car mistrustingly.

"It happened to him too," Sam whispered. "At the same time."

"Don't talk about it too much with him. We did it. It was us, it was Josh."

"Well would you mind not doing it again. It really fucking hurt," Sam stated. "And like I mean in many ways... physically and 'public disgrace' kind of hurt. How did he do that?"

"I don't know how. So it stays between us. Don't work it out with him. Play it down. It was big Sam. It was really big." Ellie shook her head in disbelief. "I have to sleep... tomorrow. Come tomorrow. Such weird shit happened tonight. I don't even know where to start."

"It *was* really weird, and now you're my uncle," Josh agreed, yawning as Ellie led him into the building. Sam watched as the door closed behind them. Faintly, Ellie pressed the elevator button. She placed a weary, soothing hand on Josh's head as he kept talking. She turned, surprised to see Sam still looking at them. Josh noticed too and waved happily, like he hadn't seen him for days, not just seconds.

"You're being creepy again!" she called.

"Piss off!" Sam called back, chuckling. "It's what we do. We're all creepy!"

He laughed as they entered the elevator. Turning to face him, Ellie delivered one, large fake smile before the life door slid closed between them. He smiled back in amusement. *Twat.*

OOO

Ellie tucked the blankets around Josh on the couch. A pillow for herself was placed on the carpet beside him where she sat.

"Are you OK?" she smiled at him.

Josh nodded, his beanie flopping further down on his lazily blinking eyes. "I'm OK. Is Nate OK?"

Nate was not OK. He was a mess. She didn't want to upset him further. How could she explain to him that from this moment, she had no idea what was going to happen to any of them?

"Yeah. I'm sure he went to the hospital. Saw the Doctor and they are fixing him up. They're nice people" Ellie replied.

"Yeah they are nice. Nate is really nice." Josh suddenly looked very sad. "Will I see them again sometime?"

Ellie thought for a moment. Josh noticed how sad she looked. He had made so many people sad lately. He wondered, when he wasn't there, if they were happier? Was Ellie happy when he wasn't there?

"I don't know. But you and I will go away for a while."

"Where?" Josh asked, frowning.

"Anywhere. We can go anywhere you want. Somewhere…"

"Sunny?" Josh's eyes shone. "With a beach?"

"Yeah," she chuckled softly. "That would be great."

Josh's eyes closed slowly. He smiled to himself with thoughts of sun and warmth. Happy things like colourful drinks and not being cold all the time. She let him sleep with this thought. As he drifted off she let herself droop across the couch, her legs underneath her on the carpet. It was then the screaming started, ever so lightly in the background - the pounding, the hollering. Bael was kneeling beside her, his white eyes burrowing into hers. She looked at the mottled, gruesome face as he towered above her, leering down. The fury was palpable. She had controlled him, pushed him and his mutt into a corner, and then Josh dispersed them. Two people had walked away.

Satisfied, Ellie looked at Bael. Lazily she reached to the side and brought her headphones to her ears. Calming music, drowning out the chaos around her.

"Goodnight fuckface" she smiled for the fifth time in one night. Closing her eyes, she quickly fell asleep.

Sam returned to the car to a different atmosphere. Jason was quiet, contemplative and gazing out the window. Sam knew there would be questions, however, he was sure that Bael was not revealed to him. Why? Although he had only known Jason for a small time, he was sure of his impertinence and brashness. He wouldn't be subtle.

"Why did the kid look like a homeless person?" Jason asked coldly.

"They had walked quite a way. It was raining."

"He was covered in shit, so was she. Like Oliver Twist and a homeless woman," he mocked. Jesus, this guy was a dick. A moment of silence passed. Jason took a large, elaborate breath. "So how did your sister last this long? How did she get out of it?"

"Stepsister. She's my stepsister," Sam answered impatiently.

"Yeah, but still," Jason seemed to not understand. "Why would you keep her around?"

The strangeness of his response made Sam unwilling to answer. Keep her around? He seriously believed that the people taken in his life were ultimately of his choosing. He couldn't ignore the niggling thought that Jason was jealous that Sam had spoken to someone else. His comments seemed designed to insult, to lash out.

He really was that needy. If they were dating, Sam would've left him at their first meeting. Red flags abounded.

The strange conversation continued until Sam pulled into the carpark of a pub he had frequented before. Pleasant, not too pricey and never too busy. Jason made a quip about 'slumming it' that Sam ignored. Making their way into the dimly lit entrance of the saloon, Sam immediately spotted a table where he and Jason could ride out this second *get-together*. Perfect location, near the door and in view of a clock. He wouldn't have to be seen checking the time on his phone. One hour was all he was prepared to give this evening.

Sam ordered drinks, two pints of the pub's own ale. The tall, frosted glass looked awkward and heavy when held in Jason's long thin hands

"Salut," Jason stated, tilting his beer at Sam and waiting for the obligatory eye contact. It amused Sam that Jason thought staring at someone menacingly was appropriate when giving a pretentious cheer, but he went with it.

"So, tell me about yourself Sam." Jason sat back, one arm crossed over the chest, the other holding his glass.

"What do you want to know?"

"Anything," he shrugged.

"OK. Um… My parents were Scottish. Grew up there until about 8 years of age. Moved here, studied accounting and finance, did…"

Jason clucked rudely, rolling his eyes, "yeah great. I mean now. I mean after your birth."

Confused and insulted, Sam frowned "My birth? I told you… I was born in Scotland."

Exasperated, Jason shook his head. "No, I mean your other birth. Your… you know…"

Sam leant forward, shaking his head wearily. Jason didn't want to know about him at all. He wanted his morbid curiosity fed.

"My other birth?"

"What about your blessing?"

"The *blessing*? Oh good God." Sam tapped the table. "OK, you wanna know about that. I was 11. It started when I was 11."

"Yeah, pretty much the same for all of us. And your parents? How long till they were gone?" Jason stared at him over his drink.

Stunned with disbelief, Sam scoffed. "You're a fucking great conversationist, seriously. Keep it light can you?"

"What does it look like?" Jason continued, unabated. *My God, this guy just didn't listen.* Completely socially inept.

"It doesn't matter what it looks like, does it?" Sam kicked back in his chair. He would try another tactic. "So Jason! What do you do with yourself?"

"Huh?"

"What do you do for work?"

"Oh… graphic design. Shit, really. Anyway, how many? What's your number?" Jason sat back as if about to duel in a video game. He was comparing scores.

"No." Sam shook his head in disgust. "I'm not giving you that."

"Why not?"

"Because I don't want to, OK? Can't you just talk like a normal person?" Sam asked.

Jason immediately looked uncomfortable, and Sam noticed. Wow, there it was. Sam had just crossed that line. If anyone else had insulted him, now would be the time he would take them. But he couldn't do that with Sam.

This is Jason when faced with someone he considered an equal. He was trying so hard to control himself. The anxiety was palpable, practically leaking out of him.

Jason scowled like a child. "I *am* having a normal conversation. I am *not* normal."

Another trigger. This guy was a loaded gun. Letting the tension sit, Sam downed the last of his pint. He would lighten the mood, let Jason off his uncomfortable hook.

"Grab another, your turn," he said, shaking the empty glass in his hand. For a moment, Jason just stared at him, awkward and uneasy, as if letting himself be guided by Sam's request, he smiled, standing up.

"Same again!" Sam called, watching Jason walk to the bar, gazing at the people around them. A collection of stereotypes all dressed in their warmest winter wear. A middle-aged couple canoodling in the corner. A collection of old, lonely men who sat in a line along the dark wood bar. Was this his future? An outcast, drinking his cares and liver away in a dark dingy bar? Who was he kidding? He scoffed to himself. He didn't have a future.

Chapter 28

Crystal ran awkwardly out of the elevator on very high heels, into the Pantheon. Where was it? Rubbing her face clean of the sticky dried blood from the episode an hour before she quickly turned to the wall mirror. Lifting her nose, she rubbed off the last small smear of blood from her upper lip. The front of her coat was speckled with the dark, crimson stains. "Fuck!" Slapping the front of her coat angrily, he tossed her bag on the couch.

Quickly checking her blonde, unmoving hair she trotted down the corridor to the room of paintings. A gentle light flickered on as she entered, sniffing and rubbing her face once more. Her eyes glowed with purpose. Her memory was hazy; the image hadn't been clear. She had seen the boy but what was that *thing* with him? Could it possibly be what she thought it was?

The scribe was Thiago. She turned to her left while scanning the archaic paintings of the ancient Scribe. There it was – it was one of the most ancient in the collection

Lobo de fuego. The Firewolf.

Crystal had seen the Firewolf, there was no doubt, and the legendary monster was attached to a damn child. A child... this, had in the past, brought advantages. If the Firewolf was here, Bael was here. For some time now she had doubted Mika's prediction as mere assumption. There was the presence of all three players, Devotees, Underlings and Ascendants in one location. The presence of a Scribe. Mika made the decision to end her... why? For God's sake why would he do that? The last Scribe possibly of their time. Aahna had been taken out for no good reason. She could have been used for years more.

Yes, all the signs pointed to it being possible, if not probable. But as time drew on, she began to question whether this was in fact the case. But now she had seen the Firewolf. Bael would be here somewhere.

What should she do with the information? Mika wouldn't be here, but he would arrive soon enough and, if he knew, he would be unstoppable. The only way he would know is if she told him. What about Luka and Chelamah? It was unlikely, as had been shown so frequently in the past, that they would have sensed what she did. She was a Devotee with the primary of Seer. Luka and Chelamah were mostly Shadows. So was this secret hers, hers alone? She had to be sure.

Crystal had found Luka, Noah and Will. She had no doubt in the power of her sight. The Firewolf was attached to that child in the other realm. Looking at the painting in front, she saw it. There it was, its eyes bright in the background of the painting, standing behind its master.

Full of anticipation, she left the hall of Scribes and entered the living room. Hesitating for a moment, she stood before the window, staring out at the bright city skyline beneath a black sky. Reluctantly she removed her stained coat and then the rest of her clothing, paying close attention to folding them and placing them in a neat pile on the seat beside her.

A tremble started in her chest, snatching away her breath making her whole body gasp. Pulling shaking hands to her side, she lifted her head and took a single large breath. Her eyes rolled over to white as her skin sank into her frame, making her skeletal, cadaverous. A piercing screech burst forth as a blackened form fell forward, out of its flesh cocoon. Stretching its long hands through the carpet, the monster lifted its round, crimson clad head to the window. With two quick movements, it kicked its back legs freeing them from its pointless, human restraint. It moved on all fours, like an animal towards the city spread out before it. Slowly it placed its talons upon the window giving three quick taps. It knew what it had to find. It knew the disposable strip of flesh left behind would see what it did, know what it knew.

With a burst of agile speed it flew forward, through the window as if it was made of black light, and into the city beyond, to hunt for the child who walked with the Wolf.

OOO

"Do you ever like, pick someone just because they've annoyed you?" Jason asked, once again turning the conversation to the extreme.

"No," Sam answered quickly. "Why would I do that?"

"Why not?"

"Because the whole damn world is annoying... what would I do? Destroy it all? No... Everyone is annoying. I, myself, am very annoying. Should someone take me out for that?" Sam replied sternly. Ellie immediately came to mind.

"Some people are just like... pointless."

"Maybe? Seriously you just... wow," Sam was flabbergasted.

Jason nodded and cast his eyes around the room. Sam watched as his eyes went from person to person.

"Some people don't really matter. Most people don't," he muttered. Sam watched with slight intrigue. He was sure he saw Jason's eyes grow dark and threatening as he scanned the room. A sudden cackle of a middle-aged woman burst forth from the bar. Jason instantly turned to look at her. His mouth smiled slightly. his eyes grew wide and darker still.

Fuck... thought Sam... *he's choosing someone.*

"What about her?" Jason gestured with a nod of the head. "That fat thing at the bar. All dolled up. Probably had five kids to five different fathers. She's kinda pointless, isn't she?"

Sam watched aghast as the slightly inebriated woman took another gulp of the pink alcohol, giggling and whispering into her male friend's ear. "You don't know her. Why would you want to do that?" he asked.

Jason shrugged. "Calm down Sam! I'm just shooting the breeze. Chill out."

Shaking his head in exhaustion, Sam leant back again. This guy was an energy vampire.

"But..." Jason muttered. "She is pointless. Most people are pointless. No-one really misses them. No-one really likes them. So would it matter if they were gone?"

Before Sam could answer, Jason shot a glance to the bar beyond the drunk couple, beyond the line of three veteran bar flies, to a small old man sitting in the corner sipping from a glass of cheap whiskey. "Like him!"

Sam didn't understand. What had happened to Jason that made him so deeply unpleasant.

"What about him?" Jason leaned forward, "Pathetic, weak and frail. Did you know that many years ago some cultures practiced something called senilicide?"

"Seriously…?"

"No, it's true. The old were just a waste of space, a waste of resources. So the tribes would take these old fuckers out and leave them to die. Keep the wealth for the young and those that contributed to their society. Made them stronger. Natural selection."

45 minutes gone, 15 more to go before Sam could take his leave.

"The Inuits would cast them out on an iceberg. They would die of starvation or exposure. Tamil Nadu in India? Their oldies would get a nice oil bath and be fed cold coconut water until they would die slowly of high temperature. It's called *Thalaikoothal*" Jason ranted, watching Sam move uncomfortably. "Like that dude. Look at him."

Unwilling, but unable not to, Sam glanced over at the lonely old man. He was leaning heavily over his glass, as if defending it, caressing it. His eyes looked empty and deeply sad.

"What's your point?" Sam snapped. "It's OK to kill people?"

"Sometimes, it is."

"Oh fuck off Jason. We don't *kill* people. My God, you know how many times I wished I could just *kill* people. They kill people. We condemn them to hell. Both fucked up, but ours is an entirely different type of fucked up. It's… evil."

"We're all a little evil Sam. All of us. Go on, choose one." Jason placed his glass down on the table before him.

"What?" Sam gasped in disbelief

"Choose one. Just one. Remember, no consequences, no returns. Choose one. If you don't… I will." Jason looked at Sam. He was serious. He was going to do it.

"Why?" Sam muttered in disgust. "Why would you do that?"

"Senilicide… for the greater good. Just think. Every drink he has is coming from your tax dollars… from your pocket. Time to put him on the iceberg. Feed him some coconut milk." Jason's voice drifted off into an angry whisper. A cold shiver ran up Sam's spine, as he noticed the familiar changes going on about him.

How would Jason do this? Why? The old man took another swig, completely unaware of the little psycho who was aiming the gun of hell straight at him. This couldn't happen, this was disgusting and immoral.

"No. Jason. I'm warning you not to do it," Sam glared at him, demanding he turn his eyes away from the target of his rage. "Stop this now." The room grew colder still.

"It's so easy ain't it? Soon he will be no-one's problem anymore. Just…" He lifted his fingers before him, clicking them loudly *"Gone."*

Talks with Ellie, theories, ideas ran through his mind. Before Sam could think about it, before he was able to consider it enough for it to scare him, he reached out, knocked his drink over and clasped his hand around Jason's wrist. Jason tried to pull away, stopping as Sam shook his head slowly. "Call it off Jason. Calm down. If you don't. I'm going with you. Your choice."

Jason looked at his wrist, then at Sam with a mixture of shock and fear. "Let me go."

The air grew thicker still. They were so close. Sam made sure not to look away, "Do it and we both go, and I don't think you want that… do you?"

"Let go of me" Jason hissed, his eyes dark.

"Stop it, Jason." He wouldn't let his fortitude fail him. Jason had to know he was serious. If he held Jason at the moment of a taking, then all bets were off, and Jason knew this. "Stop," Sam pleaded, tightening his grip. "You don't want me in there with you. Trust me, she will tear you apart."

Sam could see Jason's mind thinking, considering. What a big decision for him to make. He was being directly challenged. He did not expect this but knew the stakes.

"Will *you* be missed, Jason?" Sam uttered viciously, "tell me. How… *pointless*…are *you?*"

Sam watched with relief as Jason took a large, full breath and blinked for the first time in what seemed like forever. His lip trembled. His eyes faltered. Sam felt the air, the shadows slowly lift as the scent of alcohol and cigarette smoke seeped into his nostrils once more. Jason had backed down.

Sam slowly released his grip and watched as the old man staggered behind them from the bar towards the exit. He watched him, ignoring Jason who scowled at him.

"You are not like us," Jason muttered, trying to hide the quivering in his voice. "I don't like this. Mika wouldn't like this. How dare you…"

"I'm glad I've disappointed you." Sam stood up from the table. "Tell your Pantheon to go fuck themselves."

Jason was trembling. "Not smart Sam"

"Go screw yourself." Sam turned and left. The walk to the bar door took an eternity and once outside, he breathed in the cold air and leaned on the wall. "Jesus" he muttered, calming himself down. They were insane. Glancing quickly at the door, he made a quick jog to his car. He had to go. This fact-finding venture was over. There was no way he could possibly entertain it further. Any benefit from knowing this person was not worth sacrificing anyone for. He would go, lay low. They didn't know where he was. He would disappear for a while. He would see Ellie and Josh in the morning. From there they would make their plan. Sam would tell them what happened. They would agree that the best plan of action was to avoid these people. They would also agree that leaving for a while was best. He had just made them some new enemies.

OOO

It has been a very mundane evening at the home of his future in-laws. He had been pampered by his future mother-in-law, Julia, who insisted on adjusting his sling every five minutes. She had been in nursing school when she met her future husband, and then quickly married. She married well. This was the joke that Jess herself often made, aware of her mother's tedium. Niles always admired Lawrence's profound patience with his melancholic, nervous wife. A patience that Jess didn't share. This had been a long-standing tension.

He had been reading notes in Lawrence's study. Patients had been rescheduled, and this change of routine just increased Niles' anxieties further. He had never, in 15 years of practice, had to do this. Jessica had braved a return to their house with her brother and collected a few things. Niles couldn't stand the thought of walking in the door. Memories of his home were terrifying.

After a particularly formal dinner, Lawrence and Julia retired to the sitting room with *another* glass of sherry. He would read a book. She would gaze around the room, looking like a vacant doll. He had tried not to pay too much attention to the strange dynamic of the unfulfilled marriage until now. Perhaps it was his particularly vigilant mindset that caused him to notice. Or perhaps it was the degenerate Mika. Sighing, he shifted uncomfortably. How could he, who had sat opposite so many people just like Mika in his career, be so unsettled by this one man? Minutes earlier he had read an email sent by a previously unknown sender that he had received that afternoon. It simply read "My apologies for my behaviour Dr. Gardiner. Please feel free to contact me when you are ready."

Niles took himself and his laptop to the 'library.' The 'library', for this highfalutin couple, was simply a room containing two bookshelves. Hardly a bibliotheca, but he felt Julia loved referring to the "Library." "That will go beautifully in the Library," or "We're having some work done in the Library." This fuelled her snobbery, and he was sure that her accent even changed when she said it. Lounging upon the large couch, Niles brought his feet up and continued reading Mika's notes. Nothing to work with. The man had cleverly avoided giving any real information about himself. That was noteworthy. Every comment, every reveal had been designed to slowly introduce Will Mason into the conversation for his own means. He shivered as a sudden chill passed through him.

Looking out of the window, he gazed into the darkness of the backyard, watching the rain pelt down. He suddenly felt uncomfortable. A scene that had, at one time, provided him some comfort now scared him. What was in the dark? His rational mind fought against his fearful flights of fancy. He forgave himself. Of course, he would feel this way. He found himself seeing shapes in the black window, large foreboding shapes. The image of that man in the dark was suddenly, and inexplicably, staring at him through a pane of glass. It grew so clear in his mind, like a movie. He was sure that if he closed his eyes, he would relive the ordeal again. Feeling foolish, he quickly turned and placed his legs on the floor. The laptop fell clumsily to one side. Sighing heavily, he checked his watch. 9PM. Time for medication and sleep. Thank God for pharmaceuticals.

Walking down the hall to the stairwell, Niles walked straight into Jess' arms, burying his head in her shoulder.

"Are you OK?" she asked soothingly.

Niles nodded, "I'm fine, just tired."

Jess stroked his hair, his splinted arm pushing against her "Don't hurt yourself." She adjusted his strap as he smiled with childlike embarrassment.

"Mum and Dad are playing cards... would you like to join them?" she smiled facetiously. "You know mother would love that. Perhaps in the *Library*."

Niles scoffed, what a perfect imitation. "No, no that sounds charming but no... I think I may go to bed."

Jess nodded. "OK. I'll be up soon anyway."

Leaving Jess downstairs, Niles turned on the light to the bathroom and squinted as it struck the stark white tiles. Hazily he approached the sink and he looked at himself in the mirror. God, he looked like rubbish. His face bruised, his eyes black. He had never looked this way before. He awkwardly began preparing his toothbrush with one hand. Do this, take the medication and then sleep. He was a good mental health patient. His anxiety was peaking but he was managing to keep it at a low sweat. He would sleep soon and not wake till morning. He had had no idea how effective these meds actually were that he had been prescribing to others. Him enjoying the feeling was almost like research.

He felt that he would be able to relax more if they were not staying with his in-laws. He knew Jess certainly would. Tomorrow he would give serious consideration about their return home - for both their sake. The inane talk from Julia, the equally as boring talk from Lawrence and now the soft sound of bugle music seeping through the closed door were becoming unbearably tedious.

Downing a few little pills, he looked at his face once more in the mirror. He wouldn't scar too much, he had been told. He had the emollient ointment to pop on the superficial wounds. He was unsure how much good it would do, and it just felt terrible. His eyes turned to a reflection to his left, his breath froze in his lungs. A figure of a man kneeling on one knee, facing the wall next to the bathtub. He could see the top of his head as his face was laying on its arm. The air stilled. The room grew dark as an inexplicable and haunting military march grew louder.

Niles couldn't move. The pill bottle dropped out of his hands, hitting the floor. How could this happen? How could this person be here? Was it a hallucination? A psychotic break? The camouflage clad man rose as Niles slowly turned to look into the familiar face of his previous assailant. Towering over him, the Soldier lunged forward, grasping and throwing him against the wall. It slammed its hand over Niles' mouth, the other behind his head. Any screams were redundant as the Soldier swung him around, holding him above the white tub. Niles struck out, but as before they were useless, pitiful strikes. The Soldier lowered him into the tub. Niles fought, arms outstretched, hands sliding down the tiled wall

His head hit the back of the tub. The taste of blood filled his mouth as teeth were pushed into gums. His scream was stuck behind the restrained jaw. The Soldier pushed Niles' head to the bottom of the bathtub with a *thump*. Reaching next to him, he grasped a towel that had fallen upon the floor. Lifting it to his mottled face, he momentarily regarded the towel with white eyes before lowering it onto Niles' face. The sweet smell of blood and fabric softener filled Niles' nostrils as the fabric was held firmly on his face.

"*Stop... Stop... Stop...*" Niles screamed silently, unable to push a sound past the thick cotton encasing his face, filling his mouth and crushing his nose. With horror Niles heard the familiar sound of gushing water... he was going to drown. This man was going to drown him in the *bathtub*. Cold water ran down his face causing him to gasp. His chest heaved as water filled his covered nose and eyes. Choking, his arms thrashed frantically. His legs kicked over the edge of the tub. He couldn't move this man.

Niles couldn't tell if he was breathing in or out. His chest spasmed and his throat burnt. The water would then momentarily cease, allowing him to grasp a desperate breath before it started again. He was drowning.

ooo

Crystal saw the darkness of the streets, the passing beams of car lights and unaware people as her Shadow moved through the city. The scent was dying, and she was beginning to weaken. The kaleidoscope of lights and scenes became numbing, hypnotic. Natural. Tonight, it was lost, but she would try again. The Shadow was summoned to return.

ooo

Noah turned his head just in time for vomit to project onto the floor beside him. *Waterboarding... fuck.* He couldn't breathe, yet his lungs were clear. His chest spasmed painfully, his throat burnt and rasped. The adrenaline that coursed through him almost completely unnoticed. He had felt this before, it would pass. Not for his target, however. This was more than a vicarious nightmare for him. He would be messed up for quite some time.

317

The medication and alcohol caressed his consciousness once more. His last thoughts as the Soldier ended, as his eyes fluttered to shut, were of Mika. Fucker. Happy now, you evil piece of shit?

∞∞∞

Kept at the edge of unconsciousness, Niles took two large breaths, allowing the water to enter his lungs and then flow out from his throat. The water had stopped. His ears pulsated with the sound of his heart. Every rasping breath crackled and popped. He went to move and was able to arch his back. The man was not there anymore. This thought caused him to notice the condition of his body. Beaten, bloodied and near exhaustion. His head was still covered with a wet wadded towel. He turned slowly to the side causing him to cough hard as a mixture of water and vomit ran down his cheek. He lifted a weak, trembling hand to his face that fell uselessly onto the soaked fabric.

Someone grabbed him again; he screamed frantically, crying out for them to stop. The towel was whipped from his face, and he looked at Jess who stared down at him. Terrified, confused as she kept telling him to sit up.

The sight of her was incomprehensible. No joy, no relief. The adrenaline that coursed through him had driven him to near insanity. Jess called to her parents. She stroked his face, trying to get him to respond. He couldn't speak. He simply couldn't put words together in his mind.

Chapter 29

PLEASE. PLEASE TALK TO ME. I DON'T KNOW WHAT TO SAY TO MAKE IT RIGHT. I'M SORRY, BUT I KNOW THAT MAKES NO DIFFERENCE. PLEASE. MY LOVE FOR YOU IS REAL. ITS THE ONLY THING THATS REAL.

Noah had not seen nor heard from Chelamah since she walked out that morning a week ago. Her time was fading, as was Luka's. It was, of course, a horrible possibility that, even now, she no longer existed as he once knew her. That she had taken the final slip into the abyss. Perhaps his denial of this possibility was mere lovesick optimism. No, she hadn't gone. No, she would never let that happen without him. Wishful thinking? He had killed the mother, and then bedded her daughter not less than two weeks later. He had justified it to himself in so many ways. *It wasn't actually me. I did it to save multiple others. I was betrayed into thinking there was no other way.* Regardless of any of these, there was no reason that could possibly excuse the part he had played.

Sitting outside, in the freezing morning cold with nothing but a pair of linen trousers on, provided some relief to his sore body. With so much to think about, sleep did not happen the night before. He dragged hard on a cigarette. A habit that Chelamah detested. Leaning back, he blew lazy smoke rings into the frosty air.

Maybe with Luka's revelation there was actually some hope. Noah had no doubt that he would be able to manipulate Luka, perhaps not as efficiently as Jason, but good enough. The Soldier came from its own realm. Humans didn't go to this world. Luka, being a Devotee, had travelled there whilst Noah was strapped to a chair… feeling the brutal death of his beloved's mother. Whilst there, Luka's shadow had stashed the goods. The only way to get them back was through Luka, through the Soldier. The third attack on Niles and he would let Luka have what he wanted. They needed the secrets it held.

In that Grimoire was thought to be the accumulation of knowledge and interventions that could control and protect; provide hope of an escape and freedom. Not only for an Ace but for the more vulnerable Underlings and Devotees.

It occurred to him that the manifestations of the Oculi were a blessing for their lesser kind. The big boys, the Aces, were getting picked off by something out of all of their hands. Whilst they were busy dealing with this possible rising threat, he could make his move. If Luka didn't tell them, they would never know. They could have time to collect the Grimoires, study them, learn what they contained and then use them as a weapon against the notorious elite of the damned. Played right, the Aces wouldn't see it coming.

The morning traffic was starting to build in the distance. This was Noah's least favourite time of his day. Normal people rousing and invading his own little dark bubble. He liked the night, or more so, felt like he belonged there. Like an outcast in the shadows, like the monster he was. It felt right to be in darkness. In this dreary place, the presence of even this dim light made him feel sick and exposed.

Did he trust Luka not to take the Grimoires and run? No, of course not, but one thing Noah found interesting about Luka was the insight he had into how thick he actually was. Maybe a lifetime of being told he was stupid had finally sunk in. Even if he was smart enough to pull this off, his belief in himself was so conveniently low that he would seek out another to validate every one of his actions. There was also the very real threat that Noah could reach Luka anywhere at any time. Right now, without an Ascendant having his back, he was extremely vulnerable, and he knew it. After all, without Jason he was pathetic. The cockiness had evaporated, destroying that asshole confidence. He couldn't be in a better position to be taken advantage of.

○○○

Crystal walked slowly, cautiously down the marble steps into the sitting room of the Pantheon. This time she would find the Firewolf. She had no choice. Her mind was dark, her body numb. Multiple attempts over the course of the week had produced little results. She only had so much strength left, but there was no choice but to try again. The Firewolf was here somewhere. She had seen it. She had seen its Conduit and now, stroking the cover of the ancient Grimoire she held in her manicured hands, she hoped this attempt would be successful. Perhaps it would provide her with insight, provocation. It never had before, but now she was desperate. She had to find what she sought, and quickly, for it was guaranteed she wouldn't be the only one looking. Mika would also soon return and there was no time to waste.

Staring out of the window, her body began to hurt at the mere intention of stepping again. She chanted in her mind as the morning dawn seeped over the cityscape; with a cry of pain, she allowed herself to devolve.

ooo

Waking up and rolling over, Sam kicked his bed clothes off as he contemplated getting up. The past week he had kept to himself. He had only shared messages with Ellie, as they too were preparing to step out of the spotlight and disappear.

The old man in the bar played in his mind. Jason had been completely willing to regard that person as nothing, a plaything not worthy of any consideration as human. It made him sick and scared, how someone so revolting as this had gotten so close to him.

Rolling over, he checked the time. He had to go and see what was happening with the troublesome duo. Looking at his phone, a feeling of relief washed over him. No messages. No 50 missed calls for help. The psychopath Jason, blocked and gone for now. All was well for the moment, and he had time. Time for coffee, time for a secret cigarette on the balcony where no-one would see him. Maybe a normal start to a normal day. It had been so long.

The Child was dancing in the hallway. Switching on the coffee machine, Sam made his way sluggishly to the couch and let himself fall into it. What a night that had been. It could have all gone so wrong. Had he been prepared to do what he had threatened to do? Scarily enough, yes, he had been. This had not been a pious act or self-aggrandisement. The fact was that if a completely innocent old man was Lit, he would not have stood a chance.

321

However he, Sam, would. Testing the "Ellie and Josh" premise seemed the only option he would've had.

His eyes blurry, Sam scanned the room, listening to the sounds of vicious slaps waft airily down the hallway.

Naughty! Naughty!

Who was she beating now? What torn part of some poor fucker's body was getting pulverised? Blinking lazily, his gaze turned to the couch beside him. He rubbed his eyes, clearing the grit, before leaning to study the marks that lay, track-like across the cushion and down onto the floor. What was that? He lowered himself even further, placing a pointed finger on this stain. Gritty and hard. He scratched it, catching black scum under his fingernail and grimacing. He brought it to his nose. Immediately he recoiled with disgust.

The sickly-sweet smell of rot and decay, the putrid scent of bacteria and disease filled his nostrils. *No, no it couldn't be.*

Running into the kitchen he turned the taps to hot. Grasping the detergent bottle, he covered both hands, scrubbing them together furiously. It was the dried dribble, the bloody innards from the thing she had tortured on the couch. It shouldn't have been there. It should have vanished as soon as she did… this should not happen. The water began to burn, but he couldn't stop scrubbing off the filth. Still washing his hands, he looked up into the hallway. She was there, her hand raised and rhythmically pounding a small, trembling headless body on the floor.

Bad naughty, naughty. Bad.

Sam turned off the tap, hands still dripping as he walked towards the Child and her victim. The body rested contorted, maggot-like on the tiles. The floor around it was covered with the same grotesque shit that he just scrubbed from under his nails. Watching her, her face looked back at him in absolute delight. Her hand coming down again and again on the human grub. Sam carefully lowered himself to his knees. The grub lay a foot away from him, between him and the Child. He had to know. Hesitantly he reached out his hand. Slowly at first but then quickly he reached down to feel its cold, sickly skin. Suddenly, the familiar searing, electrifying pain shot through his palm.

"*Fuck, fuck, fuck!*" he screamed, darting back. It was really here, it was *here*. He grabbed his burning hand. The beheaded corpse stopped writhing, its muscles relaxing to the floor. Relief. For a moment, relief.

"What? What?" he kept panting, shaking his head as he pushed himself up against the wall. The Child turned to look at him, her hand raised above her head. Her face jerked into a large, crazed smile.

He's naughty. He's a naughty boy.

Leaping off the floor, Sam quickly rounded into his bedroom and began throwing clothes on his body. It was changing. It was here. Why was he so surprised? It had touched him the night near the Oculus. How long had this been the case? Was this happening to all of them? Ellie, Josh, Jason…? If so, why were they even still here? Christ what the Child would have done to get her hands on him during the Circle, and now did she have that chance? If she knew it, which of course she did, why didn't she? He would leave now, go see Ellie and Josh. He needed to talk… to work it out.

ᴏᴐᴏ

"…and then we can go to the beach and get stuff like cold drinks because it will be hot. We'll need to keep drinking because you can get sick," Josh called from the shower as Ellie packed the small, black case. Where were they going to go? She had been pondering this all week. They had to lay low. She didn't know how much room they would be given by Casey and Nate. Every time she thought of them, she felt sick. How would that play out? They would need to buy Josh clothes. Leave room in the case for them. She had washed and dried all the clothes that she had so at least they were clean. Were they going to get away with this?

"We don't want to get sick," Ellie replied absently, her mind racing. She had resigned a few days ago. She had been casual, and her resignation didn't raise too many questions. If she had thought deeper about it, it would've been quite sad. No-one would miss her, no-one would really notice she was no longer there. Josh and school? That was another problem. She had bluffed her way pretending to be Casey over the last week, saying Josh was sick. How much time would they be given?

Ellie had ID. Josh had none. Not a bad thing; they weren't planning on leaving the country. Sam was ready, and thanks to her generous parents, financially nothing was a problem. Sam had gone far down that rabbit hole. For that reason and more, they had to run. Rent paid in the apartment for 12 months as of last night, no-one would come here. No-one that would be expected anyway. Lock and leave.

323

Josh yelled sternly from the bathroom, "No we do not. This one time at swimming a kid forgot his water bottle and he got sick, and the teacher had to call his mum to take him home."

"That'll do it," Ellie sighed as if it was an obvious conclusion. "Gotta bring that drink bottle."

"Yeah" Josh nodded, rubbing the soap off his face. He lifted his hands to his nose and sniffed the bubbles. Coconut. It was going to be a very good day.

Josh had spoken of a man called Charlie. A man who gifted him the means to do whatever it was he did that night. Josh hadn't made that connection, only noticing that a "little bit of paper with nice writing on it" was gone. The black strip remained, which he kept around his neck, refusing to remove it. This was Scribe stuff. This was the type of power that existed, as Sam had told her. This man, this *Charlie* intrigued her.

"Are you finished?" Ellie called, rummaging through her backpack. One more thing to do before they left. Sam would be here soon. He could watch Josh, take him for breakfast whilst she endured her last therapy session with Niles. She wouldn't miss it. The sessions had to end today.

"Yes," Josh called happily as the water went silent.

Josh left the shower and wrapped the towel around himself, trotting on his toes to the bathroom vanity and looking at himself in the mirror. His hair looked clean. So did his face. And he smelt like coconut.

It was going to be a very good day indeed.

◯◯◯

Jason was surprised to see Crystal upon the couch, naked, clothes wrapped around her as he entered the Pantheon. She was in a ball, her eyes were open as she trembled, holding her clothing close, like a blanket. Her eyes were white as if rolled back into her head. Her head lolled atop her shoulders, staring blindly around the room. Jason smiled in amusement. He walked softly closer, trying not to wake her. Her mouth was muttering softly, dreamily. What was she doing? Where was she?

Squatting down beside her, he lifted his hand and gently tapped her vacant face.

"Well, well, you nasty little bitch" he sneered. "Where are you now?"

Panicked, Sam stepped out into the corridor, closing the front door behind him. He would go now and see Ellie. They needed to know this, and they needed to work out what it meant. To his irritation, a neighbour's door opened before him, and three young girls came into the corridor talking excitedly about brunch, their voices, like fingernails on a chalkboard. A tall dark girl he had greeted a few times in the past, turned and smiled at him. He was sure her name was Bethany. It took everything he had to smile back. He stopped to allow them to continue to meander towards the elevator in front of him.

Pulling out his phone, he sent a quick text.

OMW

Placing the phone back in his pocket, he watched the two elevator doors, willing them to open as they approached. They didn't, causing them to gather in the bottle neck of the corridor. Of course. After what seemed like an eternity and a familiar ping, the door of one slid open and the girls slowly filed in. Bethany cast a glance at Sam, smiling and expecting him to enter behind them. He hesitated for a moment. Should he enter or wait for the next? He was in a rush. It would be OK. He was not angry, only mildly frustrated, but he was seasoned at knowing his limits. He entered, turning to face the door as it closed in front of him… the Dark Child standing by the door of his apartment looked on. Small, eerie. *Creepy as hell*, thought Sam. As the door closed, she raised a long hand that had been bashing the maimed, headless living corpse across his linoleum and gave Sam a small, quick wave. Odd.

OOO

Ellie helped Joshua put on her old coat, another outfit that dwarfed him. It looked almost comical, but it would have to do. Receiving a message, she looked down. Sam was on his way. A bit late but still in good time. She would be able to make it and meet them somewhere afterwards. She had a rough plan. This afternoon she would meet with Niles and finalise her treatment order. Then, they would go north. This time of year, accommodation would be easy to acquire. No-one was holidaying in this crap weather. Once there they could work out their next move.

"Beaches have sharks sometimes, but not here. It's too cold, and sharks don't like that, do they? Do some sharks like cold?" Josh quizzed happily, asking questions to ensure they were safe, from dehydration, sharks and any other risk he could think of.

"Let's not go anywhere near sharks," Ellie dug deeper in her bag. What had she forgotten?

Josh thought for a moment. "Who do you think would win in a fight between a shark and a dog?"

"The shark, the dog would drown. Could you quickly get the small black notebook next to the bed?" Ellie grabbed the case, pulling the top over and fastening the lock.

"Sure," Josh jumped up and ran in his massive coat to the bedroom. It was dark and the curtains were still drawn. He walked across the carpet to the bedside table and reached out his hand when he noticed something odd. His eyes adjusting, he stared at the bump on the bed. Was someone sleeping? The blanket moved up and down rhythmically with the soft, rasping sounds of animal-like breathing. Curiously he stepped forward. Was Sam here?

"Did you find it?" Ellie called.

The breathing stopped and was replaced by a long, deep groan. It wasn't Sam. The covers began to lift, tenting as something rose beneath them.

"Ellie," he yelled. "There's somebody here."

OOO

Dear God, will they please stop talking. The laughing, the talking made the small space seem even smaller. Sam stared at his feet as the lift made its way slowly between floors. The slow, droning descent was calming, almost hypnotic. He leaned against the back wall and took a long, sobering breath to the background tune of Mary Had a Little Lamb. Lifting his head, the Child stood directly in front of him, but wasn't looking at him. This wasn't immediately odd. Bethany kept talking about a ring that she had seen on the finger of her friend. Her hand up, she described the ring to her companions, splaying her fingers before them. The Child bought her long, razor-sharp talons and mimicked her every move. With a final flutter of her fingers, the

Dark Child brought her hands to her side, cocking her head sideways, smiling happily.

Bethany noticed Sam staring at the floor in front of her, the colour gone from his face. Stunned, Sam looked up and they locked eyes, his face alert with panic as her bottom lip began trembling. His mouth opened; he moved forward as if to grab something bellowing "No!"

A hard thump sent Bethany falling back onto the elevator wall, her friends stunned in silence. Shaking as shock embraced her, the elevator erupted into screaming chaos as her intestine slipped from the gash in her coat and began to slide between the fingers of shaking hands that were clasped to her abdomen.

"Oh my God," Sam gasped, Bethany looked at him, her eyes wide with confusion and horror. The Child lifted her hands up, splayed her fingers once more and admired the hanging, dripping flesh caught on her knifelike fingers before lunging forward once more. Bethany slammed hard to the side, bringing another of her friends to the ground with her. She began to gasp as her legs kicked about madly while her throat was crushed by an unseen force.

"Stop!" Sam dashed forward as Bethany's eyes exploded into pools of blood within their sockets. In a mad panic, Sam threw himself on top of the girl, but it was as if he wasn't there. Someone was grabbing his hair; it was the girl behind him. Blood began to gush from Bethany's body as Sam continued screaming "Stop! Stop!" while feeling the assault being inflicted on the women he couldn't protect.

Her friend had slid to the floor, sat against the side of the elevator staring in absolute terror. The door opened allowing the bright light of the lobby into the space. Sam heard screaming as a man shouted "Jesus Christ!"

Two girls staggered out of the blood-filled cabin, screaming hysterically and looking back at Sam lying on top of their slain friend. Dumbfounded, Sam looked into the dead, eyeless head of the girl. He heard someone shout. "Stop! Don't move! Stop!" then looked up into the horrified face of the shocked building security officer.

Trying to regain his senses, Sam pushed himself off the tattered body, tumbling backwards into the elevator, only stopping when he collided with the far door.

"Stay there! Stay there!" The security guard bellowed again, pointing at Sam accusingly. More people approached. Sam could see faces, hear their gasps and shrieks of horror. The Child stood over her victim, mesmerized for a brief moment before something else caught her eye. Straddling the torn body, she brought her hand up as she extended a finger and started giggling whilst flicking blood towards the gathering crowd.

Quickly turning around on the floor, Sam lifted his shaking, blood covered hand and hit the button. The lobby erupted in chaos as the door slid closed.

OOO

Ellie wasn't sure she had heard Josh properly. He couldn't find it. It wasn't here? Sighing, she rose to her feet and walked towards the bedroom door where she froze, staring at the creature regarding Joshua. It was crouched, blackened and bent. Black matted fur-like hair across the top of a bulbous head and a moist, dribbling mouth. It squatted on all fours with its face moving closer to Josh, curious, threatening. Its eyes were white like Bael's', white like the Firewolf. Josh couldn't move, frozen to the spot with fear. He had seen eyes like this before. He knew what they meant.

"Josh," Ellie hissed from the door. "Come here, now."

Josh couldn't stop looking at it. Was this his fault too? It was moving closer to him, its eyes rolling around in its head.

"Josh... listen," Ellie spoke, calm but firm. "Run, *now.*"

Josh turned and ran for the door into Ellie's arms. The creature screeched, leapt off the bed and scurried towards them as Ellie slammed the door shut. Holding the handle tight, she lowered herself down and placed her feet on either side of the wall, bracing the door closed. Not knowing what to do, Josh grabbed the handle over Ellie's hands as the door buckled and cracked. The frenzied creature continued to hammer the other side.

"What is it?" Josh cried as Ellie furiously pulled the handle.

"Let go!" Ellie shouted, her hands began to slip. "Josh let go!"

The noise stopped. Ellie held the handle tight. It had not tried to open the door, it had tried to come through it. It wasn't smart. She glanced back at Josh. Hands over his mouth, panting loudly, he whispered, "is it gone?"

Keeping her grip and her brace, Ellie shook her head, "I don't know."

Slowly, Ellie started to release the handle. Sitting facing the door, she quietly bought her hands beside her listening for the slightest sound. It had stopped. Was it still there? There would be no way out, but then again things

328

from that world didn't require doors. Carefully she shuffled herself back across the floor, keeping her eyes on the door. No sound, she couldn't hear any movement.

"Shh," Ellie held a finger to her lips. Josh hurried forward and stood behind her.

"Is it hiding?"

Ellie shook her head. She didn't know.

"It had cat attack eyes," Josh cried, placing his hands over his mouth again as a loud, blood curdling screech echoed from the door before them.

"Go!" Ellie screamed jumping to her feet as the door swung open and the demented creature scuttled into the room.

○○○

Oh Jesus. Sam watched in terror as the Child sat before the slain women, gently tearing at her victim's torso and watching the dead face for a reaction. Suddenly, the Child leant forward, bringing her face directly above the empty eye sockets, looking down with confusion. No pain, no horror, no screaming, no writhing. She expected it. She needed it. Even in Sam's horrified mind he knew… for her they didn't usually die. She couldn't understand that this dead gift was not going to suffer for her.

The police were going to come. Fuck he was in trouble now. Barely able to balance, his legs shaking violently as his clenched hands, he forced himself to stand. The door slid open to the shocked cry of old Mrs. Howard from 502. He leapt over the corpse, shoving past the screaming woman,

"I'm sorry, I'm sorry," he gasped, lumbering clumsily down the hall to his door.

○○○

Ellie grabbed Josh and pulled him towards her. In response he grabbed her sleeve and yanked her towards the kitchen. The creature leapt at them upturning the couch. Unfazed it lowered itself again and swiftly, like a cockroach, ran forward once more. Ellie and Josh backed into the kitchen followed by the creature. It had them cornered. Slowly it rose up, unfolding on two unusually long, thin legs blocking the entrance. Joshua pushed himself against her. They both stood in silence.

It shot forward, screeching madly, hands outstretched as Ellie forced Josh behind her and waited for the attack.

 OOO

Jason watched Crystal with fascination. He had never seen this process before. What an opportunity. He moved closer, watching her pathetic state with joy. Maybe whilst she was out, he should kill her. Or at the least, smack every blonde hair out of that stupid head.

"Hey Crystal, did I ever tell you what a fucking dog you are? Your heels don't make your legs look thinner and your shoulder pads don't make you look any smarter," Jason chuckled. This was awesome.

"No... no... no" she gasped quietly. Her face contorted into displeasure, losing control.

Jason pulled back from her and smiled maliciously, "Oh dear" he jibed, "fucking up are we?"

He moved closer. What was she seeing? What he would give to have a glimpse of what this bitch was up to. God how he hated her. How he would love to see her undone, thwarted and beaten.

He jumped back in shock as Crystal was dragged off the couch. Held upright, hanging limply by her neck by an unseen hand.

"Shit!" Jason yelled before exploding with laughter. An Ace, the bitch got an Ace, and she was having her ass kicked! Kneeling in delight on the floor, he watched his gasping, choking comrade as her feet began to leave the floor. "Oh you're in trouble now!"

OOO

Ellie reached beside her. She felt Josh's head. She gave him three taps as he quickly bought his hand up, grasping hers. Bael was here restraining the creature effortlessly by its neck. In the air it hung, scared and weak. Any thought it had of defending itself seemed to have been aborted. This was a fight it could not win. Watching the monster hang in the air like this confused Josh. It was right there with them in the kitchen and then it had quickly moved to the sitting room where it... hung in the air? What had happened? What was it doing? Josh thought it was going to get them, not do *this*. Ellie had watched Bael do this in the past.

330

"Oh no," Josh whimpered. Ellie looked down at him, following his eyes as they moved down the corridor and back to the hanging monster. The Firewolf had obviously just entered.

"We need to go," Ellie said quickly, quietly. "Josh, now."

Snapping Josh to his senses, she moved in front of him and began to walk from the kitchen. Rounding the corner, fuelled by adrenaline, Ellie yelled as she made for the door "Run, run!"

ᑐᑐᑐ

Sobbing as he wiped tears from his eyes, Sam slammed into his bathroom. They would be here any moment. It was over. Years of living this life had come down to this. They would be here for him. He would be charged for fucking murder. Jesus how could this happen?

He swung open the bathroom cabinet, his hands still covered in very real blood. He cast bottles and containers out onto the floor, desperately reading the labels through tear-filled eyes. They were coming. He had to not feel. *He had to not feel.* He was fucked already, but if he wasn't prepared it would be a massacre. He could not get out of this. Sooner or later he would rouse, and she would be set loose. But he would try.

Pulling a bottle out, he quickly read the label. Yes, yes this was the one. There was no time to hesitate. Not too many. Too many and they would take him in and pump his stomach. No, he needed just enough to numb. Not kill. Not sleep. Opening his mouth, he threw the pills in and swallowed hard, coughing as they caught in his dry throat. He gripped the tap, turning on the water, placing his mouth under the flow, forcing them down.

Staring at himself in the mirror, perhaps a true reflection. Covered in the blood of another, tears of regret and guilt running down his face. Acceptance of punishment for a lifetime of perpetual suffering. He could hear the sirens now. He could often hear them, but he was pretty sure this time they were real, and they were coming for him. His thoughts went to Ellie and Josh. He was sorry. He really tried to keep it together. Now he would sit and wait. Wait for them to come and take him away. Face the consequences of a hideous action. After all, it was about time.

Picking up his phone, he called. No answer - straight to message bank. He thought to hang up but began to talk. "I'm sorry I won't be there. Somethings fucked up guys. Somethings so fucked up. I really wanted to see you today. I really wanted to just… you know… hang out and shit. Talk, be normal… be…" tears choked his voice, "myself. Just be me. I'm so tired Ellie… but I guess it's gonna end now, one way or the other. Everyone seems out to get me… literally. They are coming for me … I'm in big trouble. I'm so sorry Ellie. Tell Josh I'm sorry I didn't come. Thank you for just ya know… being you."

ooo

Crystal came crashing to the floor, her eyes opened as her Shadow slammed back into her with a rage the likes of which she had never felt before. She opened her mouth as her eyes turned from white to cold blue and screamed hysterically before collapsing with exhaustion. Her body trembled. Her throat ached. She had felt Him. His rage, His strength and His awesome magnificence: Bael. He was there. She had seen His eyes, while being held in His grasp. The child held Bael. Who held the Wolf now was irrelevant.

Breathing harshly, her chest moved in heavy ragged motion. She had found him. She slowly became aware that someone was with her. She couldn't see him clearly yet but heard a short, sharp laugh.

"Oh, hey Crystal. Well look at me, here to talk again! And no Mika, no stripping. Yes, I think now is a good time to let you know exactly how this is going to play out."

"Jason… please… no," Crystal managed to grunt into the tiles.

Jason was impressed. "Get your clothes on. Believe me, you're going to want to be dressed for this conversation."

Chapter 30

"We have to go back inside." Ellie stood on the street looking at her apartment building. "We've got no choice... we need the bags."

"No!" cried Josh. "What if the things still there?"

Sighing, Ellie knelt down to him. How could she explain to him that it wasn't the apartment that was scary. It was themselves that were haunted. Leaving the apartment didn't thwart anything.

"Josh, listen to me," she said sternly. "Everything we need is in that room. You wanna go away don't you? You wanna go somewhere nice?"

"Yes." Josh nodded, tears rolled down his cheek.

"OK. To do that, we need what's in that room." She pointed to the building. "Don't worry, it's gone now... I'm sure it's gone."

"How do you know it's gone?"

Ellie breathed out heavily, hanging her head as Bael stepped behind her. *Because the fuckface is here with us now.* "I know it's gone OK. Believe me, I know it's gone."

"Can we wait for Sam?" Josh asked, wiping his eyes.

"I don't know where Sam is. You'll have to come with me. It's alright, we'll find Sam afterwards. Right now, though, we need our bags, and we need to go." Ellie grasped his shoulders tightly, giving them a quick squeeze, "Be brave, ok? And let's not wait for Sam... he cries more than you do."

Sniffing and chuckling, Josh nodded. "Can I come with you?"

Looking around Ellie pointed to the gritty bus stop bench beside them. "No, I can be quick. You wait here for me. Don't move from here. I'll be back in one minute. *Don't* move Josh. If you move, I'll think something is wrong... so don't."

Frustrated, Josh rolled his eyes, turning to sit lazily on the bench. "Yes I won't, you don't have to say it a million times."

He watched as Ellie ran across the road. The Monster Dog stood behind him; he could hear its breathing in his ears and smell its revolting breath and sticky damp fur. Crossing his arms sternly in front of him, he didn't look back and just shook his head in disapproval.

"This is all your fault again, idiot."

Josh's legs swung to-and-fro on the bench beneath. His feet scuffed the gravel, sending bits of cement onto the curb in front of him. All sorts of horrible thoughts filled his mind. Was the monster still hanging about in the room? Why did it do that? Was it tired? Maybe monsters slept like that. He didn't know.

There was so much noise around this early in the morning. Cars and the beeping of horns and sirens. So many police sirens that seemed to be everywhere. Squinting, he looked up at what he guessed would be Ellie's little flat. He hoped she wasn't still in there. What if the monster got her? What would he do then? Maybe before the monster got her bad, she could throw his bag out the window so at least he would have his phone, but who would he call? Sam? Nate and Casey? His heart sank. No. He didn't think they would want to hear from him anymore.

Josh stood up happily as Ellie came out of the big glass door and unloaded three large bags on the sidewalk. Carefully, Josh ran across the road to meet her.

"You got it!" he cried happily. "Was the thing still there?"

Ellie didn't answer him. Josh continued talking as he pulled his heavy backpack over his shoulder, nearly toppling off the path. "We can go now, find Sam."

Ellie held the phone to her ear. Josh stopped and looked curiously at her. She looked confused, shocked and sad all at the same time. She pulled the phone down and stared into nothingness, vacant and stunned.

"What's wrong?" Josh asked. He walked up to her. "Ellie?"

Ellie looked down at him. She had tears in her eyes. She smiled but Josh had seen that smile before. Her smile didn't match her feelings. His mum had done that a lot.

"Let's go," she said, her voice breaking.

ⵔⵔⵔ

Niles adjusted himself in the chair, his free hand awkwardly gripped his tablet as the other lay redundant in its cast and large sling. The left side of his face was bruised. Ellie could see through the light layer of foundation that his fiancée had used to cover it. She had done this herself more than once, albeit much more effectively. Practice makes perfect. He smiled, casting her a glance as he steadied himself. A strange smile, a nervous smile? There was something odd about him today.

"Do you want me to hold something for you?" Ellie asked.

Niles forced a light laugh and said, "Thank you but no, I'm fine. It's just the ice on the stairs outside our house. One wrong step and everything goes from under you. I tried to grab the railing but kept falling. Hit the bottom step. Didn't notice the damage until I went to close the door. Funny, isn't it? Adrenaline!"

Ellie nodded. She would've thought being so good at deception detection he would have known better how to lie. But no. Giving a bit too much detail. A rookie mistake. Keep it simple. Keep it reductive. To her surprise he added more.

"Broken arm, fractured collarbone, and a very damaged ego. But enough about me…" Ellie settled back. Here it comes. "How have you been? What's been going on?" He smiled. Ellie suddenly felt more uncomfortable than usual. She couldn't describe the look in his eyes. Desperate anticipation? A longing to say something? He glared at her not in his usual guiding, analytical engagement but with something raw and honest. Almost like fear.

"I've been well," Ellie replied. "I'm working day shifts now which has made things a bit harder. Still not sleeping very well, but it's only for a short time."

"So sleeping's still a problem," he sympathised. *Sympathised.* What the hell was going on? Was he even aware how absolutely shit he was at masking his anxiety? Maybe, she thought, she could give him some lessons.

"Yes, but I'm managing OK," she nodded cautiously. "I'm getting enough sleep. Just changing my sleeping habits can make things hard for a time, that's all." She found herself looking around his office, avoiding eye contact. Her gut told her there was something coming. Niles moved slightly and winced in pain.

"Are you OK?" Ellie asked softly.

"Yes, I'm just a little uncomfortable, but I'm OK. Thank you for your concern." Niles gathered his thoughts. "So sleeping was an issue for you before, right? It's been ongoing for quite some time."

Ellie nodded. She agreed. It was so 'ongoing' that she had learnt to live with it, existing in a constant state of fatigue. But she was OK with it. This didn't need to be explored.

"The medication is helping?"

"Yes. It helps more now. I mean, I take it and get to sleep with no problem."

He was sitting forward uneasily. "Still waking up often?"

"Yes," Ellie nodded. Of course, she was. The noises, the banging, the cursing, the screaming, and now random creatures running around her home. Sam, Joshua, that twat Jason and the horde of monsters that now surrounded her. Bael, Firewolves and the nightly demonic social gatherings that occurred in her home. Things erupting out of cracks from nowhere, trying to tear her apart when all she wanted to do was buy some paracetamol. "But I usually fall asleep again."

With a deep sigh, Niles tapped his e-pen on his tablet. "I'd like to talk about your unsettled nights in a little more detail. We haven't revisited this for a while and now, due to changes in your schedule, I just want to make sure we are staying on track. After today your Treatment Order is due to be assessed. Keen to make sure all is well, you understand?"

Ellie's heart sank but she remained stony faced and nodded quickly.

"Now," he said quickly. To Ellie's surprise he began using the tablet on his lap. He had never done this, unless writing a prescription. She would often find it amusing that the tablet was merely a prop. But now, he was scrolling, looking. "Your night disruptions were linked originally to auditory and visual hallucinations. There was also some mention of sleep paralysis type events that seemed to revolve around a particular theme." Oh Jesus. Ellie drew a breath.

He's going to do it.

"Sorry, just give me a second. I'm just looking back to this conversation circa... a long time ago!" He forced a laugh. A laugh. He was trying to lighten the mood. "Ah here it is. Yes. The sleep paralysis seemed to be centred around a man, a bogeyman construction who, as a child, you referred to as 'Bael.'"

Horrified, Ellie nodded. A light and relaxed "Um hm" came from her lips. Play this down. What was his motive? He had asked about this before but never so clumsy and random.

"Do you still experience these hallucinations?" Niles sat back, his pen tapping annoyingly on the screen.

They regarded each other for a few moments. Niles spoke solid words, but his eyes were more uncertain. He was damaged, hurt. Something was going on. He was scared, desperate and awkward. She nodded slowly as Niles watched her sit straight up in her chair. She sighed a deep sigh before glancing around the room. Niles held his breath; he remembered *this* Ellie. This particular Ellie spoke to him as she left this office months ago, letting him know that any further poking into her psyche would be *"so bad. So bad for you."*

"Doctor Gardiner, if you have something to say to me, then say it." Niles feigned surprise. "No, I have no desire to upset you... I"

"What happened to your arm?" Ellie interrupted. "Your face. You're hurt. What happened?"

Flabbergasted, he stammered. "I told you, and this isn't about..."

"...You? Isn't it about you?" Ellie replied coldly. "I think it is. Bael has been mentioned a lot lately and not just here."

She felt sick, saying his name to someone other than her kind. Exposing herself, revealing her vile secret, but he had secrets too. If he kept requesting access to hers , then she would press for his. What new game was this that involved someone not of her kind? Not Sam. Not Josh. How did this involve him so deeply that he sat there so pitiful, terrified and out of ideas?

Niles shook his head. He was frustrated, embarrassed. "Why do you say that?"

"Have you heard that name from anyone else but me?" Ellie asked. Niles momentarily contemplated denial, but instead found himself nodding in resignation. "We have never discussed a name. Why do you want to know?"

She noticed a sudden drop in Nile's facade. For a second there was fear and unease. She could see the struggle in his small movements. *Tell her the truth... or continue this game for a while longer.* But Ellie was not in no mood for games, and though she didn't know why or how, Niles had been exposed to something that was scaring him. He needed warning.

Ellie leaned in slightly. "Do you know how many people go missing every year? Roughly 600 people a day. Some they find, most commonly within the first 48 hours of them disappearing. Some – most - are never heard from or seen again. Men, women, children. Nothing. I'm sure you know they never found my family. Not a shred after that fire, not a scrap of remains, not a piece of clothing. That new client of yours? The little boy?"

"Joshua Fielding," Niles gasped. How did she know about him?

"Where are his parents? Just gone. That's what we do to people. We make them disappear. We don't want to. It just happens. Bael, and others like Bael, are everywhere, and they come with people, like Josh, like me. Like others I'm sure you have met. We all have the same grizzly back story... well... those that make it. Most don't. We are *bound* as children and then a certain night comes when most of us don't stand a chance. But some of us make it through, becoming even more dangerous."

Ellie could feel the brewing angst within her that needed to be relieved. Keep talking... keep venting... keep distracting "Some of us are more... more *stable* than others? Not sane, just stable. Regardless, we're all dangerous in the most vile, outrageous way. If you've heard the name Bael, then you should go. Just go, now. Run. Leave this place and don't look back. Josh and I, people like us? You are no match for us." The room dimmed as a strange, creeping heat rose about them. Ellie took a deep, cleansing breath. Show him. Allow the darkness to seep in and lightly touch him. "You feel that don't you? There's nothing you can do. That line? One step and you become a *missing person*. Right here, right now."

Niles breathed softly as shadows wafted across the walls and furniture.

Ellie whispered. "You've felt this before? Maybe you just haven't noticed. But I think maybe now you're noticing? That's the beginning. All it would take now is one more little push..."

Nile leant forward, his heart in his throat. "Something is hunting me. Something is coming for me." His voice broke. "I'm losing my damn mind."

"Who asked you?" Ellie asked, her tone sharper than she intended.

Niles hesitated. "I can't tell you, that's patient priv-"

"Cut the bullshit, that doesn't matter anymore."

"I didn't say anything, but he knows I know something. If he finds me one more time, he's going to kill me!" Niles shouted, throwing his tablet to the ground. "Everyone thinks I'm losing my mind! I told him nothing, but I want to know Ellie... please. I don't know anything other than it's a name from your past and I'm getting slowly killed for it!"

"That's enough. That's all you need to know. You need to run. If some-one has said it to you, run. You're weak. For now, someone is playing with you, but your end is guaranteed. They need something from you, or you would have been gone already. But trust me… whether they get what they need or not, you wind worse than dead. Ellie stood and picked up her bag. "I want to help you, but I'm not sure I can. I might only make things worse. The reality of me, of Josh, is much worse than a couple of crazy orphans. We're as unnatural as the person who asked you, and as horrendous as the monster that hunts you."

Niles watched in dread. She couldn't leave now. He knew, if she left him now, he would be finished. "Ellie don't. Please." He blurted, standing up and following her to the door. Facing the exit, she didn't look back. Slowly she placed her head on the hard frame. Her fingers were already on the handle. Leverage. She would use this.

"Sign me off. Sign me off and never mention me or Josh again. People like us don't belong under a microscope, Niles. We belong on the outside. Do everything you can to keep us out of the system."

Turning to face Niles, who was awash with conflict, she continued. "I'm trying to do something. I don't know if I can, but this shit is closing in on me. At least set us free from this world, so we can stand a chance dealing with the other. You don't have a choice."

Releasing Ellie and a child of 8 years of age from the system would have been unthinkable, but there were so many things he didn't know. Ellie knew. Mika knew and, as unbelievable as it was, Josh knew.

"Then what?" Niles shrugged. "Then what happens?" Ellie opened the door of the office, used her hand in a simple gesture, and in trotted Josh who stood right beside her in a very big coat. She placed a hand protectively on the top of his head. Fingers fidgeting, he gave a quick wave.

"Hi," he smiled.

My God, who was he trusting? There was no logic to this. There was no science. The completely outrageous circumstances he had found himself in made him doubt his own sanity.

"Ellie," he said carefully, Joshua smiling at him. "What do I do?"

"When I leave here, you sign me off. Send me the number of the person who is doing this to you, then walk away. I'll deal with the rest. You won't survive this."

Josh glanced at the adults. That wasn't good. Was Niles sick? He hoped not... he was a nice man, and a good shrink Doctor.

"Go," Niles nodded, straining through his better judgement. Nodding back, Ellie took Josh's hand. She knew how hard this was for Niles. It was a testament to his fear and the danger he was in.

Awash with relief, Ellie took a moment to smile at him, gently, "Thank you."

Quickly she turned and led Josh from the room, who leant back awkwardly to meet the eyes of his doctor one last time. With a childlike ease he waved a small hand and simply called out: "Bye Dr. Gardens!"

To be continued...

Ingram Content Group UK Ltd.
Milton Keynes UK
UKHW040111080323
418219UK00007B/38